Leila Aboulela was born in Cairo and grew up in Khartoum. All three of her previous novels, *The Translator*, *Minaret* and *Lyrics Alley*, were longlisted for the Orange Prize. *Lyrics Alley* won Novel of the Year at the Scottish Book Awards and was shortlisted for the Commonwealth Writers' Prize. Her short story 'The Museum', from her collection *Coloured Lights*, won the Caine Prize. She lives in Aberdeen.

Also by Leila Aboulela

Lyrics Alley
Minaret
Coloured Lights
The Translator

'[A] treat – a novel that recreates the fascinating story of the rebel of the Caucasus, Imam Shamil, a 19th-century warrior who battled to defend his home against the invading Russians and united the Muslims of the region under his iconic leadership. Weaving the story of his relationship with a Georgian princess he kidnapped into a more contemporary story of mistaken terrorism, we learn much about the nature of loss, the legacy of exile and the meaning of home at a time in our world when all three are high in our minds'
Mariella Frostrup, *Guardian, Best Books of 2015*

'Aboulela's most **ambitious** novel yet ... An often intriguing story, politically relevant and historically **fascinating**' *Herald*

'The reader flicks back and forth through time, **gleaning pleasure and enlightenment** through each of the doorways as they go ... The passages are **arresting** in their descriptiveness, with **beautiful** pockets of calm in which the spiritual journey, as advocated by Shamil's Sufi teacher, is explored' *Independent*

'A novel so filled with ideas, new thoughts, images ... **extraordinary**'
Rachel Billington, author of *Glory*

'One of Aboulela's aims – apart from telling **a fascinating story with the verve and assurance of a natural novelist** – is surely to present a sympathetic picture of Islam to a western readership more accustomed to being given what, for devout Muslims, is a distorted and reprehensible version of their faith' *Scotsman*

'Aboulela's graceful writing style makes for **a pleasurable read**'
Independent on Sunday

'As Leila Aboulela's new novel reminds us, to ask where we come from, to choose where we belong, is not a simple matter at all ... An **absorbing** novel' *New York Times*

'The main thrust of this book is written from and about a historian's perspective. It's about the wish and murmur of lives lived centuries ago — what they tell us and how we exalt them, long for them, look to them to make our existence sufferable and better still, interesting'
LA Times

'**A rich, multilayered story**, a whole syllabus of **compelling** topics. As a novelist, Aboulela moves confidently between dramatizing urgent, contemporary issues and providing her audience with sufficient background to follow these discussions about the changing meaning of jihad, the history of Sufism and the racial politics of the war on terror' *Washington Post*

'Aboulela is a great storyteller, and she writes with clarity and elegance. A **pleasurable and engaging** read for fans of both contemporary and historical fiction' *Kirkus Review*

'[A] **beautiful** new book... Aboulela has written a book for grown-ups, one whose complexity is born of compassion, that **speaks more forcefully than a thousand opinion pieces.** By charting the pattern of human folly down the generations, she has done more than **breathe life into legend**. She has made the story of an obscure 19th century warrior topical and the story of three ordinary citizens in 21st century Scotland timeless' *San Francisco Chronicle*

'Aboulela, winner of the Caine Prize, pens an **ambitious** tri-continental story covering more than 200 years and tackling themes of Islamic faith, personal heritage, and the disparity between academic and personal reconstructions of historic events... **A nuanced story of identity and sense of place**' *Publishers Weekly*

the
Kindness
of
Enemies

leila aboulela

WEIDENFELD & NICOLSON

First published in Great Britain in 2015
by Weidenfeld & Nicolson
This paperback edition published in 2016
by Weidenfeld & Nicolson
An imprint of the Orion Publishing Group Ltd
Carmelite House, 50 Victoria Embankment
London EC4Y 0DZ

An Hachette UK Company

1 3 5 7 9 10 8 6 4 2

A CIP catalogue record for this book is available
from the British Library.

978 1 474 60092 7

Typeset at The Spartan Press Ltd, Lymington, Hants

Printed and bound in Great Britain by Clays Ltd, St Ives plc

www.orionbooks.co.uk

For my brother, Khalid Aboulela

'... we have to grope our way through so much filth and rubbish in order to reach home! And we have no one to show us the way. Homesickness is our only guide.'

Steppenwolf, Herman Hesse

'That the soul should be open to the Divine Light, even with so small an opening as to allow only a glimmer to pass through, was enough to satisfy the utmost aspirations and capabilities of the vast majority for the rest of their life on earth. It remained for them to treasure what they had gained and to consolidate it...'

A Sufi Saint of the Twentieth Century, Martin Lings

Contents

Contents

1
Scimitar and Son

1. Scotland, December 2010

Allah was inscribed on the blade in gold. Malak read the Arabic aloud to me. She looked more substantial than my first impression; an ancient orator, a mystic in shawls that rustled. The sword felt heavy in my hand; iron-steel, its smooth hilt of animal horn. I had not imagined it would be beautiful. But there was artistry in the vegetal decorations and Ottoman skill from the blade's smooth curve down to its deadly tip. A cartouche I could not make out. I put my thumb on the crossbar – long ago Imam Shamil's hand had gripped this. Malak said the sword had been in her family for generations. 'If I ever become penniless, I will show it to the *Antiques Roadshow*,' she laughed, and offered me tea. It was still snowing outside, the roads were likely to become blocked, but I wanted to stay longer, I wanted to know more. I put the sword back into its scabbard. With care, almost with respect, she mounted it on the wall again.

I followed her to the kitchen. It felt unusual to walk in my socks through a stranger's house. Malak had asked me to take off my boots at the door and she herself was wearing light leather slip-ons. The house suited her with its rugs of burgundy and browns, cushions for what must be a seating area on the floor and more Islamic calligraphy on the walls. One tapestry took up the whole side of the sitting room, its large rugged words stitched in green. It looked like a banner carried by a charging horseman. Whatever these letters symbolised was the reason men left the comforts of their homes for the collision of the battlefield. Or was that too idealised an interpretation? My childhood memory of the Arabic alphabet had become hazy and the letters were not easy to distinguish. Malak

3

might read the words out to me. Remarkable that a successful actor would choose to move to such an isolated farmhouse. Even the nearest town, Brechin, was miles away. And this home did not look like a bolthole, an excuse to visit her student son now and again. It looked settled, lived in. Malak Raja had turned her back on London, carried her furniture and family heirlooms north. 'I brought the scimitar by train,' she said, scooping tea leaves. 'I knew I wouldn't be able to get it past security at Heathrow.'

I took my notebook out and laid it open on the kitchen table. I thought she would be used to media interviews. But I had looked her up on Google and, surprisingly, there were none. Only a list of her roles and a brief description: *Born in Baghdad of Persian and Russian ancestry... has a diverse range of accents... trained at the Bristol Old Vic Theatre School.* Her roles were too minor to merit interviews. Perhaps the female equivalent of Yul Brynner or Ben Kingsley was doomed not to fare as well. Malak Raja had been one of Macbeth's witches on stage; she was an auntie in *Bombay Barista*, a mother in the BBC's new *Conan the Barbarian*. Recently she had played the wife of a beleaguered Iranian ambassador in *Spooks* and the voice of a viper in a Disney cartoon. Later when we became friends she told me that being a viper was lucrative.

Now at her kitchen table, instead of listening to my questions, she asked me about myself. The tea smelled of cinnamon and threatened a memory. She knew only what her son had told her. 'And you know what boys are like,' she twisted her bangles. 'They never tell their mothers everything.' She called him Ossie. His friends and teachers called him Oz. We were all eager to avoid his true name, Osama.

I too had an unfortunate name; my surname. One that I nagged my mother and stepfather to change. It was good that I did that; had I waited for marriage, I would have waited in vain. 'Imagine,' I said, 'arriving in London in the summer of 1990, fourteen years old, just as Saddam Hussein invaded Kuwait. Imagine an unfamiliar school, a teacher saying to the class, "We have a new student from

Sudan. Her name is Natasha Hussein." ' From the safe distance of the future, I joined my classmates in laughing out loud.

Malak grunted with sympathy. 'Oh they must have had a field day with you!' Behind her, through the window, the snow was falling, grey and continuous like static on a television screen.

I felt a slight drop of fatigue. I had been tense these past few days preparing for yesterday's talk. The previous night I had hardly slept, post-presentation euphoria and that unexpected new thread. I had started with 'Thank you for coming out in this freezing weather.' For a Monday at 8 p.m., it was a good turnout, boosted by the History Society's new introduction of refreshments. There was also a decent showing from the Muslim Society, drawn no doubt by the title, 'Jihad as Resistance – Russian Imperial Expansion and Insurrection in the Caucasus'. When they realised that my focus was Imam Shamil's leadership from 1830 to 1859 rather than the present, they seemed a little restless. Sensitive to their attention span, I finished ten minutes earlier than planned. The Q&A session started with predictable questions from my colleagues that reflected their own research interests. Then a young girl in hijab asked, 'Are you a Muslim?' It was easy to dismiss the query as irrelevant, even silly. I laughed and that made her face flush with embarrassment. She was sitting next to Oz and I got the impression that they had come together. He was one of my brightest students, the one who asked the good questions in class, the one I found myself preparing my lectures for, pointing out an extra reference to, making that little bit more of an effort. Like turning back to the mirror to dab on another bit of make-up before an important meeting.

Oz disappointed me at the Q&A session by not saying anything. Perhaps I even turned to him when the laughter died, expecting at least a response. But he just looked past me, out of the window, at the first flakes of snow. After the talk, as I was putting my laptop away, he came up to me and said that his mother's descendants were from the Caucasus and that she could tell me more. 'Call her,' he said, his hands in the back of his jeans, his trouser legs tucked into big white trainers. 'She can tell you more, personal stuff too.'

He took out his mobile phone. 'Here's her number, she won't mind at all. Come over and see our sword. A real one that was used for jihad, I'm not kidding!'

When I called Malak the following morning and she said, 'Come now if you like,' I jumped in the car and drove all the way with my windscreen wipers flapping away at the falling snow. I was on a high when I held the sword, knowing that it was a privilege, hoping for a breakthrough. No, I was not here to talk about myself. She had lured me this far like a fortune teller. I was usually restrained, keeping back the shards and useless memories. I had worked too hard to fit in. To be here and now. That's how I wanted to appear – topical, relevant, and despite my research interest, inhabiting the present. And now the mention of my father's name stalled me, I teetered on the brink of the usual revulsion. If I had been Dr Hussein, the girl wouldn't have asked me if I were Muslim. And yet still I would have had to explain the non-Muslim Natasha. Better like this, not even Muslim by name.

Many Muslims in Britain wished that no one knew they were Muslim. They would change their names if they could and dissolve into the mainstream, for it was not enough for them to openly condemn 9/11 and 7/7, not enough to walk against the wall, to raise a glass of champagne, to eat in the light of Ramadan and never step into a mosque or say the shahada or touch the Qur'an. All this was not enough, though most people were too polite to say it. All these actions somehow fell short of the complete irrevocable dissolution that was required. Yet children pick up vibes, they know more than they can express, they feel and understand before learning the words for a particular emotion or idea. Many of the young Muslims I taught throughout the years couldn't wait to bury their dark, badly dressed immigrant parents who never understood what was happening around them or even took an interest, who walked down high streets as if they were still in a village, who obsessed about halal meat and arranged marriages and were so impractical, so arrogant as to imagine that their children would stay loyal. Instead their children grew up as chameleons, not only shifting their colours at will, but able to focus on two opposing goals at the same time. They grew up reptiles plotting to silence their parents' voices, to muffle their poor accents, their miseries, their shuffling feet, their lives of toil and bafflement, their dated ideas of the British Empire, their gratitude because they remembered all too clearly the dead-ends they had left behind.

I was actually one of the lucky ones. I was one of the ones who saw the signs early on in the tricksy ways of schoolchildren, in the way my mother, snow-white as she was, was disliked for being Russian. I saw the writing on the wall and I was not too proud to take a short-cut to the exit.

Oz brought in a flurry of snow with him. He stood stamping his wellies, taking off his scarf and gloves. Melting snow gleamed on his hair and I could tell that his lips were numb. The news of the snowstorm was not reassuring. 'Some of the trains are cancelled; I had to change twice. Here, Malak, I got you the vitamins you asked for.' He used her first name as if he was indulging her. He seemed more grown-up in her presence. Perhaps his role was to be the steady responsible son so that she could be the ditzy artistic parent. Yet I had seen in him too the inclination for theatre. Oz liked to make his classmates laugh at his impersonations of politicians. He once had me laughing out loud when he used a clothes hanger and did Abu Hamza, the hook-handed cleric. Shaking the snow off his coat, he hung it behind the door. 'When I got out of the station the bus wasn't there and all the taxis were taken. The roads are pretty bad. I walked because it was quicker than hanging around waiting for the bus.'

'Poor Ossie,' drawled Malak without much sympathy. This was a sharper side of her, a glimpse of the mother who had handed him calmly to babysitters, tucked him into boarding school during a messy divorce, gazed past him as if he never existed while she was practising for a new role. I guessed he was not a child who was encouraged to complain, a child who learnt to search for comfort away from her.

7

He turned to me. 'Did you see the sword? It belonged to Imam Shamil.'

'We can't be a hundred per cent sure.' Malak ran her finger through her hair. 'It could have belonged to someone else.'

'You haven't told her yet, have you?' He was excited or just flushed from his walk in the cold. He drew out a chair but didn't sit down. He looked straight into my eyes and later, I would remember that focused look, the youthful energy in the voice. 'Imam Shamil is my ... is our,' a quick glance at his mother to include her, 'great, great, great – not exactly sure how many greats I should say – grandfather! We are descended through his son, Ghazi.'

My delight was muted by my mobile which, now on silent, buzzed again. It was Tony, who since my mother's death has been plaguing me with his sadness. Every other evening tears and long-winded confessions of guilt – he had not looked after her enough, he had not urged her to see a specialist soon enough. It was earlier than usual for him; on most days he only started to unravel after six. I rejected his call. I would not act as his grief counsellor today.

I said to Malak, 'Did you know that Queen Victoria supported Imam Shamil? His picture was on the front page of the London *Times* with a call for the English to be,' I made quotation marks with my fingers, ' "the generous defenders of liberty against the brutal forces of the Russian Empire." '

Malak made a face at her son. 'Queen Victoria championed a jihad.'

Oz sat down. 'Don't be naive, Malak. If Russia took over the Caucasus, it would have threatened India. Besides, the word "jihad" then didn't have the same connotation it has now.'

'Ever since 9/11, jihad has become synonymous with terrorism,' she said. 'I blame the Wahabis and Salafists for this. Jihad is an internal and spiritual struggle.'

'But this is not entirely true. If someone hits us, we need to hit back.'

'It's better to forgive.'

'No it's not. Limiting jihad to an internal struggle has become a bandwagon for every pacifist Muslim to climb on. You Sufis...' he wagged his finger at his mother.

'Am I a Sufi? Do you see me as such? Then you are doing me a great honour.'

'You're a wannabe, Malak. Besides, what choice do you have? Actresses aren't exactly welcome in mosques.' He gave a little laugh but I could tell that he was having a dig at his mother.

'I couldn't care less what conservative Muslims think of me, but a *wannabe* Sufi? Really!' she looked at me and rolled her eyes. I smiled.

'Yes, of course, with your chants and spiritual retreats,' he continued. 'Plus you're interrupting. I was saying that you Sufis play down your historical role in jihad. Most fighters against European Imperialism were Sufis. And Imam Shamil is a prime example. He was the head of a Sufi order.'

This was not new to me. But this stress on Sufism was not an angle I had previously considered to be important. I needed to reconsider. Shamil's Sufism might well be what I needed to refine my research direction.

Malak replied, 'Every fight Shamil fought was on the defence. He was protecting his villages against Russian attack. And surrender to the Russians would have meant the end of their traditional way of life, the end of Islam in Dagestan. The Russians were so brutal they often didn't take prisoners of war. By comparison Shamil's generals were scholarly and disciplined. This type of jihad is different from the horrible crimes of al-Qaeda.'

'I agree, but still it was guerrilla warfare...' reiterated her son.

'No it wasn't.'

He grinned. 'Malak, you think guerrilla warfare is what you see in the movies! Shamil understood that he couldn't pitch a direct battle against the tsar's large and well-equipped army so he lured sections of them up the mountains. He tricked them into dividing and then launched attacks at them.'

'Well, that is a clever thing to do.'

'That cleverness *is* guerrilla tactics.'

But Malak wasn't going to be shaken. 'Listen Oz, the door of jihad is closed. Jihad needs an imam and there is no imam now. Jihad is for upholding the values of Allah; it's not for scoring political points, it's not for land, it's not for rights, it's not for autonomy.'

'It's for getting us power over our enemies. Jihad is not something we should be ashamed of.'

'What we are ashamed of is what is done in its name. Not every Muslim war is a jihad. Not suicide bombers or attacking civilians.'

I said, 'The mufti of Bosnia said that Muslims shouldn't use the word "jihad" and Christians shouldn't use the word "crusade".'

'See,' said Malak with a sharp look at her son.

'Well, I shall use it,' Oz glared back at her. He sounded bitter. 'If Shamil were here today he wouldn't have sat back and let Muslim countries be invaded. He wouldn't have given up on Palestine and he wouldn't have accepted the two-faced wimps we have as leaders.'

His voice was unnecessarily loud. The slight tension that followed made me conscious of the time. 'I really should be going. If the snow is going to get worse, then I might make it if I leave now.' I stood up, but not without reluctance.

And it was perhaps because of this desire to stay that I succumbed to the following sequence of events. Their drive was thick with snow and I was unable to get my car to the main road. Phone calls to local cab companies elicited the same response – they were unwilling to venture that far out into the countryside on a night like this. Around nine in the evening, I accepted Malak's repeated invitation to stay the night. It seemed the sensible thing to do.

I ended up staying with them not one but two nights. Two days of the brightest sunshine and a record-breaking amount of snow. The university was closed and lectures cancelled; the schools and airports were also closed. It was unprecedented and for me, welcome. Briefly my normal life was suspended and I inhabited days that were elongated and crystallised; an unplanned break, a suspension of all that was routine and orderly. It would not be accurate to say that I fell in love. But I was captivated by the combination of Oz, Malak and their isolated sandstone house. I did not feel that I could outgrow them, that our conversations would go stale or that I would tire of their company. Perhaps it was because I started to search for traces of Shamil in them. Or it could have been the awareness that we were under siege, randomly brought together, an unexpected gift of freshness, more hospitality than I had bargained for when I drove out here, certainly more hours in the proximity of Shamil's sword and Arabic calligraphy.

But to go back to the first morning and my breakfast with Oz. Malak was busy with an exercise routine that turned out to be long and elaborate – an hour on the treadmill, forty minutes weight-training and a further hour split between Pilates and yoga. She also, Oz told me, had protein shakes for breakfast. He said this with a mix of wonder and disapproval. It struck me that this was what I would miss out on if I never had children – not only the baby stage, the pushchair, the school runs – but a young adult assessing me, poking me with their own personal rubric. We sat in the kitchen with stacks of toast and tea. There was honey to put on the toast; it came in a fancy jar with a London label. I had to search the cupboards high and low for a teabag that was not spiced, not decaffeinated and not organic. Oz spread peanut butter on his toast. Last night he had lent me some clothes because Malak was petite and nothing she wore could have fitted me. So now we were wearing the same GAP sweatshirts, mine grey and his green; and almost identical chequered pyjama trousers. It still felt odd to walk around in socks but it was a rule of the house. They did not want shoes indoors.

'You know,' he said, 'I was going to drop out of uni.'

I was taken aback. 'But your grades are good.'

'It's nothing to do with grades. Besides, I only bother to show up for your classes.'

'Well I'm flattered, but what's the problem? Aren't you happy with your choice of subjects? There's more flexibility nowadays in the kind of degree you can take. Have a chat with your tutor.' I should have known better than to start doling out suggestions. He seemed slightly more withdrawn, as if his gush of confidence was stilted by my presumptions.

'I'm reading all the time but the thing is I'm not reading the books I'm supposed to read.'

Inwardly I groaned. Another 'independent studies' candidate ahead of his time. 'Well, if you get through your first degree, and it shouldn't be a problem if you set your mind to it, then you can register for a PhD and read and research the topic of your choice.'

'I'm already doing that.'

'What are you working on?' I gulped my tea. It was already cooling down.

'I'm researching the types of weapons used in jihad. My thesis is that they reflect the technology of their time and are often the same as those used by the enemy.'

I chewed on my toast. 'Well, that makes sense.'

'But it violates some of the Sharia's rules, rules which have been conveniently forgotten. Such as not using fire because it is only Allah's prerogative to burn sinners in Hell. No human being should use fire on another human being.'

I saw charging horsemen wielding swords. They galloped towards enemy lines of cannons. One by one they were shot and they slid off their horses.

'Would you look at what I've already written and give me feedback?' he was saying.

'Sure. Email it to me.' I started telling Oz of a Russian film I had seen. It depicted Shamil's battles and the camera was angled behind the cannons facing the charging highlanders.

'Like cowboys and Indians,' said Oz and made me laugh.

But he was not so off point. The comparison had been made before by sympathetic historians. The Caucasus represented as Russia's wild west, Shamil the noble savage, as magnificent and inscrutable as a Native American chief.

Not shy of sounding abrupt Oz asked, 'Why are you so interested in Shamil?'

'From a purely secular perspective, he was one of the most successful rebels of the colonial age.'

'Why do you have to say "from a purely secular perspective"?'

I paused, momentarily caught out. I put down my piece of toast.

'Do you assume that I am religious and so you want to distance yourself from me?'

I did not want to distance myself from him. I shook my head.

'You're different from the other lecturers,' he went on. 'A Muslim talks to them and they put on that wide-eyed tolerant look, quick little nods and inside they're congratulating themselves thinking, "Look at me, I'm truly broad-minded, listening to all this shit and not batting an eyelid." Whereas you're the opposite. You pretend that you're sarcastic but deep down you have respect. Am I right?'

He was like his mother, wanting me to talk about myself, but I was not ready to answer his question. I concentrated on chewing toast and finishing my tea. Then to break the silence I said, 'Here is something about me that is odd. I dream of historical figures. I've dreamt of Stalin and Rasputin.'

He smiled. 'It's because you were reading about them.'

'But I've never ever dreamt of Shamil.'

'Not everyone can dream of Imam Shamil,' he said a little coolly.

'Why not? Is he a prophet?'

'No, but people like him don't just pop up in anyone's dreams. Only in those who've achieved a certain spiritual level.'

He made it sound like a video game. I decided to humour him. 'Has Shamil ever visited you in a dream?'

He looked at me as if to test whether I was teasing him or not. I kept a straight face.

'No,' Oz said. 'I have often, though, wished that I lived in his time.'

'To fight with him?' This was one of the leading questions. Without meaning to, I found myself asking him one of the questions the trainers suggested we put to our students. I hadn't intended to test if Oz was 'vulnerable to radicalisation', but the question presented itself now, appropriate and easy.

He said, 'What I like best about his days is the certainty. Every-thing was clear cut. Shamil and his people were the goodies; the Russians were the baddies. The Caucasus belonged to the Muslims, the tsar's army were the invaders.'

So, according to the guidelines, how should his response be classified? Did he tick this particular box or not? According to the guidelines, a student was who 'vulnerable to radicalisation' would have symptoms of regression, a hankering for an idealised past, a misguided belief in authenticity.

In the afternoon, Malak and I went for a walk leaving Oz shovelling snow in front of the house. The shining sun was no threat to the packed snow. We sank into it with our boots and messed up its neatness, beating down a path all the way to the main road. Paths, grass and asphalt were all one and the same. I breathed in the freshest air and put my gloved hands in my pockets. My mobile phone rang and it was my stepfather again. I ignored him. Nothing must break what felt like a spell. I vowed that tomorrow morning I would wake up at dawn to milk every minute of it. Here in this setting, with these two people, sleep was a waste of time.

'Do you ever go back to Chechnya?' I asked Malak.

She shook her head. 'But I have cousins there and we keep in touch. During the war I was always worrying and calling them. I tried to help them as much as I could; I still send them money.'

The name of Shamil hovered over the recent Chechen rebel wars. The militant leader Shamil Basayev was responsible for the terror-ist attacks on the North Ossetia school and the Moscow theatre hostages.

As if to dispel the negative images from her mind Malak said, 'One of the most popular films in Chechnya in the 1990s was *Braveheart*. Hundreds of pirated videos were sold.'

Probably young Chechen men saw themselves as the William Wallaces of the Caucasus. I smiled and we spoke a little bit about the film. It was interesting to hear her opinions, an insider's view of the film industry that I was not familiar with.

We came across another farmhouse; a neighbour shovelling snow. Malak stopped to chat. She sounded comfortable as she swapped updates about the weather and introduced me as a house guest. I gathered that she had only met this particular neighbour once before. She was still relatively new in the area. It made me wonder at her motives for leaving London. It was a brave step to take, to live in such isolation, to start anew. Though I appreciated the peace and fresh air, this lifestyle was not for me. I needed the anonymity of the city. Here I was conscious of being African in the Scottish countryside, of the need to justify my presence.

To avoid small talk with the neighbour I stepped back and took out my mobile to answer Tony's calls. He probably needed reassurance that I would drive up with him to Fraserburgh for Christmas with Naomi. She was his daughter from his first marriage. It was an annual tradition to fill the car with presents and spend Christmas with her and her husband. They were a generous and good-natured couple, but this year for the first time, we would be visiting without my mum. The telephone rang in the house but it was the Polish cleaner, Kornelia, who picked up. I asked her to pass on a message explaining my predicament. That was how I made it sound, an inconvenience; a tiresome pause in my usual, busy life. Sometimes a lie makes more sense than the truth. Often the truth is irrelevant.

The sun started to set, still bright through the trees. We walked back to the house and stopped when we saw what Oz was doing. He had built five snowmen so crudely that they were almost columns. None of them were taller than him. He was holding the sword in his hand, the same one I had held yesterday and imagined to be Shamil's. His coat was open, his scarf covered his mouth and his woollen cap was low over his eyebrows. His feet were deep in the snow and with the sword he was swinging away at the snowmen. One after the other – hacking, thrusting, lopping off their unformed heads. There was no passion in his expression, only concentration, as if he was practising, as if he was trying out new tricks.

'Are you out of your mind?' Malak walked towards him. 'It's hundreds of years old, you'll ruin it.'

I had not seen her angry before. She moved to snatch it away from him so abruptly that for a minute I was afraid she was going to get hurt. He turned to her and because only his eyes were visible, the smile in them had a mesmerising, distant quality. He hid the sword behind his back and with the other hand pulled down the scarf so as to say, 'Malak, don't fuss. A little bit of snow won't hurt it.'

It disappointed me that he would lack such appreciation. I thought he would value Shamil's sword, cherish and respect it.

'What would the neighbours think seeing you so violent?' Malak sounded exasperated now. If he were still a child, she would have snatched the forbidden game from him, hauled him yelling and kicking back into the house.

'They'll think I'm a jihadist.' His voice was deliberately loud, deliberately provocative. Then he changed his tone so that it was theatrical, bordering on comic. 'They'll think we've set up a jihadist training camp out in the countryside, aye, that's what they'll ken.' He added the accent, a thread for her to catch on.

She softened and cuffed him on the shoulder. The three of us walked towards the house laughing. We stood at the door in the blue cold dusk, stamping our feet to get rid of the snow. But the next day when the men made their way to the house, it didn't seem funny after all. They rang the bell, they came in and they asked not for Oz and not for Ossie. They said the other name.

2. Akhulgo, the Caucasus, 1839

Eight-year-old Jamaleldin, clambering with his friends, followed by his toddling brother, could see a cloud approaching. Then he was in a white mist, the highest snowy summits invisible, the neighbouring peaks and gullies fading to a blur of reddish browns and greens. He crouched down, waiting for clarity, for the sight of the Russian battalions stationed far below. The word Akhulgo meant 'a meeting place in time of danger' and now the Russians had laid it under siege. It was a natural fortress, high on one of the peaks of the Caucasus, six hundred feet above the river Andi-Koisu. The river looped around its base on three sides; only horses trained for such a twisted, vertical ascent could reach Shamil's aoul. This made Jamaleldin feel safe. The Russians' horses were not trained; if they ever came up here they would have to come on foot.

He turned and held his brother in his arms, leaving the older boys to collect more stones. Ghazi was still plump but he could talk fluently. 'Don't take me back to mother. I am old enough to fight too.'

Jamaleldin laughed. 'A murid would have to carry you on his shoulder if you want to even toss a pebble.'

'I'm not afraid.' Ghazi wrenched himself free and scampered away.

Jamaleldin admired his daring. He himself was an able rider and a fair marksman. He could use a dagger and had ridden with his father in several raids but he was cautious by nature, reliant on practice rather than aggression. Watching Ghazi leap away from him, he could sense that his sturdy younger brother was of a different nature, living up to his Arabic name of 'Conqueror'.

Jamaleldin had been named after his father's teacher, Sheikh Jamal el-Din al Husayni, the gentle Sufi scholar who preferred books to war. Everyone knew that Sheikh Jamal el-Din was special because he was a friend of Allah. Whenever he prayed for something, it happened. Shamil's strength came through him. That was how he had become Imam of Dagestan and was now leading the tribes of the Caucasus to fight the armies of the Russian tsar.

When Jamaleldin thought of his father, the feeling of pride made his chest big. Every cell in his body strained for his father's approval. It was as if Shamil's love was his nourishment and Shamil's admonishments his understanding of Hell. It was incredible to Jamaleldin that some men disobeyed his father. The wars against the Russians went on and on and some of the tribal chiefs were weakening; they were trading with the Russians, paying taxes and even spying on Shamil himself. Jamaleldin wanted to trust everyone around him. Sometimes, though, he would notice a villager with shifty eyes, an elder with a haughty look and he would wonder if they were the hypocrites. If they were the traitors who had sold their souls to the White Tsar.

'The world is a carcass and the one who goes after it is a dog.' This was what Sheikh Jamal el-Din taught, and his young namesake repeated it to himself though he was not quite sure what it meant. Long ago, Shamil swore an allegiance to Sheikh Jamal el-Din and became his follower. For years he lived the austere life of a student, learning the Qur'an and how to bow his will, through his spiritual teacher, to the will of Allah. Today after the dawn prayer, the men of Akhulgo and sleepy Jamaleldin too, renewed their oath of allegiance to Imam Shamil. But Shamil himself would remain obedient to Sheikh Jamal el-Din. When father and son had last visited him in his aoul, Jamaleldin had seen his towering father – who could make grown men tremble at the sound of his voice – bow down and kiss the feet of his teacher.

Jamaleldin continued to fill his basket with stones for the coming battle. He could hear the murids chanting, churning in themselves the spirit to fight: 'Under the infidel's supremacy, we would be covered in shame.' 'Brother, how can you serve Allah, if you are serving the Russians?' Then the prayers rising up: 'Preserve us from regression. Bring us the longed-for end.' *Preserve us from regression.* Jamaleldin looked up to see his father's younger wife Djawarat, carrying his sleeping half-brother on her back and stuffing her pockets with rocks. He liked Djawarat because her face reminded him of a rabbit and because she often gave him tasty fried grain sprinkled with salt. 'Do you think the Russians will be able to come up here?' he asked her.

She looked down at the ground. 'If only it was winter and the mountains covered in snow. If only, like long, long ago, they fought with swords and not gunfire.'

But it was June and the Russians had more artillery than they did. Jamaleldin regretted his question.

'It is Allah's will that we fight,' continued Djawarat. She straightened up and put her hand on his shoulder. He gazed at her big, attractive teeth, her eyebrows that were high and thick. 'Jamaleldin, when the Merciful honours a slave with His power, then no other creature can ever humiliate him. This is how it is with your father.'

They both knew that Shamil was backed by mystical powers – the kind that could make him tame a jackal or bless a handful of millet so that it would feed five men instead of one. Djawarat sat down on the rocks and put her baby on her lap. 'Remember when he leapt over a line of soldiers who surrounded him...'

'They were just about to fire on him...' The story was in Jamaleldin's mind as if he had been present.

'He whirled round and struck two with his sword.'

'Three,' Jamaleldin corrected her.

'The fourth one hit him but he pulled the bayonet blade from his own shoulder...'

'Jumped over a five-foot wall.'

'Seven,' Djawarat corrected him.

'In one leap.'

Djawarat was smiling. She bent down and gave her baby a kiss. 'No one is like your father, little one.'

And there was Shamil now, tall and still, as if he had willed himself into this particular place and time. He was dressed for battle in a long cherkesska and a large white turban, the end of which hung down his neck. Two black cartridge pouches crisscrossed his torso and a leather halter held his scimitar. Jamaleldin moved forward to kiss his hand. The familiar warmth emitted from his father, an energy that surfaced in his dark eyes. He lifted Jamaleldin up; it had been a long time since his father had carried him. He was a big boy now, not a baby, not like Ghazi. He heard Djawarat laugh but he was too full to make any sound. His father's beard, his smell, the groove under his cheek. Jamaleldin felt a slight pressure on his stomach; it was his father's cartridge pouch digging into his own skin. 'If only they would leave us in peace,' his father whispered and then he started to pray, 'Lord, this is my son and he is under Your protection. Oh Lord, shake up our enemy...'

The attack started almost gently. The Russian soldiers would try to scale the bluffs and slip. They climbed on each other's shoulders to reach ledges and any rocks that protruded as footholds. Shamil and his murids bided their time and held their fire. When the soldiers came close, they drove them back with rocks and burning logs, javelins and daggers. A soldier only needed to lose his balance once. By nightfall three-hundred and fifty Russians were killed. Akhulgo had stood firm but, after a lull of four days, the Russians changed their tactics. Batteries were manoeuvred into better positions out of reach of the murids' range. Cannons started to blast the walls of Akhulgo and bury the murids one by one under the rubble.

Day after day Jamaleldin woke up to the stifled sobs of women mourning their men, to the clap of gunfire, to the ugly moans of the wounded. Shamil and his murids fought on, charged with energy, flooded with a strength that seeped too into Jamaleldin. He pitted rocks at the climbing soldiers, large heavy ones he would not normally be capable of raising high. He threw daggers and didn't miss. He heaved burning pieces of timber and didn't wince when his palms got scorched. Yet there was no time or occasion to exult; the mere pressure of his father's hand on his head or his mother,

Fatima, saying, 'Eat now,' gave way to the sudden submersion of sleep. Days punctuated by prayers taken in turn, a rawness in the chest, a cleaving to everyone who was around him; men, women and children in stress.

Week after week, with less food and more wounded, a jagged airy sensation was felt all around when their outer defences came down and left them exposed. The Russians were looming nearer. But Shamil still resisted with a firmness his enemy had not been prepared for. The tsar's army had not counted on losing so many officers. Reinforcements were brought in, a forced march of troops from the north. They divided into columns and approached Akhulgo from different directions.

In desperation, women and children joined in an ambush. To fool the Russians that they had more fighters, Djawarat and a group of women dressed like men. Reluctantly their husbands, fathers and brothers shared battle tactics and turbans, lent them swords and sharpened daggers, whispered advice. These were dark times, indeed (but temporary, they reassured themselves), when even the prettiest could not be spared the proximity of the enemy. Yet, these wives and daughters were as eager as any man to pitch themselves at the enemy, to help protect their homes, to win the day. And if they died in battle, they too would become martyrs, granted everlasting life. A ferocity was rising up in them, like mothers in the animal kingdom baring their teeth and hissing to protect their young. Jamaleldin's mother, Fatima, was pregnant and she stayed behind with the younger children. Djawarat called for Jamaleldin and they lay in wait on a ledge overhanging a precipice. Djawarat crouched next to him, praying softly to herself. If she died, her baby would scream with hunger. Jamaleldin could feel his heart beating; he held a dagger in each sweaty hand. 'Bend down below their bayonets and aim at their bellies,' Djawarat said. 'Wait, wait till they come close, take them by surprise. This is your advantage; they tread unknown territory while you stand on higher ground, your own higher ground, your home.'

He heard them approaching, voices in another language, a thud of boots, the lethal metal clank of their weapons. Bend down below their bayonets. Spring together. The blinding gleam of the sun on a bayonet. Shock in the wide eyes of an enemy. A roar in Jamaleldin's ears. A gun had gone off and the smoke choked him. Where was the bayonet he must bend under? All his strength and that terrible sound of his dagger ripping flesh. But it was either them or us. Them or Ghazi. The women around him brandished swords; one threw hers aside and, grabbing a soldier's bayonet, used the weight of her body to pitch him headlong over the cliffs.

The Russian column retreated and Djawarat burst into tears. Dazed and shaking, Jamaleldin stumbled back to his mother talking gibberish. He had wet his pants as if he was little, but she did not scold him. There was not enough time to rest and forget, not enough time to heal properly. Hungry and feverish, the nightmare weeks blurred. His father and his naibs deep in discussion, changing tactics, arranging for the wounded to be smuggled out of Akhulgo, arranging for reinforcements to sneak past the Russians. Already two months – for how long could they hold out? The summer sun was merciless, the well was drying up, there was hardly any food left and no timber to reconstruct. Typhoid swept through the Russian forces while in Akhulgo men, women and children were slowly starving. Death below and with them – carrion birds circled above.

Preserve us from regression, was the desperate prayer. *Grant us an honourable death.* Then a lull in the fighting. The Russians were willing to open negotiations. At last, at long last, peace was near. But as proof of Shamil's good intentions, the Russians wanted Jamaleldin as a hostage.

'No,' was Shamil's reply. 'Not my son.'

Jamaleldin heard his name mentioned in the naibs' council and sensed the concern in his father's voice. Soon the whole of Akhulgo bristled with the news. The women held their breath. The children stared at Jamaleldin in a way that made him feel important. Pleas were sent to the Russians to accept another child, a nephew or a cousin, but they would accept only Shamil's eldest son. Jamaleldin wanted to talk to Djawarat but it was as if she was avoiding him.

At home, the naibs came over to argue with Shamil. He refused again and this time angry voices were raised. When the naibs left, Fatima started to cry. His parents talked in whispers until his father got up and left the house.

Because he couldn't sleep, Jamaleldin sat outdoors. The summer sky was clear but there was a bad smell, the stench of war and waste, of fire and his own unwashed body. He knew the custom of hostage-taking during negotiations. Hostages were treated well; they were given clean clothes and food. At the thought of food, his stomach rumbled and there was moisture in his mouth. Pancakes in butter, rolled-out bread with honey. The Russians would give him cheese. But he could not imagine being away from his father, living in a place where Shamil did not command and forbid. Jamaleldin did not want to leave Ghazi, he did not want to leave his mother or Akhulgo or Djawarat.

He dozed, his head lolling on his chest, and found his father sitting beside him, propping him. It was all he wanted, to be in his father's arms, to be approved of, to be safe.

'I lost my finest men,' Shamil said and there was a catch in his voice. 'When I think of each of them, when I think of his qualities, I know that he cannot be replaced. He was worth ten or more, a hundred even. Now the others are becoming too feeble to fight. I can see it coming. In days, in a week or so they will no longer gather for battle. They might not even show up at their posts.'

Jamaleldin understood but what he understood could wait – there was no need to voice it, no need to put it into words. He wanted these moments to continue. His father talking to him as if he were a man, recalling the brave, strong fighters who were now granted eternal life; men who had once jested with Jamaleldin, who had taught him how to wield a kinjal, who had carried him on their shoulders. Father and son listened to the sounds of the night.

'Tell me the story of the chicken, Father.'

Shamil smiled in the dark and Jamaleldin felt the warmth coming from him, all the memories of peace. 'Long ago before you were born, when I was a young lad, our people, sadly, allowed themselves

23

to forget Allah. Instead of the Sharia they followed the adaat. Do you know what the adaat are?'

'They are our ancient customs and laws. They told people to worship the forest and the trees but they also taught us hospitality and honour.'

'Yes, the adaat were a mixture of good and bad,' Shamil continued. 'A mixture of Allah's laws and the traditional laws of the tribes. They taught us to be brave warriors but they allowed us to ferment grapes and get drunk. And worse than that the adaat supported blood feuds. Once a man stole a chicken...'

Jamaleldin smiled and drew nearer for here the story was starting.

'He stole a chicken from his neighbour's village. In reply the owner of the chicken stole a cow. The first man got angry and said,' Shamil's voice rose, ' "A chicken is a chicken. It is not a cow!" In revenge he stole the man's horse. When you steal a man's horse it is as if you are stealing his honour. The horse owner went and killed the thief. Blood was spilled, it was serious now. The families got involved. A vendetta began. Generation after generation carried on this feud. There were raids and fires, there was kidnapping and treachery. Hundreds of men died, all because of...?'

This was the pause that had delighted Jamaleldin when he was little. That part in the story where he would chip in and squeal out loud, 'A chicken!'

It had been Shamil's predecessors, Ghazi Muhammad (after whom little Ghazi was named) and Hamza Bek, who had first urged the people of Dagestan to stop the blood feuds and obey the Sharia. To draw strength from Allah's laws, to tap into His power and push away the Russians. The invaders set aouls ablaze and destroyed crops; they were even destroying the forests in order to build their military roads. And when they captured a village, they defecated in the houses as if to mark their territory. At times they would also foul the wells. But it was not always easy to resist the Russians. Many tribes did not have the strength. They shirked the hardship involved or were lured by the riches of the red and white coins the Russians promised. Some succumbed to the pressure so wholeheartedly that they even joined in the aggression against their fellow highlanders. These traitors would ride with the severed heads of their own people dangling from their saddle bows.

Ghazi Muhammad al-Ghimrawi preached from region to region and from aoul to aoul, 'What kind of repose could there be in a place where the heart is not at ease and the authority of Allah not accepted? Grab the strong cable of Islam and our enemies will not even find a weak protector!' Ghazi Muhammad mobilised an army in which Shamil was a young naib. In one battle after another they took back the villages that had fallen to the Russians. But Ghazi Muhammad was martyred and his successor Hamza Bek only ruled for two years.

When Shamil became leader, he did not find support in Gimrah, his birthplace. The villagers insisted on obeying the Russian commander's order of supplying five donkey-loads of grape vines and fruit. Shamil argued and threatened but he could not convince them. This was Jamaleldin's earliest memory – his mother and father packing throughout the night. After the dawn prayer, Shamil came out of the mosque and addressed his fellow villagers. 'I am leaving you because I am unable to uphold the faith among you. After all, the best of Allah's creation, the Prophet Muhammad, peace be upon him, left the best of cities, Makkah, when it was no longer easy for him to maintain his faith there. If Allah wills the faith to be strong in you, then I will return. If not, then what can you offer me, you whose houses have been smeared with the shit of Russian soldiers!'

The family moved to Ashilta and had to move again – always fearful of the Russians and suspicious of the hypocrites who were tired of fighting, who were bitter against the strictness of the Sharia. 'Would the Russians have advanced so far without collaborators from among us?' The answer was a painful no. That was why Shamil taught the prayer, 'Preserve us from regression. Don't try us, Lord, beyond our means.' Too often the villagers would listen to Shamil preach his resistance and say ruefully, 'What is he saying, when we can't even defend our women against the Russians!' It was the modern cannon that filled them with dread, the 'Father of the Guns', that beast set to devour them. Then when the tide turned, in twists and surprising turns, Shamil would leap from one victory to another and the spirit of resistance would rekindle in men's chests. They would swell with pride and remember the old days of freedom. They would move to join Shamil and be among his murids. An autonomous Caucasus would shimmer in the horizon, credible again.

The morning after sitting outdoors with his father, Jamaleldin watched his mother, Fatima, sob as she handed him his best clothes. A white tunic and a high lambskin papakhi. He must look his best today even though he was thin and fatigued with dark shadows under his eyes. 'Take your kinjal with you,' said Fatima, controlling herself. 'But never use it against your captors.' She was eight months pregnant and her face was puffy. 'You must always act honourably, with courage and patience. Never cry. Never let them see you crying. Remember, you are an Avar. Remember always that you are the son of Shamil, Imam of Dagestan.'

Jamaleldin adjusted the halter around his neck and put his kinjal in place. He was ready to go now, his mother breaking down, his father's hand on his shoulder. The whole of Akhulgo was gathered and Shamil lifted his palms up in prayer. 'Lord, You raised up Your prophet Moses, upon him be peace, when he was in the hands of Pharaoh. Here is my son. If I formally hand him over to the infidels, then he is under Your care and protection. You are the best of guardians.'

Ghazi tugged at his brother's sleeve and said with characteristic bravado, 'Let me go instead of you.'

'Don't be silly. I am more valuable to them.'

There was Djawarat giving him a small handful of fried grain with salt as a goodbye gift. Her sweet smile and her sleepy, docile baby.

There was Akhulgo ugly around him. A woman crouched over a dead relative raised her arm up to flap wildly at carrion birds. Keep off, keep off, she repeated, keening softly. The siege had prevented them from burying the dead. They lay in piles, decomposing and starting to smell, shameful under the morning sun.

Fatima was still clinging to him and crying; Djawarat was by Fatima's side, her arms around her.

Three of his father's naibs escorted him away, carrying their banners. They guided their horses down the tricky slopes and Jamaleldin breathed the air of the lowlands. Akhulgo was above him now, and here, at last, were the Russian lines. The enemy, smiling men who held their arms out to their prized hostage. Tears of anger rose to Jamaleldin's eyes but he would not break down. The naibs were lowering their banners in a final salute; they would go back and tell his father that Jamaleldin was brave and did not flinch. He walked into enemy territory with his kinjal at his side. They would tell Shamil that the Russians treated his son with respect and did not disarm him.

Forward now into a mass of tents and horses, men whose words made no sense. Their large beardless faces; their own particular smell. They stared at him and some laughed. Laughter was a language Jamaleldin could understand. Some of it was good-natured; he was, after all, a symbol of the ceasefire, a reason to celebrate. Tonight, they would be issued extra rations of vodka and there would be songs around the campfire. But there was another kind of laughter. He was little and they were grown men. He was something and they were something else; men who made faces and pretended to snatch away his kinjal.

'Watch him. He's like a trapped animal.'

'He'll use his dagger on you given the chance.'

'Give me that!'

Jamaleldin leapt at the soldier, punching and scratching. Without the kinjal he was a mere prisoner. Without the kinjal he was a disgrace. Jeering, the worst kind of laughter.

'We'll tame you, you little savage. We'll tame you in no time.'

'Look at these wild eyes!'

'Enough. Give him back his kinjal, Alexi.' Always, as Jamaleldin was to learn, there were kind ones embedded among the rest. They would pop out like secrets, ready to make a difference.

Inside a Russian tent, the size of it, a world so much softer than the houses made of rock. The pistols of the soldiers, their boots. To see a cigar for the first time. It smoked and glowed! An object that entered the mouth and was neither food nor a twig for cleaning your teeth. The sun moved in the sky, shadows lengthened and no Russian stood to make the call to prayer. His father would be at the mosque now, Ghazi too. Were they thinking of him? He stared at two lamb cutlets, he sniffed the porter wine. This was not for him. Where was the cheese and the flat bread? Where were the honey and the pancakes? His stomach growled and for the first time in that long clumsy day, he burst into tears.

The negotiations lasted for three days and failed. Jamaleldin should be handed over now, like any other hostage voluntarily turned over and held temporarily during a ceasefire. No ransom was demanded from Shamil, no ransom was expected to be paid. Instead Jamaleldin found himself in a carriage. He had never been in a carriage before. Next to him a Russian staff officer sat with his legs wide open, taking up more space. The wheels rattled and Jamaleldin listened to the hooves of the horses through the forest and on a newly built road. If he tried to escape now, he would be able to find his way back to Akhulgo. But it would be dishonourable to do that; he must wait. 'Where are we going?' he asked but the staff officer only smiled and gave him an apple. Jamaleldin was leaving Dagestan. He was no longer a hostage now, he was being kidnapped away from his father's territory. On to the misty unknown, to the city of the tsar himself, St Petersburg.

3. Akhulgo, the Caucasus, 1839

Shamil fought and when he despaired of winning, he longed for martyrdom. During the negotiations, the thinness of his fighters was visible and there were more damning reports from the Russian spies, the collaborators who circled among Shamil's forces pretending to be translators and intermediaries for the peace process. It became known that Shamil's men were weary and restless. The front lines of Akhulgo were destroyed and the corpses piled up. This was too valuable a prize for the Russian generals to pass. They changed their plan. Instead of a surrender on their own terms, they would aim for a bigger prize – a complete collapse of Akhulgo and the humiliating capture of Shamil. This would crush the resistance once and for all. The negotiations were halted and Jamaleldin was sent away. Then the Russians hit with their greatest force.

For a week the highlanders fought back. Every reinforced position was destroyed and yet the murids would stay up all night trying to rebuild. But it was useless now. Too numb to fear the Russians, they feared instead their own spiritual weakness. Defection loomed at them as the ultimate temptation, the dishonourable outcome. With everything slipping away, arms, homes, families and properties, only the spirit was left and that spirit belonged to Allah and was created to be free as the eagles that circled the mountains.

Shamil sat on the cliffs in full view of the Russians. Below were green groves and the foaming river. He prayed out loud for an enemy bullet in the middle of his forehead. The treachery of the Russians devastated him. He had been ready to surrender in return for permission to live in Dagestan and to have Jamaleldin back. Reasonable demands, but the Russian general had deemed them insolent. The Russians wanted to drag Jamaleldin across the country, all the way to the tsar himself. And they were not above mocking the divisions between the highlanders and the way the naibs, even during the negotiations, voiced their individual opinions. The Russians, on the other hand, were one force, an organised, powerful entity united in loyalty to the tsar, obedient to authority.

Shamil accepted their demands of sending away the families for whom Akhulgo was not home but the Russians granted nothing in return. Instead they acted swiftly and cruelly, dispatching Jamaleldin without Shamil's permission, treating him like a criminal, not a worthy adversary. The Russians were, he said to Fatima, as poisonous as the snakes that crawled in the steppes.

On the last day before the Russians finally took Akhulgo, Shamil made a decision. His family would elude the soldiers and escape on foot by nightfall. As for himself, he would fight to the end. Many years later he would recall that time with pain and wonder. How he dressed for battle and headed to the stables intent on slaughtering his horse so that it would never carry a Russian rider. He stroked its mane and when it turned to him and whinnied, he felt sorry and spared it. He stood in his house and looked at his books. One of them was especially precious to him – *Insan al-'Uyun*, copied by the scholar Sa'id al-Harakamil. Shamil held it in his hand. Who would read it again? Who would value and appreciate it?

He gathered his remaining followers and issued his harshest orders. 'Avoid capture at all costs. Escape from the Russians or fight with the last ounce of your strength. If you are wounded, throw yourself in the river.'

In small groups, for they could not all stay together, Shamil's family groped their way down the cliffs. They clung to the rocks, often treading on each other's feet, pressing their bodies against the mountainside. It was slow progress, with the river gushing below and the Russians swarming up the cliffs. They would hide in caves and emerge to move again. Arguments on how to proceed, true and false alarms, Fatima holding on to her belly, Ghazi still clutching a kinjal in his hand.

Shamil's naibs urged him to escape. They knew that as long as he lived, the resistance would continue. They persuaded him to join his family who were hiding down in a ledge and by doing so he missed the Russians' ultimate entry into Akhulgo. Those that stayed behind, too wasted to escape, hid in caves in order to ambush the Russians. Others pretended to lay down their arms only to turn on their captors at the last minute. Young women, fearing rape, covered their faces with their veils and jumped into the river. In every trench, in every stone hut and cavern, women and children fought desperately with stones and kinjals. One child after the other fell. One mother, insane with sorrow, picked up the dead body of her son as if it were a weapon and heaved it at the soldiers.

Akhulgo was reduced to what the Russians wanted it to be; the stench of the corpses, the wailing of children, houses and stables turned to rubble. It had cost them half their forces and lost the highlanders hundreds of families. The siege had lasted eighty days, far longer than expected. But it was all worth it to be able to report to the tsar that Akhulgo had fallen and that Shamil had been captured. The soldiers were instructed to turn over every corpse, to search in every nook and cranny, to question all who were alive and could speak. It was inconceivable that he had eluded them, that he had got away to continue to be a thorn at their side. He must be hunted.

The enemy was now above Shamil. When he caught up with the group that included Fatima and Ghazi, they hid for three days in a cavern halfway down the mountain. Djawarat and her baby were missing. One of his uncles had been martyred. His sister was one of the women who had covered their faces with their veils and drowned in the river. Grief seeped through his pores, the claws of death so close that he could almost hear them scratching. He held Ghazi close, desperate for the sweetness the child offered, his youth, his soft cheeks, his innocent voice. The void of the missing baby, a picture of Djawarat the last time he had seen her, frantically sewing something or the other in preparation for the escape. It was warm and claustrophobic in the cavern. Fatima slept most of the time.

He dozed next to her and dreamt of Djawarat. She had fallen on the ground and their son was crawling over her. It was not a good dream. But how could he go back and search for her?

Light-headed from lack of food, they groped their way in the moonlight. They crossed a ravine by balancing a tree trunk from one side to the other. He thought Fatima, heavily pregnant, would not be able to make it but she did. He carried Ghazi on his back, his shoes in his mouth. Dawn, and from high up came a volley of shots, the blur of Russian sharp-shooters among the sycamore trees. They were after him. The only solution was to hide again. Ghazi was wounded in the leg. He cried out, 'Throw me in the river,' remembering his father's orders at Akhulgo.

It became a pattern to hide by day and move by night. They paused when they reached the river and, to fool the Russians, they built a raft and filled it with straw-stuffed dummies. They launched the raft at dawn and while the Russians fired at it, Shamil and his group waded upstream.

Making wudu in the river, the truncated prayers of the traveller, and inland through dry brushwood, thirsty again, sucking water from the hoof-prints of mountain deer. Steadily they reached the summits and sandstone of Chechnya, crossing for days the looped river; wading, climbing and clinging to the cliffs. The mountains closed in against them and, looking above, the sky was a jagged strip between two cliffs, but these moss-covered boulders were their refuge too.

Resting one day at noon they were fired at by a group of villagers from Shamil's birthplace, Ghimra. These young men had defected to the Russians and were hunting Shamil. He recognised their leader and called him by name. Shamil pulled out his sword and raised it high, shouting, 'One day, soon, I will stab you with it.' He was bolstered by a vision that one of his men had seen. A great river rushing over Akhulgo drowning everyone except Shamil and a few.

It was not only the Russians they were fleeing from but, as with the Ghimrans, their allies too. Leaders who had defected to the Russians in return for keeping their chiefdoms. They wanted to hand Shamil to the Russians, and knowing the mountains, they were more than qualified to track him down. Shamil spotted two of his adversaries, Ahmed Khan and Hadji Murat, who had raised a party and succeeded in coming close to Shamil's group. He prayed that Allah Almighty would veil their eyes and weaken their resolve, and they did not fire a single shot.

Fatima pale, her stomach protruding from her skinny body. Ghazi crying from hunger, unsteady even though his injured leg was healing. Shamil picked him up and Ghazi dropped his head on his father's chin. 'My neck isn't strong enough to carry my head,' he said. Shamil held him all night. He was the only child he had now. Jamaleldin out of reach and Djawarat's baby dead. The sad news had come from Akhulgo carried by a fighter who caught up with them on horseback. Djawarat had been hit by a bullet in her chest. She lay partially trapped under the rocks while her baby, as in Shamil's dream, crawled on top of her body. For three days, she called out for water and chewed on the fried bits of grain she had sewn on the borders of her veil.

The next evening bullets whizzed past the group as they walked exposed on the top of a hill. No longer able to hide, Shamil and his companions attacked the Russian picket and sent the soldiers running back to camp. Shamil paid a mountain shepherd to carry the wounded on horseback. He paid for water too. But lagging behind with Fatima, he later discovered that everyone in the group had drunk their fill and forgotten Ghazi. He cursed them and carried Ghazi again through the night.

'I will die of hunger, Father.'

'No, look ahead.' He pointed to the top of the mountain. 'When we get there we will feed you bread and all sorts of good things. You will feel full.'

They prayed fajr and climbed the last mountain as the sun was rising. A rider headed towards them. He had been searching for them and his saddlebag was full of bread and cheese for Ghazi. 'At last we are free of the Russians,' Fatima sighed, but Shamil broke down and wept. 'I wanted to fight till the end. Where will we seek refuge and settle now? In this world there are only those who hate us.'

True, many villages, fearing reprisals from the Russians and their allies, would not take them in. Yet in others they were made welcome. In Tattakh a bull was slaughtered for the travellers and Fatima gave birth to a healthy baby boy, Muhammad-Sheffi. But they could not settle there. Shamil had to search for a more permanent home, a place where he could, insh'Allah, gather more fighters and rebuild.

At times he felt like a discarded rag, denied not only military success but the blessing of martyrdom. Perhaps he had not done enough and his fate was to fight on, his duty to do more. What did he possess? Where were the men who would fight with him again? In years to come, children like Ghazi would grow up and lead his armies. Women would give birth to new heroes. Now, though, it was a time to heal, an inward time for prayer and seclusion. He was surviving on the love of the Almighty, fuelled by the urge to win back Jamaleldin, shaded by the martyrs of Akhulgo.

It was weeks later, after all the fighting had died down and the Russians abandoned Akhulgo, that Shamil was able to go back in search of Djawarat. He walked around asking one survivor after the other until he came to an elderly man whose rheumy eyes had witnessed. The man's voice barely rose above a whisper. 'Your son crawled over his mother's body until he too perished and was carried away by the water.' The man pushed himself up to totter on spindly legs and pointed out where Djawarat had fallen. As he came nearer, Shamil recognised her clothes under the rocks and silt deposited by the flooding river. He knelt next to her and lifted up the stones that were crushing her. He cleared away the pebbles. He cleaned the mud away from what he was realising was a miracle. Yes, there was no rigor mortis for the martyr, no putrefaction or decomposition. In this way they are rewarded. Shamil had come across this phenomenon in some of the fallen bodies of his men. But Djawarat was his first woman martyr. It was usually during childbirth that women attained martyrdom. And yet, here was his own wife, on a battlefield. As honoured as the sincerest of warriors.

She had not wanted to die; she had wanted to see her baby grow up. He lifted Djawarat and her body was as supple as he remembered it. He wiped her face and her skin felt alive under his fingers. His warm, heavy breath on her hair, ears and eyelashes. She was living, living with Allah, though Shamil knew she was dead. Even her lips, resting evenly on her teeth, were soft with moisture.

II
The Days Before

1. Scotland, December 2010

There is something about waking up in a room that one has not seen by daylight. It comes sharply into its own, mocking first impressions. This one was untidy, a work-in-progress and I guessed that I was the first to use it. It looked almost like a store room; several boxes were stacked on top of each other, an exercise bike was facing the wall, a large painting lay face down on the floor. A faint sound of machinery came from downstairs, a steady thud. I tugged open the curtains. The sun reflected on the snow and hurt my eyes. The path and garden were even more packed than yesterday, in confident clumps several feet high. My Civic was completely covered, which meant that it had snowed again during the night. It made me wonder whether I would be able to leave anytime soon. Far to my right the hills were a sweep of white and then below, the river was clean and flowing rapidly. A movement close by caught my eyes; powdery flakes drifting from a black and white tree. A strip of white on the black branch. My eyesight blurred and I moved away before an aura fully developed. I could not cope with a full-blown migraine now, not when I was away from my flat.

I had thought that if I discovered what made me anxious, I would be able to find a cure. But all I could do was learn to control it. The symptoms started when I was young. At a fancy-dress party, I kicked and screamed at a child with the head of a wolf and the body of a seven-year-old-boy. I knew that the wolf's head was fake. I myself was wearing a Red Indian wig with two thick braids pleasantly heavy on my chest. I was not even unduly frightened of wolves. Whether stalking the three little pigs or behind bars at the zoo, they were thrilling and worthy of respect but they did not make me ill. It was the disproportion of the wolf's head to the child's body, the shock of the half-human, half-beast, the lack of fusion between the two. There was no merging. It was a clobbering together, abnormal and clumsy, the head of one species and the body of the other. Later, a picture of a centaur in a library book and I vomited over the pages. Then as a teenager, a scene in a horror film of a dog with a man's head made me faint. The video was the 1978 version of *Invasion of the Body Snatchers* – the product of an innocent time when aliens from space were more threatening than Muslims from al-Qaeda.

The explanation became clearer as I grew older. I was seeing in these awkward composites my own liminal self. The two sides of me that were slammed together against their will, that refused to mix. I was a failed hybrid, made up of unalloyed selves. My Russian mother who regretted marrying my Sudanese father. My African father who came to hate his white wife. My atheist mother who blotted out my Muslim heritage. My Arab father who gave me up to Europe without a fight. I was the freak. I had been told so and I had been taught so and I had chewed on this verdict to the extent that, no matter what, I could never purge myself of it entirely. My intellect could rebel and I was well-read on the historical roots and taboos against miscegenation (the word itself hardly ever used now), but revulsion and self-loathing still slithered through my body in minute doses. The disease was in me despite the counselling and knowing better. Natasha Hussein would always be with me. I could glimpse her in the black-white contrast of a winter branch that was covered on one side with snow.

The machine noise and the thudding turned out, on investigation, to be Malak on a treadmill. I stood and watched her. She was wearing a black training suit and there was an olive bandana around her hair. She jogged for two minutes, then walked for one with the machine up on an incline. I had never visited a gym and so the procedure was intriguing. We talked about the snow, how it was even worse than yesterday, how the television had reported that a few had died, some were in hospital and commuters stuck in their cars for hours. I told Malak that I had called work but it was hard to get anyone at the department to pick up the phone. I had tried again with no luck to get a taxi to come and pick me up. Malak told me I was welcome to stay and sounded like she meant it. I had thought of walking to the nearest village but I didn't really want to leave. Besides, I argued with myself, I had my laptop with me and could get quite a bit of work done here. It was an opportunity to see what Malak had among her family's belongings that could shed more light on Shamil.

Over breakfast Oz asked me about my old name. Natasha Hussein explained my frizzy hair and the flat disc of my face, my skin that was darker than one parent's and lighter than the other. 'My mother is ... was Georgian,' I told Oz, 'and my father is Sudanese.'

'Is that where you were born?'

'Yes, Khartoum. After the divorce my mother married a Scottish man and we came to Britain. They actually got married in Tbilisi – that's where we went, Mum and I, after leaving Khartoum. We stayed in Georgia a few months. In between. It was boring until Tony came. He adopted me and gave me his name. We lived in London for a few years then moved to Aberdeen.' It was an effort formulating this summary, explaining myself. I preferred the distant past, centuries that were over and done with, ghosts that posed no direct threat. History could be milked for this cause or that. We observed it always with hindsight, projecting onto it our modern convictions and anxieties. When I was doing my Highers, the subject became my passion, a world that kept me awake at night; that claimed me, without conditions, as a citizen. I could lose myself in it and forget to visit my mother. I could memorise the dates of battles and the details of treaties so that I could blot out my father, so that I could be without a childhood self. The taunt 'swot' was the only one that never bothered me.

Oz passed me the peanut butter. He put more bread in the toaster. 'Do you have family in Khartoum?'

'My father is still there. He remarried and has a son. My father,' I expanded, knowing Oz would be interested, 'is Muslim in name only, unless he's lately changed. He didn't care about religion. He was a member of the Communist party and they gave him a scholarship to Russia where he met my mother and faith was not an issue for them. So I wasn't brought up Muslim even though we lived in a Muslim country. But I was aware of Islam around me. You can't miss it in Sudan. My grandmother prayed. When she came to stay with us, I would taunt her and push her as she prayed just because I knew she wouldn't leave her prayers and punish me. She used to swipe at me, though, while she was praying.' I mimicked my skinny grandmother flailing her arms.

Oz laughed. 'That's so mean.' He sounded like a schoolboy.

'During Ramadan,' I said, now that I was on a roll with memories, 'none of us used to fast, not even my father, but instead of eating lunch at the usual time before siesta we would eat around sunset. My father insisted on it. He liked the special drinks and foods of Ramadan. You've never lived in a Muslim country, have you? Culture and religion are so entwined that sometimes people can't tell the difference. At sunset, the special Ramadan cannon would go off. It was a relic of Turco-Egyptian rule. I would hear that one bang as I was playing in the street. The other children were fasting and we would each go to our own homes. Sometimes I fasted like them just so as not to be different, but it annoyed my mother.' Those were the years when I had hope of fitting in. Then awkwardness became my home.

'Do you think if you stayed with us here, you would change?' He stirred more sugar into his coffee, splashed a drop of milk on the table.

'What do you mean?'

'If, just to say, the snow lasted for days and days. If you couldn't leave, would you come closer to faith, just by being with the two of us?'

I knew that I should resent his suggestion. Its echoes of compulsion and submission. 'No matter how long the snow lasts, it will melt and I will leave. Then I will go back to my own life and this will be a memory. Do *you* find yourself easily changing? Do you match the company you keep?'

'Yes,' he said. 'I guess I do or at least did. I would like to be braver. I would like, just as an example, to be assertive enough not to mind my name or not to care what others think about my mother's job.'

'What's wrong with her job?'

He sat up straight and didn't reply. I could hear Malak in the next room close. At last he said, 'It is not others that are the problem. Their thoughts become my thoughts.'

'You're young,' I said and that was not the right thing to say. He felt somewhat rebuked.

Malak came into the kitchen, her face shining with sweat. She refilled her water bottle from the tap. 'Ossie, show Natasha the flag that was sent to Shamil from England,' she said as she walked out again.

In the living room, he moved a tartan rug from the top of a trunk and knelt down to open it. I sat next to him on the floor and it had been years since I had done that. My knees creaked and I shifted my heaviness on the carpet. He showed me portraits of Shamil; sketches and paintings made by Russian journalists and artists who accompanied the troops. They were orientalist in ethos: one of him standing alone in prayer while behind him his men were on horseback, swords drawn, ready to charge. In others, he was a hawk-like figure, with brooding dark eyes. In a family album, someone had collected fragments of the comments written in the West about Shamil. Oz read them out loud and when Malak joined us, she supplied the appropriate accent and I was soon laughing.

A French accent for Alexander Dumas: 'Shamil, the Titan, who struggles from his lair against the tsar.'

The MP in the House of Commons lauding Shamil's stand as a check to tsarist designs in India: '. . . a really splendid type who stood up to tyrants . . . and deeply religious even if he did have several wives . . .' The Caucasus blocked the route to Delhi and Shamil was their man.

'Look,' Malak said and took out a scrap of material preserved

43

in a sealed glass case. Three scarlet stars stitched on a dull beige background that must have been white at the time. 'This was part of a banner that was sent to Shamil as a token of support. Imagine a group of English ladies, a sewing circle, stitching away in a parlour. Wasn't it good of them, Natasha?'

Oz shook his head. He was right to be sceptical. These tokens were not enough to save Shamil. All the newspaper articles that extolled Phoenix rising from the ashes of Akhulgo, all the calls in Parliament for an independent Dagestan, all the collections for the 'poor, brave Caucasians', the talk of training from Indian army officials on modern artillery methods, at the end only provided him with moral support.

'These three stars on the flag,' I said, 'probably represent Georgia, Circassia and Dagestan even though Georgia had ceded to Russia.'

Oz showed me sheets of music enfolded in a romantic colourful cover of warriors with their swords and Arabian steeds. The title was *The Shamil Schottische* and Malak gave us a demonstration of the dance, a slower polka that really needed a partner, she said, but Oz would not oblige.

It was part of the magic of the day, to watch her dance and laugh, to listen to Oz teasing her. She was light on her feet, saying 'The composer was English and to use Shamil's name to market the tune must mean that he captured people's imagination at the time.' The sun shone on the sweep of her black hair, her jade earrings. The sight filled me with a sense of privilege, a gratitude I had not felt for a long time. Here we were, the three of us, fascinated by a common past – faithful to it, even. I at least to the history, they to an ancestor they were proud of. It was only in a specific period of Shamil's career that he won British favour – the years after Akhulgo, the politics surrounding the Crimean War, up until Princess Anna Elinichna entered into the picture. It was precisely because of a Georgian princess that the British representative said, 'Shamil is a fanatic and a barbarian with whom it would be difficult for us... to entertain any credible or satisfactory relations.'

2. Georgia, June 1854

In order to nurse the baby while sitting on her favourite armchair, Princess Anna had gone through considerable effort. Neither David nor her sisters could understand her insistence on taking this particular armchair from Tiflis all the way down to the Tsinondali estate. The chair had to be hoisted on top of an oxen-cart with the ikons and the silver samovar, covered in old sheets to protect them from the dust of the road. Even though the Chavchavadzes spent every summer in the country, this year the move had been spiked with doubts. The military governor had refused to sanction it, citing the increasing raids of the highlanders. However, Anna had insisted. It was too hot to stay in town and there was much that needed doing at Tsinondali; to give it up one summer would amount to neglect. Besides, it was only in the countryside that she felt at ease, able to wear her national costume and speak in her mother tongue, garden and supervise the estate. Luckily David had supported her. He was to be nearby throughout the summer commanding the local militia, a line of forts along the river that protected the lowlands from any invasion by the Caucasus highlanders. On a good day he could reach them by dinner, and at the slightest inkling of danger he would be the first to know. Still, though, their summer move raised frowns. There was gossip that Anna was headstrong and manipulative of her husband. Relatives hinted that they would not visit as often as they usually did and her sisters teased her about the armchair, which she would have to abandon in case of a hasty return to town.

The chair was upholstered in a material that was gentle on the skin and easy to wipe clean in case of spills. Its design of lilacs and

45

roses was pleasing and it was comfortable enough to sleep in on those difficult nights when Lydia was colicky and refused to settle. Anna would hold her as the baby sucked on and off, swallowing lazily because she was not really hungry, dozing into the kind of sleep that was so light that Anna knew if she even tried to move her to her cot, she would shriek into full consciousness. 'You are spoiling her, Your Highness,' the new governess had said. If Anna had been less confident she would have minded. But she had been a fine mother to Alexander and there was no reason to doubt her abilities with Lydia. 'You French have your ways and we have ours,' she answered Madame Drancy, not so much as to put her in her place, but to nip in the bud any undue harsh discipline.

Drancy had had no previous experience with children. She arrived in Georgia with the intention of opening a bookshop. French novels were much in demand, especially as the Crimean War had stopped many from travelling. But the war itself made her project fail. She was unable to import any books, the French Consulate closed and, reluctant to return to Paris as a failure, she had little option but to seek employment as a governess. French tutors and English nannies were in high demand. Anna, though, was relieved that she had been able to talk David out of the need for a nanny as well as a wet nurse. She would not give up this close contact with her children. A governess was enough for their small family and Drancy was hardy and adaptable. In Tiflis, when their move to the countryside had been debated, a staff officer presented Madame Drancy with a dagger and recommended that she learnt to use it before venturing out to danger. To her credit, Drancy had airily remarked that the dagger would make a useful letter-opener. And ever since they'd arrived at Tsinondali, she had not stopped admiring the gardens and the fruit trees, the vineyards and the jasmines.

From her armchair, with Lydia swallowing rich, early-morning milk, Anna gazed down at the big courtyard, the garden where David had played as a child and where Alexander now picked a pear from the tree and walked, eating it. She could see the whole estate spread out before her. Greenery on one side and the dark mountains on the other, the ravine that marked the limit of her afternoon walk. There she would lean forward to look at the running stream, a small tributary of the Alazani, the water washing the rocks, pushing away at the mountain sides. As a child David had learnt to swim in this river and years later on their honeymoon (yet another reason that Anna was fond of Tsinondali) they had spent many laughing hours in the water. Easy days when it was just the two of them, enamoured and young, before the responsibilities of children and households.

At Tsinondali they were seven miles from the nearest town and the house was self-supporting. They raised their own cattle and made their own bread and wine. There was much to supervise including the staff of head cook, under-cooks, grooms, dairy maids, farm-hands, gardeners, carpenters and scullions. Yet all this was preferable to the social rounds of St Petersburg, the predictability of court gossip, the formality of being 'at home' on Thursdays or Mondays. She was, it seemed, the only Georgian princess who had not enjoyed being a lady-in-waiting to the tsarina. Anna was often homesick and had no patience with the games and side-stepping needed to catch the eye of an eligible bachelor. She wanted to marry a Georgian prince and did not understand the need to go all the way to Petersburg to find him. Now gazing into baby Lydia's eyes, she knew that she would rather be here than anywhere else. 'Wake up, don't doze again. I'll change you and take you out in the sunshine.' This was the best feed of the day when her breasts were full and she could revel in this natural, maternal generosity, this abundance that was making her daughter content and languorous, this nourishment that would make her tiny limbs strong. When she changed Lydia's nappy, Anna bent down and took deep breaths of the yoghurt smell that came from a baby who had not yet tasted solid food. It was as exhilarating as a perfume, a sweetness that locked them together, that sealed them as mother and child.

In the evening, after Anna had made the sign of the cross over

Alexander and kissed him goodnight, she stayed up playing the piano, but Madame Drancy was restless. The governess kept getting up to walk to the window and peer out from behind the curtains. It made Anna lose her concentration. She stumbled twice on the same note and gave up. 'What can you see out there?'

'There is a light; it might be a Chechen campfire.' Drancy's fair hair was held firmly away from her face and she dressed in sombre colours as if she was always conscious of being a widow.

Anna moved over to the window. The moon was covered by clouds but she could see a cluster of orange flames up on the mountains. 'They are on the other side of the river.'

'They can cross it.'

'Cross the Alazani!' Anna pulled the curtains closer together and walked back to the piano seat. 'It's the deepest of rivers. Besides, with all the rain we've been having, it's swollen.'

Madame Drancy followed her. 'There is talk that Shamil and his men are descending from the mountains to take Georgia.'

Anna tidied her music sheets. 'It's just servants' gossip. You mustn't pay attention to it.' She looked up at the clock. It seemed a little slow; it needed winding. 'I must remember tomorrow to send for the clockmaker.'

But Madame Drancy was not to be distracted. 'They say Shamil is a monster who eats Russian flesh.'

Anna laughed. 'An educated woman like you believing such nonsense!'

'But how else can one explain the uncanny way he escaped death and capture! Time and again. It must be that he has made a pact with the devil.'

'I doubt it very much, Madame Drancy.' Anna's voice was deliberately calm. It would not be right to lose patience.

Madame Drancy clutched her hands together. 'He's a savage with insatiable needs.'

Anna sighed and started to offer more reassurances. The Chechen campfire, if it was really that, was definitely across the river. There was no need to panic and yet, she told herself, the anxiety would always be there, a risk she had taken when she insisted on coming here for the summer. The military were concentrating their efforts in the Crimea. It would be a strategic moment for Shamil to attack and yet many believed that he was in too poor a shape to do so.

'More and more of his men are defecting, Madame Drancy,' she said. 'It is true that after the defeat of Akhulgo he did, against all expectations, gather strength and numbers. But that was fifteen years ago and unless the Turks or English bolster him now, he is not in a position to attack Georgia. And they are putting all their resources in the Crimea.'

Madame Drancy settled back in her chair and even picked up her novel again. She looked her best when she read, the way she held up *La Dame aux Camélias*, the curve of her neck, the slight tension in her shoulders. Anna continued to play but the conversation had affected her. For the sake of prudence, she would, first thing tomorrow morning, send a message to David.

A day later, he joined them for dinner. It became almost festive because of his presence but in order not to frighten Alexander they avoided talk of the mountain campfires until they were alone. Their bedroom had nets around the four-poster bed. There were three large chests of drawers, a mantelpiece that had belonged to David's mother, and Anna's armchair near the window. She pushed it so that it would not be in David's way as he looked out of the window. Anna said, 'One of the maids walked out on me this morning. She refused to say why but I think she was frightened.'

David looked out of the window. 'Two campfires tonight.'

She moved and stood next to him. 'You are sure they are on the other side of the river?'

'Definitely.' He turned away from the window and went to sit on the bed. 'Shamil cannot take on Georgia. Marauding bands up and down the river, that's all he's capable of. A skirmish here, a run-in there, just enough to keep us on our feet and persuade us that we're a little bit more than a token force.' David sounded resentful. He would rather have been sent to the Crimea. The David Anna had first married used to be more good-natured, more inclined to enjoy life. There was an added seriousness in him now, new ambitions.

'It is such a comfort to me that you are near.' She crawled on to the bed, bunching up her nightdress so that it wouldn't entangle her. Her dark hair fell from the chignon she had pinned up for dinner.

'Don't worry. If I was worried, I would tell you to leave.'

She hugged him. 'Thank you for understanding that I need to be here.'

He did not return her embrace and instead lit a cigar. 'In truth I don't understand. It is a mystery to me.'

She sensed that they were stepping into the murky area of their marriage. That cove which nurtured differences, rather than peace. Further in and they would reach the point where everything she could say was of little use; everything he could say was hurtful.

Yet she had to speak, 'Because this estate is the most beautiful place in the world. Because it's been in your family for years. It's our children's heritage. It's what we are.'

'Then don't complain. I've tried for years to loosen your attachment to it and convince you to move to Petersburg. You've chosen the edge of civilisation so you must accept its hazards.'

She drew away from him. 'What is that supposed to mean?'

'It means a country lady should learn to look after herself.'

'I will. I will look after myself and our home and our future.'

He looked at her as if he was sorry for her. Then with a gesture of impatience he picked up an ashtray. 'My future and my children's future is Russia.'

'Why are you differentiating yourself from me? We are the same – we're Georgians, not Russians.'

He shook his head. 'Your own grandfather, a wise king and a man of peace, ceded Georgia to Russia. He spared us bloodshed. Look at these Chechens, hard-headed as the mountains that bred them, fighting years on end, and every day I lose one lad after the other. Every day my clerk writes a letter to the family of a Seregin or a Panov, telling them that their son has been killed defending tsar, fatherland and the Orthodox faith. Why all this waste, why does Shamil continue when common sense says that we will win, when common sense says that they are resisting all that would be good for them?'

'What good?' She was sullen now, the arguments narrowing around her.

'What good?' he snorted. 'Peace for one, prosperity too. Modern roads, sanitation, education, enlightened thinking. Everything that is uncouth and reprehensible to be replaced by what is civilised and rational. No one in his right mind, given a choice, would choose primitiveness over advancement. You can't live in the past, Anna, you can't be like them.'

Tears came into her eyes and as if in sympathy her breasts, though not full, started to leak. Lydia's milk. She would like to feed her now, to douse the baby's thirst and her own anger. Instead it was her nightdress that was becoming wet. Not every Georgian was glad to submit to Russia. But David deliberately shunned those objecting members of the family who had had their lands confiscated and were held in Moscow against the threat of political intrigue. It irked Anna that her grandmother, the dethroned Queen Maria, was commanded at times to attend court for certain functions, then ridiculed for her clothes and tanned skin. Why did these humiliations not touch David too? In Petersburg society, hangers-on went around describing themselves as 'Georgian princesses' as if the phrase had no protection or use. In Anna's case, the title was a right – she was granddaughter of George XII, the last king. David would accuse her of being proud if she mentioned this. In turn she would defend herself by saying that she wanted simplicity and closeness to the peasants, that she worked hard and did not indulge herself in luxuries. Then they would argue even more.

She looked at him now, holding his cigar in one hand, the mother-of-pearl ashtray in the other, and saw what she had not wanted to acknowledge. This was not the bridegroom she had exchanged vows with in church, the husband who brought her to Tsinondali, the lover who swam with her in the river. It was not only that he was older, the lustre lost from his hair, the boyish look in his eyes replaced with the keen desire to advance. His beard was gone; his clothes, his concerns, his watch with the double chain and seal, his manner of speaking, were more Russian than she could ever be.

3. Petersburg, June 1854

Jamaleldin, granted an audience with the tsar, waited in the reception room on the upper floor of the Winter Palace. His uniform was that of a young officer in the Imperial Escort. He had even volunteered to fight in the Caucasus and was awaiting the tsar's consent. All this would pave the way to his marriage to Daria Semyonovich. It would subdue her parents' doubts, manifested in the cool reception he often received from Daria's mother, the veiled comments about his slanting eyes. To fight the highlanders would seal his loyalty; it would, he believed, dispel the memory that he was Shamil's flesh and blood. Let everyone know him only as the tsar's godson. Let them remember his outstanding performance in his military examinations, his accomplishments that included astronomy, painting, a fluency in English and French, and not least his horsemanship. When he was with Daria they spoke of their love and not his past, they dreamt of the future, and unlike other girls he had known, she did not pry with questions about his family or where he was born. Daria was content to listen to him praising her eyes and her lips, her little hands and the curls that fell naturally on her wide, smooth forehead. She lapped up his devotion with a serenity that was part of her nature; a silence that hinted at either emptiness or pliancy.

It might be a long wait. The minister of war was inside, briefing the tsar, and Jamaleldin did not know how long it had been since their meeting began. He could ask the duty officer, a newly appointed aide-de-camp, whom he had never met before, but he preferred not to. The sound of murmured voices and the scratch of the officer's pen, while inside fates were being decided. Troops deployed, peasants made to run the gauntlet, promotions and demotions. The atmosphere was solemn and strangely foggy. Jamaleldin stared at the portrait of Emperor Alexander I, his reddish sideburns and an enigmatic smile on his lips. *May Allah have mercy on his soul.* The phrase, learnt in Arabic as a child, bobbed up unbidden. It was a natural, internal reflex. The sort of response he must not say out loud. He worried, sometimes, that these words would slip out of him on their own accord. It was for this reason that he never allowed himself to get drunk. There were limits to how much he could reveal, restraints that he imposed on himself in order to continue to succeed.

During his long journey away from Akhulgo, he had expected his father to rescue him. Spending the night at a military garrison near Moscow, he boasted of this and they took away his kinjal. He lashed out at his minders, biting, kicking and screaming. They locked him up and punished him with hunger and a darkness in which evil spirits thickened and floated because there was no lamplight to drive them off. Surely Shamil would not allow this injustice to continue. Surely he would save him. Jamaleldin waited, strained for the sounds of horses, prepared himself for a raid in which he would be carried off back to safety.

This episode of harsh discipline turned out to be a solitary one, condemned by the tsar, and never repeated. When Jamaleldin finally reached Petersburg, it was decided that military quarters were no longer suitable and that a family would foster him. A town house for him to live in, children who grudgingly shared their toys and clothes, parents who were not his parents. Better the kind nanny with the kerchief tied around her wide face. She reminded him of the peasants of the lowlands; she knew how to talk to him – not in the Avar language, but words didn't matter – he understood the tone of her voice, the clucks and music in her sentences. She held him on her lap and sang him lullabies as if he were still a baby, as if he were a newborn. He was exhausted. Exhausted from the assault of newness; of space, sounds and smells betraying him, food not being food and speech not being speech. All this strangeness demanded his attention, all these new people in his life drew him out, pushed or goaded or cajoled him. His mother had told him not to cry, he was an Avar, he mustn't cry. All that Jamaleldin had to do, he told himself, was wait, watch out and wait, be alert, be ready.

An invisible leash kept him tethered to his enemies, kept him cowed and conscious of his weakness in comparison to their strength, of his smallness and what he quickly realised was his ignorance. He must learn, they kept telling him, not only the Russians but the Caucasian chiefs who had allied themselves with the tsar and were now brought to meet him, those Asiatic princes who looked like him but had betrayed his father. You must learn to speak Russian, they all said. You must learn these modern ways so that one day, when peace comes, you will go back to your people and help them.

During the day, he became too busy to watch out for his father's rescue. Night became his time to wander free. He could lie very still and strain his ears for the soft leather steps of a highlander, anticipate a midnight raid. Which of his father's men would come for him? He went through them, exercising his memory: Zachariah who was the bravest, Abdullah who was more reliable, Imran who could speak Russian and come in disguise. Or it could be Younis, who used to visit him in the Russian general's tent in Akhulgo, following an arrangement made by his father. Younis taught him more of the Qur'an and made sure that he was keeping up with his prayers. This, perhaps, was why Younis's face and voice remained longer in Jamaleldin's memory. For slowly, as week followed week, he forgot to expect the relief expedition, although there still lingered a faint hope for it to surprise him, to take him unaware; as if he had just been momentarily distracted and everything would go back to how it had been before.

Later, when he was eleven and sent to the Cadet Corps, he toyed with plans of escape. The urge to flee would only come when he was reprimanded by a teacher or set upon by a bully. Humiliated, he would plot to steal a horse, wrap food in a rag and set off back to the Caucasus. But he was an able student, an amiable schoolmate and soon puberty brought with it a self-absorption that calmed him down. What felt like an alien challenging prison became a home with known boundaries, tightly filled with much to keep him exercised and amused.

And he was special, after all – he was the tsar's ward, he had a place in court. A palace he had only encountered in the descriptions of Paradise. Gliding staircase, glittering chandeliers, beautiful women, their breasts cradling jewels, dressed in rustling silks, who caressed his hair and cooed in their own language. The military parades, the steeplechases, the labyrinthine, teeming streets, of the city; magicians and clowns, a trip to the theatre, sledges, and girls peering at him over their sable muffs. Slowly, the present, the here and now, asserted itself and shoved all else to the back of his mind. Jamaleldin began to enjoy the fact that he was an intriguing figure at court, that others were drawn to his difference. Soft-spoken and even-handed in his dealings, he got along well with young men his age. He possessed, too, the keen ability to ferret out the best in others. It suited his patrons/captors to think that he had forgotten his past and it suited him to maintain this impression.

But his memories of Akhulgo were vivid and when alone with his thoughts he could smile at his brother Ghazi, he could smell his father's beard and breathe the cloudy air of the highest peaks. The images he recalled were tied to the past. He could not speculate on how Ghazi looked now as an adult or how much Shamil's new home in Dargo resembled Akhulgo. Jamaleldin was not interested in his family's present, a present he could not access. Nor would he bite the hand that fed him. His captors' values must be his values, their rules obeyed, their aspirations supported. This was why he offered to serve in the Caucasus. He would be a link between the two sides, he would carry peace and modernity to the highlands. Greater Russia's goal, the subjugation of the mountain tribes, had become, for him, an abstract attainment. He did not have the tools to question it or doubt it. It was too much a part of the larger scheme of life.

*

The Emperor Nicholas was seated behind his writing table, dressed in a black frock coat. The long pale face Jamaleldin had grown to resent and revere, to fear and to serve, the familiar moustache curled at the ends, the fresh scent of eau de cologne and sense of physical wellbeing. The tsar's hair was combed forward to one side in an attempt to hide his bald patch.

A voice in Jamaleldin's head said in the Avar language, '*Praise be to Allah. Observe how a mighty king with endless riches and power over people's lives is helpless before the ravages of Time.*' The humorous tone was familiar. It was an elderly man's voice Jamaleldin was hearing and not for the first time; a man with a turban and a long white beard who was not necessarily addressing Jamaleldin specifically. He was addressing a whole group; he exerted no pressure on Jamaleldin to listen nor needed a reply. Sometimes Jamaleldin absorbed every word, often he pushed the voice away; but he was unable to silence it. These observations, sometimes exhortations, he knew, were ghosts of his previous life. They disturbed him because, unlike the phrases he had learnt as a child, these observations were fresh and relevant to the moment. Perhaps it was the voice of his father's teacher Jamal el-Din, the Sufi sheikh he had been named after. Perhaps he had been endowed with the gift of communicating with souls across time and space. But that was far-fetched. Rationally, the composer of these phrases must be Jamaleldin himself and yet why would he have such strange, unbecoming thoughts? He must never speak of them. They were like a squirrel hidden in the breast pocket of his jacket, threatening to wriggle out, not particularly to escape but to cause the greatest of social embarrassments.

Nicholas gestured for Jamaleldin to sit down. He looked fatigued and Jamaleldin wondered if this was perhaps not the best of days to approach him. Nicholas pushed aside the papers he had been working on and said, 'I am sending you tomorrow to Warsaw. You will be with the Vladimirski Lancers.'

The disappointment caused Jamaleldin to lose his natural reserve. 'But Your Majesty, I had hoped to serve you in the Caucasus.'

'You will, but not now. It is not the right time.' Nicholas folded his plump hands together. 'I do not doubt your loyalty but I have other plans for you. When we subdue the Caucasus you will play your part. It will not be long now. We destroyed their supplies and laid waste to the forests. Our strategy has worked! And we will continue to harass them. We will tighten the cordon around them and only then, Jamaleldin, will I send you there.'

'I hear and obey.' It was the right thing to say, the only choice.

Nicholas's curled moustache twitched. 'You will rule Dagestan and Chechnya on my behalf. No one will be able to win the tribes' loyalty and trust more than Shamil's son.'

At the mention of his father, Jamaleldin felt as if he was forced to put on his best woollen coat in the height of summer. Shamil was not for him now; he was a legendary name, a lost love, as close and as far as an organ inside Jamaleldin's own body, deadly to reach. He believed in Shamil's eventual downfall; this belief came from the palace walls around him, from the roads he walked on, the artillery he handled, the teachers who taught him, the existence of cities such as Petersburg and Moscow, of the opera and the skating ring, the horse races and a pair of binoculars, a dance at the ball, the railway lines. Shamil's defeat was in the trajectory of Jamaleldin's life. Yet he flinched whenever Shamil was portrayed as an ogre. And he felt proud when he heard tales of his heroic resistance. Jamaleldin's heart would contract and all the Arabic words, all the Avar phrases, would frolic above a whisper and it would require extra effort to control himself, to maintain his usual non-committal expression. He was too intelligent to indulge in undue insistence or exaggerated displays of his loyalty; these would only attract more attention. Instead, he trod softly, careful to hit the right notes. Unlike the Central Asian princes who wore their native dress when they came to court, Jamaleldin did not even wear a cherkesska. Every conscious thing he did reflected his conversion to the Empire.

But it was not enough. Nicholas sat back in his chair and lowered his voice, kind and firm. 'As for the other personal matter you petitioned me on, there can be no union between you and the

Princess Daria Semyonovich. You are incompatible in status and background.'

Jamaleldin flushed. It was as if Daria herself had scrunched his love like a handkerchief and thrown it in his face. He now wanted this audience to be over. He wanted to grab his dashed hopes and run away.

Nicholas chuckled. 'So Russian women are to your taste ... eh? Well, go ahead, have as many as you like, why not? But marriage, no. You must marry from your own kind. A tribal chief's daughter, perhaps. Or an emir's. This would further increase your acceptance among the highlanders. Think of the future,' he concluded with a flourish. 'You will be my mouthpiece in the Caucasus. You will bring enlightenment to your own people. For this I have fashioned you.'

4. Dargo, the Caucasus, June 1854

In his teacher's home, Shamil could put the war behind him, give up the burden of command and learn again. He reached out and took over the cleaning of Sheikh Jamal el-Din's shoes. The elderly man's long white beard rested on his chest, his bright penetrating eyes were sources of light. Outside in the night air an owl hooted.

'The great Shamil is cleaning my shoes!' There was a warm jocular tone to his voice, one that listeners never forgot.

The two of them sat cross-legged on square cushions, a rug spread out in front of them on the earthen floor. The door of the house was open to let in the summer breeze and every once in a while it creaked on its hinges nudging shadows across the room. Shamil's rifle and sword were hanging on a nail dug into the plastered wall. In any other house, they would have been next to the master of the house's weapons but here there was only the washbasin and pitcher used for wudu.

'In your presence, I am not great. I am the young boy who came to you in Yaraghl with neither knowledge in my head nor much strength in my body.' These were sharp memories as all memories of awakenings are, that time when the swirl of unnamed desires settles into the focus of purpose. Shamil had been a moody child with a sense of loneliness so acute that it resembled arrogance. The cheerful pastimes of others his age left him baffled and disdainful. When one day the neighbourhood boys ambushed him and left him bleeding from a dagger wound, he had been too proud to seek help. Instead he had staggered to a cave in the mountainside and fastened his torn skin with the mandibles of ants, applied crushed herbs and rested until his wound healed. But instead of returning home once he recovered, he set out to seek physical and spiritual strength. He found it in the mystic teachings of the Sufi sheikhs of the Naqshbandi Tariqa.

'I recall,' Jamal el-Din said, 'that you had fight in your soul. You were disciplined, too. When it was time for books, you were studious and patient. When it was time for athletics, you were energetic and sturdy.'

Shamil smiled. 'I used to repeat the prayer you taught me. 'Lord, make me grateful and make me patient. Make me small in my own eyes and great in the eyes of the people.'

'And today the Ottoman sultan has nominated you as the Viceroy of Georgia.'

Shamil laughed, 'You have heard already. No news escapes you! Advise me. Shall I accept?'

'It is only a fine title. The sultan is offering you what he doesn't possess.'

'He is anticipating victory.' Shamil's voice quickened. 'If the Ottomans and their allies, Britain and France, launch an attack on Tiflis, I can attack from the east and cut off the Crimean peninsula from the rest of Russia.'

'If they attack Tiflis . . .' His teacher's voice trailed off and then he started again. 'Has Queen Victoria replied to your letter?' Jamal el-Din had written the letter himself for his calligraphy was outstanding, and despite his age, his eyesight was strong. The letter would reach her through the British general-consul in Baghdad, who advocated supplying the mountain tribes with ammunition against the Russians, and was fluent in Arabic. *Our resistance is stubborn*, Shamil had dictated, *but we are obliged, in winter, to send our wives and children far away, to seek safety in the forests where they have nothing, no food, no refuge against the severe cold. Yet we are resigned. It is Allah's will. He ordained that we should suffer to defend our land. But England must know of this . . . We beseech you, we urge you, O Queen to bring us aid.*

'No, I have not received a reply.' Shamil sounded more subdued.

'Lord Palmerston was working on our side. His opposition

to Russia is deep but he is no longer foreign secretary. As home secretary, his influence is reduced.'

'I fear that the right time has passed,' said Shamil. 'That all of Britain's efforts have sunk into the Crimea.'

Sheikh Jamal el-Din was quiet. He patted his hand on his knees and his head sank deeper into his chest. At first the prayers he was saying were inaudible, but Shamil caught the recitation of the beautiful names of Allah.

When Jamal el-Din finally spoke, he said, 'I am filled with foreboding about this war in the Crimea. There will be much bloodshed and misery.'

This was a point of disagreement between them; Jamal el-Din the more peaceful of the two, the more eager to reconcile, negotiate and forgive.

Shamil repeated what he always said in these situations. 'Wars are never won with kindness. If men respected compassion I would have been the first to grant it. But even our own warriors are only in awe of power.' Nothing was more damaging than the weak Muslims who defected to Russia, who gladly or by force marched with the tsar's troops. Or they became spies, hypocritically claiming they were on Shamil's side and then reporting his secrets to the enemy. Or else they deliberately misled him so that he would walk into an ambush or launch an attack based on misinformation. He must always be on his guard, he must take nothing at face value. He must distrust.

'The world is a carcass and the one who goes after it is a dog,' Jamal el-Din murmured as if to himself.

'Men of bad character punish their own souls.' The leather shoe in Shamil's hands was becoming darker in colour because of the varnish. Sometimes he was not sure who was the scourge of his life, the Russians or those who betrayed him?

As if reading his mind, Jamal el-Din said, 'To get what you love, you must first be patient with what you hate.'

Shamil shifted his position so that his back was closer to the wall. 'You speak the truth.'

'Was it gunshots that I heard earlier in the afternoon?' Jamal el-Din turned to look at him.

'Five prisoners of war attempted to escape by smuggling a letter in a loaf of bread. They gave the loaf to a Jewish peddler and he was carrying it as part of his provisions for the journey. I will not tolerate treachery.'

'A loaf of bread,' Jamal el-Din repeated.

His tone made Shamil uneasy. When a prisoner faced his death sentence without flinching, Shamil spared him and gave him his due praise. But those who wept and fought were deprived of his mercy. Was he truly just? There was a hole in the heel where the leather was eroded. He searched the room for the necessary needle and began to mend it.

'Come with me to Mecca,' said Jamal el-Din. 'Let us visit the house of Allah together.'

The words, the prospect had an instant effect on Shamil. He felt light and carefree. 'Oh what a pleasure that would be, to put down my sword and take off my turban. To become a simple pilgrim dressed in rags chanting, "To you my Lord I come".'

'To you my Lord I come,' Jamal el-Din repeated. 'So what is holding you back?'

'My son Jamaleldin...' The words were heavy on his tongue, his fingers slackened. He felt it on his skin, that tingle of humiliation always associated with this particular defeat, this constant, eroding loss. 'I wonder sometimes how I am able to sleep at night, to eat, to make my wives smile while my son is worse than dead.'

Jamal el-Din stiffened as he always did when he heard what he disliked.

Shamil continued, 'I fear that not only is he a hostage but that the infidels have corrupted his soul and taken away his religion.'

'Malicious gossip.'

'It has been fifteen years. Fifteen years without my care or guidance. A strong adult might withstand such a trial but he was just a child.' The sense of injustice was always fresh, never faded or stale. 'Now on a night like this, I think *what* is he doing? How can the son of Imam Shamil be unclean and not pray five times a day? Even our language, he must have forgotten it by now.'

Jamal el-Din closed his eyes. 'There is no strength or might except with Allah.'

Instead of repeating after him, Shamil said, 'I will get him back. I will return him to Islam.' For how long has he been saying this and every plan was thwarted, every hope turned to nothing? He had promised Fatima that he would bring her eldest child back to her but he had failed. Nine years ago, as she lay dying, she wept and called for her son and though she did not name him, everyone knew it was not Ghazi or little Muhammad-Sheffi that she wanted.

Shamil was on the battlefield. He had lured the Russians across the mountains, up to ten miles from his stronghold in Dargo. He had been patient, tiring them out as they made their way down the steep descent with their heavy baggage trains and lengthy lines. He had cut off segments of them by blocking the mountain paths with tree trunks and while they figured a way to overcome these barriers or broke into confusion, he sent his horsemen in a full attack or fired at them with hidden sharp-shooters. Disorder broke out as one Russian column after another fell back, low morale set in as the dead piled up and the chants of the Orthodox funeral services merged into one another. Shamil and his men were attacking them from every side and they could now barely resist or fight back. With ammunition and food supplies running low, they remained under siege for several days.

It was then that the news reached him of Fatima's death. At first Shamil continued as he was, sending one of his men to see to the funeral. He was needed here where his own troops too were worn out and so hungry that they had taken to grilling the corpses of Russian horses. But his naibs urged him to return home and promised that they would, on their own, be able to defeat the besieged enemy. However, no sooner had news of his departure reached the Russian camp than the celebrations started. They banged drums and played their pipes. The following morning they had even more to celebrate. The relief force they had given up hope on finally arrived from the town of Gurzal. But it ended up being a costly, indecisive battle that left both sides entrenched in bitterness. And Shamil was left without Fatima, his link to Jamaleldin, she who kept alive the hope that he would return. Now Shamil was solitary in his memories, for very few liked to speak of his missing son.

He finished cleaning the shoes and broached the subject he had especially come to talk about, 'Sheikh Jamal el-Din, I seek your permission to appoint my son, Ghazi, as my successor.'

His teacher turned to look at him with questioning eyes as if waiting to hear more.

'It is unseemly to praise one's own offspring but the lad has demonstrated courage, horsemanship and skill.'

'I know,' Jamal el-Din nodded. 'Ghazi does not act arrogantly and he has insight and compassion. But you must gather the scholars and the naibs. Let them consider the matter and deliberate among themselves. Do not impose your choice upon them.' He raised his palms up in prayer. 'Lord, give Ghazi the strength to promote Your religion, to guard his community and to act with caution and justice.'

The joy and pride Shamil should have felt was weighed down by the implications of this step. He was admitting his loss in public. Not specifically that Jamaleldin would never come back, but that even if he were to return, he would not be fit to take his father's place.

As if sensing that it was Jamaleldin and not Ghazi who was in Shamil's thoughts, the elderly man asked, 'What came of that hostage that you were going to exchange him with?'

'He was not valuable enough. I ended up exchanging him for some of our men. But I will not give up.' He needed someone more valuable. This was the plan he had been working on. And today he had sent out scouts.

III
Crossing the Frontier

1. Scotland, December 2010

I told Malak that I had seen, from the upstairs window, little islands of snow floating on the river. They must have fallen from the Grampians. We were sitting in the kitchen without the lights on, just the pale dawn from the window. Melting snow meant clearer roads. I could leave today and get to work. There was no excuse to stay here longer.

'Would Oz like a lift to the university? I can wait for him to wake up.' She agreed that it would be helpful, especially with the semester exams starting next week, and wrapped her shawl closer around her, held her mug with both hands. I was stalling for time, unloading the dishwasher, cleaning the coffee maker. Outside one side of the sky was completely dark, like it was still in night. But it would not be left in peace for much longer; daylight was ready to enter. If I looked closely I could see new vulnerable depressions in the snow, areas of relative warmth. The edges, too, were melting away, the solid mass shrinking. Yesterday evening I had offered to pay for my board and lodging but Malak refused. 'We are happy to have you as a guest. We are enjoying your company.' This was generous of her because I hadn't really contributed anything; I should have, but I hadn't, even offered to cook dinner. All I gave them was my interest in their past.

It had been a special evening, like a celebration of sorts, perhaps an unspoken agreement that it would be my last. Oz lit the fire and we sat on the cushions on the floor. I looked up at Shamil's sword and down at the flames and I felt confident about my work, that I was on the right track, that I was worthy of my chosen subject. If I could get four papers on Shamil published in prestigious journals,

69

I would have a bigger chance of promotion. I was saving too for a trip to Dagestan, to climb the Caucasus. 'Come with me,' I urged them both. The invitation tripped out spontaneously, so unlike me. I could tell by their eyes, by the way they exchanged glances that the idea piqued their interest.

Oz stood up and fetched his laptop. 'Yes, let's go this month, over the Christmas holidays. I'll bet we can find cheap last-minute flights.'

'It would be better to go in the spring,' said Malak. 'Early when the swallows fly back. There would be snow on the highlands, but the lowlands would be clear.'

'Easter then,' I said, my voice different with happiness. This would be my ultimate journey, my pilgrimage and they would lead me to Shamil, to knowing him better, to seeing the world through his eyes.

Oz, laptop on his crossed knees, was doing the research. He read out, 'Tindi is a small picturesque aoul with a historic minaret, in the south-western mountains close to the Georgian and Chechen borders.'

'That's our place then,' I said.

He kept on reading, 'According to Wikivoyage, travel to Dagestan is extremely dangerous and strongly discouraged. And here's the latest headlines: *Russian security forces clash with militants in Dagestan, nine killed.*'

This dampened us for the time being. I was and had always been a coward. Malak said there were plenty more ways to spend a holiday than courting danger. Only Oz, all bravado, still seemed keen. 'You can't believe everything you read,' he argued. 'Besides, we're not tourists.'

'What are you, Ossie?' his mother smiled.

'I won't look out of place.'

'You only have to open your mouth,' she said. 'Besides, your fancy trainers will give you away.'

He scowled at her. 'I'll get new ones from Primark.'

She laughed. 'What a comedown!'

He was, I had noticed, proud of his clothes. But then many students nowadays were. They surprised me with their Uggs and Hunter wellies; their leather jackets and mobile accessories. The markets had them by the throat; they might be in debt, they were surely struggling, but they needed what generations before them had easily done without.

Perhaps if I wasn't there they would have argued about his allowance. Instead Malak started to speak about her parents and grandparents; all those descendants of Shamil that history didn't record. Stories that Oz hadn't heard. It was a pleasure to watch a mother hand over strands of the family narrative to her son. She was talking to him as much as to me. 'Our side of the family,' she said, 'followed the fatwa that with the collapse of Muslim rule in the Caucasus they should emigrate to the Ottoman Empire. Others stayed on and were deported by Stalin, and those who stayed struggled throughout Soviet rule. The mosques were shut down, it was forbidden to read or write Arabic and practising Islam had to be done in secret. Only the very tough could resist; most ordinary people lapsed. When I hear Muslims in the West complaining, I have no sympathy for them . . .'

Oz interrupted her, 'Come on . . .'

'I mean it,' she said. 'We have the freedom to practise and teach and bring up our children in our own faith. Can you imagine, Oz, what it is like when generation after generation grows up with all their Islamic teachings muddled up and pushed to the far side of memory? Snatches of verses here and there, a vague idea of Ramadan, no solid scholarship to back them, none of the blessing that comes from reciting the Qur'an. It is the biggest loss to become religiously illiterate, to be left without a choice. This is why my side of the family packed up and left. To spare themselves all this.'

I was surprised by her deeply held convictions. Too often she came across as malleable. Oz seemed surprised too but in a different direction. 'You always said that your parents weren't religious.'

'They weren't in the sense that you would understand it. My mother didn't wear hijab, for example. But their faith mattered to

71

them. I was the one who was the rebel. I ran away from home because I wanted to become an actor. I broke their hearts because I had grand ambitions.'

I would have liked her to say more but Oz stalled her with his question, 'But they forgave you, didn't they?'

'Of course.' She smiled at him. A smile I would always remember because of all that it held. 'Parents will always forgive their children, no matter what.'

It mattered to him that she said that. I wondered what he had done wrong or what he considered to be wrong or what he believed would hurt her. I envied them the ease between them. I could not reconcile the idea of forgiveness with my own parents. With my mother who left my father for Tony. The sensibilities of 1980s Khartoum were mine against my will. That world where men owned the streets and women pretended to be shy even when they weren't. That time and place where sparks flared up at the slightest provocation; where words like 'betrayal' and 'disgrace' undid lives. Over the years I had tried to rid myself of such baggage but never fully succeeded. I understood my father's feelings of shame and, later, my own failed romantic attachments seemed like an apt punishment, because although I went through the motions, these casual relationships never felt right.

Nor could I reconcile the idea of forgiveness for my father whom I hadn't seen in over a decade. He visited me once when I was in university. He came, he said, all the way from Khartoum especially to see me. I kept telling him I was busy with exams and I only met up with him twice. The first time he was waiting for me outside the library and I was ashamed to be seen with him around the campus. He was wearing flimsy clothes in one of the coldest springs, his English was rudimentary and I had, by then, almost forgotten my Arabic. So ironically my mother's language became our only way to communicate. We must have looked weird. On the grounds of a Scottish university, an African father and a mixed-race daughter, dodging the rain and speaking Russian. I told him that my graduation was next week but I did not even ask about my grandmother or my old friends. There was only the resentment at his presence, the impatience to get rid of him. 'I will attend your graduation ceremony,' he said.

'You can't,' I replied. 'The seating is limited and I only have tickets for Mum and Tony.'

The second and last time we met he took me to lunch and I ate in silence, barely answering his questions. And yet on that occasion I was more relaxed; I even smiled at one of his jokes and noticed the new white in his hair. When he warmed up, he called my mother a whore and Tony a racist. 'A thief,' my father spat out, spittle flying from his mouth, who stole her away from him, as if she didn't have a will of her own. As if she and I didn't spend afternoons in Tony's villa, me in the swimming pool hugging a Tweety inflatable ring, the chlorine jamming my nose and the two of them upstairs, behind a locked door with the air-conditioner humming. But I wouldn't defend the indefensible; I tucked into my meatballs and left him to rant.

'I should not have let you go with them,' he repeated. 'All my friends advised me to keep you but I didn't listen.'

I sounded grown-up when I replied, 'It's been good for me to come here.' I sounded confident, as if I had moved on and the past hardly mattered to me at all. I was doing well in my studies and this impressed him. He had little to offer me if I chose to return with him. Sudan was in a state of economic collapse, the civil war against the south was raging. He had, as expected, failed in every business venture he started – he had neither the necessary political connections nor the dogged perseverance – his was another brilliant mind burned out by a dysfunctional post-colonial state. The house he was building was still incomplete, his only car a wreck, his debts mounting. I was much better where I was. At the end of the lunch, which didn't include dessert, my father gave me money. Five twenty-pound notes in a grubby envelope. Tony had stopped supporting me since I turned eighteen and I worked part-time in the student union shop, so I hesitated a little but then I took his gift.

*

Malak, sipping her green tea, said, 'I should wake up Ossie so that you're not delayed. It would be better for him to get a lift from you in case the buses are still disrupted. And it would be good for you to have company in case your tyres get stuck in the snow.' Her face was still puffy with sleep, gentle without make-up.

I assured her that I was not in a great hurry. I stood up to make myself another mug of coffee and to wash my cereal bowl in the sink. In the first orange rays from the rising sun I saw the car approaching. So for sure the roads were clear enough. No more doubts, no more procrastinations. I could leave, I should leave. The car came closer, but later I realised there must have been another car, one that was already parked out of sight of the house. My telephone buzzed. It was a message from Tony. *Need to talk to you. Bad news from Khartoum.*

I looked up and through the window saw two policemen. Before I could tell Malak, they rang the bell. She went to answer it and then everything happened very fast.

One of them speaks and says the other name instead of Oz. His voice is loud, says they have a warrant for his arrest. Malak asks why and the answer starts with 't', ends with a suffix and she draws in her breath. I am glued to the kitchen floor, mobile phone in my hand, open at Tony's message. They are everywhere now, lots of them, not two, with their shoes clomping, but Malak doesn't say take your shoes off. They leap up the stairs, I catch a blur of dark uniform. Footsteps above me. Malak is calling Oz. This makes them angry. They think she is warning him off and two of them run, banging the bedroom door open. I hear him say, 'What the fuck!' I hear a scuffle but then Malak's voice, telling him to be calm, to best do as he's told. I walk to the landing but one of them is holding the sword in his hand, the sitting room is in disarray, one of them comes up to me, his large face looms close. He carries two laptops – mine and Oz's. The white one is mine, I say but he takes my mobile too. His voice is loud but he just wants my name and my address. I tell him why I am here, but still my laptop gets carried into their car. They clamber down the stairs, Oz in handcuffs, Malak following.

Oz is wearing his coat over his pyjamas. His lips are dry and his eyes, his body, the tilt of his head, are rigid with anger; anger a crust pressing down fear. Before they prod him out of the house, he looks at me and I have nothing to say.

Because the front door had been open all the time the police were here, the house was freezing. Blasts of air swept through; there was sludge on the carpet. I closed the door, I locked it too. I started to tidy up. I was shivering and my fingers were numb. Malak sat on the bottom step hugging her knees. 'It's a mistake,' she repeated. 'They've mixed him up with someone else, I'm sure.'

I reassured her as best I could. I picked up her shawl, which had fallen on the ground, and tucked it round her shoulders. I could not bear the chaos surrounding us, the way the house had been violated. I started to tidy up, putting everything back in its place. I pulled the vacuum cleaner from the store cupboard. I mopped up the shoe stains on the kitchen floor. I wanted everything to look and smell and feel like it had before they came.

I walked past Malak, who seemed to be glued to the stairs, and carried the vacuum cleaner up. Oz's room was in complete disarray. Every drawer had been turned out, every poster pulled down from the wall, files and books scattered, clothes on the floor. I folded his clothes and put them back in the cupboard and drawers. Unable to stick the posters back on the wall, I rolled them up – one black and white image of the Kaaba during a freak deluge, pilgrims swimming around the cube instead of walking, two *Spider-man* posters, one of *X-Men Die by the Sword 5*. As I worked, the room lit up with the morning sun; it felt warmer than anywhere else. It had really happened, they had taken him away and the magnitude of the charge against him was pitch-dark and shameful. *What have you done, you stupid, stupid boy?* I could no longer move, I slumped on the bed, willing myself to calm down, to be rational. *What have you done…*

I stretched out on the bed, the sun coming straight at me through the window. I could smell him on the pillow, I could see him putting the kettle on in the kitchen and I could hear him call his mother by her name and I tried to push away the fear, to ignore his last look. I must forget their clomping shoes, their big faces and the invasion that had happened. Soon, I would wipe away all traces of them, vacuum the fluff that had fallen from their uniforms and the shedding of their skins, open the windows and flush out the smell of them. I closed my eyes from the bright sun, I saw blotches of colours, my fingers pressed down on the duvet. There was no sound from downstairs, the peace of shock. My body started to feel heavy, my stomach relaxed enough to start digesting my breakfast, my bladder to start filling up. I dozed and I was standing on one of the peaks of the Caucasus, balancing on the edge of a ledge. From the top of my head all the way down in one straight swoop, I split in two, half-human and half-reptile. In the logic of dreams it made sense that my left side was human because that was where my heart was. In the logic of dreams I was not embarrassed that I was naked, nor that a part of me was inhuman. With my left hand I ran my fingers over a pattern of scales on my right shoulder, ridges of shell, leathery grooves. In the logic of dreams what perplexed me the most was that I had split vertically rather than horizontally. It was natural to be like a centaur or a sphinx; it was usual to have a full human head. But I had failed; I had morphed into something completely different. A man was coming behind me and I was reluctant to turn around. Below me was a sheer drop into rocks and burning forests. I lost my balance and jerked awake.

I sat up and remembered Tony's message. I fished in my pocket for my mobile and realised that it was going to be a real nuisance not to have it. I could not remember Tony's number off the top of my head. This was the result of years just pressing a button, instead of dialling. Of course there were other ways of getting hold of it and most likely I had scribbled it down in an old Filofax. But I wanted to hear that news from Khartoum. And how exactly had it reached Tony? Maybe Grusha, my mother's friend, had called him. The news would be about my father – who else? I put the vacuum cleaner on and tried to remember Tony's home number, the number I used to call Mum on all these years. 01224 was the code but the number itself was muddled.

When I went downstairs, Malak was locked in the same spot, her knees bunched up, her face expressionless. When she finally spoke, her voice sounded strange. An accent had crept in. Shock did that to people, it hurtled them back to their mother tongue. 'They took the sword,' she said.

'They took every CD you have. They took my mobile phone and my laptop.'

'I am sorry, Natasha. I hope you will get your things back soon.'

Tears came to my eyes. I wanted to speak to her like I had never spoken to anyone before. Instead I said, 'I have to go.'

'Can't you stay a little longer?' she whispered. She looked pathetic huddled in her shawl. She stood up and for the smallest fraction of a second, lost her balance and then regained it again. That wobble added years to her age, a slip-up as if she had been acting all the time, playing the role of a London actor, a glamorous woman of the world and now this was her real self. One of those who don't matter, who shuffle down the street, reeking of failure if not trouble, suspect and unwanted. One of those people I never wanted to be seen with. She said, 'Let's make a pot of tea, shall we?'

Weren't these the words I had longed to hear? Where did I have to go that was better than here? But the warning said get away, don't get dragged further into this – it's bad enough that you're already involved; save your skin. I recognised this pragmatism, these tropes of survival. It made me grab my coat and head towards the door. Malak stood up and followed me. Her movements were slow and tentative; she was not herself. In a high querulous voice she repeated, 'It's all a mistake. They've made a mistake. They've got the wrong person I'm sure.'

I didn't allow myself to speak, I didn't look at her. Guilty, I got into the car and drove straight to work.

2. Georgia, July 1854

She walked through grass that reached her waist. It tickled her arms and almost covered Alexander to the brim of his straw summer hat. He let go of her hand and ran in the direction of the soldier galloping towards them. Anna opened her mouth to call him back then closed it again; she shaded her eyes from the sun. These maternal flickers of anxiety flared with varying degrees of intensity through every stage of his life. Sometimes they were justified, often they weren't, but cats had nine lives and children didn't. What if the soldier didn't see Alexander or Alexander didn't stop running early enough? At the same time she did not want him to be timid, to be tied to her apron strings as no boy should be. So she must grit her teeth as he exposed himself to a thousand and one dangers.

During her pregnancy with Lydia she had been less alert, and after the birth too, she was immersed in that satisfaction that only comes to mothers with copious milk and a healthy feeding baby. In that period Alexander had flourished, benefiting from less of her attention, venturing further away from the radius of her vision. Here in the countryside, he had grown fitter and more hardy. Apart from Madame Drancy's lessons and the requirement to speak to her in French at all times, he was allowed to do as he liked. It was as carefree as a summer should be, despite the rumours that Shamil's men were set to descend from the mountains. Such an invasion had never taken place throughout history and was, Anna believed, just as unlikely to happen now.

The horseman had seen Alexander. She could tell by the way he straightened up in his saddle. Anna could breathe more easily now, continue walking towards them for surely the soldier was bringing a message from David. She was conscious of the fullness of her body in last summer's dress, aware of the absence of Lydia, neither inside her nor in her arms, and still it was a surprise. She felt less weighed down but at the same time incomplete; the distance from the garden to the nursery where the baby was sleeping seemed excessively large. If Lydia woke up and cried now, she would not hear her. Her ears, though, strained for that familiar high note and now it felt as if she was playing truant, exploring the furthest end of the leash that tied her to her daughter. The gardener, Gregov, reached the rider first and turned to bring her the message. Despite the white in his hair, he was strong and quick in his movements. She must ask him why he had delayed cutting the grass. It had not rained yesterday.

Gregov gripped his hat in one hand and handed her the message. 'Should he wait for a reply?'

She hesitated before saying, 'Yes.' It meant cutting her walk and returning to the house. She preferred writing leisurely long letters in the evening. Now it would have to be a hurried note. Still, David would want her to reassure him.

Gregov hovered over her as she read the message. His avuncular right or just a natural eagerness for news from the local militia? *There is no occasion for uneasiness*. The sentence was underlined and she read it first. Then she went back to the beginning.

She said to Gregov, 'The fortress at Shildi was attacked by a large number of Lezgins but they were repulsed and they took heavy losses.'

'Shildi must have been Shamil's target then.' He twisted his hat in his hands.

'Would that explain the campfires on the mountains?' There were four of them last night and Madame Drancy even more edgy. 'How far is Shildi from here?'

'A good thirty miles. The Lezgins are the most lawless of the tribes that follow Shamil.' Gregov shook his head. 'My cousin was taken by them as prisoner. They threaded horse-hairs through his heels.'

'Whatever for?'

Gregov narrowed his eyes and replied coolly, 'So that he wouldn't escape, ma'am. The wounds fester and make walking horribly painful.'

She looked towards Alexander. He seemed to be enjoying a new friendship with the soldier, who now dismounted and lifted him up to take his place.

'The Lezgins keep their prisoners in pits,' Gregov continued. 'What would they know of Christian compassion?'

Anna turned away from him. Sometimes she felt like she was part of a great charade. An essential pretence that Russia was winning the Caucasus, that every encounter with Shamil was a resounding victory. And yet thousands of lives were being lost and the mountains still did not belong to the tsar. David too, talked this optimistic language. He had to, he had no choice. This awareness of the pressures he was under caused a rush of love for him. This and the relief that he had not fallen into the hands of the Lezgins swept her back to the house and into writing him an effusive message urging him to come as soon as he could, even though they were all safe and well.

In the evening as she was putting Lydia to bed, Madame Drancy came in to say that Gregov wanted to talk to her. Lydia was not fully asleep – her eyes fluttered open as soon as Anna put her down in the cot. She tiptoed out of the room, Drancy close behind her. It was on the tip of her tongue to say, 'Stay with Lydia until she is deeply asleep,' but Madame Drancy bristled whenever she was asked to do anything that remotely resembled a nursery maid's duty. Besides, she was clearly eager to hear what Gregov had to say. He had never asked to see Anna at this time in the evening.

'There is a man at the gate asking permission to spend the night,' Gregov said. 'He is an Armenian merchant.'

'Where did he come from?'

'He says he swam the Alazani.' Gregov stressed the word 'says' as if he didn't believe it.

Neither did Anna. Most travellers were heading in the opposite direction.

'He says he was evading Shamil's men and he's soaked to the skin.' Gregov's tone softened.

Madame Drancy, hovering behind Anna, blurted out, 'At a time like this? We certainly should not trust him!'

Her outburst made the two Georgians close rank. 'We can't turn him away, Madame Drancy. It is not our custom.' She turned to Gregov. 'Give him supper too, but watch him.'

'I will disarm him,' said Gregov. 'And if he tries to escape, I will shoot him.'

She had been brave in front of Madame Drancy but she did not feel comfortable with the thought of the stranger spending the night on the estate. Sleep eluded her and at last when she drifted off, she heard a shot. It could well have been a dream but Madame Drancy banged into the room without knocking.

'Princess Anna, wake up!'

She scrambled to her feet. 'Did you hear that?'

Madame Drancy's face was visible in the bright strips of moon-light that bordered the curtains, 'Yes, I was walking in the garden. I just couldn't sleep. It's so hot. I saw a man – the traveller who was spending the night. He had a gun – he must have hidden it from Gregov. I saw him make for the woods.'

Anna put on her dressing gown. 'He must have fired that shot.'

'Why? What does it mean?'

'He's a spy.' The word was heavy in her mouth, the consciousness that she was turning a corner. 'He fired the gun as a signal.' She let duty dictate her next words, not her preference, not her need. Left to her own devices she could cling to Tsinondali and grit her teeth, pray that the threat would go away. 'We must leave for Tiflis at dawn. I'll have to start packing. We must bring down the big trunk from the attic.' She would pack with precision and care; she would not scramble off dishevelled, leaving behind what was precious and

81

irreplaceable. Back to face the smug 'told you so's of Tiflis, her flight a smile on everyone's lips.

'There is something else.' Madame Drancy drew in her breath. 'Something I didn't tell you.'

'Well, out with it.' Anna's hand reached out to the back of her favourite armchair. How could she leave it behind?

'The moon is so full tonight, I could see across the river. The water has definitely subsided. Two men were leading their horses along the bank searching for a place to cross. I saw their weapons.'

Anna stood up, the sense of urgency finally taking root. 'They must be scouts. Wake the servants up. We have to be ready by dawn.'

But they were not ready by dawn. The ikons needed wrapping, the bedding needed folding, the maids panicked and slipped away which made the process of packing even slower. Anna made sure that all the silver was put away in the trunk. Her dresses and the children's clothes. She made Gregov carry the armchair and hoist it up on the oxen-cart. He grumbled and cursed but he was too loyal to leave them at a time like this. The younger gardeners had already disappeared without even saying goodbye, so had the grooms and the field-hands. Gregov was the only one left guarding the estate; he would be at the gate now. When all this was over, she would tell David and he would reward him.

Alexander pushed his father's pistol against Madame Drancy's back. 'I am the dreaded warrior, Shamil,' he shouted.

'Mon Dieu!' his governess squealed and dropped the ikon she was wrapping. It shattered on the ground.

'How dare you, Alexander! Is this a time for games?' Anna snatched the pistol from him. 'Apologise to Madame Drancy.'

She accepted his apology. 'Now that you're up, you might as well be packing instead of creating mischief.'

He smiled, 'I will pack my summer hat.'

'Off you go then,' said Anna. 'We are leaving soon. Be sure the flowers on your hat don't get crushed.' Afterwards she would think, if I had not cared about the flowers, the silver, the packing, how much time would I have saved? Horsemen at full tilt on the plains and she was giving Lydia her morning feed. Her breasts not as full as they usually were, the milk sensitive to the sleepless night, the disjointed nerves.

Could the trunk take one more tablecloth? 'Just push it in.'

Madame Drancy kneeling to lock the trunk, held herself still. 'Can you hear it?'

'What? No. If we both sit on it, it will close.'

Sitting on the trunk, she heard the unmistakable galloping. Madame Drancy ran to the window, her voice squeaky as a girl's. 'They are here! They are here! We must run to the woods.'

Anna was conscious of her own heaviness – baby, Alexander, belongings. 'No, it's too late. It's best to hide in the attic. Fetch Alexander from the nursery.'

Under the low ceiling of the attic, they crouched among the dust and what looked like rat droppings. Anna loaded the pistol and looked out of the window. The shock of the actual sight of them storming the gate – their turbans, some green, some white and patterned; their guns and sabres, their mouths stretched open, war cries in another language, a sense of chaos and tense power. There was Gregov carrying his gun, his familiar cap, white speckled hair, his compact figure, running towards them and shouting, 'God save us. The Lezgins!' He stood and fired. Then she saw his body receive the pain of a bullet and slump to the ground. She turned her head. If they were going to trample him with their horses, she could not watch.

She rocked Lydia while Alexander and Drancy peered out of the small window. The clatter of hooves on the cobbles of the courtyard. 'Get back, they will look up and spot you,' hissed Anna.

But that crash was the downstairs door being broken down. They were in the house now and Anna started to buzz with fear and indignation too. This violation of her property; their paws on her furniture, their hooves treading her carpets. Alexander came close to her, pushed his head against her arm. 'Don't be afraid. They won't find us.'

She didn't need to whisper. It was pandemonium below, glass breaking, the sounds of furniture being demolished, crockery smashed to the floor. So destructive, so destructive.

'They will loot and leave. What would they want us for? They will take as much as they can and leave.' She was speaking out loud and she jumped at the sound of the piano. One of them must have slammed his hands on the keys.

That quickening was them mounting the stairs. The voices coming closer, up to the attic. 'Shush, not a sound.' But Lydia was whimpering. Anna held her close. Madame Drancy was moving her lips in prayer. The doorknob juddered. A substantial group was at the door. A shout as they started to break it down. Once, twice, the door held for some time. More shouts and the wood cracked. Madame Drancy screamed as the men spilled into the attic.

Anna grabbed the pistol and started to shoot. She was not aiming, just pushing them away, wanting them down and out the door and out the gate and off the estate. A grunt as she wounded one of them. Smoke and the acrid smell of it and their smell too as the pistol was yanked out of her hand.

A Lezgin glared down at her. He had to stoop so that his head would not hit the ceiling. His turban was tight across his forehead, black beard and a snarl. 'Enough. Not a single man among you and you think you have a chance!'

His Lezgian accent was heavy but she understood what he was saying. She could not, though, grasp the babble of the other men, all speaking at the same time as if making opposing suggestions, the word 'Chavchavadzes' chilly and odd in the middle of their sentences.

'Take them downstairs,' their leader bellowed.

She was lifted, Lydia and all, and when she resisted was dragged out of the attic, her elbow banging on the door, her toe scraping the floor. A raider lifted Alexander, who kicked and screamed.

'I'm a French citizen,' Madame Drancy was shouting. 'Put me down. How dare you do this to me!'

Lydia was crying too. It took all Anna's effort and concentration to keep her safe in her arms. Alexander bit his captor on the shoulder. He was punched in return and groaned from the pain. Grunts of laughter from the men. 'That little devil has sharp teeth!'

'Don't fight him, Alexander.' She was already downstairs, calling up. She was being pulled out of the house. It was as if there were a hundred of them crowded on the stairs. It was not only Madame Drancy and Alexander that they were carrying, but whatever they could loot. Without discipline, without logic, grabbing this and that, armfuls and their clanking weapons. The ludicrous sound of the piano as it was leant upon, fallen over or even used as a foothold. Loud jarring notes among the whoops of triumph. One of them leapt down the side of the staircase as if he were still on the mountains, jumping from boulder to boulder. Anna turned to see the heavy trunk being rolled down from the upper landing. The combined weight of people, goods and weapons brought the whole staircase crashing to the ground.

Dust rose in the centre of the house. Anna gasped at the ugliness of the splintered wood and the rubble, the strangeness of an upper storey that could not be reached. She screamed but her voice meant nothing; her orders, 'Get out of my house', did not raise the slightest interest. Nonchalantly, the highlanders picked themselves off the ground amidst grunts and lazy recriminations. In a flash they were looting again and she was pulled out the front door and into the courtyard.

It too was alien, crowded with their sweaty horses. The cart that carried her favourite armchair had been overturned. The familiar upholstery, the roses and lilac design was smeared with mud and horse manure. In the middle of the courtyard, Anna and her children were thrown in a heap. She examined Alexander's arm. 'Move it for me. Good boy.' It was bruised but unbroken.

'You are brave,' she told him. 'Papa will be proud of you.' Her own back ached but she scarcely noticed it. One of the sleeves of her dress was torn. She could put Lydia down on her lap but she still clutched her. Around them more highlanders jostled each other to enter the house; those who had already been inside squabbled over their spoils. It was as if this was not Tsinondali any more, this was not the same garden trampled and muddied, this pillaged house not the same house, these were not the same stables, doors wide open, the horses tied up, men and more men swarming all the way to the gate. The men brandished their sabres even though they faced no resistance. No villagers had rallied round, no field-hands, no one.

Madame Drancy was being pulled and dragged between two men who were exchanging curses. One of them held her right arm; the other hooked her left arm over his shoulder and was grabbing her by the waist. A cold understanding seeped through Anna; these two were fighting over Madame Drancy. The tall Lezgin, who had taken the pistol from Anna upstairs, strode towards the scuffle, shashka in hand. He was, Anna guessed, their leader. He bellowed at the two men and they reluctantly let go of Drancy. She was dragged, instead, by her hair and thrown down on the ground next to Anna.

Lydia was whimpering and twisting her head, rooting for her next feed. It came as a surprise to Anna that several hours had already passed since she had last fed her. But yes, it was time again. Lydia started to cry, the distressed wails of a justified hunger. Here, in the middle of this, Anna must undo her bodice. She crouched behind Madame Drancy and tried to be as discreet as she could. But the Lezgin leader came over and leered down at her. With the tip of his shashka, he pierced the knot her hair was tied in. When it fell on her shoulders, he lifted a strand, the blade now touching her neck, inches above Lydia's head, perpendicular to Alexander's neck.

Madame Drancy shouted, 'Get away, you turbaned monster.' She leapt up but he pushed her down with his free hand. The blade vibrated against Anna's cheek.

'Well, you're the pretty one, aren't you?' He hooked the shashka under the shoulder strap of her dress. It tore with the slightest of tugs.

'How dare you do this to me! You don't know who I am.'

He smiled, 'Oh, but I do know, your Highness. I know it and it is a shame that I am under strict orders. You see, you are precious.

Too valuable for a Lezgin like me. Maybe this one will do. If she is worth it!' He turned to Madame Drancy and with a downward swoop of the shashka tore her dress in half. She was now in her corset and petticoat. She leapt at him, clawing at his face. 'You butcher, you animal, leave me alone.'

Another highlander, with a bare shaven head, dropped the candlesticks he was holding and cut Madame Drancy across the shoulders with his whip. She fell down crying and huddled against Anna.

The Lezgin squatted down and brought his face level with the two of them. 'Listen, you are my captives now. Until I take you up the mountains and hand you over, you will obey me. Understand. You will obey every word I say. This is better for you and easier for all of us. So now you sit here, you don't move and you keep quiet. We have not herded your cattle yet.'

'You will not get away with this,' Anna said. 'There are posts up and down the river and you will be captured. Is it brave to hit women and children? You're a lowly criminal.'

'Yes, I'm a bandit. I will be paid when I hand you over. But I'm following orders too. Don't touch the princess, don't hurt her children. But if you provoke me, you'll see the worst side of me.'

He walked away and Anna turned to see that Madame Drancy's shoulder was badly cut. She comforted her as best she could, her words sounding feeble even to her own ears. Had he really said *take you up to the mountains*? Would there be more of this, more of them? She had thought they would loot and leave, leave them humiliated, leave them hurt but leave without them. She started to fix up her own dress and managed to tie it up with a pin from Lydia's nappy. Her toe was bleeding. She could not remember when and where she had injured it. If she wanted to change Lydia's nappy now, how was she meant to go about it?

'That's my hat,' Alexander called out. He ran towards a raider who had just stepped out of the house wearing the straw summer hat. Its flowers, crushed and askew, were dangling over his turban. Anna shouted, 'Alexander, come back.' But he darted ahead and managed to reach the man without being stopped. Instead of giving him his hat back, the man pushed him away. It was as if they were two children squabbling. Soon, Alexander was carried back and dumped next to Anna. She rebuked him for endangering himself. 'They will hurt you, Alexander, they are merciless.' Tears welled in her eyes. If anything should happen to him . . . but just thinking about it was unbearable. She hugged him close to her, finding comfort in his shape and the familiar sensation of his hair against her cheek.

'Look, Mama.' He pointed at two men who were sitting cross-legged examining their new belongings. One dipped his fingers in white powder and tasted it. It was the chalk from the schoolroom. Another one was licking Anna's face cream.

'He thinks it's food.' There was wonder in Alexander's voice. She should laugh too, but the reflex let her down. She stared at their questioning, ignorant faces. What would they deduce apart from the realisation that chalk and face cream were inedible?

'Grotesque,' Madame Drancy whispered. She muttered to herself in French.

There were more men now in the courtyard, fewer in the house. Some were already mounted, leading behind them a new horse or cow. The Lezgin approached them. 'Come on, it's time to get out of here. Each one of you will ride with a different horseman.' He reached out to take Lydia away from Anna.

'No. My baby stays with me. I will not hand her to anyone else.'

There was no expression on his face. 'Very well. Then you both ride with me.' He dragged her away before she could even say goodbye to Alexander. 'Mama, wait for me. Where are you going?' But already one of the men was hoisting him off.

Anna shouted back, 'Don't be afraid, Alexander. I will be with you soon. Don't fight so that they don't hurt you.' She wanted to tell him that David would come and rescue them. Soon. This ordeal would be over and everything would go back to how it was before. Surely David would not allow this to happen to his wife and children. But she was afraid to mention his name in front of the Lezgins. Let them be lulled into thinking that they had succeeded.

She turned to look back at the estate. Her favourite armchair toppled over on the ground, dirty and abandoned. The stables were set on fire, the shimmer of burning grass, pigs out of their pens roaming. Anna closed her eyes when she recognised the lifeless heap that only this morning was the loyal, active gardener; Gregov's cap and his greying hair.

They rode at a moderate pace towards the river, towards those mountains that hosted the campfires of the past days. The sun was high in the sky; it made her head start to hurt. The cattle of the estate, rounded close together, bellowed and stirred the dust of the road. The gush of the water became louder and there was the Alazani, rushing over the boulders, foaming and deep.

'Can you swim, Princess?'

She did not answer him.

'Then hold on tight and keep your baby close to you!'

Everyone had told her that the Alazani was too deep to cross this time of year. David had said so, Gregov had said so. She had believed it and now these riders were patting their horses with encouragement; they were tensing up as if for an adventure.

'Too deep for *your* horses,' the Lezgin said. 'But ours are trained. You will see how they will swim.'

When they entered the water, the riders fell silent. There were no more shouts and boasts, no argumentative exchanges and in-decipherable grunts. The horses were indeed swimming even though they were weighed down with their riders and the cattle they were pulling. Anna's lower half was plunged into the cold water. It filled her shoes and pulled down her petticoats and dress. She turned and saw the amazement in Alexander's face. He had forgotten his fear and the bruise on his arm. Anna lifted Lydia even higher.

A sound of a splash as Madame Drancy fell into the river. The men burst out laughing while she flailed in the water shouting for help.

'Hey, drag her out . . . enough,' the Lezgin ordered and they obeyed, good-natured and at ease. It filled Anna with loathing and the urge to escape. Then panic rose in her throat like vomit. She was away from home now, floating weirdly on water. This Lezgin and his devilish horse were keeping her alive. Where were the Russian defences? She wanted the nightmare to end. Enough. Lydia was fidgeting against her. She needed her nappy changed.

Madame Drancy was now up behind her captor; she was breathless and soaked. Anna shouted out, 'Are you all right?' The spluttered reply elicited another foreign joke.

At the other side of the river, they stopped while the men made their ablutions and lined up to pray. Alexander took an interest in what they were doing, watching them from a distance. Anna took the opportunity to clean Lydia's nappy but she did not have a change of clothes. She did her best under the circumstances but was not satisfied. The baby's skin was sensitive and it would chafe. She washed the dirty nappy in the river and wrung it out. She hung it on a bush but they did not stop long enough for it to dry. She had to carry it damp.

'You should give your baby to one of the men,' said the Lezgin. They had been coming up to Anna with pantomime gestures, offering to do so.

'Never.' She held Lydia closer.

'Suit yourself.' He adjusted his turban. 'It will be a dangerous climb.'

Lydia slept but was jolted awake with every leap and jerk of the horse. She started to cry, working herself up to such a pitch that her face turned red and her body rigid. She was so loud that some of the other riders heard her. They turned around and made lewd gestures as if to instruct Anna to feed her. She did eventually because she had to, because there was no other way to make this piercing, frustrating sound stop. Lydia was so overwrought that she could not at first settle and suck. The unsteady movement of the horse over the rocks made matters even worse. Still whimpering as if feeling sorry for herself, as if berating and reproaching her mother, she finally was able to draw in and swallow. But true satisfaction didn't come. Anna's milk was watery and insufficient. So long ago, it seemed, she had skimped breakfast in order to start the packing. Since then she had not had anything except gulps of water from the river. Lydia squirmed, sucking intensely until it made Anna's nipple sore. She strained her ears for the Russian picket; surely they were stationed near, surely they would come to rescue them.

When the sun started to set, they made camp on the mountainside. It startled Anna to see Madame Drancy in a burka. It belonged to her captor and he had flung it over her to keep her warm. 'The water was freezing,' she said sitting down next to Anna, and arranging the folds around her. 'Hideous outfit.'

They sat in front of the fire. A campfire like the ones they used to see from the windows of Tsinondali. 'The water made my fingers numb,' said Anna. 'I had trouble holding Lydia.'

'Luckily Alexander didn't get wet,' said Madame Drancy. He too was wrapped in a burka, sound asleep.

Anna's stomach growled. She had pushed away the dinner of dried millet they had been offered. It was unappetising and touched by their dirty fingers. Lydia was asleep now but she would not stay asleep for long; fretting and hungry, she would want to be nursed all night.

'They say the journey up the mountains will take five weeks.' Madame Drancy spoke in a matter-of-fact way.

Anna could not even visualise one week. She turned to look at Madame Drancy's face. It looked fresher and leaner, like she had been on a brisk walk.

Madame Drancy said, 'I wonder if one of these highlanders would be sympathetic enough to help us escape. I can teach him a little bit of French. We can bribe him...'

'With what? They've taken everything.'

'We can promise to reward him once we are free.'

Anna sighed, 'You are so fanciful. We will be rescued. Surely by now David will have heard of our predicament.'

'It's only been a few hours,' was the governess's terse reply.

Of course it felt more than that. The night was long too. Anna couldn't sleep even though she was exhausted and bruised. It was uncomfortable to lie on the ground without a pillow. The moonlight was too bright and there were the menacing sounds of the forests, the torrential river, the snores of these violent men. It seemed that whenever she dozed, Lydia would wake up whimpering and whenever Lydia fell asleep, Anna lay anxious, alert to the dangers around her. Images of the day pounded the gap between wakefulness and dreams; the pistol snatched away, a cow being dragged from the stables, Gregov's body sprawled on the ground. She closed her eyes and saw Madame Drancy fall in the river. The water had been icy, it had chilled Anna's legs and when her hands got wet, her fingers became numb. They felt clumsy and fat and it was awkward to hold up Lydia. She had been afraid that she would let her slip, straining all the time to keep her from sliding, forcing herself closer to her captor's back because that was the only way to keep the baby safe.

Anna finally fell asleep a little before dawn and woke up to a foreign chant. It was some of the men praying. A part of her had hoped that she would wake up in her bedroom in Tsinondali and all of this would have been the longest of nightmares. Her body was stiff as she followed Madame Drancy deeper behind a clump of trees. This was their toilet and surprisingly the men were decent enough to stay at a distance. Perhaps they judged them too weak to escape or else they knew she would never run off and leave Alexander.

He was faring better than her and did not complain. He ate the food they put before him and drank a mug of tea. 'I have to eat for Lydia's sake,' thought Anna. No food and drink meant no milk. It was as simple as that. She forced herself to eat. Her stomach felt full even though it wasn't; her mouth was dry. One of the highlanders shambled close and pointed at Lydia, making gestures as if he wanted to carry her when they next rode off. His plebeian face was in smiles and he spoke in a dialect Anna couldn't understand. She held Lydia close and waved him away, shaking her head.

He persisted, trying to ingratiate himself by bowing and begging. Exasperated and eager to get rid of him, she took off her pearl earrings and tossed them to him. The bribe worked. He put them in his pocket and turned away.

When it was time to mount again, Anna retched out her breakfast. It splattered on her dress. She used to be clean and sweet-smelling. And Lydia too, used to be clean and sweet-smelling. Now her wispy hair was matted against her scalp, there was congealed milk behind her ears and in the folds of her neck. As expected, her lower half had risen in a red rash that extended even to the folds around her knees. She needed a bath, talcum powder, a change of clothes. But where would these come from?

Although their progress was slow, the higher they climbed, the more Anna's heart sank. They were venturing further and further towards Shamil's territory. This was the border that David was meant to be protecting, this was the line where the river forts were stationed. Around them was nothing but the forests and the mountains, familiar to these men; their natural habitat.

She dozed against her will and woke with a shock to find that her arms had gone slack and Lydia was wedged loosely between her and the rider, the trail of her nappy dangling over the saddle. The baby was wide awake, gazing up with large wet eyes at the green swirl of the trees, the sun filtering through.

They reached a clearing, a stretch of flat ground and suddenly there was a whizzing sound that made Anna turn her head. Were they being followed? The loudest cry from the Lezgin as his horse wheeled and broke into a gallop. 'It's an ambush. Go, go, go.'

Anna felt her whole body sway backwards, her arms instinctively jutting out for balance. 'Stop,' she screamed, 'I'm not holding her properly.'

Lydia was loose in her arms, a lopsided bundle, as bullets zinged past them, as the highlanders dispersed, yelping and working their horses up to a frenzy. One of the riders was shot. He groaned and fell to the ground.

'Hold your hostage close!' the Lezgin shouted to his men. The horses of their pursuers could be heard now. They were gaining on them. A bullet hit a horse and it skidded and crashed down, flinging its rider.

'Stop,' she screamed. 'Please stop.'

'Hold tight to my belt, Princess.'

'My baby is slipping from me. Stop now, I beg you.'

'Soon, soon we will stop.'

I am holding her, aren't I? She is here and we are being rescued.
The Lezgin suddenly reeled his horse to the right and dashed into the forest. The movement guaranteed their escape but Anna swayed and nearly tipped over. He reached behind to steady her but only succeeded in knocking her elbow. Lydia slipped from her arm. 'My baby!' she screamed. She screamed and the sound pressed close, her nerves vibrating. The bundle fragile on soil and leaves. Her wrong empty hands. It was as if her own insides squished and bled. Her own spine cracked and the thud was thunder in her inner ear.

IV
Further Than the Outpost

1. Scotland, December 2010

'Can I have a word with you, Natasha?' Iain put his head through the door. It meant he wanted me to come to his office. 'Any time within the next hour,' he added. He drummed his fingers against the doorknob. As always, his clothes hung on him as if they were a size too large. His hair, too, always seemed big for his face, a throwback to the 1980s. The formality of his request surprised me. A dull ache started behind my eyes. I was still shaken by what had happened this morning.

After leaving Malak, I drove through slush, streets that were busier than usual now that the snow was melting. The need-to-catch-up mood reached me through the edgy shoppers impatient to cross the road and the announcement on the radio that Debenhams would stay open till ten. The Christmas songs were familiar and reassuring. I found that I had an effortless memory for past Number One hits. Given a year, I could guess either the song or the artist, sometimes even both. When it was time for the news I found myself gripping the steering wheel. But there was no mention of dawn raids or of Oz.

Today I had my own catching up to do. I had missed one full day of work and most of the morning. Next week, exams started and there were plenty of emails from my superiors to wade through first, answer or file before I turned to the students'. Without my laptop, I would have to get through them at the desktop in my office. Even my personal emails. I tried not to think of the files on my laptop that I had not backed up.

There was an email from the Classic Car Club saying that tonight's Christmas dinner was cancelled because of the weather.

Lucky for me that I wasn't in charge this year. These kinds of decisions were not easy to make. Last year I was events secretary and that party was a success. It was disappointing that this one was cancelled. I had been looking forward to it, a chance to show off my 1960 Czechoslovakian-built Skoda after all the work I'd had done to it. I was much less hands-on than the others, who tended to do all the work themselves and devoted more time to their car. It cost a fortune at the garage but I would not begrudge my heroic Felicia, which made it to the West at the height of the Cold War.

When I sat in the armchair in Iain's room, he said, 'It's not good news about Gaynor Stead. They've decided to uphold her complaint.'

Gaynor had been my student last year. I had judged her to be the stupidest person to have ever stepped into university. It baffled me that she survived until third year after repeating both of the previous ones. Too often I had watched quirky and brilliant students crash and burn. Instead it was the doleful and dogged Gaynor who was the survivor of the species. She never missed a class – perhaps that was her secret. Or because she knew her rights and felt entitled to a degree as if she were a client and the university a service. She had failed my class, but that was not the issue – her work was poor without question. Instead she claimed that I had sat on top of her desk and broken one of her fingers! It was a seminar and there were only about ten students, the desks arranged in a rectangle. While answering a question, she stumbled over the pronunciation of a Russian name and clammed up, refusing to speak any further. Instead of asking her to spell the name or leaning over to look at her notes or just moving on to someone else, I perched on top of her desk and picked up her notebook. She was clearly irritated by my proximity, swinging her hair back sharply and muttering something under her breath. But there was no cry of pain, nothing about a bruised or injured finger. And I was sure, as much as I could ever be sure, that I did not sit on her finger or even her pen.

'Iain, this is ridiculous. She never left the room. Would anyone with a broken finger continue to take a class as if nothing had happened?'

'She has a letter from her doctor.'

'On that same date?'

He spoke slowly. 'The school is going to look into all that. It's going to take time. In the New Year there'll be another meeting and they'll decide then whether to go ahead with any action.'

There was a picture of his wife and two children on his desk. His wife was wearing a purple jumper; the little boys, only a few years apart, resembled her in that they both had red hair. The photo, taken in front of their new house, seemed recent because of the snow. I too would like to leave my flat and move to a house. I could sit in the garden with my laptop. This was not likely on the pay scale I was on now and the expense of keeping two cars. I would have to be a professor, like Iain. In time I could become one; there was nothing wrong with my abilities. 'This isn't the first time Gaynor has complained about a member of staff. How come this time she's being taken seriously?' My voice sounded sharp to my ears.

'She's complained twice before,' he said. 'Different lecturers.'

'So I'm her third time lucky!'

'I can understand your frustration.'

'What do you think will be the outcome of the meeting?' I might have to fight and the prospect of battle was in itself repulsive.

'It depends,' he said. 'Often these things just fizzle out.' He was giving me his full attention. 'Are you a member of the union?'

'No.' It was not the answer he wanted. Suddenly I wished I was sharing this with Malak and Oz. Malak would laugh and Oz, who probably knew Gaynor, would say something mean about her.

'Iain, I didn't break her finger. I'm sure of it.'

'I believe you and I'm sorry that you have to go through this. It might never come to a hearing though. I know the stress of waiting will be hard but don't let this get to you. That last publication has put you in a strong position.'

At the mention of my paper on Shamil, I brightened up. Every seven years the university submitted its best work for the Research Assessment Exercise. My paper, 'Royal Support for Jihad – Victorian Britain and the Russian Insurgents', was my third to be published and I had another one 'Jihad as Resistance' pending publication in a journal that had previously included Iain's work. They had asked for amendments and I was planning to work on the revisions over the holidays.

Iain went on, 'I've heard good things about your talk last Monday. You're doing well. I can tell you that for this cycle, you're one of our few people with a strong hand.'

Despite the news about Gaynor and what had happened this morning, Iain's last words gave me a sense of safety. 'You're one of the few with a strong hand' played in the background of the afternoon. I could hear it even while I was teaching. It wrapped itself around me when I stood in the kitchen making coffee and chatting with Fiona Ingram. Fiona was the closest friend I had in the department, though her demanding husband and even more tiresome children barely left her room to socialise. We often had coffees together in the staff room or in our offices, like true workaholics. Whenever one of us was having a particularly difficult day, the other would mention the one or two lecturer friends in our separate circles who still couldn't find a full-time job in academia. This morning Fiona was fretting that some students might not make it to the exams because of the snow-blocked roads. I wondered to myself whether Oz would be released on time.

Fiona had the same concern for all her students that I felt only for Oz. She was one of those well-meaning lecturers who could never get to grips with the irony that students were not why we were here. As a result her research was not up to scratch and now Iain would load her with more teaching hours. She did not mention my latest publication but I could tell that she knew about it. Envy gleamed through her mascara. It gave me more satisfaction than anything she could have said. It even cushioned the clunk of finding an email from Oz, which he had sent last night from his personal, not university, email address. His username was SwordOfShamil and the subject was 'Weapons used for Jihad'.

Natasha, here's what I've been working on. Thanks for agreeing to look at it. I listed my sources. Most of them were from the library but I downloaded the al-Qaeda training manual from the US Justice Department website and I didn't even have to pay for it!

My email address, now added to the list of SwordOfShamil's contacts, was bombarded with a stream of spam: *Take the quiz: Muslims dropped the atomic bomb on Hiroshima. True or False? Muslims killed 20 million Aborigines in Australia? True or False? Muslims started the First World War? The Second World War? Muslims killed 100 million Native Americans? True or False? Sick of the hypocrisy of the West? Angry that right now in Iraq and Afghanistan they're killing your brothers and sisters? Then why aren't you doing anything to stop it ...*

My flat was on the top floor and climbing up the stairs I realised how tired I was, in need of a bath, my own cooking, my own toiletries and clothes. The last two days were still bright in my mind. I wanted to go over them, to hear the conversations again. I wondered if I would be able to do so without Oz's arrest burning out the details, rendering our time together as random and obsolete. I reached my landing at the very top floor and froze. It was as if my door was not my door. It was half-open and inside was chaos. A hole in the roof so that I was staring straight up into the dark attic, foot marks on the carpet, my television and DVD player gone, my iPod, even the microwave and the electric blanket. It was a robbery and they had broken in through the roof.

I banged on the door of my neighbour across the hall, but no one was in. I forced myself to walk through the damage, to fight back the tears. It made me queasy that someone had fingered my things, been through my possessions. It made me feel soiled. I called the police and, twice now in the same day, I was in their company, not the same armed officers but still their bulky presence, the hiss of their personal radios, the dark uniforms. How did the robbers get in the attic? How do you think they got on the roof to begin with? How come the neighbours didn't notice? I wanted these answers but they were asking the questions. I started to feel nervous, the truth forcing itself out of my mouth as if it were made up on the spot.

Too quickly, too easily; gently, politely they pushed me back into the old roles. On cue, my skin flared in their presence, it became more prominent than what I was saying; and I was now an impostor asking for attention, a troublesome guest taking up space. They had better things to do and worthier citizens to protect.

I rattled off my mobile number, knowing they would not be able to contact me through it, but unable to explain. Why tell them if they didn't ask, that my phone was bagged and sealed in the possession of the counter-terrorism unit? I needed to focus. Situations like these required an extra effort, an assertiveness I usually brandished with acquired practice. But the day was catching up with me; I stammered and couldn't meet their eyes. My mother's accent crept into my voice, her fear of authority, her tendency to regard questions as interrogations. Growing up in the Soviet Union, state repression was as natural to her as the mountains; it was in every brush with bureaucracy, it was in the factories and offices and even the stairway of my grandparents' block of flats. She would grip my shoulders as we stood in front of Tbilisi's passport officials. She would lower her voice when she criticised anything or repeated gossip. My mother told me that a mental hospital could serve as a prison – one of her classmates, a dissident, had been punished with the vague diagnosis of 'sluggish schizophrenia'. She explained to me that a career could come to an end if you held the wrong political views – early retirement, extended sick leaves and transfers to obscure posts were codes for falling out of favour. Looking around now at the mess of my belongings, my privacy exposed, I remembered my mother. Much more paranoid than me, she would have dealt with this better. 'You are too trusting of authority,' she used to say to me. But all my colleagues were trusting; my teachers and bosses were decent and fair. I missed my mother, she was my first home and now, until the roof was fixed, until the gas and water pipes were checked, I would be homeless.

'You're better off staying over with some friends,' was the police verdict, a notebook being shut. 'Call your insurers.'

The friend, from my PhD days, who would most likely offer me sympathy and help was over two hours away in Dumfries. It was the worst time of day to call Fiona. She would be putting the children to bed, exhausted from washing up after the evening meal. I packed a bag and checked into a hotel. I ordered room service but I was too hungry to wait. Instead I raided the mini bar, my body more responsive than usual after all those non-alcoholic evenings with Malak and Oz. The bottles felt small in my hand as if I were a giant, handling doll-sized utensils. The nuts were stale and the crisps not in my favourite flavour. From the next room I heard the sounds of television. I should put mine on too and catch the news. Instead what was obvious but felt like a brainwave had me moving to the telephone. I could get hold of Tony's number through Directory Enquiries. He picked up immediately and the old-man tiredness in his voice lifted when he realised it was me.

'How come you haven't been answering your mobile?'

'Long story.' I told him instead about the robbery and that diverted him.

'Drugs related,' he said. 'This time of year, everyone is short of cash. Where are you going to stay until your roof gets fixed? You can't stay all that time in a hotel. I suppose you can come here part of the time.' His voice trailed off as if he wasn't sure if this was an invitation he wanted to issue.

To commute from Aberdeen every day would be hectic. But perhaps I could do it for part of the week. I swallowed and asked, 'What's the news from Sudan that you needed to tell me?'

'Your father's in hospital. He's got kidney failure.'

When I was doing my PhD and out of work, I had asked my father for money but he never sent any. When my mother was ill, I wrote him several letters but never got a reply. When she died, he didn't bother to offer his condolences – and that for a Sudanese could not be a casual omission. He had another wife now, he had a son. They were his real family, while my mother and I were the old mistake he wanted to forget. The blood rushed to my head. 'Well, I won't donate him my kidney if that's why he called you.'

Tony sighed. The elderly closing ranks against the younger

generation. He would want me to be reasonable; he would expect me to take appropriate action. 'There is a possibility they would fly him to Jordan for a transplant but it might be too late.'

'How did you find out? Did he call you himself?'

'No. It was Grusha Babiker who did.'

Grusha used to be my mother's best friend in Khartoum and they had stayed in touch. She too was a Russian married to a Sudanese. Her son, Yasha (real name Yassir) was my first boyfriend. They crowded around me now, these names and faces from the past – my reproachful father, Grusha who succeeded where my mother failed and Yasha who probably didn't use his nickname any more. He became a successful lawyer, I had heard; he became more Sudanese as the years passed. Perhaps we half and halfs should always make a choice, one nationality instead of the other, one language instead of the other. We should nourish one identity and starve the other so that it would atrophy and drop off. Then we could relax and become like everyone else, we could snuggle up to the majority and fit in.

Tony said, 'Natasha, you need to speak to Grusha. She will tell you more about your father. He really isn't well at all. I gave her your number. She said she would call you.'

But I did not have my phone so I would not get that call. Dear Aunt Grusha. You were my role model all those years ago. Physics lecturer at Khartoum University, the only woman in the faculty. You dressed like Thatcher and went to war against the Sudanese dust so that your house could be impeccable. I missed the only cake she knew how to bake, her signature honey sponge on every birthday table and event in which she was asked to bring a dish. I missed her Arabic with its Russian accent, her deep gold hair, her son who held me when I cried about my parents' divorce.

Tony started to talk about next month's Southern Sudanese referendum. He was always even more up-to-date than I was. Predictably he slipped into talking about his time there. He was another Tony then, suntanned and exuberant, not the unremarkable pensioner pottering in his garden or walking in Duthie Park. I remembered him in a Hawaiian shirt, open at the neck, hairy chest and a silver medallion, drink in hand, dancing with an Ethiopian beauty (the last girlfriend he had before my mother). He was on top of his game was how he described it. There were expatriates who hated Sudan for the obvious reasons – the heat, the incompetence, the shortages, the boredom; and for other reasons – the political uncertainty, the racism against the Southern Sudanese and the way grudges were held for the pettiest of reasons. There were also those who understood and loved it or more likely the other way round, loved it first and then understood it. For it was too proud a place to explain itself without that first admission of love. Tony unravelled the Khartoum code. 'It's all about mixing with people,' was how he put it. Initially arriving as an engineer with a multinational company, he stayed on past his term and ventured on his own. There were rumours that he was in the arms trade, that he was a spy, that he was a smuggler. Whichever was true, he made good money out of it and it was his house with its own swimming pool, his latest Mercedes, his frequent trips abroad that first attracted my mother.

I ate the stodgy lasagne I had ordered and drank enough to shed a few sentimental tears over Yasha. It had been twenty years since I last saw him. I wanted to dream of sitting on his lap like I used to. How we would both be dusty because a sandstorm was blowing, how our pores would be open, our skin damp, my scalp wet, the back of his shirt in patches and we wouldn't feel there was anything wrong with that. It was as if we bypassed the stage of making a good impression; there was never a need for pretence between us, never a need to seduce. There were no edges between us, no sparks, we flowed, we fused, so that one day glancing at our reflection in the mirror we looked like Siamese twins joined at the waist. I even hesitated to draw away from him then, thinking irrationally that my skin would tear. But the moment passed and time proved that we had taken each other for granted and that I, at least, was unable to replace him. He was too diffident to assume that he was the love of my life. And I was short-sighted – I thought there would be other more exciting alternatives. I thought I deserved better than the obvious family friend.

A few years ago Yasha's life was hit by tragedy. His wife and five-year-old daughter died in a plane crash, a domestic flight from Port Sudan to Khartoum. Compelled by the understanding that condolences were the most important of Sudanese social obligations, I phoned Aunt Grusha. 'Yasha is in a world of his own,' she said, her own voice thick with sorrow. 'I thought I would stay with him for a few days because he's still not back at work. He keeps himself locked up in his room; I might as well go back to my own house.' She insisted though that he would want to speak to me. She knocked on his door and I heard her whisper, 'Natasha Hussein, calling from Scotland.' It felt strange to hear my old name, to realise that no matter what, they would only know me as such. It was a long time before Yasha picked up but he was only able to garble, 'Natasha . . .? Thanks . . .' I could have called him again after a week or a few days. Instead I dropped off his radar.

Tonight I nursed my memories. Random images of his Afro comb, his tennis racket, his Bee Gees cassettes. How when he was seven he came over to play, stayed the whole day and then went back home and complained to Grusha that we hadn't fed him enough. I remember Grusha indignant and my mother embarrassed. Now the memory made me smile but at the time harsh Russian words were exchanged all round. When Yasha was fifteen he would take his father's car without permission and we would sneak off for drives. He would have one hand on the steering wheel and the other resting on the open window. We would talk our own mix of Russian, Arabic and the English we learnt at school. He was the same species as me – I could sprint through the added contradictions of what I knew and what I had inherited and he would keep up the pace, he would know the terrain; he could do Sudan through Russian eyes and Russia through Khartoum eyes. Tonight I wanted to reach, through sleep, to the comfort of how we used to be. Instead I open a drawer and I am appalled to find a baby, a naked baby I put away in the drawer and forgot about.

The baby is dead, it must be dead. Is it dead? I can't find out, I can't lift it out of the drawer. I can't look at it properly. I must close the drawer. I must close the drawer and move away and pretend that I never opened it in the first place.

I surfaced into tears. When I dipped down again it was Gaynor Stead who barged through my dreams.

Gaynor Stead talking about me to Fiona and saying, 'Natasha put her fat arse on my desk...' 'Interesting,' was Fiona's characteristic reply, warm and understanding, eager to help. 'Black arse ... fat arse...' Gaynor was younger in the dream and Fiona, with her arm around her, was older. 'They are mother and daughter,' I realised even though in real life they were not. 'How could I have missed it before?' my sleeping mind insisted on the connection. 'They are really mother and daughter.' 'Black arse ... fat black arse...' The words looped and steadied, they became rhythmic. I woke up warm with humiliation, not sure where I was.

I tried to find Malak's number through Directory Enquiries but she was not listed. I would have liked to speak to her now, not to tell her my dream but to listen to her voice. She would tell me that dreams mattered to Shamil, that they influenced decisions he took and manoeuvres he devised. I rummaged in my bag and found my notebook. In it I had written some of the things Malak had said. 'Sufism is based on the belief that the seeker needs a guide. Even Muhammad, on his miraculous night's ascent through the seven heavens needed Gabriel as his guide.'

In the margins I had scribbled the word 'guru'. And so how would it work in modern life? I taught for a living but it was learning that had always been more fulfilling. Malak the actor, Natasha the teacher. Sufism delves into the hidden truth behind the disguise. Perhaps Malak was only an actor in disguise. Perhaps Natasha was acting the part of a teacher. If I ever started to seek the kind of knowledge that couldn't be found in books, who would I want as a guide? Does the student seek the teacher or the other way round?

2. Georgia/Dagestan, July 1854

Anna stumbled around, repeating the same question to anyone who would stop and listen – Avars, Lezgins, Russian prisoners of war, serfs from the Tsinondali estate who had been captured in separate raids, wounded Armenians and Georgian villagers who, with a shock, recognised her – she would clutch their arm and say, 'Have you seen my baby?'

The hostages were in Polahi now, a Russian outpost that had been captured by Shamil. His troops were stationed around the watchtower and the surrounding areas. The attack on Tsinondali had been part of a series of raids into the Alazani Valley. Now some of the men brandished severed heads as trophies; they herded cattle, slaves and horses up the mountains.

'Have you seen my baby?' Anna's words did not need to be translated, they were understood, but no one wanted to answer her or even meet her eyes. Madame Drancy straggled after the princess. Sometimes she succeeded in leading her back to where they were camped. Sometimes she crouched helplessly, watching Anna, on hands and knees, sifting through rocks and brambles looking for the impossible. 'Be strong for Alexander. Look at him. See how distraught he is to see you like this.'

Anna turned dutifully towards her son. She understood the logic of Drancy's argument but she could do nothing about it. A storm was inside her and she could not subdue it. If she could be sure, if she could hold Lydia again, if she could kiss her cool cheeks, if she could put her finger on that mouth that couldn't swallow, that couldn't cry, that no longer needed her, that no longer knew her, then maybe she could settle down. Hope was the devil, hope wrestled with her and wouldn't let her rest. 'Someone saw her fall and picked her up. Someone found her, someone saved my daughter.' How could she not believe this? Why should she not believe it? No one dared, not even Madame Drancy, to contradict her or to say that they had seen the horses ride over a bundle that should never have been on the floor of a forest.

'Come and lie down, Your Highness. Come and have a rest.'

When she lay down, the tears started. 'I had her by the leg. But I couldn't keep holding her,' she mumbled over and over again. She dozed but jerked awake. 'She is too small ... too small for all this ...'

Alexander snuggled close to her, his head pushing her stomach. His tears were those of fear rather than grief. So much was happening around him that he could scarcely remember his baby sister.

The next morning Anna's breasts were hard as rocks. She needed the baby to relieve the discomfort but now she was on her own. Expressing the milk gave her a few lucid moments, a recess from grief. She knew from her experience of farming that if a cow was left unmilked it would eventually dry off. But the process had to be gradual otherwise the milk would curdle, there could be an abscess with fever setting in. She lay down on her side and let the milk seep into the burka she had been given to use as bedding. One of her breasts already had less milk than the other; it would dry up first. When Lydia came back to her, what would she feed on?

'Madame Drancy, why have we stopped?'

'The men seem to be expecting someone of high rank to come and see us. It might even be Shamil himself, as they say he has come down from the mountains to inspect his troops. I am terrified of him. He sounds like a monster by all accounts.' The governess sounded more curious, though, than anxious.

Anna, still lying down, told herself, 'In this audience I will not be a prisoner. I will be what I really am, a princess of Georgia.' But it was as if she could still hear herself weeping, it was as if her heart still beat the words Lydia, Lydia.

'Heathens,' Madame Drancy was saying. 'All these men revere

Shamil as if he is God's representative on earth. Just the mention of his name and they're mumbling salutations and chanting.'

Despite the language barrier, Madame Drancy was communicating with the men. This was done in a mixture of sign language and the little Russian that some of the men spoke. The ordeal seemed to have awakened in her an anthropological interest, an intellectual ability to detach herself and make observations. She had even taken to wearing the burka, stretching inside it as if she were under the bedsheets. It soothed Anna to listen to her voice.

'Do you know what one of their laws is, Your Highness? No woman is allowed to remain a widow for longer than five months. I might end up in a harem!'

'Oh you are fanciful.'

'But I wonder though. We seem valuable to them. Didn't you notice, yesterday when we entered that village and we were surrounded by crowds, our captors shouted, 'For Shamil Imam' and then everyone stepped back?'

Anna couldn't remember passing a village. Two days or more were a blur, as smoky and as eerie as a nightmare. She turned to wake Alexander up with a kiss, to reassure him that his mother was still with him.

It was not Imam Shamil who came to inspect them but a young man with bright eyes and a roughness to his skin that contrasted with his easy smile. He bowed to Anna. 'My name is Ghazi Muhammad. I am Imam Shamil's son and the viceroy of Gagatli and the governor of Karata.' He spoke Russian poorly and with a heavy accent. Her full concentration was needed to understand every word.

Ghazi went on, 'These incursions into Georgia are aimed at inducing the population to join our resistance. On behalf of my father, I welcome you as our guests.'

'Guests! Is this the treatment of guests?'

He said lightly, 'Clothes will be provided for you to replace your torn ones. And warm food too. I will immediately order this.'

'This is not enough. Not after what we've gone through. I lost my daughter because of you.' She must not let her voice break, she must not show weakness in front of him.

He looked more sombre now. 'Your Highness, what happened to the little princess was not at all our intention. Indeed, your lives are precious to us.'

The words 'little princess' made her breasts leak. She would not risk speaking now.

'It was Russian bullets that were fired at you, not ours.' His voice turned cool with this defence.

She hardened against him. 'They did not know that we were your captives.'

'Perhaps so. If it will comfort you, I will immediately order a party to search for your missing child.'

Hope would keep the wound open for longer. Her voice rose. 'I have done nothing to deserve this. What wrong have I and my children ever done to you?'

Ghazi folded his hands on his belt. 'Believe me, I am saddened at how much you have suffered. My father is going to be very angry. I blame all this on the brutality of the Lezgins. They are uncouth soldiers of the line. But we were unable to spare my father's elite force.'

Momentarily he looked young and unguarded. It gave her a surge of strength. 'You will pay for what you have done to us. Do you think His Majesty the tsar will sit back and do nothing? Do you think my husband, Prince David, will not try to rescue us?'

Ghazi shifted and stood up straighter. 'You are distraught, Your Highness and understandably in pain. I promise I will do everything I can for your wellbeing. My suggestion is that you rest and once you're suitably dressed, I will take you to meet my father, the Imam of Chechnya and Dagestan. He has summoned you.'

'What does he want?'

Ghazi smiled. 'To speak to you, of course.'

'I will not go to him.'

The young man raised his eyebrows. 'He is Imam Shamil.'

With all her strength, she held herself straight. 'And I am a princess of Georgia. I will not be summoned by him.'

Ghazi bowed and withdrew. She had won a very small victory.

They were given millet bread and dried apricots. It was good to see Alexander eating. He had been dreaming of cake with sugar on top. Anna still dreamt of Lydia, that she had been found, that she was safe, after all, lying on the armchair among the lilac flowers. In the morning she watched Alexander wander off and join the men. Madame Drancy, sensing her disquiet said, 'They're only showing him their horses.'

'Still. I don't trust them.' When Alexander was a baby he had looked exactly like Lydia, the same colour hair, the same long lashes.

Madame Drancy was still speaking. 'We're going to be given face veils when we meet with Imam Shamil.' The new clothes they had been given were nothing but ill-assorted rags. Loose Turkish trousers and a sack full of left-foot shoes. Madame Drancy, who had been stripped to her corset, was grateful to have them. Anna, though, refused to change.

She looked around her as if for the first time. The condition of the other prisoners was worse. They had been made to march on foot and many were ill with dysentery and typhoid. No patience or special treatment was given to them. Insolence was dealt with by a scimitar thrust or a shove off a mountain ledge. Women were snatched as handmaidens and children set to work as slaves. The friendliness Shamil's men showed to Alexander, the relative respect she and Madame Drancy received was denied to the others. Innocent Georgian villagers and serfs who had nothing to do with the war between Russia and the Caucasus. Their crime in the eyes of the Muslims was that they had succumbed to Russia and were now her ally. Georgia had not resisted as it should. Anna bit her lips. Weren't these the same words she had said to David? The thoughts that could not be voiced in public, the resentment that must stay hidden. We are Georgians, not Russians. But for the sake of peace her grandfather had ceded the throne and here she was, caught up in the war against Russia.

The Georgian prisoners raised their voices up to lament their fate. They started to sing of home and pain, of orphaned children and of how low their princess had fallen. It brought tears to Anna's eyes. *The flower of Kakheit has fallen into the Lezgins' hands. Pray for our princess...* She wished she could have protected them, she wished she could have spared them all this. Her helplessness frustrated her. But not all of the Georgian prisoners regarded her with goodwill. An elderly peasant woman was livid that the princess had been given a horse-cloth to lie on. She railed out loud against the injustice, decrying the privileges of royalty. When she attempted to seize the horse-cloth by force, Anna let her have it.

She had heard of the tower of Pohali, after which the fort was named, but it was the first time she had seen it. The top storey had been demolished by Shamil's artillery. Behind it the mountains rose, arrogant. If she narrowed her eyes against the sun and looked up, she could see clumps of snow on the peaks. Ahead of them was a journey of more than three weeks. If David was ever going to rescue them, he would have come by now. The further they travelled up the mountains, the more difficult it would be for him to reach them. And when they arrived in Shamil's stronghold at Dargo-Veddin, it would be too late.

Fresh horses, new captors and it was time to climb again, up steep zigzagged paths, through bushes that tore at her clothes, around ugly rocky aouls where strangers lined up to stare. In some of these villages, they would find kindness and hospitality. They would be welcomed into the most peculiar of designs: a hill inside a courtyard, which had to be climbed in order to reach the upper floor. Rooms without windows and only a door to a large balcony. The grudging shelter of stables, spending a night next to asses and oxen. And that was preferable to the hostile aouls, where the villagers crowded to throw stones at them. Her back ached, her toe was still sore. Now lice in her hair. She scratched until there was blood under her nails. They must dismount because the horses could

113

not manage these dangerous paths. Wading in deep mud one day, crawling on hands and knees over a ravine. Surprising avalanches of snow, gifts from the summits, that were not expected to melt until the middle of July. She began to hate these rocky barren mountains; they were endless and cruel. She screamed, she could not help it, as she was led to mount a horse that had a severed hand dangling from the saddle. The hand was Georgian, she knew, because of the wedding band. 'Assassins,' she yelled at them and they laughed. Men with faces blackened by gunpowder. 'To prevent sunburn,' Madame Drancy explained to her in a moment of clarity.

Anna noticed a small swelling in her breast. Despite expressing every day, the milk had clotted and now her skin burned. Feverish, she started to ask again, 'Have you seen my baby?' But she asked in a feeble voice as if she was not expecting a reply, as if the words were a lament rather than a question. At long last there came news from the search party Ghazi had sent out. Servants from the estate had picked up Lydia's body. She was buried in the neighbouring church of St George, one of the few buildings that had escaped the burning and looting.

The truth was a blow even though a part of her had expected it; a part of her had longed to be free from the daily tussle with hope. She wept continuously without any sound. Tears flowed freely until she could scarcely see ahead of her. Stumbling in a mix of sweat from the fever and pain from the news. Dragged tottering across a tree bridge, she lost her footing and had to be carried the rest of the day. Alexander needed her; she must be stronger than this. There he was, eating handfuls of snow, chewing on rhododendron leaves. His hair was riddled with vermin but he did not seem to care.

'I wonder if my mother knows that we've been kidnapped,' Madame Drancy was saying as she put a wet rag on Anna's forehead to bring down the fever. 'I have never let a week pass without writing to her.' Anna hung on to every word. Conversation and prayers were the route to normality. 'The news must have reached France by now. We've been climbing this mountain for nearly a month.'

They had set up camp at night and when Anna woke up, weak

and clammy but no longer burning, she found herself in an area of absurd beauty. Waterfalls and ferns, vineyards and herds of healthy cattle. Madame Drancy and Alexander picked nosegays and azaleas, bunches of perfume and silky texture for Anna to bury her face in. When she washed her hair, when she finally changed into the clean loose trousers that they had been given, she felt more refreshed. It was as if every drop of liquid had drained from her body in tears and milk; she was now as dry and as light as a piece of cotton.

'Why have we stopped?' she asked Madame Drancy.

'They are waiting for confirmation that Imam Shamil has reached Dargo-Veddin. It would be wrong according to their customs for us to arrive there first.'

They could see the aoul now above them, the rock fortress embedded in the mountain, so much a part of it that it was almost invisible. Why did Shamil leave this green area and huddle inside an ugly gated stronghold? But she did not want to think of the future, of the entry into this prison and whether they would come out again. For two strange days, she let go of the past and the future. She pushed away death and surrendered to her five senses. The colour green, the sound of a waterfall, Alexander sitting by her side. Nothing made sense except existence, feeling the grass beneath her bare feet, the sun on her hair, the taste of water through her parched lips.

But too soon it was time to climb again. The dreaded burkas, new black silk to cover their faces and soon enough the gates of Dargo closed behind them. A world made of stone, houses like caves, hardly any two at the same level. The villagers crowded to look at them and to welcome home their fighters. Imam Shamil had ordered that they be housed in his own home, among the women of his family. They were to be, like Ghazi had promised, guests in the harem.

A tall woman in veils and Turkish trousers led them to their quarters. Anna entered a long dark low-ceilinged room that did not have a single item of furniture. A felt rug was spread on the ground and piles of bedding were folded up on shelves that ran around the walls. There was one small window, with shutters instead of glass. This was a prison even though it opened out into a gallery that, she found out later, adjoined the rooms of the other women. Their rooms were just as bare, their windows just as small. Anna could hear a raven outside and the sudden call to prayer from the mosque.

Their hostess lifted up her black veil. Her movements were graceful and economical. Her lips did not stretch into a welcoming smile but there was a glow in her heavy-lidded eyes, an almost masculine strength in her prominent nose. 'My name is Zeidat,' she said in careful Russian. 'I am Imam Shamil's first wife and head of the household.'

Behind her, two other women stood at the doorway. Their faces were lit up with curiosity as they almost tumbled into the room, giggling and flouncy in wide white and blue trousers, rainbow veils and ankle bracelets. 'You are very welcome, Your Highness,' said the older, plump one, bobbing down in a clumsy curtsey. She held out a box of sweets. 'All the way from Tollet, really. Please have some.' Her name was Chuanat and she was the most beautiful of the three.

Ameena was the youngest. She had excessive kohl around her eyes. When she took Anna's arm, her grip was light but clingy. 'It is so nice to have company – you must tell me all about Russian life. We can become friends.' Her use of Russian was fluent, confident.

Zeidat gave her a cold stare. 'Since when do we make friends with infidels, Ameena!' She spoke Russian deliberately, with a quick sideways look at Anna.

'They are Imam Shamil's guests and he is furious at the way they've been treated. We have to make amends, or have you forgotten his orders?'

'I never forget his orders.' Zeidat turned to scrutinise Anna. 'But I think that no matter how well we treat the princess, it will not be good enough. It will not be at the standard Her Highness is accustomed to. I did say to him, "Husband, pampered Russian royalty can hardly be expected to accept the austere conditions we're accustomed to."'

Anna struggled to understand their accent when they spoke among themselves: clusters of foreign words, repetitions and hand gestures. She relied on their facial expressions, their ages to gauge their hierarchy. Chuanat stood out, European, the only one fluent in Georgian. With her box of sweets, she was stroking Alexander's hair and urging him to have more. Several children came into the room now and they absorbed the attention of Alexander and Madame Drancy.

'It is nice for us to have company,' Ameena persisted. 'And such a special guest too.' Ameena squeezed Anna's arm and gestured towards an array of cushions laid out against the wall. Was she sixteen or seventeen? Not more than a child, but the eyes were quick and knowing, unstable too.

Zeidat, with one deft, unexpected movement, picked up a louse from Anna's hair. Anna flinched and stepped back. Indignation melted into embarrassment as Zeidat squeezed the insect between her fingers. 'You will need to help your new friend clean up,' she smiled at her young co-wife. 'Lice are contagious.'

'This is not good manners,' Ameena's voice rose. 'Zeidat, you know this is not how you are meant to behave!'

Zeidat turned to leave the room. 'Imam Shamil won't be in Dargo for long and when he goes away I will know best how to treat this Russian captive.'

Chuanat gestured for Anna to sit down next to her. She had quickly made herself comfortable on the ground with her back against the wall and her legs crossed in front of her. 'Don't let Zeidat frighten you. She can be bossy and harsh but there is no evil in her.'

Ameena flung herself on the ground next to them. 'Oh indeed! You are the angel who refuses to see badness in anyone. Zeidat is a shrew and what makes her more bitter is that she knows Imam Shamil doesn't love her. He only married her because of her father.'

Chuanat shook her head, 'You're such a gossip! You know very well Imam Shamil treats us all equally. Besides, you're disturbing Princess Anna with details of our personal life.'

Instead all this was a welcome diversion.

'You must be exhausted after all you have gone through.' Chuanat's eyes were misty. 'I am so sorry for all you have endured. I was a captive once too, long ago and...' She faltered, lost for words. Instead she loosened her veil and her thick auburn hair fell around her cheeks.

'You are not Chechen, are you?' Anna's voice sounded to her ears as if she were in a drawing room making polite conversation.

'No, I'm Armenian. Years ago, I was captured in a raid with my family. They returned but I stayed on.'

'I'm so sorry for this.' No, she was certainly not in a drawing room sipping tea. The fear was all too close. A captive that couldn't escape, was never rescued, never returned. That must be the saddest of fates.

Ameena laughed. 'Oh, Chuanat does not deserve your pity. She *wanted* to stay. Her family raised a ransom for her, they went through all the hardship of negotiations and her poor cousin risked his life climbing up these mountains to rescue her. Remember what he said about passing the Russian lines?' She turned to Chuanat. So much ease between these two.

Chuanat smiled, 'The Russian sentries crossed themselves and spat on the ground when they saw my cousin riding up the mountains to meet Shamil Imam's horsemen. They thought they would never see him alive again. Instead he returned with gifts including a fine Arabian mare.'

'But why didn't you leave with him? Or were you not allowed?'

Chuanat looked at her as if she was gauging her understanding, as if pondering how much to share. 'I could have left if I had wanted to. It's a long story. I will tell it to you another day.'

'No, it's not a long story,' Ameena contradicted her. 'It is straightforward. Hannah, as she was called then, fell in love.'

'Ameena!' Chuanat reproached her. 'I said I would tell her myself in my own time. Besides, when are you going to learn to practise some discretion? You're no longer a child.'

'Don't try to sound like Zeidat.' Ameena helped herself to some of the sweets. 'It doesn't suit you.'

Anna turned to her and said, 'Well, Ameena, maybe you can tell me about yourself.'

'Very well,' she spoke with her mouth full, the sweetness sticking to her teeth. 'My family are originally from Bavaria. But I was brought up in Imam Shamil's household.'

'Spoilt and pampered, if I may say so,' Chuanat added.

Ameena sounded more thoughtful. 'He treated me just like one of his children. They were my playmates.' She turned with a mischievous look towards Anna. 'Then, as you can see, I matured and turned into a striking beauty.'

Chuanat rolled her eyes and Anna laughed. She had not done so for a long time. It made her feel generous towards the young girl. 'I agree. I have been admiring you since you came in and took off your veil.'

Ameena narrowed her eyes. 'But it was my beauty that ended my childhood. Imam Shamil could hardly pretend that he couldn't notice me and so he took me for his third wife.'

'Still she was such a baby that she kept crying and saying "I miss my mother",' Chuanat said.

Ameena laughed. 'Shamil Imam brought her here for me. She is always with me now and I am well looked after.'

All this sounded strange to Anna. A part of her recoiled, a part of her noted the frankness. Their friendliness and their difference made her conscious of herself. Who she was and what she looked like. She must rid her hair of the lice. She must look presentable. They believed in her as a princess and they were right to do so, that was who she was.

'But Anna . . . Can I call you Anna? You will have to tell us your story too. All your experiences at court.'

'Yes, please,' Chuanat added. 'We know you were lady-in-waiting for the tsarina.'

It was such a long time ago, before she was married. An adventure of bright nights and the grandest buildings, dresses and jewels, Moscow balls and all the thrills of coming out into society. Even though she was homesick for Georgia, even though she knew that she did not belong at court, she had revelled in the music and the dancing. The steps came naturally to her, the fluid movements, her gown lifting, the music passing through her skin, flushed afterwards, pretty and thirsty, reaching for a drink. She tried to remember herself then, what her body felt like before it was touched by David, before her stomach filled out strong and large with babies. But she must not let her mind wander in this particular direction. Only mention the tsarina's diamonds, officers with sideburns, a morning spent ice-skating.

'Did you ever see Jamaleldin?' asked Ameena.

Anna could not see that there could possibly be any connection between an acquaintance of Ameena's and the Winter Palace.

'Imam Shamil's eldest son,' explained Chuanat. She lowered her voice. 'He is the tsar's godson.'

A figure, a name, a face shaped itself in the shadows of Anna's Petersburg memories. Had she known then that he was Shamil's son? Perhaps she had and the knowledge had not interested her, had not mattered, except to explain that he was 'Asiatic'. He was different, but not different enough – eyes that were not like hers, but nothing in his manners, his speech or his conduct that set him apart. He was certainly not a highlander; he was certainly not the enemy. 'Yes, of course, he is an officer,' she said. 'I danced the Mazurka with him once.'

Ameena gasped, her face alight with excitement. 'Oh this is shocking. Imam Shamil's son attending parties and dancing with strange women!'

'What is so strange about me?'

Ameena laughed, 'There is nothing strange. You are perfect. By strange I meant you're not related to him. You're not his wife or his sister.'

'But these are our customs and Jamaleldin is a Russian gentleman.'

Chuanat turned towards her with soft eyes. 'This is not how Imam Shamil sees it. You will understand when you meet him tomorrow. He will explain everything to you and you can ask as many questions as you like. Today, though, you must rest. How exhausted and hungry you must be!'

She was hungry but the meal provided disgusted her. Goat's cheese that smelt too strong and bread baked in such a way that it had an outer layer of thick grease covering the crust. She had to pare off the crust in order to reach the crumb. Even the tea tasted odd, smoky and strong. Hunger, or the stale-smelling mattress, was keeping her awake. Madame Drancy had spent a long time saying her prayers and was now fast asleep. Alexander tossed and turned, sometimes whimpering, sometimes thrashing his arms as if he was fighting. It was hot in the room. Anna stood up and opened the shutters but the ventilation was poor. A tree blocked the air and up through its leaves she caught a glimpse of the night sky. The staccato sounds of the mountains pressed in, frogs and insects, a jackal howling for its mate, but instead of posing a threat, the animal sounded distressed. She put both of her arms through the window. It would be possible for the three of them to squeeze through one after the other and then what? She could hear the footsteps of the sentries, back and forth at a leisurely rate. They might have lacked military precision but they were wide awake.

She found herself pacing the room. The treatment she had been given for her head lice, a mixture of butter and brimstone, was starting to melt over her face and neck. The smell was unpleasant but it was worth it if it would rid her of all the irritation and scratching. She found herself measuring the room: length eighteen shoes, width twelve. She pressed her palms against the stone wall. Such thick walls, only a cannon could burst them. The thought of a Russian attack filled her with dread. She did not want to remember their last attempt at rescue, if it was such, its failure and huge cost.

The next morning she met Shamil. He did not consider it polite to come into her room and impose on her privacy so a chair was placed for him in the gallery. Anna saw him through the face veil she and Madame Drancy were instructed to wear. It was as if a film of smoke dimmed her eyesight. Shamil was accompanied by his steward and a Russian defector who was to act as their translator. Shamil's white turban contrasted with the darkness of his thick eyebrows and beard. He was unarmed, wearing the highlanders' long cherkesska over leggings, his feet in leather slip-ons that were stretched tight over the arches of his feet. Afterwards Madame Drancy would describe Shamil as a lion with eyes in the shape of scimitars. Anna's impression was of a tall, slim man hemmed in by his surroundings, forced into an extraordinary stillness, a pooling of shadows and energy, a lull of density and strength.

'Anna, Princess of Georgia.' He looked at her when he said her name. The rest of his speech was translated. 'I have captured you for a specific reason. Usually I employ prisoners to build or repair roads or to work in the quarry but you are valuable.'

Though she knew that he had more to say, she spoke up. 'I have been dragged here against my will. I lost my daughter.' She paused but the translator did not translate. So the imam could understand her. He was deliberately choosing not to use her language.

She continued, 'I have done nothing to deserve this. I ask you to return me to my home. I do not belong here.'

'My son Jamaleldin was innocent too when the Russians captured him. He was eight years old. You are a mother, you have a young son. Tell me, is it right, is it fair to pull a child away from his parents?'

She hesitated before she replied. It would not be right to criticise the tsar and at the same time use him as a threat against her captives. Her ambivalence towards Russia must never show. She had said to David, 'I am Georgian, not Russian.' But here, in this stone world, in this war, with this enemy she was as Russian as she could ever be.

He lowered his voice. 'Answer my question.'

She was conscious of the brush of silk on her cheekbones and nose. 'No, it is not right to hurt any child in any way.'

He bowed his head in agreement. 'For years, I searched among my prisoners for someone of importance. Prince Orbeliani was my captive for six months but he was not weighty enough. I could only exchange him for some of my men. But you, Anna, Princess of Georgia, are distinguished. You are valuable. This is my hope.'

After his words were translated, he seemed to reconsider. 'Not my hope, my conviction that you would be valuable enough to the tsar. You will be exchanged for my son Jamaleldin.'

Would the tsar exchange his godson for a woman and a child? Maybe, maybe not. Her voice was a pitch higher. 'If the tsar doesn't accept? What will happen then?' It was as if she had asked an embarrassing question. The lips of the translator twitched. One of the guards looked at her, his eyes bold as if he could see through her veil.

Shamil sounded distant when he replied, 'Our customs and laws will prevail.'

She shifted in her chair. It was wooden and crude. She had not sat in a chair since they had left Tsinondali.

'I have waited fourteen years,' Shamil was saying. 'You are the granddaughter of the King of Georgia. You are a fit person to write to the Russian sultan. Let him return to me my son Jamaleldin from St Petersburg and I will free you on the hour. I am giving you my word and I am a man true to my promise.'

'The tsar will not give up Jamaleldin easily. He is his protégé and his favourite.'

'And I am his father. He is my flesh and blood. Wouldn't you do the same for your son?'

She did not have an answer. Not for him. Lydia's blood was on his hands.

He said, 'You will now sit and write a letter to the tsar begging for your release. Tell him Shamil demands his son and tell him my people also demand a ransom. The details of the ransom will follow. Write to your husband too, Prince David, that if my demands are met I will return you pure as the lilies, sheltered from all eyes like the gazelles of the desert.'

She wanted to laugh at his lilies and gazelles. But if she started to laugh, she would cry.

123

'There is another matter that you need to know of,' he continued. 'I abhor trickery. I can forgive anything except deception.' His voice rose as if he was giving a sermon. 'Deceit is an offence against Allah and his servant Shamil. The first time I find you plotting to escape I shall have you killed. To cut off heads is my right as imam.'

If he expected to frighten her, she was unmoved. 'You need not threaten me. My rank and upbringing forbid me to lie. I have no intention of tricking you.'

'Then what is this?' Shamil opened his palm and his steward handed him a letter. 'I have letters addressed to you which I have had translated. But this letter is neither in Russian, nor Georgian, nor Tartar. What is this script? Are you trying to trick me?'

'No, I am not. Show it to me.' She stood up and pushed aside her face veil. The script was clearer now. And without the black silk barrier, Shamil seemed closer, his eyes lighter, all his features more in focus. She reached out for the letter.

He could see her face now and later she would wonder if his expression changed in any way. But he tore the letter in shreds. 'It is a coded message and you will not be seeing it.'

Her eyes fell on a fragment on the floor. 'This is not a coded message. This is French, a foreign language. It is written to my son's governess by her mother in France. How dare you destroy it! Madame Drancy is another of your innocent victims. This letter is addressed to her. It is not yours to dispose of.'

'Understand my rules, Princess of Georgia.' He still remained seated but he did not look up at her. 'You will neither send nor receive anything which my interpreters cannot translate for me.'

The translator gestured for her to return to her chair. But it was too late, she was too angry to sit. 'I cannot be held responsible for what others send me. As for your staff, they are surely limited in linguistic ability if they cannot tell the difference between French and a secret language!'

In the pause that followed, it occurred to her that she had now provoked his anger, now she had gone too far. He rose and they stood facing each other. She was conscious of his height and his mass, his aura of mountains and war. When he spoke, he spoke in her own language, the interpreter made redundant. 'You will be given the letters after I have read them. Conduct yourself well, Princess, and you shall have nothing to fear.'

3. Warsaw, September 1854

Jamaleldin's face remained hot as he wrote his dispatches, as he walked to the stables and as he patrolled this city that bristled in Russia's grip. He was stationed in Warsaw, with the Vladimirski Lancers. In the mornings when he faced the mirror to shave, his face felt especially hot, and when he let his mind wander, his hand went slack and the razor cut his chin. Yet, to be honest, he was not completely surprised by the news of the kidnapping. He was like a child who had committed a misdemeanour and after a longer than average reprieve was finally caught. It was bound to happen. His father reaching out to claim him, the method brutal, their names linked and on everyone's tongue. It was bound to happen, and now this was the chosen hour.

Jamaleldin walked into the officers' mess and headed towards the dining table. He avoided the group who were bunched avidly over the latest newspaper from home. Thankfully, there were not many of his friends left. Most of his regiment had been despatched to the South Crimean front. Once again, as was the case in the Caucasus, his request for active service was denied and he was now part of this token force that had been left behind to assert Russia's hold over Poland. Jamaleldin sat facing the opposite direction from the group of officers and ordered a steak from the waiter. He could hear a game of billiards in the adjoining room, the click of the balls against each other, the occasional high cry of success. When his dish came, he whispered *bismillah* like his mother, Fatima, had taught him years ago. Most of the time he forgot to say it, but these days the past was easily accessible, the Caucasus clearly visualised. In his dreams, his father's men surrounded him. Imran, Abdullah,

Zachariah, Younis. They beckoned and shouted in a language he could no longer understand. His teeth mashed the food as if eating was a duty.

Here was the companionship he wanted to avoid. Two strolled over and joined him. They recounted the previous night's adventures and how Pavel, another officer, had lost a huge amount of money at the gambling table. He was now bereft not only of his month's allowance but of his watch, his silver cufflinks and his mare, a beauty they had been admiring all summer. And where was Pavel now? He was still asleep in his cot, not yet recovered from his hangover. 'Will he remember that he has gambled away Sultana?' This was said with a laugh. Jamaleldin smiled as he swallowed. Not much of a response was expected from him. Appreciation for this latest gossip, a suggestion to send seltzer water and lime as a remedy to the unfortunate Pavel, or at the most a jovial dash over to Pavel's quarters to throw cold water on his face and witness his first agonising wakeful moments? Instead as Jamaleldin was cutting another piece of steak, the old solemn words fell out of his mouth, the kind of sentences he had made a career out of holding back. *The world is a carcass and the one who goes after it is a dog.* This was what Sheikh Jamal el-Din had taught his disciples and this was what Shamil repeated night and day.

'What language is that?' Good-natured curiosity, a trusting smile.

Jamaleldin knew he should dismiss the question and change the subject. It was the best way for the slip to be forgotten. But something had changed and he was less in control. Or something had changed and he had less to lose. He said, 'The Avar language. It means "The world is a carcass and the one who goes after it is a dog."'

Bafflement in the eyes of the two officers and the expected drawing back. Jamaleldin's face was now hot and tipped towards his plate. He could feel them exchange looks and yearned towards them. He yearned towards the steady ground under their feet and their one-dimensional vision. He wanted to be them and he was tired of this wanting. Unease – that feeling of panic before it

127

sharpened and rose, before it ballooned and caught in his throat. A slight nausea as he lifted another piece of steak to his mouth and chewed. He had slipped up because his ears were straining for the tsar's summons.

'See you at the ball tonight,' one of the officers said as they drifted away to give him the wide berth he deserved.

Yes, he would be at the ballroom tonight. He would dive into all that Warsaw could offer, a city more elegant, closer to Western Europe. The railway line ran to Paris and the theatres staged all the latest plays from Germany. Quick, time was running out. His days in Warsaw were numbered. The summons would come soon and he would be in a troika heading back to Petersburg. So he should waltz tonight. Here it was danced in a faster manner; a livelier twirl was the norm. His arms around a girl, spinning her out of control. A girl who didn't resemble Daria, a girl who was just a waist, her face a blur, her name quickly forgotten. He still had Daria Semyonovich's letters and he reread them once in a while. But it was as if he was playing the role of the jilted lover – in reality his heart was distracted, his thoughts about her starting to curl bitter. After the tsar had refused them permission to marry, Daria's mother forbade her daughter to meet Jamaleldin or write to him. And Daria, a good daughter, had acquiesced. Out of clumsiness or misery, Jamaleldin had refused to give her back her letters. There was no dramatic scene of farewell between them; there should have been. Tomorrow he would tear her letters and throw the pieces in the Vistula. And tonight, which might be the last night of freedom, he would indulge himself without pleasure.

There was a mosque in Cracow but he did not visit it. There was a Tartar colony in Vilno but he had learnt early on that success was correlated to the distance he must keep away. He was on his own. His passions, his thoughts were so often held in check because language (which one?) could not come to his aid. And he did not, above all, trust his own loyalties. *They* trusted him, though; in one magnanimous sweep they were inclusive and tolerant, but that was

128

not from any merit in him. It was because of their own convictions of superiority, their own sweet arrogance.

In Poland's courts, petitions were heard only in Russian. Interpreters were not provided for the prisoners. Polish youth were conscripted into the Russian army, revolutionary dissent was squashed and every independent institution was systematically weakened. This was why the Poles smiled at the news coming in from the Crimea. They took deep breaths of the wind that was blowing in favour of England, France, Turkey and their allies. There were even rumours of Austrian troops marching into St Petersburg and talk of the tsar's abdication. In the slums of Moscow and the vodka cellars of St Petersburg they were saying that he had failed the country. It touched Jamaleldin that his patron was weakening. It altered the chemistry of the situation. The tsar was ailing and, from high up in the mountains, Shamil was calling him back.

He pushed his plate away. If he was truly courageous he would join the others bent over the newspaper. Instead he listened to the sound of the billiard balls and he drained his glass of water. How thirsty he had been all this time without knowing it! The news was not only in the Russian papers; Europe's too were shouting.

Princess of the Blood Royal prisoner of barbaric tribesmen.

Savagery in Russian Territory – French citizen abducted for ransom.

Only the Turkish newspapers put forward a reason: *Shamil Imam, Viceroy of Georgia, has made a successful sortie into territories seized by the infidel invaders and is holding a Christian family as hostages against the return of his son Jamaleldin, torn from him by the infidels and brought up in the Christian faith since 1839.*

V

When the Sugarcane Grows

1. Scotland, December 2010

A few minutes into the lecture, I ran out of words. I stalled. I left the subject I was teaching and stood staring. Gaynor Stead was sitting in my class. She should not be in this room because this was a second-year class and she was repeating third year. It was really her, not a lookalike. No one else had that dopey look or that shaggy hairstyle. But, it flashed through my mind and made my shoulders weak, perhaps I was the one who had walked into the wrong room, I was the one who was going over revision questions on the Crimean War instead of the Bolshevik Revolution. I searched the faces of the students for some indication. They seemed undisturbed at my presence, yawning this early in the morning, pushing away damp fringes from their eyes, hunched as usual over laptops and notes. The room smelt of cheap shower gel, a mix of deodorants and styling mousse. 'Excuse me a minute,' I said. I took my bag and left the room. I stood in the corridor, I checked my timetable, I checked the room number and completely reassured of my sanity, I walked back in. Laughter gurgled in my throat now. Gaynor Stead must have surpassed the breadth of her own stupidity. She was now sitting in classes she was not required to take, listening to a course she had (disingenuously, erroneously, miraculously) been awarded a pass for at one resit or the other.

As the students filed out at the end of the class I was tempted to stop her. But I did not trust myself. Could I be civil after she had falsely accused me of breaking her finger? She, on her part, did not acknowledge me in any way. I gathered my lecture notes and with them I saw a pro-life leaflet that didn't belong to me, a picture of a foetus in sad blue tones. One of the students must have put it there either when I was out of the room or earlier when filing in. Perhaps it was Gaynor out to intimidate me. Perhaps that was why she was here. To target me. But this was a ludicrous idea. How on earth would she know? I was being paranoid, too easily rattled.

Surgical instruments used in the abortion process. I put the leaflet away and for the first time felt the urge to escape. But where to? To go back to Malak and see the vacuum Oz left behind? To fly to Sudan and sit at my father's deathbed? Instead I went into town because I needed to be surrounded by people, by normal life.

I needed tea and cake, not proper food, and I found a shop that specialised in cupcakes. All kinds of them were set out, with different coloured icing and flavours: lemon, chocolate and raspberry. My mother, to make life in Khartoum less austere, had at one time started her own cake business. She baked at home and then delivered by car but it was not easy. There was a sugar shortage; cooking gas was difficult to get – she had to sit in the petrol queue for hours in order to refuel. I helped her as much as I could. In the kitchen, answering the phone for orders and going with her in the car to deliver. We had to be nice to all the customers. This was difficult when they cancelled orders after my mother had started baking or they delayed bringing back the containers in which we had delivered the cakes. When we passed by to pick them up, they would spend ages searching their kitchen and end up saying, 'Oh, we must have lent that tray out.' Then my mother would raise her voice to harangue them and they would take offence, punishing us by withdrawing their custom.

My mother knew how to make only three cakes: chocolate, which was popular; pineapple upside down which needed tinned pineapples – and these, being imported, were not always available at the grocers; and a honey one that was inferior to the one her friend Grusha Babiker specialised in. It upset my mother that Grusha would not share her recipe. Even though Grusha had none of our income woes, she insisted on keeping her recipe a secret. I remember my mother talking to Grusha on the phone and then crying afterwards. But she could have been crying about something else and not what Grusha had said. She could have been crying about the time a good batch of baking had used up all the gas before she got round to cooking my father's lunch. He came home to find the table set but with bread and cheese as the meal. He banged the table so hard that some of the plates shattered to the ground. Then he walked out of the house and no matter how hard I tried, I couldn't remember his return. Most likely he came back late, after I went to bed.

My mother had trained as a physiotherapist. She met my father when he tore his rotator cuff playing volleyball. He was in the university team, conspicuous because he was black, he would say. Conspicuous because he was handsome, she would insist. He was shy undressing in front of her. Women, where he came from, did not treat men, did not touch their naked shoulder. My mother found his shyness endearing, his inhibitions intriguing. Their courtship was not smooth. He blew hot and cold but she pursued him. 'I was smitten,' she later said. 'I didn't think.' He did, though. He thought that she would come to her senses. He depended on this and eased himself into the relationship, allowing her to treat his shoulder and type up his thesis. There were romantic photos of that time, cigarettes in their hands, smiles, hers always broader and more optimistic. In the wedding photo, a civil ceremony in Georgia, an almost bewildered look in my father's eyes, as if time and circumstances had caught up with him. As if what he had judged to be inexorably shifting and amorphous had unexpectedly crystallised.

They arrived in Sudan together. He had omitted to tell his family of his marriage and presented them with a pregnant wife. The muted celebratory homecoming was adjusted to include a Sudanese wedding. My mother objected to being decked out as a Sudanese bride. She hated the henna, the sandalwood and the gold. She wouldn't fit in. What did she imagine? What were her expectations? I know because she spoke about them; they remained vivid in her mind, for years, because they never materialised.

My father, despite his PhD from the Soviet Union, against all

135

the odds of his generation, struggled to earn a living. This was the reason their marriage failed. Nothing else. Their quarrels were in tangent to this and so in the sporadic times of plenty, there were happy moments, humdrum silent days, stretches of peace. The three of us slept outdoors in the front yard, just below the high wall, my father dragging out the three beds and spraying water on the red bricks of the ground. Thinking I was fast asleep, they would go indoors to their bedroom and then later come out to lie down with their cigarettes and talk in low voices. I liked dozing to the sound of their voices, the pink glow of the cigarettes in the dark. They wouldn't talk finances at that time of night; instead they spoke about films they'd seen or exchanged news of friends and neighbours. My father, for all his seriousness, enjoyed satire and rumours.

He made a mistake when he prohibited her from working as a physiotherapist. He should have defied convention but maybe the foreign marriage itself was his limit. It would shame me, he said to her, if you touched other men's backs and shoulders and legs. He did not object to the cake business but my mother registered the curtailment of a vocation she loved. She held it against him, drawing it out in subsequent quarrels, making digs whenever she could. Ironically, when she married Tony and moved to Scotland, her Russian qualifications also hindered her ability to work. But by then, she cared less and felt too old to retrain. By then, even without a divorce settlement from my father, she was content with coffee mornings and shopping, and crucially, Tony was earning enough.

It was not through the cakes that my mother first met Tony. But he ordered a pineapple upside down so that he would see her again. I sat in the car while she rang the doorbell of his villa and went in. The reason I remembered that day was that his was the only villa in which the railing running over the front wall was shaped in letters from the English alphabet. It was as if the villa had at one time been a nursery. For a time I enjoyed looking at the letters while sitting in the front seat, then the back seat, then the driver's seat until I got hot and bored. I hooted the horn and felt foolish when the few people walking down the street stared at me. At last I got out of the car and rang the bell. Instead of yelling at me, my mother came out animated and smiling. To placate me she bought me a Pasgianos from the corner store. The bottle was warm and I drank it all in one go.

Before the baking, when I should have been in nursery school but I wasn't, my mother used to lie in bed during the day and read novels in order to improve her English. The bed was in the sitting room because we didn't have proper furniture. It was something that annoyed her but my father said, so what, very few Sudanese had chairs and sofas in their sitting room, just string cots pushed against the wall. Aunty Grusha and Yasha had a dining table and everything in their house was neat and modern. But we were different; we were unlucky because my father was unlucky. He was on the wrong side of the government and the wrong side of the market. So my mother would lie down in that sunny sitting room, the fan spinning above us while I played on the floor with a jigsaw puzzle. The puzzle was of a scene in *Bambi* and some of the pieces were missing. It didn't matter to me, though, because I knew which pieces were missing and I worked around these absences. The sand of our cement floor poked up in between the greenery of a European forest but Bambi and his mother were whole.

Once I looked up from the puzzle and stared at the cover of the book my mother was reading. The large capital letters in green and orange nestling close together and the little picture at the bottom that was hidden by her fingers. I was happy that she was settled in one place. I could work on my puzzle and then look up to catch her turning a page or circling her ankle as it rested on top of her knee. Her toenails were the exact colour of Little Red Riding's hood, another jigsaw I had. I liked the way my mother's hair fell over the pillow. She had yellow shoulder-length hair, but near her neck the hair was darker. And her eyebrows too, which she plucked diligently, were darker. My own hair was different – it was like my father's even though I was a girl and it should have been like hers;

137

instead it was a mistake, a bush to touch and in photographs, a cloud. Like other white mothers with black daughters, my mother had no clue how to deal with it. It left her bewildered and helpless, it made her feel incompetent.

I was searching for the piece of Bambi's eyes which was central to the whole jigsaw when I noticed a movement and saw that my mother had raised one knee and hugged it to herself. The dress she was wearing slipped and her thighs were white and smooth all the way to her grey underpants. Milky white, not like her face and arms, which were regularly touched by the sun. A pressure rose in my chest but also a glow as if I was wearing a golden necklace that weighed too much. Even though I was with her, even though I could move towards her for a cuddle and a kiss, I was not like her and might never be, I was in another place, lonely because she would never join me. I stood up and walked to the bed. With my whole hand, I pinched her inner thigh as hard as I could, until she cried out and dropped the book and scolded me – but she was laughing now and tickling me, tickling my stomach, feet and armpits until I was squealing. When I burst into tears, she thought that it was because I had laughed too much.

One day my mother wanted to go and see a film at the cinema but my father didn't. They argued about it and instead my mother went with Grusha and her husband. I didn't like that: to stay a whole long evening with my father all by ourselves. He didn't speak to me. There was a power cut so we sat in the moonlit garden. He with his drink and radio and I with nothing to do but look at our tall metal door and will my mother to walk through it. There was talk coming from the radio and military music among the static. My father didn't walk indoors to the bathroom. Instead he stood up and peed into the flower bed. This upset me and he laughed, saying it was good for the plants. He gave me a sip of his drink and it tasted like perfume. I didn't understand what the radio was announcing but it couldn't have been anything cheerful because he became sullen again. It was as if I could read his thoughts and this made me anxious. I wanted to help him but at the same time

I wanted to move away. I wanted to be her daughter, not his. Yet I empathised with him, I knew that he was uneasy about my mother and this, in turn, made me worry that she would not come back from the cinema. I went and stood by the door, leaning on the warm black metal, aching to run out and search for her. Years later, when Tony appeared on the scene, I spent many such evenings alone with my father. We never spoke about her but she was the tension between us, the new meaning of shame, a restrained lurid excitement. I felt that I was her accomplice because that metal alphabet on the walls of Tony's villa beckoned me to a better life, the first rung on the ladder of opportunity, and my father was the one we both kicked away.

These dips into the past guzzled time. Three cupcakes for lunch and I drank my last mug of tea without sugar and milk. More people were coming into the café carrying their Christmas shopping; I should leave to make room for them to sit. Instead I looked out of the window and saw the girl in hijab who had come with Oz to my talk on Monday. She was crossing the street with the calmest of expressions. Most likely she had not heard yet about Oz's arrest. The belt of her coat was undone and her purple Uggs looked like they were brand new. She saw me and smiled a little, like there were no hard feelings between us, like there could be a beginning. Behind her two bearded men walked in the same direction. This was a higher than usual rate of Muslim sighting for our small town. It was Friday of course and they were heading to the mosque. I thought of Oz missing this prayer and of Malak praying for his release.

On the way out of the café, I threw the pro-life leaflet into the bin. A friend once said to me, 'You're not the first or last woman to have had an abortion. Get over it.' But I was a Sudanese woman or at least, when I learnt the facts of life, I was preparing to be one. No matter how much I changed when I came to Britain, changed my behaviour and my thoughts, there would be layers of me, pockets, membranes and films that would carry these other values and that other guilt.

The thought of guilt led me back to Oz. What if he wasn't innocent? How could I be sure of anything? Sit on the fence and be neither this nor that, believe in everything, believe in nothing. Know only excess and hunger. Too much sugar in my blood and a need for a roof over my head. The repairs to my flat were likely to take weeks, delays because of Christmas, delays because it was winter. Until then I would be a nomad, living in temporary accommodation and on the weekends with Tony or friends. The afternoon sun was hidden behind more snow clouds. It was time for me to head back to the university.

Iain walked into my office and closed the door behind him. He said, 'I've just had two officers in my room interviewing me about Oz Raja.'

Why Iain? Because even though he was head of the department, he was Oz's tutor too. I should have expected this.

'What did they want?' I wanted my voice to sound casual. Business as usual, as if this was another administrative issue, serious and urgent, but not out of the ordinary. I noticed that Iain's hair was even bigger than usual today. He must have been a Duran Duran fan back in the eighties.

'They wanted to know if Oz had been behaving suspiciously. They wanted to know if he drinks alcohol.'

'He doesn't.'

'They wanted to know if he has a girlfriend.'

I paused for a second and then I said, 'I don't think so.' Why drag the girl into this?

Iain shifted his weight. He pressed his back against the door. 'They wanted to know whether he had always worn a beard.'

On another day, on another occasion we could have been laughing. All of this was the stuff of jokes. 'Yes,' I replied. I noticed Iain's shirt was striped and his tie was striped, navy bars straight and slanting.

His voice rose a pitch higher. 'They wanted to know why in the reports we submitted about the students vulnerable to radicalisation, Osama Raja's name never showed up?'

I had written these reports. Two of them. I had written them well and I had written them with care. But I had not written them about Oz.

'I had everyone backing out of this saying they won't spy on their own students.' Iain spoke more softly. 'You volunteered for the training course. You wrote these reports. So what happened?'

He was right, hardly any academic member of staff wanted the added task of monitoring their Muslim students. 'This is Scotland, not Bradford,' was one of the comments, and 'We don't have enough Muslim students to justify the time and effort.' I remembered Fiona Ingram saying, 'I will not shop my students and end up losing their trust in the process!'

But I had no qualms. I had figured out, long ago, that it paid to do what the competition found difficult, distasteful or even just a waste of time. Besides, we had to show, in addition to our publications, that we were undertaking Continuing Professional Development. Attending this training course would count as such. It was held at another university and I went by train. It was only as I gazed out of the window at the Scottish green and shimmering grey sea, that I admitted to myself that I was doing this to distance myself. From Hussein and from the titles of my papers. The two consultants who led the workshop were 'industry specialists' and not academics. It was assumed that we agreed with the effectiveness of the strategy to prevent radicalisation and by extension another terrorist attack. I remember thinking, 'If you say so.' I remember knowing that I was a hypocrite; I remember the reach to grab yet another opportunity. But the awareness was banal and familiar, like the fact that I was overweight, another fault I could live with.

Later, I applied what I had learnt at the course and referred two students. One of them was an international post-grad who was skipping classes. The UK Border Agency had already suspended one Scottish university's licence to sponsor overseas students – so it was right that I should expose any irregularity. The other student, son of a halal butcher in Glasgow, was a nasty little number. Misogynist, anti-Semitic and homophobic, he had no qualms in sharing with me his extremist views. Instead of trying to argue some sense into him, I let him speak his mind and ended up writing a report that swarmed with details. There was no point in attending a training course if I was not going to put what I had learnt into practice.

I opened my mouth to explain but Iain went on, 'Why couldn't you identify Oz as being at risk, when now the police have him in for supporting websites that recruit Chechen Jihadist fighters who are linked to al-Qaeda? And what on earth were you doing in their house when he was arrested?'

The last question was the easiest to answer. To start with my research on Shamil was the sturdiest of footholds. To talk of the snow, their house, their connection to Shamil soothed me. He heard me out without interrupting.

'Oz didn't tick the right boxes,' I said to Iain.

He remained standing and I remained sitting. The stripes of his shirt dazzled my eyes. They merged and moved. 'Oz wasn't lonely, he wasn't depressed or isolated. He didn't seem to me to have more political grievances than average. He wasn't disadvantaged, and he wasn't estranged from his family. His parents are divorced but his father supports him. His father is, as far as I gathered, a successful businessman in South Africa and his mother's an actor, so I judged Oz to be integrated and well adjusted. They're pretty well off. I mean, how many people can afford a state-of-the-art treadmill in their house?'

My last sentence didn't soften the mood. Iain's head was tilted down towards me. I noticed that he was holding a pen in his hand. 'Natasha, if this boy is found guilty how are we going to look?'

'He's not guilty,' I said.

'The police don't go around arresting people at random.'

'It still doesn't make him guilty.'

Iain spoke to me as if I was someone else. 'You aren't answering my question. So I will ask you again. If he goes down, how are *you* going to look?'

'Not good.'

'That's right. And I don't want that and you don't want that. So here is what you're going to do. You are going to write me a report on every conversation you've had with Oz Raja. I want every email he sent you and every paper he's ever submitted in your course.'

So I would write that he made snowmen and ~~chopped~~ practised cutting their heads off with a sword.

So I would write that he ~~joked~~ spoke about setting up a jihadist camp in the countryside.

So I would write that he was researching weapons ~~used~~ to use for jihad.

I must have scowled. I might have even shut my eyes. I couldn't look at his shirt stripes any more. They were like electrical circuits.

Iain said, 'I think the police might want to ask you more questions and check your desktop. I hope they won't decide to seal off this room. Everyone walking down the corridor will want to know why!' His tone then became friendlier, as if we had finished a meeting and now we were chatting informally. He even put his hand on the back of my chair. 'Natasha, you're astute enough to know what needs to be done. You've always been an asset to us and I want you to continue to be so.'

He turned to leave the room. He put his pen in the pocket of his shirt and his hand on the doorknob. 'And I don't need to remind you that your contract of employment warns you against bringing the university into disrepute.'

No, he did not need to remind me. And I noted that he had not mentioned Gaynor Stead or the fact that her complaint had been upheld. A complaint against me was already in the system, being examined, being processed. Iain would expect me to feel grateful that he hadn't brought this up. He would expect me to respond.

2. Dargo, the Caucasus, September 1854

Quickly it became also about money. Zeidat towered over her. 'Shamil Imam doesn't want it for himself; he doesn't care.' Her Russian had improved or more likely Anna was finding it easier to understand. 'Look how we live!' Zeidat's hand swept over the bare room ridiculously referred to as the guest quarters, the walls stained with damp, the tired cushion Anna was sitting on. She was mending a ragged piece of netting brought in to protect Alexander from the flying insects that bit him through the night.

'Look,' Zeidat repeated as if Anna, in this confinement, had not noticed the broken chimney or the small lopsided window – and this room, as she had found out, was one of the better ones.

Anna continued with her sewing while Zeidat paced up and down. This flexing of muscles, her voice louder than usual, was because Shamil was away. His departure, a dawn gallop of horses, had not woken Anna. After bedtime, she would listen to Alexander's steady breathing and to Madame Drancy who snored softly in her sleep. For hours, Anna would vibrate with injustice until, in the middle of an unspoken accusation, sleep would dunk her down and keep her oblivious to the break of dawn and the early movements of the aoul. 'Lazy,' Zeidat had said in front of the other women. 'Brought up in the lap of luxury, never done a day's work. Satan pisses in her ear, that's why the infidel can't hear the call to the dawn prayers,' she would laugh to the others, who always objected, who often defended Anna. Shamil's orders were that she be treated as a guest but she was not fully shielded from Zeidat's daily knocks, her twists of the mouth and sighs of exasperation. Today she was even more reckless because she was the one solely in charge now, she commanded and forbade. So breakfast had been water and dried bread for the hostages, no tea. Later, Anna guessed, it would be tepid unappetising soup or even no dinner at all.

Zeidat swept down and squatted in front of her, her breath dry and sour. She clicked her fingers in front of Anna's face so that the diamond on her ring flashed. 'Recognise this!' It had belonged to David's mother; it was looted from Tsinondali. 'Your husband is rich, isn't he? So he needs to pay us. We must have fifty thousand roubles. We need to build our villages again, the ones you burnt down, the trees you cut down, the crops you destroyed, the pastures you razed, the cattle you did not pull away like decent warriors but shot down for no reason other than that you are evil Russians.'

I am Georgian, not Russian.

It was difficult to stop the words from coming out but still it was a challenge that she welcomed. Being able to restrain herself was itself a reassurance that she had control. She needed these proofs throughout the day. A little while ago, when Zeidat walked in, Anna had ordered Drancy to step out of the room and noted with bitter satisfaction the reply of 'Yes, Your Highness'. Insisting that Alexander continue with his lessons, asking him to speak French at all times with Madame Drancy. She was clinging to who she had been, insisting on being more than a prisoner. 'Anna, Princess of Georgia' was how Shamil had addressed her. He knew who she was.

'Write a letter,' Zeidat hissed.

'I have written to my husband.'

A smirk. 'And he has not paid up. Maybe your husband has forgotten you. Write to that rich tsar of yours. Tell him to pay your ransom. Beg him for help.'

'No.' She should have heeded the warnings and stayed in Tiflis for the summer; later on she should have escaped immediately to the forest. Now, especially, she could not approach the emperor when he was so troubled by the campaigns in the Crimea.

Zeidat looked like she wanted to hit her. She opened her mouth but Anna interrupted, 'The tsar will not hand over Jamaleldin.' She remembered him clearly now as the exotically handsome aide-de-camp, walking two paces behind the tsar. 'And Jamaleldin himself would never want to come here.'

A vagueness skimmed over Zeidat's eyes. Jamaleldin was not her son; perhaps that was why she cared more about the money. But Anna had heard Shamil say, 'I want my son back.' She had understood him because of Lydia.

Zeidat cocked her head to one side. 'The tsar will return Shamil Imam's son. And your husband will pay the money.'

'My husband does not have fifty thousand roubles.'

'Liar,' Zeidat snorted.

'I am not a liar. His wealth is in the land.'

'Then he will have to sell it, won't he?'

'We don't sell our land. It belongs to our ancestors and to our children. It is more than a possession.' Tsinondali was vivid to her, more so than the present. Tsinondali was big and bright and waiting for her. When she was young, her father would speak disapprovingly of a neighbour who sold his land to cover debts, of a cousin who neglected his estate, of a friend who mistreated his serfs. The land was a responsibility, part of the fabric of the family. Not for sale.

Zeidat stood up. 'Haughty, haughty. Do you think I believe such nonsense? Sell, borrow, steal, we don't care. We want both: Jamaleldin and the money. Otherwise what will happen? You asked Shamil Imam this when you were presented to him and what did he say? He said "Our ordinary laws and customs will apply." Did you understand what he meant? Of course you didn't. Well let me explain. It means no more of the "guest" nonsense. It means you are a prisoner-of-war, like any prisoner. How do you treat us, you Russians, when our men fall into your hands? When our women fall into your hands?' She squatted down again close to Anna. 'Let me tell you, I lost sisters in Akhulgo dear to me, one a cousin and another a close friend. When the village fell, they could see the Russian soldiers climbing up, coming close, they could not escape and so they knew the Russians were going to capture them; do you know what they did? They covered their faces with their veils and

146

jumped from the cliffs.' Zeidat's voice rose to a pitch. 'Because being captured by the Russians is worse for a woman than death. Do you understand what I am saying? If the negotiations fail, you, Anna, would become a prisoner-of-war. You would be tossed out of my home and I would do it gladly. If the money isn't paid, if Shamil Imam doesn't get his son back, he will hand you over as a gift to his favourite naib. You understand, Anna, what I mean by the word "gift" – of course, you are not a child. That is our custom. Already every day now one of his naibs approaches him with an offer to purchase you. So write to the tsar.'

Anna pressed her hands together to hide their tremble. Her fingers were slippery. 'I will not write to the tsar asking for a ransom and if you refuse to take the lead from Imam Shamil and treat me as a guest, then the least you can do is address me as he does, *by my title.*'

Zeidat picked up Alexander's netting and stood up. It was one agile movement, a smoothness in her voice. 'Maybe when your son is itching and crying, you will start to see sense.'

In this room, which was poorly lit even in the daytime, Anna had strained her eyes repairing the bigger holes in the netting. She now watched Zeidat carry the material out of the room. The sewing materials were one of the few things David had been able to send. Along with combs, soap, towels and a shawl. A serf from Tsinondali had made the perilous journey and had been allowed to speak to her for a few minutes, though not in private. He reassured her that David and all their friends were doing all they could to secure her release. No doubt the serf would go back and report on how thin she had become. She gave him a letter to David but she was only allowed to write about the ransom, nothing else. With a wooden pen and piece of wool soaked in ink (the only writing materials provided), she had managed a few stilted sentences, no information about their life, except that they were in good health, well looked after.

She read David's letter only once. It made her stay awake at night, silently shouting at him. On the day of the kidnapping, he said – *I thought you had escaped to the woods when I saw the flames rising up from the direction of Tsinondali.* Why he had not rushed back home – *the correct military procedure was to lie in ambush waiting for the enemy's return.* Why he had not attempted to save her – *I know from experience that they prefer to slaughter, God forbid, their prisoners rather than loose them, I could not take such a risk.* How the serfs found Lydia – *they recognized the lace shawl . . .* Where she was buried – *in the Church of St George which has escaped the fire.* When he found out about the burial and the kidnapping – *two days later, when it was safe for me to leave the fort.*

When it was safe for me to leave the fort.

The lace shawl.

She had wanted to tear up the letter. But she had controlled herself. Why make Zeidat laugh at her? Why upset Alexander? She had not torn it up but she had not read it again. David was telling the truth, she knew, when he said, *I am doing everything I can to secure your release* but, strangely enough, she did not believe in him. Nor did she doubt him, or question his abilities. He was telling her the truth but the truth did not always inspire faith. That was what she lacked often these days after the denial and the extravagant hope had passed, especially after the ransom sums were bandied about, more extortionate, it seemed, by the minute. Was it greed or compensation? She was not sure. Crops burnt, villages destroyed, forests felled . . . why? Her faith was wavering, not only that they would go back to Georgia but in who was right, who was winning; what was it all for?

Madame Drancy was better than her in this respect. She impressed Anna with her determination to be a true Christian, patiently carrying her cross. She would read aloud from the *Imitation de Jesus-Christ*, the only book that managed to reach them. 'This is my true comfort,' she would say, a little dramatically, tears in her eyes. Often she gave in to sobs and hysterics whenever she missed her mother or fell ill. These easy feminine tears made Anna envious. She was all dried up after Lydia, too angry to cry.

Of course David was doing everything he could to secure her

release, but every day he seemed further away, detached from this strange new life. She would not even want to tell him about it, ashamed of what she had been reduced to. But again, his letter should have given her nourishment. One would think, she mused, that such a letter would be my lifeline, my consolation, my link. Instead its words rattled rather than soothed her, kept her awake, her body lengthened with passion, her dreams, when they finally came, carnal and unfulfilling. The nights were hot and the room poorly ventilated. Thighs stuck together, sweat pooling under her breasts, her hair damp on the pillow. Last night she had sensed a familiar tug that folded into a gentle ache, a promise of a trickle. It had been more than a year since she had leaked this monthly blood, since first carrying Lydia. Welcome old friend. To reassure her that she was still fertile. To promise her future princes and princesses.

When they had first arrived in Dargo, it was stifling nights following long empty days. Total imprisonment in this one room for at least two weeks. 'Is this how you treat your guests, Imam Shamil?' she had berated him the next time they met, finding herself matching his tone, using his words. 'No fresh air, no sunlight, no exercise. No wonder we are poorly.' He relented immediately; Anna and Madame Drancy to have full and free access to all of the women's quarters, Alexander to play outdoors with the children of the aoul, even all day if he wanted to.

What did they do with themselves, Shamil's women? Anna's hosts were themselves like prisoners huddled in these quarters. Rooms of stone that opened into a gallery, screened by a high wooden fence, through which they could look out at the rest of their household. Shamil had his own separate building adjoining the mosque, a reception room in which he conducted meetings and received visitors. His rooms, which roused Anna's mild curiosity, were not shared by any of his wives. Instead he visited them in turn, knocking on their door, waiting for permission to come in.

'Is it true,' she asked Chuanat, who arrived sneaking in another netting for Alexander, cake and tea for his mother, 'that you ransomed yourself to Shamil to save your family?'

Chuanat smiled with her usual warmth. 'That's what I wanted them to believe but, no, I fell in love with him. I could not leave him.' When they had first arrived in Dargo, Anna had noticed that Chuanat was plump. In fact she was pregnant and now due to give birth. Her trousers were hitched above her bulge; she needed extra pillows to lean upon.

Anna had plenty of questions. How could Chuanat bear this life? Did she not mind sharing Shamil with Zeidat and Ameena? Does not love wane after years of marriage and children?

'When he comes back safe from battle, I am so relieved. It is as if I am seeing him again for the first time, fresh feelings and we start all over again. He is so handsome, I sometimes think he has bewitched me. If the story about the mountain lion is true, then it would be easy for him to ensnare a young girl. The first day I saw him, the way he looked at me, it was as if he knew everything about me and I didn't have to explain myself. I was young when I was captured. Treated fairly well on the journey, no one laid a finger on me, but I cried for my family. Then he became my family. He replaced everything I lost, and more. He never asked me to change my religion. 'Chuanat, my Christian wife', he made everyone say it, like him, with respect. 'We worship the same God,' he told me, 'and when you are ready I will show you shorter, quicker, more direct routes to Him. I will lead you.' My mother had wanted to give me to the church. Yes, I had been destined for the Armenian Church – but I had my own misgivings though I kept them to myself. I loved my Lord and wanted to serve Him; I even liked how the nuns lived, how peaceful they were and orderly. I liked their clean life removed from the bustle of the markets, away from the competition and envy and always wanting more. But I wanted children, I imagined myself a mother and that made me think that I would be out of place in the convent, I wouldn't be able to keep up with the other nuns, somehow, I would let them down. Now here I have everything I wanted.' She laid a hand on the bulge of her stomach. 'They are all inseparable, the baby and the prayers.'

'But it is so basic, this life. How can you bear it? No music, no rides, no books. These stone rooms. The food is horrible, the clothes are horrible.'

Chuanat nodded, 'Yes, I wish Shamil would permit us to dress better. A bonnet and a cloak – I would like that. But not the other things, not at all. It would have been basic too in the convent. Now I feel I have plenty. The outside world doesn't interest me. When I pray behind him I am happy. I am peaceful. Shamil has brought me closer to God, because he is close to Him. And there is such a blessing in being with him, in serving him. It is a kind of intoxication that does not diminish or become stale. It is as close as I can get to Heaven. He is gentle with us. Have you seen him with the children? He always gives them fruit and toffees.'

Anna had seen him once carrying a pretty girl, while her crippled leg hung over his arms. She was his daughter, from Zeidat. His two older daughters were from the late Fatima; they were thirteen and ten.

'He is one thing at home and another outside. He has never raised a hand against any of us. He knows when I am tired, he knows when I am remembering my family; he understands when someone has upset me.'

'And the others?' Anna prodded. Polygamy disgusted her but at such close quarters it was interesting.

'Zeidat's father is Sheikh Jamal el-Din, Shamil Imam's teacher. Zeidat could not find a husband because of her sharp temper and difficult ways – so in gratitude to his teacher and to ease his mind, Shamil married her. I did get jealous when he married Ameena. But she is too young, she does not appreciate him. I don't know what is wrong with this girl, she is moody and doesn't know what she wants. You know she once set fire to Zeidat's room! Over a quarrel about a piece of silk! She flew into a rage and burnt all of Zeidat's clothes. And Imam Shamil did not punish her.'

Ameena visited Anna later that day. She often did, keen to hear stories about Petersburg and the tsar's court or to ask Madame Drancy about Paris. Anna found her a harmless distraction as well as a welcome source of information about the household. It was

Ameena who told her that the elderly lady, Bahou, was Jamaleldin and Ghazi's maternal grandmother, mother of the deceased Fatima. The one who looked like Ameena was her mother, the middle-aged Tartar was the governess of Shamil's daughters, the steward's wife, a visitor and so on. Today Ameena took Anna by the arm. 'Come, let me show you something special.'

They walked through the gallery to the building that housed Shamil's quarters. Anna began to feel wary even though she knew he was away. Curiosity kept her from turning around. Ameena pushed open a door and they were in Shamil's room. In the dim light Anna smelt cloves or camphor. When her eyes adjusted she saw, hanging over the fireplace, a scimitar, a sword and some pistols. The pistols were Georgian, mounted in silver. The sword had an Ottoman cartouche and there was gold Arabic calligraphy inscribed on the blade. The hilt was of animal horn and there were vegetal decorations on the crossbar.

The walls of the room were a simple white and there were a few Caucasian rugs on the floor, a wooden trunk pushed against the wall, a copper basin and jug. What surprised Anna most were the books, manuscripts and journals lining the shelves of more than one wall. There was a stack of the St Petersburg paper, the *Russki Invalid*. It was a simple room, no opulent chair, no desk, no clocks or cigar boxes, no globes and no decoration. And yet she wanted to linger, to absorb the solemn atmosphere, the stillness that almost had a colour. She looked more closely at the books, their Arabic script, a stack of letters, ledgers full of accounts. Ameena moved towards the trunk and said, 'Come and see his clothes.'

Anna shook her head but Ameena had already lifted the lid of the trunk open. Anna looked down at green and brown woollen cloaks folded neatly, the heavy twisted white that made up his turban. She flushed because she was snooping and she should not be. She had told him that first time, *My rank and upbringing forbid me to lie. I will not trick you.* Ameena was naive to bring her here; perhaps she would be punished for it.

'Let us go back.' She turned to see Ameena holding a pistol in her hand. There was a strange expression on her face. She pointed it at Anna. It could not be loaded, but the sudden fear made her whole body tingle. 'Put it back, Ameena.'

'Why?'

'Because it is not yours.'

'Or because your life is worth thousands of roubles? How much do you think my life is worth? One thousand, five hundred? How much is a childless wife worth?'

She did not feel frightened any more. 'You are still young, Ameena, there is plenty of time for you to have children.'

Ameena mounted the pistol back on the wall. 'I was teasing you,' she said. She linked arms with Anna as they left the room. 'But you weren't afraid at all. If this were Drancy, I would have laughed my fill at her hysterics.'

The next day Chuanat gave birth to a girl. She lay propped up on cushions, dark shadows under her eyes but smiling, the baby swaddled in her arms. Her room filled up with women and a tray of rubbery Turkish Delight was passed around. The celebration would have been bigger had it been a boy. 'We are waiting for her father to name her,' Chuanat smiled. 'I have already sent a message to him. Would you like to hold her, Anna?'

She could not refuse, though it brought back gusts of disbelief, one battering memory after the other. She had crooked her arm in exactly the same way, made sure Lydia's head was supported, felt her own body large in comparison, a bulwark against harm. All babies were alike but not identical. There was the delicate skin, dewy, sometimes flaky, hair on the arms like threads. There were the exquisite movements, the slight toss of the head, mouth open rooting for milk, a yawn, a push of the elbow, a drawing in of the knee; these exact same movements the mother had felt in the womb. And then there were their eyes, large and steady because they held knowledge of other worlds. Later, in a few years' time, they would carry names that defined them; they would find out on which side of the war they belonged. Later they would learn the legends and the proverbs, hear them from an older cousin or a younger aunt. *When will blood stop flowing on the mountains? When the sugarcane grows in snow.* But not yet, in these early days of their life – they were above it all, pure and holy.

Chuanat's eyes were on the baby. She was a new mother, attuned to her infant's needs, the two of them in harmony with each other, understanding and possessive. Anna handed her back the baby and left the room.

She went up to the roof, another concession she had fought for and won – fresh night air. She walked slowly around, breathing, wishing it were a full moon so that she could see more of the mountains. It had been almost four months since they were kidnapped, three months in Dargo. How slowly time passed! She must think of Alexander and not of Lydia. She must talk to Alexander more. He was left too often with the other children, fussed over by the women of the household. Madame Drancy had been shocked to hear him speak their captor's language but Anna did not object. She was relieved that he was adjusting to this new situation better than she was. Last month he had been ill and it had intensified her anger to watch him suffer, away from the amenities of home and reliable medical care. It was true her captors were deeply concerned but their strange herbs and concoctions alienated her further. Nor were such cures successful. Shamil slaughtered a sheep and wrapped the feverish Alexander with its skin. It was the best cure, he explained to Anna, but it only partially reduced his temperature. 'He must sleep in the gallery,' she had insisted. 'It is the stifling air in the room that is bad for him.' Shamil agreed and checked on Alexander several times a day. 'See how kind he is,' Chuanat was quick to point out. 'He loves children.' But Anna was more sceptical. In this war of kidnaps and ransom, Alexander was a valuable hostage.

Madame Drancy joined her on the roof and they circled around, walking more briskly. Sometimes they counted the rounds they made, sometimes they timed themselves and kept going for a full hour. 'I want to go for a walk,' she had demanded of Shamil and he had not understood. 'Is there nowhere to go? Is there no such thing here as an outing? Perhaps I can walk through the village.'

He relented and left it to Chuanat to organise. But it required such extensive arrangements, deliberation on who would be included in the group, what route they should take, what time was best, which of the guards could be spared to accompany them, that by the time they set out a heaviness weighed down what should have been a recreation. The village was all narrow steep roads, poverty-stricken families who either stared, jeered or followed.

The houses embedded in the mountains reminded Anna of burrows. Uneven, lopsided, with no sense of symmetry or continuity. She stumbled over the rocks, her burka (non-negotiable) dragging her down. Of course there were no parks, no pavilions, no fountains, no boulevards. What did she expect? It was a relief to return to the house. She never asked to go out again.

Madame Drancy, matching Anna's wide strides with quick short steps, was assessing the consequence of Chuanat's confinement. 'We are fully at the mercy of Zeidat now. No tea, she insists. It is bad enough that there is no morning coffee at all, but why no tea? And this will continue for six weeks. Really six weeks of confinement for a new mother is too long. Another peculiar custom is that they bury the afterbirth. Is that not quaint?'

'It must be the practice of the mountain tribes.'

'Onion water for dinner! I went to the kitchen to see if I can find any scraps but the cook barred my way.' She slowed a little. 'I am not valuable to them, Your Highness.'

This was true and Anna was unable to contradict her. She wanted to keep walking, the movement soothing in itself. She did not want Drancy to lag behind. 'We must keep our strength up, Madame Drancy. Exercise and fresh air. At least Zeidat gives Alexander a proper meal.' Once or twice she had found herself asking him to save her a boiled egg or an apricot. It shamed her to do so.

'I thought I could make myself valuable by teaching Shamil's daughters French. But the only book I have with me is the *Imitation*. They object to its content and I cannot risk it being taken away from me.'

Anna remembered Drancy in the drawing room of Tsinondali,

her neck bent over *La Dame aux Camélias*. The Crimean War had ended her plan to open a bookshop in Tiflis; now the highlanders had disrupted her career as a governess. She said, 'Madame Drancy, I will do everything I can to compensate you for this predicament.' She paused and reminded herself to say 'when' and not 'if'. 'When we go home, I will insist on you accompanying us. I will not leave without you. You will receive your full salary and I am sure that Prince David is taking you into account in the negotiations for our release.' Madame Drancy's thanks did not lessen the listlessness that crept over Anna. It had not been easy to make these promises; her pace became slower as a consequence.

The heavy footsteps of the sentry could be heard coming up the stairs. Soon it would be the end of their outdoor session. They would be locked up for the night, another of Zeidat's provocations. Make the most of these last minutes, breathe in. A northern cloud had the inflated shape of a churn of cream in the kitchen of Tsinondali and that star reminded her of the diamond badge of office she had worn when she was presented at court.

3. Dargo, the Caucasus, October 1854

Shamil visited his teacher first before he went home. He felt Chua-nat waiting for him, eager to show off the new baby, but a vague sense of unfinished business drew him to Sheikh Jamal el-Din. Grimy from travel, the din of battle still in his ears, he needed the calmness that the elderly man possessed. Sitting on the floor, they ate a meal of pilaf and raisins. Jamal el-Din said, 'In your absence another message came through from Tabarsaran wanting you to send a representative with an army. They want Sharia rule so that they can be strong enough to resist the Russians.'

'I will send them three thousand troops and three naibs. One will not be enough.'

'Good. Is it true that you dismissed Umar al-Salti?'

'He turned back on the road.'

Sheikh Jamal el-Din chuckled. 'They say it was because he had recently taken a new wife.' Saintly and learned, but he was partial to gossip.

Shamil frowned. 'Is that an excuse? I appointed him as a naib, heading over a thousand, I tell him to set up camp up on Rughchah and he turns round!'

'He was more suited to overseeing the gunpowder factory.' Jamal el-Din had always been impressed by how the river's current power-ed the machinery.

They spoke of the martyrs of the battle. Muhammad al 'Uradi al Hidali, a scholar. Batir al-Militi, renowned for his courage, had been injured and died a few days later. Youth they did not know personally, brothers, sons, husbands and fathers. Winners who had been granted a life unlike this one, men who were to be missed and envied.

Jamal el-Din complimented him on Ghazi's latest success in Shali. 'At first,' Shamil explained, 'he was forced to retreat and rode through the night back to the mountains. He fell asleep across his saddle but a rider caught up with them saying that the Russians were in pursuit. The men gathered around him and started to sing *Sleep no more, Ghazi Mohammed/ Sleeping is done/ The Russians are upon us/ There is a war to be won.*'

'And win it he did,' said Jamal el-Din, taking a sip of water. 'Now Muhammad-Sheffi will train even harder to catch up with his brother.' He was Fatima's youngest son, born in the difficult days after they were driven out of Akhulgo.

'He rides well but his shooting is still mediocre.' Shamil chewed on a raisin that was particularly tough.

'Once,' Jamal el-Din swallowed his last mouthful, 'there was a man strolling through his grounds followed by his slave. When he reached the vegetable garden, he cut off one cucumber from its vine and took a bite. It was bitter so he gave up on it and tossed it to his slave. The youth ate it all up. Surprised by this the man asked, "Why did you eat it? Didn't you find it bitter?" The slave replied, "Yes, it was bitter but you have been so generous to me and every day you give me the most delicious food so I felt ashamed to refuse something which, for once, was not tasty." '

Jamal el-Din sat back, gesturing for Shamil to wipe clean the dish. 'The man turned to his slave and said, "You have gained your freedom. Go now as you please." '

Shamil fetched water and a basin so that they could rinse their hands. He would drink tea later with Chuanat. She always had the samovar ready by her side.

'You did not consult me on the kidnapping of the princess,' Jamal el-Din said.

Shamil bristled but he understood now why he had been drawn here, to face the disapproval he had suspected. 'With due respect my master, but I do not usually go over with you every raid and operation.'

'If you had asked my permission I would not have given it. And that is why you did not ask my permission.'

Shamil felt young, like a child caught out. He expected to receive a loving reprimand, a chuff on the shoulder, a gentle tug to his ear. 'She is valuable,' he said. 'High enough to shake the tsar.'

Jamal el-Din's eyes widened. He leaned forward. 'You're not going to ask me why I would have withheld my permission.'

'It is too late to ask.' His voice was louder than he expected it to be.

'This is a new arrogance in you, Shamil.'

'I want my son back.'

'You want your son back?'

'Yes, I want him with me where he belongs.'

'You want. You want. Weakness lies in desire.'

'I see no harm in trying, in making another attempt.'

Jam el-Din raised his voice. 'All this and no harm.'

Shamil flinched. 'I was appalled at how much she suffered on the journey. And the loss of the daughter was unfortunate to an extreme. But now she is in my house, living with the same amenities as my family. I have ordered my wives to treat her as a guest.'

Jamal el-Din interrupted him with wide eyes, his tone slightly mocking. 'You entrusted my daughter as a hostess!' He knew Zeidat's faults, indeed they were well known. How the gentlest of men could father a shrew, how an upbringing steeped in wisdom and compassion could produce a fanatic, was in itself a curiosity to puzzle over.

Shamil's voice took on a more defensive edge. 'I myself make sure that the princess gets good food. Her son was ill and I fetched him the rarest herbs but they didn't cure him. At last I sent down into Tiflis for medicine. What more can I do?' He was speaking too much and he was conscious of his voice getting louder. 'If Her Highness continues to suffer it is not my fault but the fault of the pampered lifestyle she has been accustomed to.'

'I see no blessing in this risk you are taking. My heart is not at ease.'

Shamil glanced at his old teacher, the delicacy in him that came from a life of peace, eyes toned by books, tongue moist from reciting the praises of Allah, sensitive fingers that tended plants, milked goats, folded prayer rugs. He said, 'Sheikh, leave warfare to me. I know more about it.'

'Who is the go-between in this?'

'Isaac Gramoff, an Armenian interpreter serving in the Russian army. He knows our dialect.'

'From where?'

'He's lived among the mountain tribes all his life.'

Jamal el-Din sat back and closed his eyes. 'Return her to her husband.'

Shamil lifted up his hands in exasperation.

Jamal el-Din opened his eyes, pointed his finger and raised his voice. 'I am telling you: return her to her husband.'

It was a direct order and Shamil stood up. 'No.'

Jamal el-Din looked up at him with eyes that still requested, that still held out. 'What do you mean, "no"?'

'Until my son comes back, she is staying.' He picked up his gun, which was hanging on the nail on the wall, and walked out of the door.

He walked out of the door without kissing his teacher's hand, without begging as he had always done these past thirty years for blessings, for support, for prayers to grant continuous triumph in battle, without humbling himself to kiss his sheikh's feet, knowing that only in this humility, in this love could the spray of a miracle reach him, to anoint him invincible in the face of the enemy. He walked out of the door into heat, haste and darkness; it was several yards before he stopped and collected his bearings. The night was dense, moonless. The crescent to herald the new month, a sacred one, had not yet appeared. Autumn was holding off this year – usually by now the nights were pleasant. He needed a bath but a bath would not resolve the angry sadness he had landed in. This grappling with ugliness, this touch of inner disease. There was no merit in a student defying his teacher, no sweetness in a murid disobeying his sheikh. In his own aoul, his wives five minutes away, his children waiting and yet he veered into exile.

Decades ago Shamil had sworn allegiance to Sheikh Jamal el-Din. He had soaked up the sheikh's Sufi teachings, eager for enlightenment, eager for the grace and strength that came from the Creator. Ghazi Muhammad al-Ghimrawi, too, had been a disciple. Together they had stood up in prayer and gone into seclusion; together they chanted and studied. And they had known that perfection could not be reached without the instructions of a master; they were seekers and Sheikh Jamal el-Din their spiritual guide. Keeping company with him yielded more than reading one thousand books; loving him was the gate to a higher love. Yet Ghazi Muhammad al-Ghimrawi dared to stand up to his teacher, opting for action when the older man favoured passivity. Al-Ghimrawi threatened the tribes that did not implement the Sharia; he raised the banner for jihad against the Russians. After his death, Shamil had succeeded him; by then the foundation of resistance had been laid down, the jihad in full swing.

Now stopping on the outskirts of the aoul, feet away from the sentry who would think he was inspecting them, he tried to calm himself with this thought. Jamal el-Din had always disliked war and hostage-taking; he had always turned away from conflict and strife. But I have a son who belongs with me, I have a son in need of rescue.

He could retrace his footsteps now and continue to reason with Jamal el-Din. He could beg for forgiveness and then explain. But what was there to explain and why was it that Jamaleldin's return was an urgent priority only for him? It was the pressure from the naibs for a high ransom that was stalling the negotiations. If it were up to Shamil, it would be a straight hostage exchange. And yet his hands were tied; the community privileged over the individual, and the People's Council was in need of funds. 'Be patient and fear Allah in the hope that you will flourish and He will remove the evil with which the infidels oppress you.' Is that not what he told his men? 'Do not lose heart and do not grieve, for you are the exalted. We are servants of Allah, all-powerful Victor over all, who resists those who oppose his Sharia. Peace be upon those who hear the word and follow its best meaning.'

He turned and started to walk home, still troubled. Fear did not usually steal into him so easily and yet here it was. It had slung itself around his neck as soon as he left Jamal el-Din's home. If the sheikh now held off his spiritual support, would Jamaleldin not come home? Would the hostage negotiations fail? Until now there had been not been a single word from St Petersburg about the return of Jamaleldin. Shamil walked faster to shrug off the pessimism. He was driven to succeed and through Allah's will he would succeed. He must not contemplate failure.

It was Zeidat who met him at the door. He said, 'I will inspect the guest quarters now. Announce me.'

'There is no one there. The Russian is visiting Chuanat. Have a bite to eat first while I heat up the water for your bath.' She tossed the invitation out with more efficiency than concern. He knew that the usual wifely duties held no interest for her. Dishevelled more often than not, jingling her keys and bossing the servants, she was more fulfilled priming his pistols and sharpening his sabre. Nothing pleased her more than sitting with him to mull over the administration of his troops or to assess the merits of a particular naib. She had sharp opinions on everything from battle tactics to who should be promoted and who should be punished. With time, the care of their permanently disabled child had, thankfully, mellowed and restrained her, thickening also the bond between them. He loved her best when she stirred his resolve with eloquent elegies of the martyrs; her fine eyes, the only likeness to her father, glowing and sincere. But not today.

He strode past her and walked into the guest quarters. 'What's this?' he bellowed and kicked over a rusty pot of dirty onion water. 'Is this supposed to pass for soup? Is this what you have been giving them?'

Zeidat's protests did not have the slightest effect on him. 'Since when did the chimney break down and why wasn't it fixed straight away?' Now both of them were shouting at the top of their voices; soon Zeidat was reduced to tears.

He ignored her and headed towards Chuanat's room. In her was his comfort, in her was tranquillity and what was beautiful in this ugly world. Charged with self-doubt, restless, saddened, he felt himself pouring towards her, mother of his newborn, his pearl and gentle friend, who never thwarted his desires, never contradicted, never held back loyalty and love. But when he entered her room, it was Anna who caught his attention. Anna standing up holding the baby, the light of the fire on her hair and foreign dress. She turned and looked at him with the haughtiness of the injured, the stark knowing eyes of a parent who had lost a child. He sensed in her what she had not yet acknowledged; her need to conceive was only dormant, poised to unfurl. 'What will happen to me if the negotiations fail?' she had asked the first time they met and he had felt bored by her question. 'Our rules and customs will prevail' meant handing her over to the chief of one of the dithering mountain tribes not yet won over to the resistance. Now, seeing her turn towards him with his newborn in her arms, royal blood rising to her cheeks, he changed his mind. Anna, Princess of Georgia. If the negotiations failed, he would not give her to anyone else.

VI
A Glimmer Passes Through

1. Scotland, December 2010

It was a spur-of-the-moment decision, to check out of the hotel, to get in the car and just drive. I had been unable to sleep and couldn't bear any more the raspy blow of the heating, all the coughs and noises from the other bedrooms. My mind was switched on, uncontrollably scanning the events of the day. In the afternoon, the police had come to the university and checked my desktop; they searched my office and asked me question after question. On the titles of my papers, *Royal Support for Jihad* and *Jihad as Resistance*; on my political opinions, on my other nationalities and, of course, on Oz.

They sealed the entrance and though my colleagues were restrained in their curiosity, I shrank. Every step climbed, every achievement, every recognition – all that hard work – had not taken me far enough, not truly redeemed me, not landed me on the safest shore. The skin on my skull tensed so that I could not form a facial expression; even pushing my glasses up my nose felt strange, as if my skin was both numb and ultra-sensitive at the same time. To have your personal files examined, to reveal what is exceedingly intimate – a password and search engine history – felt a hundred times worse than having luggage examined at the airport. Perhaps Oz's email to me was worth their search. *I downloaded the al-Qaeda training manual from the US Justice Department website and I didn't even have to pay for it!* They didn't say and I didn't ask. I could not bring myself to speak naturally to them. When they finally left, hours later, the corridors and rooms around me were empty. In the floor below, the sociology department were finishing up their Christmas party. I walked out of the building as if it was the end of

167

just another ordinary week, as if I had not had my dignity shaken and my balance broken.

I drove into Aberdeen a little after 3 a.m. I crossed the dark river, its surface surprisingly still, like a creased sheet of metal. Orange streetlights on the black roads and the hidden white buildings. Despite the ice warning, I had been speeding all the way, enjoying the emptiness of the dual carriageway, overtaking one truck after another; Amy Winehouse on full volume, the heating just right. Now South Anderson Drive swept up ahead of me, the smooth curves of one roundabout after another. I owned the brightly lit road and could drive longer, all the way to Inverness and beyond. I slowed down, reluctant now to reach my destination, still without the pleasant tiredness that preceded sleep. Tony was not expecting me until Saturday afternoon but I had the key to the back door. I had kept it all these years and when I parked across the road I lingered in the car, remembering other homecomings. That early switch from new independence to entering the life Mum and Tony continued without me. The time I had come from the hospital stunned and still bleeding but I never told them why, just stayed in bed for a whole weekend. Fast forward to finding Mum ill and in her dressing gown, the evening I found her wearing a wig. Back to less dramatic times: coming home from a club on the night bus, the weather blustery, and fiddling with the back-door key, knocking my handbag against the wheelie bin. Birthdays that were boring, gaps between moving from one set of digs to the next, storing my things. A whole summer in which I worked in Waterstones and took driving lessons in long sunny evenings.

I let myself in through the back door into the kitchen. It looked messier and barer than in my mother's time. A sudden pang of hunger made me open the fridge and sit at the table, still in my coat, helping myself to potato salad and cream crackers. My old room, now the guest room, was on the ground floor. I had liked that a lot, being downstairs by myself, away from the two of them, close to the kitchen, close to the road.

I rolled my suitcase into the room and decided to nip into the sitting room to see if Tony had some vodka in the cabinet. Then I heard a noise from upstairs. I was sorry I had woken him. The sound of a door opening, a whisper and I stepped into the hallway, stood at the foot of the stairs. Up on the landing he looked vulnerable, not at all as if he was about to confront an intruder. His longish grey hair was dishevelled, his pyjama trousers sagging. 'It's me,' I called out loudly. 'I'm sorry I woke you up, it's just I had the worst night. That hotel...' I stopped when I saw her behind him. For a minute my blood went cold. But it was not my mother, healthy and young again. Of course. It was the cleaner, Kornelia, in a satin nightdress.

I turned and headed towards my room. Tony shouted down after me, 'You can't do this! You can't just barge in here in the middle of the night. Who the hell do you think you are? First thing in the morning you give me this key back, Natasha. Bloody inconsiderate.'

I heard the whisper of Kornelia's soothing words, her accent. I imagined her holding his arm, pulling him back to bed. It turned my stomach. I stumbled into my room – something was on the floor blocking my way. It was only when I switched on the light that I saw that the room was full of boxes, suitcases and clothes. They covered the whole floor area without even a path to the bed. My mother's things had been tossed into reusable shopping bags. Her cardigans, her shoes, her toiletries. Long evening dresses lay across the bed. Her fluffy slippers, a belt in leopard print, the belly-dancing outfit (she had taken classes at one time and purchased this on holiday in Istanbul), her curling tongs, hairdryer, fake fur, real silk. Photos of family members in Georgia, photos of me as a baby and at school, my graduation. Things from way back, *I Can Make You Thin* and things she had used at the very end – the wig, the hot-water bottle and the walking frame. A lifetime of possessions had been dumped here. A testament to a mania triggered by having financial access to shopping centres and channels after a communist upbringing. My poor mother who, as a child protégé in the Russian Olympic team, returned from the games in Rome with a doll, only to have it confiscated at the airport. She never got over the resentment, what she felt as a theft. But it was not dolls that she wanted when she came to Aberdeen, it was all this. What lay now before me, valuable rubbish. Tony could never have risen to this task by himself or even taken the initiative. It was Kornelia who had done it, I was sure, to evict every trace of my mother from the master bedroom.

For the first time since her death, I cried. I cried over the wasted time, conversations in which all I did was mock her accent and taste; time wasted in aching to be white like her and blaming her for the failure as if she were the one barring me from entry into a privileged world, as if she were begrudging me a gift she could give.

It was noon when I woke up, the pale light coming in through the curtains. The house around me was silent. I walked around and there was no sign of either Tony or Kornelia. In the kitchen I made myself breakfast and was annoyed that there was only one bun left in the bread bin. Where did this entitlement come from? It was as if I had regressed to a younger version of myself, lost my bearings, and was coming back expecting to recharge. But so far this was not the homecoming I expected. The things in the room were still there, even more numerous in daylight. The telephone rang and I picked it up. It was Grusha Babiker and I felt a sense of relief, as if she, from her home in Khartoum, was coming to my rescue. We had not spoken since my mother died. Now the words tumbled out of me; I told her about Kornelia, about my mother's things dumped in my old room.

'They are yours – you must not let this Kornelia take them. Listen to me, Natasha, you need to go over everything carefully. Take the valuable things and give the rest to charity. Do it now, do it today. You are actually lucky, you arrived just at the right time. That woman must have been plotting to remove them out of the house and taking them downstairs was just the first step.'

I managed to laugh at her paranoia, her willingness to think badly of Kornelia. What did I know about her? She was the only cleaner Mum hadn't found fault with. We bumped into her once at the Bon Accord Centre, all decked out, almost unrecognisable.

Her English kept getting better with time. She had a son in Torry Academy and a husband still in Warsaw. Every Christmas she gave Tony and Mum a box of chocolate liqueurs.

'Tony is gullible,' Grusha was now saying. 'I've always said that about him. A simpleton where women are concerned.' She knew things about him from way back before he met my mother. I had heard variations of these 'Tony, the playboy of Khartoum' stories before. 'But really, now, he could do better,' she concluded.

I agreed with her and promised to deal with my mother's belongings. It was my responsibility after all. I should have done it months ago. But this was not why she was calling. 'I tried your mobile,' she said. 'The number that Tony gave me. But it was off. For days now. So I am really happy to find you at last. Not that I have good news. Your father is not well, Natasha, and he is asking about you. If you can't come then at least phone him, Skype with him in hospital. It would mean so much for him just to hear your voice, just to know that you are well. He is proud of you.'

Anger made my neck stiff, my voice impatient to end the conversation. I decided to change the subject. 'How is Yasha?'

She seemed taken aback, her voice distant as if she was thinking of something else. 'He's busy, you know. More and more, he is involved in human rights abuses and with these recent upheavals there's been more for him to do and more cases to defend. I will tell him you asked after him.'

Galvanised by this conversation, I rolled up my sleeves and started to work. Immediately I found what I badly needed, a laptop and a mobile phone. I could get myself a temporary pay-as-you-go SIM card, I could download my work from a USB onto this laptop. An hour later Tony found me cross-legged on the floor, still sifting through things, but I had already filled three black bin liners ready to give away.

He stood at the door of the room. It seemed he was alone, but I was not going to ask him about Kornelia. 'If we pack my car and yours,' I said, 'we could take the bags to a charity shop.'

'Sure.' He looked surprised but also relieved that I was doing all this.

'Unless you have something else in mind?' I folded a purple dress. I folded a pair of leggings.

'No. It's got to be done.' His shoulders were slumped but he looked better because he had gone for a haircut.

'Remember,' I picked up a deep red velvet dress. 'She wore this not last Christmas but the year before.'

He shook his head and stepped into the room, sat on the bed. 'Keep it. Don't give it away.'

At least he had stopped saying, 'I'm gutted.' I must have heard him say it a hundred times. On and on like a mantra. 'I'm gutted, Natasha.'

I stood up to try on a black jumper. It looked baggy enough to fit me. Just about. A large A5 envelope caught Tony's attention. He extracted it from the box it had been thrown into, pushed down by a travel pillow.

'X-rays,' he said. 'That time she twisted her ankle in Prague. We had it X-rayed. Do you have a bag for rubbish?'

I pointed to the one nearest the window. He dropped the envelope into it and turned back to pick up the travel pillow. 'I suppose I could use this, no?'

'Of course,' I said. 'The more you keep the better. I just thought you had gone through all this stuff?'

'No,' he said, rummaging inside a shoulder bag. 'Kornelia did it all.'

Now that her name was mentioned there was an opportunity for him to expound. But I sensed a weariness in him and I accepted it. He did not owe me an apology or an explanation.

'Would Naomi like these?' I pointed to a pile of fitness-related things – a Slendertone Abs Belt, a power ball, pieces from a dumb-bell set.

'Yes, I think she would. She said she might drop by tomorrow on her way into town for more shopping.' He was beginning to systematically look through the box nearest to him.

Naomi was a good ten years older than me. I had always looked up to her and she was generous, giving me time and encouraging my studies. Often I did things to impress her, feeling that she knew more than me, that she had an edge and access to privileges that were beyond my reach. If she was not who she was, down-to-earth, accessible, without malice, I would have envied the uncomplicated way she got on with her life, the sense of rootedness and belonging that was out of my grasp. I would even have envied her closeness to Tony. 'Will the boys come with her?' I asked him now.

'Not this time.' Tony adored his grandchildren. I had never seen him happier than when he was playing football with them in the back garden or taking them out for the day.

'Look,' he said, holding out a large baby doll dressed in a white christening dress. I had never seen it before. 'I bought it for her on eBay,' he said and smiled. 'Vintage 1960s. To substitute the one that got confiscated at the airport.'

'You knew that story too?'

'Yes, she told me she never got over it. It still made her angry. She had felt chuffed with herself, participating in the Olympic Games in Rome, coming home to a special welcome; instead they confiscate her new doll at the airport. So I got her to describe the doll and we went online together so that she could show me what it looked like. She didn't imagine I would actually buy one for her until it came in the post.' He tilted the doll and the eyelids with their thick lashes closed over the blue eyes. The hair was also plastic, shaped as if it were combed back. 'Do you want it, Natasha? She would have liked you to have it.'

He held it out for me and even as I took hold of one hard, chubby arm, I felt a stab of irrational dislike. A familiar envy. Yes, this was the baby my mother would rather have had, creamy pink with blue eyes, a child with blonde hair that she could comb straight and pat down, not me.

We worked together, Tony and I, until it became dark outside. We packed the two cars and headed into town, braving the Christmas rush. We made it in time to the charity shop before it closed. Buoyed by a sense of achievement we decided to go for a drink and a bite to eat. It was not easy to find two parking spots but we managed in the end. The road in front of the vodka bar was thronged with a farmers' market. Various stalls sold cheeses, organic vegetables and fish. It seemed like a long time before we were seated with a menu in our hands.

Near the end of the meal Tony said, 'Yesterday I went to my solicitor and changed my will. I had to because of how everything is different now. I've left the house to the two lads with Naomi as their executor in case they are not yet of age before my time comes. If I don't overstay my welcome and spend left, right and centre, there will be a bit of cash left over for you.'

The house had been in his name, never my mother's. I swallowed, thinking that the former playboy of Khartoum would indeed find himself spending left, right and centre, especially if Kornelia started to make demands.

'Thank you, Tony, for all you have done for me,' I said flatly, wishing that he would not want to be thanked. But he did. I saw it in the way he put down his knife and fork and sat back. I managed a few more sentences, a more genuine show of gratitude. Something was slipping away from me, an opportunity I had never acknowledged as such.

The next morning Tony went swimming at his gym and I read the Sunday papers. It was there, why shouldn't it be, pared down, words standing up thin on the page like spikes. *A twenty-one-year-old man is being held at a high-security area of Glasgow's Govan police station after officers raided a property near Brechin on Thursday. His arrest is understood to be related to downloading radical Islamist material.*

He should not have been downloading material. He was looking into weapons used for jihad. That's what he told me.

After lunch, Tony suggested we visit the Garden of Remembrance in Hazelhead. We walked around but the atmosphere was heavy, toxic. We did not stay long. 'I don't think I will come again,' he said when we got back into the car. And I felt the same way. He dropped me back at the house and stayed away most of the afternoon. It felt strange without my mother, as if the house was full of her and drained of her at the same time. It struck me for the first time as strange that we always went to Naomi's for Christmas dinner. Why didn't they come to us? It must have been a throwback to Tony's time in Khartoum. He would come for a short holiday and spend it at Naomi's house in Fraserburgh. Even after he married Mum and after they moved to Aberdeen, he kept the same habit. Perhaps Mum wasn't confident of pulling off a British Christmas dinner. Perhaps she didn't mind falling into his regular routine.

Naomi didn't drop by as promised and I was disappointed. I had always liked her because she was not presumptuous. She had a talent for accepting others as they were, on their own terms. Tony must have been like that in Khartoum – no wonder he was popular. When I went into the kitchen to make dinner, I overheard him talking to Naomi on the phone. I burnt the onions hearing him mention in the same breath Kornelia and Christmas in Fraserburgh.

'I don't want her to be there,' I said when he put the phone down. 'This is the first Christmas without Mum. It's not right.'

I had misjudged. His anger was swift, as if it had been building up all weekend. His voice rose sharp as a slap and everything he said was the truth, no exaggerations, no lies. 'Listen, you can't suddenly turn up and tell me what to do. I call you and you don't pick up, you don't get back to me. Where were you when your mother was in hospital, when she needed you, when I needed you? She was dying, for God's sake, and you just went on with your selfish life. I had to practically beg you to come up for the funeral. So now back off and let me do what I like.'

Early the next morning, I let myself out quietly and pushed my key through the letter box. My car was full of those things of my mother's I had decided to keep. When I stopped for petrol, the clock in the shop showed 5.50 a.m. I bought a new SIM card, a buttery and the new edition of *Classic Car*. I was going to visit Malak on the way. This was how I got through the night, thinking of her and her house and how good I had felt staying with her and Oz, like I was worth something and we were ringed by wider spaces, the past, the future, the Caucasus, the Grampians, my memories of Khartoum. It should not have ended, not in the way that it did. I had not been able to speak to her since the police took our phones. Now I wanted more news of Oz. And she always got up early to pray so I would not be disturbing her.

It was a little after dawn when I parked in front of her house. Without the snow, the fields and the house itself looked bleak. She came out of the front door or at least it seemed to be her. Her appearance was noticeably different. Hair straight as a helmet, pencil skirt, leather jacket, boots reaching her knees. It was as if she was dressed for a part – what part, I wasn't sure.

'I thought you were the taxi,' she said and explained that she was going to Glasgow for a few days.

I persuaded her to cancel the taxi booking and that I would give her a lift to the station. We went back indoors so that she could use the phone. I was grateful for those moments inside the house, to wander around and recharge myself. I was looking at the empty space on the wall where the sword had been, when she joined me. 'My great grandfather said that he got it back from the Russians. This is the sword Shamil wanted to fight with until it was shattered into pieces. The fact that it is whole represents the sacrifice he made. The other day when Oz was playing with it in the snow, he wasn't respecting it enough. He has – as I have – a heritage which is moral and thoughtful and merciful. Did he honour it? Or did he choose to go along with those who claim they're acting in the name of Islam and at the same time don't follow the principles of submission and restraint?'

I was taken aback. 'You don't believe he's guilty, do you?' Maybe she knew more than I did.

She tensed a little. 'He's involved. But I can't be sure. It's all moved online these days. You can do it all on a laptop – run a website, fundraise, send money abroad, post this and that. Search for whatever needs searching for. He's ruined his life; how will he ever get out of this?'

She was not asking me a question. She went on, 'Or I think "that little squirt ruined *my* life". Because I forget he is old, I forget that to the world he is a man. I keep going back to when he was little, when he was nine, fifteen. My memory mixes all these versions of him together. And I feel the same anger that I felt for him when he muddied his brand new trainers or went out without locking the front door. Then I shake myself, this isn't a prank … I keep going back over things he said, the way I brought him up. I don't believe it. Except that I remember one time. There was something on the radio about a suicide bomber and he said "cool".' She looked down to the ground.

I could imagine him breathing the word without smiling, without intending to shock. 'So what did you say to him?' I asked.

'I let it pass. We do that sometimes, we mums, we pretend not to hear.'

That stung. We mums. As if I would never find out, as if I would never be part of that group.

'We bury our heads in the sand,' she continued. 'Because we are busy or we can't be bothered to start an argument or because we can't keep tabs on every little thing. And they do pass, these fads and moods. They go through phases. He went through a phase, I remember, of believing all these conspiracy theories about 9/11 – that it wasn't Muslims that did it. I argued with him then, I talked him out of it, or at least I thought I did.'

I too had my misgivings about Oz. No situation at any given time is entirely new; the constraints and conversations are different, the fears are different, but still today is a ripple of former times, a version of what has been passed down. Supposing Oz was neither completely guilty nor completely innocent. Suppose he had done something wrong but that something might not be what he was arrested for, might not be what he would be punished for. And at the end of the day we would all accept what was happening. We would all have a rationale for it, a way of putting it into perspective.

I said, 'We should go. I don't want you to miss your train.'

She picked up the house keys. Her movements were a little nervous, her shoulders dropping. Despite the effort over her appearance, she looked the slightest bit gaunt, she looked her age. 'I've got an appointment with a London lawyer who specialises in terrorist arrests. He's coming up to Glasgow to meet me and talk to Oz. They haven't charged him with anything yet.'

It was when she started talking about Oz that I guessed the part she was dressed up for: activist mum campaigning for the release of her son.

I gave her my new mobile number, she gave me her house phone and the number of the hotel she was staying at in Glasgow. We would be in touch from now on. I drove slowly, wanting her company but unable to tell her about the last few days.

'I was in denial when he was first arrested,' she said. 'Then I told myself I have to help him in every way, every possible way. I have to get him out of this mess. I can't just sit back and cry. What good would it do? Yes, it's been a shock for me but it's not about me now, it's about him.'

Light was beginning to gather around us but below the clouds I could still see the full moon. It looked like a sun. 'I haven't spoken to him,' she said in reply to my question. 'They wouldn't let me. And they wouldn't let me take him anything. No change of clothes, no food, no nothing. I called his father in Cape Town.' She sounded breathless, maybe because she was speaking too fast. 'Instead of getting on the next plane, he says, "They might drag me into it and then what use would I be to him?" Can you believe it!'

Yes, I could believe it, but I kept my eyes on the road. She sighed and touched her forehead. 'So I'm on my own now in this. But I know people in London. I know people in the media and in human rights groups and I am not going to take this lying down.'

We were inside Montrose now, passing the caravan park, empty now, nothing like in the summer. She said, 'You don't look well, Natasha. You look like you haven't been sleeping properly.'

I told her about my flat and the nights in hotels. I told her why I couldn't stay with Tony any more.

'Come and stay with me,' she said. 'When I get back. I mean it.'

It touched me, this not unexpected invitation, but I would need somewhere closer to the university. I felt heavy with what I couldn't tell her – the mistakes I had made; my conversation with Iain, all the reports I had written on the 'vulnerable students'. I stopped the car in the parking bay of the train station. She undid her seat belt.

I wanted to tell her that the days I had spent with her and Oz were special. Days in which I needed neither drink nor medication. Days in which I liked myself – no, that was not what it was; it was days in which I was free of the burden of myself. Instead I blurted out, 'Malak, I've committed a sin.' Since when did I use such language! Gaynor's pro-life leaflet had hit me where it hurt.

She laughed and turned towards me, touched my arm. 'Only one? You're lucky.'

I pressed my lips together. The impulse to confess passed.

Her voice changed. 'Don't do it again.'

I looked at her dark eyes, not fierce like Shamil's, not as wise, not as profound, but still there was something weighty there, the smallest remnant of power, just for me. I asked her, 'Don't do what again?'

'What you believe is a sin. And don't even talk about it. Let it go. Many things in life are out of our control but our egos insist that they are leaders.' She stepped out of the car, the first rays of sun making her hair gleam. 'Better a sin that leaves us broken-hearted, than a virtuous act that puffs us up with pride,' she quoted. In this small Scottish station there were, directed at her, a few glances of surprise, glances of not quite admiration but an acknowledgement of that special quality she carried.

2. Dargo, the Caucasus, November 1854

In spite of the fog, she insisted on her regular walk on the roof. Exercise was the cure for her restlessness, the outdoors an escape from the smoky chimney, the sound of the wind banging the doors and windows. But today the mountains were not visible. Holding Alexander's hand, they could only see a few feet in front of them. Enough for a slower than usual walk, not too brisk, not like the other time when they ran a race. It made them feel as if they were entirely alone, in the kind of privacy they had been accustomed to in their life in Georgia and were now, as captives, deprived of.

The fog thinned and Anna could see the curved edges of dense clouds trapped between the lower peaks. Then all became grey again. We could be anywhere, she thought. This silvery blindness was a neutral surface she could impose her imagination on. The garden in Tsinondali, Alexander in his summer hat. She must talk to him about home so that he did not forget. She must talk to him about his father.

But Alexander could not be pinned down to the subject of home. He surprised her by asking, 'Is Baby Lydia in Heaven now?'

It had been a long time since he had mentioned his sister. 'Yes,' Anna replied. 'Yes she is.'

'Is she happy?'

'Yes, she is well and happy.' She squeezed her son's shoulder. When he looked up, she bent down and gave him a kiss. It was a comfort to her that, despite everything, *he* was well and happy. Her own hair was falling out; all she had to do was run her fingers through it for strands to loosen and fall. Dampness had crept into her chest so that she often coughed and wheezed through the night.

A heavy downpour the previous week had caused the courtyard to flood; all became mud and dirt, dankness a smell she couldn't shake off. Since Shamil's arrival, their food had increased but it continued to be unappetising and limited in variety.

'Imam Shamil said he would let me ride his horse tomorrow,' Alexander was saying. 'If the weather is good. He really said that. He promised.'

'Aren't you afraid of him?' She was a little. The stories his wives liked to recount of his mystical abilities made her nervous. At first she had mocked them saying, 'If he were so holy, he would bring my daughter back to me,' but the way he looked at her on the few times they met made her feel that he knew more than he should.

'Why should I be afraid of him? He gave me sweets today,' Alexander said. 'He gave all the children sweets. We had to stand in line. And I got extra because I was a guest.'

'Lucky you.' She meant it. Sometimes the craving for toffees and chocolates made her dizzy. At other times she desired nothing, her body arid and flat as paper. In the Eid al Adha oxen and sheep were slaughtered and there was enough meat for all. But the smell of the meat had made her crave wine and the feast did not feel like a feast without it.

Alexander said, 'When he is not speaking, he looks like a lion.'

'So you are afraid of him?' She could just make out the stairs, which meant they had come full circle. For the sake of variety, she switched sides with Alexander. He was now on her left.

'No I'm not. A lion who is very quiet. You almost think he's asleep.'

She smiled. 'When did you ever see a lion?'

'In a picture book.'

'Poor Alexander, you must miss all your books and toys.' She wanted him to talk about his playthings but he suddenly cried out because he had seen something that she couldn't. He let go of her hand and surged into the milky space ahead. The sound of an unfamiliar laugh as Shamil lifted him up off the ground. This is what Anna could see now. Shamil, with one arm, holding Alexander

181

up high. His hand supported her son's chest. Alexander lifted his arms out to the side, his legs straight out behind him. 'Look Mama, I'm flying like an eagle!' She caught the pleasure in his voice and laughed out loud as Shamil bent so that Alexander swooped down and Shamil twisted and moved so that Alexander, the eagle, veered left and right, weightless and free.

When he put him down, gently in case he was dizzy, Shamil took out of his pocket a few pieces of dried fruit and gave them to Alexander. He turned to her and said, his Russian words carefully chosen, his accent familiar to her, 'Would Anna Elinichna, Princess of Georgia, like some figs?'

She warmed to the way he addressed her. It had a meaning these days, in this place; it was necessary that who she was should be acknowledged. She liked figs too, but pride made her say, 'No, thank you.'

Alexander wandered off with his mouth full. The fog thinned; he spotted the sentry and walked towards him.

'Alexander and I have become friends,' Shamil said.

'Yes you have. In Georgia he used to hear that you eat Russian children.'

'Raw or cooked?'

She smiled. 'I am sure this particular rumour is untrue.'

'What else have you heard about me?'

'That you miraculously escaped more than once.' She started to walk and he fell in step with her.

'They are cumbersome and slow these Russians. Heavy-handed bombing, brute strength – that's what they're good at. But you are right. I escaped by the will of Allah Almighty; my abilities are not enough.'

'Did you really jump over a line of soldiers who surrounded you, slashed two with your sword...'

'Three,' he corrected her.

'...and then over a five-foot wall.'

'Seven.'

'With one leap?'

182

'I was young then. What else?'

She flushed, sensing that she had been praising him and he was enjoying it. 'That's all. Do you keep your word?'

'I do. And if my demands are met I will set you free.'

A coolness settled over her. He was reminding her of something she would rather have forgotten. But she was the one who had asked the question.

'Does Anna, Princess of Georgia not believe me?'

She turned to look at him, beard, turban, worn-out coat; no weapons. 'Yes, I believe you.'

'Nothing has caused me so much pain as treachery. If the Russians would fight me honourably, I would not mind living the rest of my life in a state of war. But they tricked me; in Akhulgo they treated me like a criminal, not a warrior, and they sent my son far away to St Petersburg.'

She could imagine how he must have felt. It was not difficult. 'My grandfather, George the twelfth, did not want to go to war. He did not want his children to live in a state of war. This is why he bequeathed Georgia to the tsar.'

'Is that what you've been told? He had first wanted protection from the tsar but instead Georgia was annexed.'

'For the sake of prosperity.'

'Are you sure?'

As a child her instinct had been repelled by the loss of the Georgian throne; Georgia distinctive, whole, should not be swallowed up. Her questions were at first received with indulgent sighs and then disapproval – it was unbecoming for a young princess to express dissatisfaction with the king's will. And so now she repeated to Shamil the answers she had received over the years. 'My grandfather believed in progress. Progress meant following Russia. It meant education in the European manner. It meant change for the better.'

'You do not sound convinced.'

'My husband is more European than me. He often remarks that I am too Georgian, too traditional.' She regretted the confidence immediately. It felt as if she had tripped.

He caught her in time. 'Here in Dargo, you are more modern than any of us.'

She stopped walking. 'I should not have said that about my husband. It was not my intention to sound disloyal.'

'You are not disloyal.'

She nodded and moved briskly away, stumbled in the mist, scraped her shoulders against the wall, until she found the stairs.

In the evening Ameena tiptoed into her room. Her ankle bracelets jingled, the kohl rimmed around her eyes made them wider. 'I will hide with you, Anna,' she said. She had a gleeful smile on her face. It made her look like a child set on a prank. She drew the door behind her but left a crack open, flounced down on the floor and peered out. Anna joined her. She could see the entrance to Ameena's room across the gallery. 'What's going on?'

'Shush,' giggled Ameena. 'Wait and see.'

Anna saw Shamil approach Ameena's room and knock on the door. Ameena shifted on her knees, breath held. Shamil stood in his long white coat, head bowed; he knocked again. Finding no response, he stood waiting at the door.

Anna whispered, 'Why doesn't he just walk in?' The key was visible in the lock.

Ameena breathed in to supress a laugh. 'He's waiting for me to let him in.'

Time passed and yet there was no expression of impatience on Shamil's face. He did not knock again on the door, he did not fidget or stamp his feet. Yet it must be cold to stand so still. Anna drew her shawl closer around her. She watch the breath come out of him like smoke.

'I'm going to keep him waiting and waiting.' Ameena's voice was a pitch higher. Would he hear her, would he sense her? If so, Anna would rather she was not with Ameena, giving the false impression that she was her accomplice. She moved away from the door and went back to where she had been sitting on a cushion on the floor. Chairs were one of the things she missed but it no longer hurt her thighs to sit on the floor. Not like when she had first arrived – the pins and needles, the stiffness in standing up again.

Ameena turned and beckoned. Anna quickly took up her position behind the door again. She saw Shamil turn the key of the room but instead of unlocking it and walking in, he locked it, put the key in his pocket and walked in the opposite direction.

Ameena groaned. She was now locked out of her own room.

The following morning Alexander insisted that she accompany him to the goodbye gathering in the courtyard. Shamil was riding out to battle or so Anna assumed. He could be going to inspect troops or visit other aouls but she did not want to ask. Ameena was indiscreet and often let slip the kind of military information Anna should not know about, but the others were tight-lipped, Chuanat out of fear for his safety, and the snippets Zeidat dropped were deliberately guaranteed to lower Anna's morale. 'We must stand in line to see him ride out,' Alexander insisted but Madame Drancy refused to budge and it was Anna now, shivering in the cold, who was crammed with the whole household, children, servants and an added group of eager beggars. The weather was brighter today and she could see all the way down to the successive stone walls that circled the aoul, each with its wide low entrance. The mountains beyond and all around were covered in snow, the sky a bluish grey in contrast.

Anna had woken up to a busy household. From the window, she watched Zeidat, with full concentration, saddling Shamil's horse as if she wanted to ride out herself, before walking off shouting at the servants for their tardy packing. In the meantime Shamil was indoors, spending a long time visiting the elderly Bahou in her room. When she shuffled with him to the door, Anna saw him kiss her hand one last time and ask for her blessings. Then he sat with his crippled daughter, Najdat, who was unwell, crooning to her and feeding her breakfast. Now in his long sheepskin coat, his scimitar held by a leather halter, a tall Circassian hat on top of his white turban, he carried his newborn baby and walked slowly in the windy courtyard bidding everyone goodbye and asking them to pray for his safety.

'I should not be here,' Anna thought but the delight on Alexander's face made her stay. Tugging at her hand, he was caught up in the thrill of the moment. Shamil's white Arabian stallion, now led from the stables, had a red bridle and a bright crimson blanket under the saddle. More horsemen gathered outside the gate. The canter and snorts of their horses filled the air. They carried banners and a few began to chant. The whole aoul, it seemed, was out and Anna felt nervous of the fervour that was building up. The repetition of *La ilaha illa Allah* rose up around her and even Alexander joined in. Later, when he kept on singing it, Madame Drancy, ever sensitive to religious differences, would scold him and in vain teach him *Cadet Roussel* as a substitute. But now Anna looked at his animated face and could not bring herself to censure him. To see him enjoying himself was enough and when they went home, she deliberately reassured herself, all this would become a childish memory.

Shamil, in what must be a farewell custom, handed out pieces of cotton cloth to the beggars and servants. He seemed reluctant to leave. The fervour of his men, the excitement of battle had not yet reached him. He was giving pieces of silk to his wives when Chuanat burst into tears. She took the baby from him and, overcome, had to be helped indoors by Ameena. Sweets for the children, and Shamil was now in front of them both. Anna could see the fringes of black fur around his collar and sleeves. He was more distant than he had been that day on the roof, but his sadness weighed him down and bobbed him towards her. Alexander was cheeky enough to demand his extra guest's ration.

'You are right, young prince,' said Shamil. 'I owe you two coloured creams instead of one.'

In imitation of the other children, Alexander bent and kissed his hand. Thank God Madame Drancy didn't see this, thought Anna. Shamil turned to her now, looked straight into her eyes. 'Anna

Elinichna, Princess of Georgia, I have no gift worthy of you. I am not a rich man.'

She remembered her rude refusal of the dried figs, opened her mouth but there was nothing to say.

'So instead I will send you a dream.'

Later she would wonder if she had heard him correctly. Later when she waited for the dream and rebuked herself for waiting for the dream and marvelled that she was waiting for a dream. Later she would doubt that she had heard him correctly. He must have meant something else, a weakness in his Russian, a misunderstanding. But she was almost sure he had said it. 'I will send you a dream.' And then it was all over immediately, the individual and collective farewells, the melancholy air, the mixture of anxiety and loss. He turned and leapt on his horse. The chanting rose like cheers. He gathered speed and cantered towards the gate. Joined now by the other men, he galloped towards the outskirts of the aoul. The portal was too low for him to ride through and yet he didn't slow down his pace. At the very last minute, to the thrill of the crowd, he pitched himself low over the horse's side. Once through the first portal, he stood up on the stirrups of the speeding horse, and again, this time with Alexander gripping her hand, swung himself to the side of the horse just in time to pass under the second entrance. The chants grew louder as the riders, crouching low over their saddles, followed him out of the aoul and into the distance of the lowlands.

'Madame Drancy, you certainly missed a show of equestrian skill today.' Anna was flushed from the cold. She stood by the fire rubbing her hands. Madame Drancy, bent over the *Imitation de Jesus-Christ*, looked up at her with tears in her eyes. 'If Imam Shamil dies in battle, we are completely lost.'

'What do you mean?'

'If he is killed, they will cut our throats. Zeidat said so.'

'To frighten you, I am sure.'

'I told her I would rather die than live here the rest of my life.'

'And what did she say to that?'

'She flew into a rage. But I am not afraid of her. If she wants me to despair, I will not.'

Anna felt the familiar soberness creep up on her, the duty to bolster Madame Drancy. 'You are right, we must not despair.' She sat down next to the governess. 'Tell me about your book. Have you been thinking more about it?'

Madame Drancy was planning to write about their kidnap and captivity. Sometimes when she could get hold of ink and paper, she scribbled down notes. But a carefully drawn map of the compound had been confiscated by Zeidat and there would have been dire consequences had not Chuanat intervened. 'It is always on my mind,' Drancy said. 'I am constantly recording all that I see and hear so that I don't forget. Remember that pit we saw when we went for our walk?'

It had been a large empty pit and they had speculated about its use.

A faint expression of glee crossed Madame Drancy's face. 'There is a woman in it now, a young woman with a baby in his cradle.'

'Whatever for?'

'She killed the murderer of her husband. Her punishment is to stay there for four months. After which she will be promptly married off.'

The marriages of widows was a subject that fascinated Madame Drancy. 'I have never been in such close proximity to a people so different from me. It is a marvel.'

A marvel. For a person to send another a dream would indeed be a marvel. Anna waited a day, a week. She slept better than she had ever slept before but in the morning there was nothing to remember, only fragments of sights and sounds, poor in quality, nothing wholly formed, nothing distinct.

Shamil's absence meant reduced rations at mealtimes, all of which were poorer quality. There was also no response to requests for an extra blanket or for a coat for Alexander when it started to snow. Shamil's absence meant longer visits from Chuanat and her baby, Ameena showing off her talent to sing, egging Drancy on for more

188

descriptions of Paris, insisting that Anna teach her the difference between the mazurka and the quadrille. His absence meant that when the sound of gunfire echoed around the mountains, Chuanat would cry, Drancy would cross herself and no one would want to talk. His absence meant no protection from Zeidat. She banged into the room one morning brandishing a copy of the *Russki Invalid*.

'Read this!' She pointed at a paragraph. It was an article about Queen Victoria granting sums of money to the Crimean War.

'See,' said Zeidat. 'This is proof that such big sums of money do exist. If the Empress of England can pay millions so can the Empress of Russia. You were her lady-in-waiting. She will pay if you ask her.'

Anna wondered if Zeidat was serious or merely bluffing. 'The empress will not be fooled into paying such exorbitant sums.'

'Well, your family can. Today I spoke to the mother of a man who has been to your estate in Tsinondali. Such riches and trees and gardens. With all this evidence I will put pressure on Shamil Imam to raise the ransom to sixty thousand roubles. And his naibs will support this. See if they won't!'

'Do you understand these figures you are talking about? No one has so much money.'

Zeidat stabbed the newspaper. 'It's right here.' She sat down cross-legged on the floor and lowered her voice into a whisper. 'Listen, Imam Shamil wants his son back but we've been hearing reports about Jamaleldin. What good is a man who drinks wine and dances with half-naked women? What kind of fighter will he be? I cannot say this to my husband but I am telling you now, woman to woman: what use would Jamaleldin be to us? I say better a larger ransom than such a son.'

Anna tried to hide her dismay, to sound calm and confident. 'My husband will not be able to raise sixty thousand roubles.'

Zeidat folded up the newspaper. 'You think I am an ignorant tribeswoman, don't you? You think I can't think and I don't know. But I do. Your husband married his sister off to none other than the Prince of Mingrelia – so tell me that you are poor!'

Anna sighed. 'The Prince of Mingrelia is an honorary title. It does not mean he is wealthy. You might find this hard to believe but I am telling you the truth.'

'The truth,' Zeidat snorted. 'The truth is your husband is not eager to have you back. Unlike you, he is completely Westernised. He has acquired all these Russian tastes and you were unable to keep up with him.'

'How dare you talk about my private life!' She stood up. 'Get out of here. At once.'

It worked. Zeidat did leave the room and later Ameena tossed the words out in passing, as if they were not poison, as if they did not turn the day inside out, 'She's jealous of you. That's why. She knows what's on Shamil Imam's mind. If the ransom isn't paid, he will keep you for himself.'

She dreams of Georgia. All of it. Its Alazani river, gardens, Tsinondali. Riches spread before her. Vines, grass plateaus, forests. She can see it all because she sits on a cloud. It is comfortable, voluptuous. She hovers over this beauty knowing that she is part of it. She dangles her feet, she rolls. She moves her body without the fear of falling. One time running her fingers through the river, one time picking up a flower with her toes. The cloud holds her up with the most gentle of pressure. It responds to her desire to rise or move. Time passes and there is only more to enjoy, more to look at. The silver, blue, grey, cream colours of the water, the breath of air. There can be no doubt. Only Georgia smells like this, feels like this, has these shapes and sounds and tones. Her presence here is enough, without language or tasks or aspirations. Without hunger. Only harmony. Only light. Time passes as it would for a child. Everything is close, larger, infinitely interesting. Jasmine, fruit, fish. There is no gap between herself and her surroundings. The fibres of her body, her skin, her pulse, her blood spring from this water and soil. It is the longest dream she has ever had.

When he came back, she wanted to thank him but did not get the chance. He was superficially wounded but many of the other fighters were in a more serious condition. The hushed atmosphere of the aoul, the intermittent wailing from families who had lost lives, the darkening of Zeidat's face could only mean that the battle had not gone well. 'Their loss, our gain,' Madame Drancy whispered and Anna wished it was as simple as that. Was anyone really winning? *Yours kill ours – ours kill yours.* What would it take to raise the white flag of peace? Madame Drancy was keeping a close watch over the dates. Unless she had miscalculated, Christmas Day was next week.

Ameena was unlike herself. She no longer played with the children. Anna tried to cajole her. 'What's wrong? You have not sung to us for a long time. Nor are you climbing to the roof or playing with Alexander.'

'Shamil offered me my freedom,' she said. 'A divorce. This is because I told him I was not happy. I told him I would rather be with someone my age.'

Anna was taken aback. 'He must have been furious.'

'No,' Ameena said. 'He was very gentle. We've been married for four years and still no children. He said I could go back to my tribe but I really don't want to go away. I want to stay here in Dargo.'

The arrival of Ghazi Muhammad brought more cheer to the household. Anna had disliked him when they first met at Polahi but now she was ready to reconsider. Arms were fired in his honour, the villagers vied to kiss his hand and he strode into the house full of smiles. His grandmother, sisters and stepmothers were all eager to see him and there was much coming and going, gifts shown off and special meals cooked. The marks on Ghazi's face that had given him a rough appearance were scars from the pox. He might have resembled Shamil physically but his disposition was considerably jollier. Like his father too, Ghazi had a talent for winning the affection of children. Alexander was soon following him around. One clear afternoon, he dragged Anna off to watch Ghazi give the youth a fencing lesson. Soon, Shamil joined them and stood next to Anna, watching the young men.

At last she had the opportunity to say it. 'Thank you for the gift.'
'The gift?'

The clink of sabre against sabre and her face started to go hot. He had forgotten? She had conjured it all herself? And now to explain by saying, 'Thank you for the dream,' would be utter folly.

'Ah,' he had remembered. 'A throne for Anna to sit on.'

Relief made her limbs loose, the start of a laugh in her throat. 'Oh no, it was a cloud.'

He heard her but did not hear her. Instead he turned his back to the lesson. Eyes to eyes, like a pledge. He said, 'The throne of Georgia is for you. We defeat the Russians and then there would be justice. What they have taken would come back to us. And you too would be lifted up high. To become Anna Elinichna, Queen of Georgia.'

She felt herself fall, even though she remained standing. Alexander thrusting his body in imitation of Ghazi, the sunny shine of steel, the snow-capped mountains – all folded back like a curtain and there was only a glittering darkness. He had excavated an ambition from deep down. He had picked out one nebulous desire and given it a name. The throne back to Georgia, as it should be. Georgia, free and autonomous, as it should be. And she would be the one to make this happen. She would be worthy of it. Anna Elinichna, Queen of Georgia. She could feel Shamil place the crown on her head – the weight of one hundred and forty-five diamonds, fifty-eight rubies, twenty-four emeralds. Russia was losing the Crimean War, he explained. Soon, the Allies would take over the Black Sea Coast and drive the Russians out of Georgia. The throne would be restored.

She should know better. There was another name for this kind of talk and these kinds of alliances. Treason. For centuries Georgia was a Christian nation at the mercy of its aggressive neighbours, the Persians and the Ottomans who were, like him, Muslim. She should know better than to trust him.

3. St Petersburg, January 1855

Jamaleldin sat by the tsar's bedside. The figure on the bed was wasted, eyes sunken into dark sockets, wisps of white hair on the satin pillow. Jamaleldin had been told that Emperor Nicholas was ill, possibly dying, but it was still a shock to see the alteration, this accelerated aging, said to be exacerbated by the bad reports coming from the Crimea. The familiar scent of the tsar's eau de cologne struggled to mask the odours of a sick room. Jamaleldin wished he was somewhere else. He needed fresh air and brightness.

With tremendous effort, Nicholas was telling Jamaleldin the story of the kidnapping. He was croaking it out as if his health depended upon it. Jamaleldin, who already knew the details, flinched at every mention of his father's name. The tsar's attendants and nurses glanced at their patient from time to time, followed the inflection of his voice for signs of agitation or deterioration. He was a vulnerable man, at the mercy of bad news from the front. The war he had passionately believed in had played out in such a way that the admiral of the British ship that reached Kronstadt was boasting that, come May, he would be toasting Queen Victoria's birthday in the Winter Palace. Nicholas raised his head and attempted to sit up higher. The nurse rushed to rearrange the pillows. Jamaleldin moved, pressing his back against the chair.

'David Chavchavadze came to see me,' Nicholas said. 'He is mortgaging his estate to pay for the ransom. But the ransom is not enough. Shamil wants you. I told David I cannot order you to make such a sacrifice. It is too much.'

Jamaleldin said, 'I was not given a choice when I came here. I do not have a choice now.'

Nicholas's fingers grabbed at the sheets. He tossed his head impatiently from side to side and moaned. 'Show more gratitude. It took David a long time to approach me. He knows how dear you are to me. He did try to rescue his family but failed.'

Jamaleldin felt conscious of his well-shined boots, his leather gloves that lay across his knees. The distance between him and Nicholas was growing. There was a time when it had all been much simpler. He rescued from the wild, Nicholas the benevolent godfather. He the pet, Nicholas the mighty. He the puppet, Nicholas the conductor, the thrower of crumbs, the arranger of roles, the changer of destinies. Jamaleldin the chess piece, and now Shamil had changed the rules of the game.

'Sire,' Jamaleldin said, wanting more than anything to stretch his legs, to run down the stairs. 'I will not shy away from my duty.'

The tsar raised his hand. 'You do not have to give me your decision now. Go away and reflect on the sacrifice that is asked of you. I will give you two days.'

To reflect – was that to realise that he would not be entering the military academy, that he would never serve on the staff, that in terms of his career in the Russian army this was the end? Or to reflect that if he did not buy an atlas and take it with him, he would never see one again? Or to attend the ballet one last time, really the very last time? Or alternatively to think "I will see Ghazi again" and laugh out loud in a rush of elation? Or to reflect that if he fell ill in Dargo, there would be nothing but herbal concoctions and superstition? But these recent pangs of hunger to hug his little brother again – how else could they be subdued? No, he did not want two days to reflect. He could not visit this sick bed again.

Jamaleldin fell to his knees. 'There is only one right thing to do. I will use the two days to prepare for the journey and say my goodbyes.'

The tsar blessed him and gave him a parting gift, words to keep hearing in the mountains. 'Never forget that I made you a civilised man.'

He walked down the stairway, of course, he did not run. The

palace was gloomy; for some time now there had been no balls, no receptions, just echoes of better days. Near the archway, Jamaleldin had a sudden memory of Anna. Ever since he had heard the news, he had searched his mind for a recollection of her, sure that he must have met her at one point. Now her face and figure slotted into place under this particular chandelier. Slightly older than him, too beautiful to be considered dowdy, but still the provincial had cast a pall over her. He had danced the mazurka with her once and found her distracted, a little awkward, not Russian enough. She did not fit in and this had lowered her instinctively in his estimation. Perhaps she reminded him of himself, perhaps in his competitive desire for court approval he surmised that her acquaintance could not be an asset. And now, exponentially, she would be his downfall. But blaming her was hardly chivalrous, let alone logical. His father. This was all about his father. His father's love had done all this. But what took you so long? Why not after six months or a year or even two, when I stayed up at night listening out for your men's footsteps then cried myself to sleep. Before I forgot your language.

Once in his first week at the *Kadetsky Corpus*, on a particularly windy night, the branches of the tree kept tapping on the dorm window. Jamaleldin had imagined it as a code. He crept out of bed and crouched by the window. 'Younis,' he had whispered and then in the Avar language, 'Is it you?' until the cold sense of his foolishness sent him back between the sheets to dream of the last highlander he had seen, the teacher who gingerly made his way down the mountains, passed the Russian lines and visited him in the garrison at Akhulgo, to lead him in prayer and continue with the Qur'an lessons. Younis, who left one day saying, 'We will continue tomorrow insh'Allah', but by tomorrow Jamaleldin was on his way to Moscow, without ever saying a proper goodbye. At cadet school the following day, hardened and grateful that no one had seen or heard him talking to a window, he plunged into the race to prove himself. No time to be homesick, no time for memories. So why now, after all these years? Because Anna Chavchavadze had not heeded the military governor's warning and stayed in Tiflis. Or because, when the raiders came, she didn't escape to the woods in time. Or because, as his father would no doubt say, it was Allah's will and nothing could be done to change it.

Jamaleldin packed his drawing materials, he packed books and what he reckoned he would not find in Dargo, what people carried from civilisation to the back of beyond. A clock, a globe, a music box. The tsar signed a travel order, a small group of Cossacks of the imperial escort were gathered, a troika with a bearskin rug was prepared and Jamaleldin sat in it. The journey south, via Moscow, took him along the river Don. When the Caucasus came into view, the awe he felt was mixed with oppression. The peaks were higher than he remembered, barren, stony. The troika, rendered fragile by the landscape, was exchanged for a tarantass. On and on, he travelled. It took a month to reach Vladikavkaz. There David Chavchavadze was waiting to meet him and say, 'I cannot thank you enough.'

Jamaleldin noticed the anxiety and pain on the prince's face. He was tall and rangy, too direct to be clumsy and too socially aware to be deep. Ironically he had recently been awarded the Order of St Anna and raised to the rank of colonel for his heroic defence of the river forts against Shamil's invading army. That very same invasion which had carried off his family and killed his daughter. Entering David's solicitous care and companionship, Jamaleldin could not help but think that it was only these peculiar circumstances that had thrown them together. Ordinarily he would not merit the prince's attention or presume upon his time.

During a walk by the Terek river, David updated him on the negotiation process. He said, 'Your father has been informed that you are on the way.' Six months since the princess was kidnapped, one month on the journey and five in Dargo. 'She is suffering,' David said and Jamaleldin did not want to hear the details, did not want to dwell on the spot she would be giving up for him.

In the evening a dinner at the commanding officer's house was arranged in Jamaleldin's honour. Thirty ladies and gentlemen, lulled by the monotony of this outpost, deprived of the pleasures of the metropolis, seized on the diversion of Jamaleldin's arrival. They were curious too and he sensed the hush when he and David walked into the drawing room, noticed the plump red-headed woman who turned away from the window. Soft introductions and then time to walk into dinner where instead of sitting on the far end of the table with the other young aides-de-camp and officials, he was seated in the middle of the long side. Prince David was across from him. Next to David was the wife of a general, a tall, heavily bejewelled woman. Jamaleldin took note of all that was to pass away: the footmen in their livery, the silver tureen and the shifting breasts of the red-headed woman inches away from his left elbow.

The conversation looped reluctantly around the tsar's health, the further bad news from the Crimea, until the general launched into a first-hand description of Hadji Murat's defection in 1851, lauding the highlander's courage and humanity. It must have been a story he had told often before or it was familiar enough to his audience, because no one paid much attention. It was only when Jamaleldin spoke out that everyone turned and gave him their full attention.

'After failing in a mission, Hadji Murat was removed from office by my father, who also publicly forgave him. Instead of accepting this decree, however, Hadji Murat defected. This show of ingratitude brought down on him the charge of apostasy.'

'An unfair charge,' said the general, moustache bristling. 'Everyone who was with him could see that Hadji Murat was fastidious in performing his prayers. He did not give up his religion.'

'A pragmatic man then,' said Prince David. 'An opportunist who shifted his alliances when necessary.'

The general launched into an account of Hadji Murat's unfortunate demise and Jamaleldin wished he hadn't spoken out. He was able to give them extra information, the view from Shamil's side, but they preferred their own speculations and opinions. They knew best. Jamaleldin turned to the lovely lady next to him and whispered, 'I am a condemned man. But it is worth it for the pleasure of sitting next to you.'

She smiled and put down her knife and fork, turned to him with shining eyes. 'I have never met anyone as self-sacrificing as you. Never.'

He decided to push further. 'To spend my last days of liberty in company such as yours will help me bear more stoically my impending return to the wilds. Would you deny a dying man a drink of water?'

She was visibly moved but prevented from answering by Prince David, who stood up to propose a toast. He cleared his throat and said, 'My joy at the prospect of regaining my family is only matched by the anguish I feel on behalf of my deliverer, our guest tonight. I have only known him a very short time but I can confirm to you all that I have never seen a Muslim with so little of the Tartar about him. A young man whose opinions and manners are completely and truly Russian!'

While the toast was being drunk, Jamaleldin felt queasy at the praise that was not praise, the compliments that were intended as compliments but settled inside him like stones. What a freak he was! Better to focus on the luscious lady whose hair was the colour of autumn and whose loneliness, her lieutenant husband being away on duty, was a distracting temptation. Coffee in the drawing room, a seat at the card table. Jamaleldin added a pack of cards to his list of things that must accompany him to Dargo. He sucked on a cigar, knowing his father had outlawed smoking in all of his territories.

There were more of such dinners as he continued on his journey south accompanied by David. The garrisons on the Georgian Military Highway all the way to Tiflis threw parties in his honour. It was as if every officer stationed in the Caucasus wanted to meet him, every young woman wanted to dance with him, and every matron wanted to indulge in sentimental tears over his 'sacrifice'. Jamaleldin, the deliverer, the hero, worthy of toasts and curiosity. And always by his side the watchful and grateful David Chavchavadze, too cautious to indulge in premature celebration, patiently tolerating and certainly not impeding what had turned into a spectacle, the procession of a champion, the last free frolics of the sacrificial lamb.

In Khasavyurt, at the frontier of Shamil's territory, a ball was held in Jamaleldin's honour. The opportunity to show off his dancing skills, his manly elegance and his natural handsomeness inherited from 'he who must not be named'. By that time he had perfected his lines with young debutantes and bored army wives, with blondes and dark-haired Georgians, with seasoned beauties and those hovering on the edges of style. 'Would you deny a condemned man a drink of water?' He spun around the room with a Marta or a Maia or was she a Vardo? Marta, Maia or Vardo had full rosy cheeks, so large and firm that he wondered if they obscured her vision. Another turn and he noticed a movement in the window, the sway of the bushes and what could be a flash of cloth.

At the end of the dance, he excused himself and went to investigate. In the cold moonlit February evening, the sound of music and conversation followed him. He felt heady with a sense that he had done this before, he had seen something through a window, someone who beckoned to him, someone who wanted him. He moved around the building, approached the same twitching bushes he had seen from inside, wished that his progress was not so noisy. Spurs on the path, the swish sound made by moving his arm, the thud of his boots. A movement ahead of him. There was definitely someone there. In the splash of moonlight he could see that there were even two. They speeded up and he surged forward in pursuit, circling them so that instead of the forest, they were forced to head to the garrison wall.

No sounds from them, not a whisper. Their soft, soft steps in the leather slip-ons. He could see them clearly now and his heart skipped a beat. The two men of his dreams, their turbans, the folds of their cherkesskas, their sabres hung in a halter-neck. Before they reached the wall, before, as he knew, they would deftly climb up and over it, he called out. 'Younis!' The word was heavy in his mouth. He had said this before and now it was time to say it louder again, summon the old language and give painful birth to it. 'Younis. Is it you?'

The older of the men stopped and turned around. The other one stayed by the wall. The older man came forward. His breath was heaving, beads of sweat between the bushy eyebrows, eyes scanning the background to check that there was no one else. 'Jamaleldin?'

They had come for him at last. His father had sent them and here they were. A flood of Avar but he could understand this hug from Younis, this kissing of his shoulder. Embraces that pressed his body and hurt as if he were fragile. The other man, a youth, approached open-mouthed, then kept his distance.

'Your father sent us to check that it was really you. That the Russians weren't tricking us.' Younis had hardly changed over the years. Only more white in his beard, more fatigue in the lines of his face, a thickness in his bearing, but the same voice, the same manners. More kisses. 'Oh, he would be happy. Oh, I would say that I touched you too!' He was talking to himself, 'It's him, it's him. Subhan Allah. I was sure of it as soon as I saw him.' More squeezing of his arms, tugging of his hair, pinching of his cheeks. 'Look at you! Look at you all grown up. Praise be to the Almighty. Subhan Allah.'

Jamaleldin was floating, he felt drunk. With wine, yes, but also with this apparition, this dream come true. Was he speaking Avar or just understanding or both? Or laughing like a simpleton? The youth, Younis explained, was his nephew Mikail. 'I taught him the Qur'an like I taught you.' He gestured for Mikail to come forward. The youth obeyed but his expression was sullen. He was held back by the Russian uniform, repulsed by the imam's son they had just seen dancing with a woman in his arms. He did not utter a single word of greeting.

For an instant, Jamaleldin's sense of superiority flared. Who was this boorish highlander to disrespect him? An air of forest and swamp came from Mikail, the smear of mud where he had pressed his forehead on the ground, those nostrils flaring like an animal.

'We must go now,' Younis said. 'There are others. You will see them soon. They are in charge of the negotiations. I am here tonight only because Shamil Imam specifically wanted someone who knew you from when you were young.'

He embraced Jamaleldin one last time and the magic returned, the dream come true. 'We must go. Our work is done.'

The two stole back into the night. Unlike in the dream, they must leave him behind. He stood watching them leave; he kept standing even after he couldn't see them any more. The moon disappeared behind a cloud, the shadows shifted. He could hear frogs and from further away the howl of a wolf. A powder puff of snow blew from the mountains. The cold seeped through his uniform. Unbearable to return to the ball; this starlight was enough.

His father had sent spies who watched him through the window. What were they saying about him now?

'Do we report, Uncle, the wine drinking and the dancing?'

'We report.'

'And Shamil Imam cuts our tongues off?'

'Fool. He will order us to pray for his soul.'

'He's not one of us. Russian, I swear. Can't see any difference between him and an infidel.'

'Mikhail, I will be the one to cut your tongue out if you say this again.'

VII
Homesickness Is Our Guide

1. Scotland, December 2010

First semester examinations began that week and brought more normality. I found the daily routine of invigilation soothing and welcomed the concentration needed to start marking students' papers. My colleagues, busy themselves, oscillated between sincere shows of solidarity against last week's police search of my office and the natural instinct to keep their distance. I wanted nothing more than to pretend that everything was normal. In the staff room I found a stash of pro-life leaflets, identical to the one put on my desk. Fiona Ingram said they had been left there by a pro-life student and distributed to all the classrooms. She showed me Gaynor Stead's paper, which she had been marking. She had tried, she said with a straight face, but could not give her more than a four out of twenty. Last year I had given her a zero. 'That girl does not belong in a university,' I said and Fiona sighed because she did wish all her students well. The news that another of my papers had been accepted for publication (with only minor revisions) arrived as a much-needed boost to my confidence. Iain was pleased but it did not stop him from saying, 'Let me have that report on Oz Raja by the end of the week, latest.' This was the moment I should have said no. This was a chance to back out, but now that things were settling, I did not want to rock the boat.

Wheels were set in motion for the needed repairs to my flat and for the insurance payment to kick in. The workmen would only come after the New Year and I had to face the task of finding a temporary place to stay. Luckily, Fiona knew an elderly couple willing to take in a lodger. I drove out to visit them. The room was small but sunny and I would not have to share a bathroom. I agreed to take it straight away and was disappointed when they said I could only move in after the holidays as they had family members spending Christmas with them. They were happy, though, for me to move some of my things in and this eased my situation a little.

In the hotel, I stayed up marking exam papers and putting off writing the report about Oz. I brooded over where I would spend Christmas. Put up with Kornelia in Fraserburgh or try, at this late stage, to find an alternative? All my friends had other arrangements and to impose on them would entail a fee of confiding my latest troubles. Now that I had my mum's laptop, I surfed for last-minute Christmas travel deals and considered what I could afford of sunshine and seafood. There was still also my urge to visit the Caucasus. In the museum in Makhachkala I would be able to see Shamil's saddle covered in crimson velvet and the medals sent to him by the Ottomans. He never wore any but he gave them to his naibs to signify their rank. For a long time I gazed at pictures of the mountains and the Caspian Sea but I was unable to commit to anything.

On Wednesday I found myself invigilating a class in which Gaynor sat next to Oz's friend, the girl in hijab, whose name I never learnt because I had never taught her. Gaynor was diligently writing away, her greasy hair falling over the paper, blocking the light necessary for her to write in. She was her own worst enemy. She looked up suddenly and caught my gaze; it made me nervous. I turned away and walked to the back of the room.

We were only halfway through the allotted time and Oz's friend had her head on the table. She had pushed her paper to the side and laid her cheek on the desk. Her eyes were closed. I went up to her. 'Are you all right?'

'I have a bad headache,' she said, looking up. 'I can't focus.'

'Do you want to go out for a short break?'

There were dark shadows under her eyes. 'I'd rather stay here and rest a bit more. Maybe I will be okay in a few minutes.'

I could hear Gaynor behind me starting to mutter. We were

disturbing her. She might complain about me afterwards. It would be like her to do so.

'Let me know if you need to leave the room,' I said to the girl. 'Raise your hand.' I would then have to call the Registry to send in an escort to supervise her until she returned.

Thursday was only a week since Oz's arrest, though it felt like a month. I started to feel uneasy that I had not yet written the report. I met the girl as I came in through the car park. 'Feeling better?'

She smiled. 'Yes, fine. Exam tension, I suppose.'

I started to walk away when she said, 'Do you have any news about Oz?'

I repeated what Malak had told me but it did not seem new to her.

'He missed the exams.' This was said in such a poignant tone as if it alone underlined the seriousness of his predicament.

'He can resit them,' I reassured her.

'The police questioned me,' she said. 'They questioned all of his friends.' She told me the details, speaking in a matter-of-fact way as if she was neither intimidated nor surprised. But her voice hardened when she said, 'My parents told me to unfriend him on Facebook and not even to try to get in touch.'

'They're concerned about you.'

She rolled her eyes.

It was gratifying that she was open with me. 'Was Oz very active in the Muslim Students' Society?'

'Not really. He's different from everyone else.'

'In what way?'

'The way he was brought up. His mother's an actor and for a lot in the MSS that's not how a good Muslim woman should be. I remember, once, an invited speaker came to give a talk and afterwards Oz was one of those who took him back to the station. Apparently he spent the whole ride telling Oz that it was his duty as a son to convince his mother to quit her job! He got to him so much that he was almost crying.'

I could imagine the scene, the packed car, shoulder to shoulder and knee to knee. The colour rising to Oz's face, the clenched fists. 'But Oz and his mother are descended from Imam Shamil. Surely that counts.'

She gave a little laugh. 'Not to that lot. They hate the Sufis.'

She was putting it bluntly. Theologically, Sufism's veneration of its saints and the belief in their mystical powers was problematic. In modern times as Political Islam embraced transnationalism and activism, the Sufis were perceived to be not only passive and traditional, but often, also, reactionary and neo-cons.

'That speaker shouldn't have been invited in the first place,' she was saying. 'He's on some list or other.'

'What was his talk about?'

She made a face. 'I don't know. I arrived late, slipped into the first free seat on the front row and he suddenly stops talking and says to me, 'Move to the back with the other sisters.' It was so embarrassing. Everyone turned to look at me. I hadn't even noticed that the seating was segregated! I felt like an idiot so I just got up and left. But he's not going to say anything controversial in a lecture hall, is he? They save that kind of thing for private meetings in peoples' homes.'

'Could Oz have gone to such a meeting?'

'Maybe. Do you think that's why he's in trouble? But why him? There are others.'

Perhaps he did something rash as a way of showing off, just because he was keen to fit in, to prove himself. He had struck me as being proud of Shamil, deeply loyal to Malak. Still, I knew that ache to belong. When you're young, it could drag you against your better judgement.

I wrote the report that night. I could not put it off any further. On Friday morning I dithered before emailing it to Iain. Three hours later I clicked the send button. Then I waited for something to happen. I wanted something to happen. A penalty. Not this silence. Sometimes we do get what we want. My mobile phone rang. It was Grusha from Sudan. I had previously texted her so that we would stay in touch. Although she said the same thing she had said before – 'Your father is getting worse. Can you come and see him?' – this time I answered differently. I said yes, I would be there as soon as I could.

My request for compassionate leave was granted. Now that Iain had his report he inclined towards generosity. There was one more week to go before the holidays. Fiona would take over my hours of invigilation. As always, because her output was poor, he threw every extra administrative and teaching task onto her.

I was just heading out for lunch when I found a voicemail message. 'Natasha, it's Malak. I'm back home, not in Glasgow. Oz was released yesterday. We're home now. He's not talking to me. He's not leaving his room. He won't eat . . . I don't know what to do. Can you come over? Maybe he'll talk to you.'

I drove to Brechin straight away. I still had time before I needed to catch the overnight train to London. I was lucky with the traffic. Oz was innocent and that made me smile to myself. I had sensed the relief in Malak's voice despite the concern. The countryside was still covered in snow. It ceased to amaze and was now part of the landscape as if it had always been there. I counted the days Oz had been held – eleven. They must have felt longer to him.

Malak opened the door. She was pleased to see me and her warm welcome lifted my spirit. 'It took you no time to get here,' she said. 'Easy and smooth.' This house had cause for celebration but she spoke in hushed tones, as if there was someone ill inside.

'We came back yesterday,' she explained. 'I hired a car because he refused to take the train. He said he didn't want to be around people. All the way in the car, he lay in the back seat. He wouldn't speak to me. He said he wanted to sleep but I could tell he wasn't asleep. I could tell he was just tense, staring in the dark. I put on the radio and he shouted at me to turn it off. Rudely. Not like himself at all. Then when we came back, he wouldn't eat dinner. He wouldn't shower. He just went to his room and stayed there. I knock, he doesn't answer. But he is there. I hear him moving around. I eavesdropped.' She ran her hand through her hair. She looked like she too hadn't slept well.

'You have to look after yourself,' I said to her. 'How can you take care of him, if you are in a state?'

She shook her head. 'I need to take the rented car back into town. And the day after tomorrow I have to fly to London to record a radio play. How am I going to leave him like this?'

'He's had a bad experience. Give him time. Why don't you grab yourself a bite to eat and I'll stay here while you take the car back into town.'

'Thank you, Natasha. I'll pick up a few groceries for him too.'

I left her in the kitchen and went upstairs. I knocked on the door of his room. 'Oz, it's me, Natasha.'

There was no sound from inside. Perhaps he was asleep. I stood at the door not sure what to do next. Then I heard him moving, getting up from the bed, walking around. I knocked again. 'Oz, I know you're not feeling well. But do you think you're up to coming downstairs and lying down on the sofa for a bit? I'll wait for you downstairs. Your mum is just going into town for a bit.'

In the sitting room, I sat staring at the empty space on the wall where Shamil's sword had been. The sun shone at an acute angle low in the sky. A flash of brilliance before the early darkness.

Oz came down in his pyjamas, wrapped in a blanket. Unshaven, his hair greasy, streaks of dark skin under his eyes. He sat on the sofa, drew his feet up underneath him and bunched up under the blanket. He lowered his head.

I told him about my father being ill and how I was going to Sudan. I spoke about the weather. He listened to me or at least to my voice. He emitted anger and some bewilderment.

When he finally spoke, he said, 'I'm not going back to uni. If that's why you're here.'

It seemed an odd thing to say. I chose my words carefully. 'There is no rush to go back to uni. You've missed the first week of the exams and I wouldn't advise you to try and sit for the second week.

What you would need to do is fill out an Extenuating Circumstances form—'

'Extenuating circumstances!' He looked straight at me for the first time and gave a forced laugh. 'Oh yes, I was just pulled in for a whole ten days of fucking questions. One stupid question after another. They locked me up in a tiny room. I couldn't even sleep. They were watching me every single minute of the day, writing things down, every little thing I said or did...' He stopped abruptly and looked out of the window. A bird had flown past and made him nervous.

'What sort of questions did they ask you?'

'Don't you start asking me questions! That's what Malak was doing and I can't stand it. One question after the other. What did they feed you? What did they say? What did you do to make them suspicious? I don't want to answer any more questions. Enough.' He put his head back on his bunched-up knees.

'You are out now,' I said. 'They've released you without charge. This is excellent.' I tried to sound pleased or at least grateful. The room was getting darker.

He spoke without looking up and his voice was muffled. 'I shouldn't have been there in the first place.'

'You've had a terrible experience. In time you will get over it. A few weeks' rest and recuperation is what you need. You can even take the next semester off. Why not? Just start the new academic year fresh in September.'

He shook his head, threw the blanket on the floor and stood up. 'I'm not going back there.' He headed towards the kitchen. I heard him rummaging in the fridge then slamming shut the door of the microwave. 'Good,' I thought. 'At least he is starting to eat.'

I drew the curtains and switched on the lights. These were the shortest days of the year.

2. London, December 2010

I went to the Sudanese Embassy to get a visa. My Sudanese passport had expired years ago and I never renewed it. I actually didn't even know where it was. Lost over the years. In one move or the other. In it my name was Natasha Hussein. But on everything else – my British passport, my Russian passport, my driving licence, PhD – I had a different surname. In the spatial details of the embassy, in its hue, tones and pace my planned destination started to take shape. Men who spoke like my father, a woman in a tobe coming in to renew her passport, pictures of the Nile on the wall, younger versions of Tony waiting to collect their visas. A certain casualness, a slower tempo, a difference that made me, for the first time, excited to be travelling.

'Your visa will take four to six weeks.'

I was taken aback. 'But I need to go now. My father is seriously ill.'

'Are you Sudanese?'

Why ask such a difficult question?

'When was the last time you were there?'

'Twenty years ago.'

I also, they said, needed a sponsor. On Cleveland Row, I called Grusha. She told me not to worry. She said that Yasha could pull a few strings for me at my end. I was to fill out the form and wait a few days in London.

In my hotel room I surfed for news of Oz's release without charge. His arrest had been a news item; would his release also be one? There was nothing among the snow warnings, cancelled flights and delayed trains. I had been lucky to get here. Instead a news item from Sudan caught my eye, a video posted on YouTube of a woman being whipped by the police. She is unrestrained in her cries, pleading and shuffling on her knees, raising her arms uselessly to obstruct the blows. A small crowd watches. The scene is slow and saturated in humiliation, a world removed from valour or decency. The policeman is laughing at this vocal plaything rolling on the ground; the sun shines on his blue uniform and on the white of a nearby parked car. I don't want to go there.

I spent the following day at the National Archives among the correspondence of the Foreign Office. Here was the response of the British ambassador in Turkey to the news of the kidnapping: 'Shamil is a fanatic and a barbarian with whom it would be difficult for us ... to entertain any credible or satisfactory relations.' Lord Clarendon, the foreign secretary, certainly agreed, calling it an 'atrocious and revolting outrage'. This was the end of British support for Shamil. His reputation, strong in the previous decades, was shattered. The admiration he had roused after Akhulgo turned to disgust. Did he guess this would happen? Did he care? Or was Jamaleldin more important to him? I might never know.

As I left the archives, I 'heard' my mother talk about shopping. She had loved London, loved Harrods. And now the city went on without her. Of course it did. The whole world had. On Oxford Street I joined the Christmas shoppers, looked at the window displays, wondering if I should buy new Sudan-friendly clothes, but I did not want to be stuck with them if my visa didn't come through. Instead I bought gifts for Grusha and Yasha; I bought a dressing gown for my father. I could post them if I ended up not going.

With time on my hands, I called Malak. She asked me to meet her tomorrow in the Starbucks near the BBC. She would be finished by six, she said. I got there before her and waited for quite a time. She came in looking tired and distracted after a whole day of recording. She said she was playing the part of a Jewish postmistress in 1940s Poland but did not give more details. 'It was hard to leave Oz though he insisted he would be fine,' she said, sitting back in the sofa, the mug huge in her hands. She was wearing layers of grey and blue, loosening the scarf around her neck, pulling strands of her hair behind her ears.

'He needs a good rest,' I said.

'Yes. I lost my temper with him, though. I shouldn't have but I did.'

'What happened?'

'He told me he wanted to leave and join his father in South Africa. Give up his studies, give up his whole life here. Just up and go!'

'What's he going to do there?'

'He doesn't know. He hasn't thought about it.'

'He'll come to his senses. Give him time.'

'He's not thinking things through. As if the authorities won't be watching him! He's been given a police warning against accessing prohibited materials online. Why suddenly leave the country? That would raise their suspicions!'

We fell silent after that. I ate more of my cake.

Malak sighed. 'I am the one being asked the questions now.'

I raised my eyebrows.

'Yes,' she said. 'The money I send to my relatives in Chechnya.' She put on an accent. 'It better not be funding terrorism.' She was more rattled about this than she was letting on. It was in the way she held her mug, the slight tremble of her lips before she bent her neck down to sip her latte.

And here I was with my laptop still held by the anti-terror squad, applying for a visa to a pariah state. We were both tainted.

Should we swap reassurances or bolster our defences? Quickly she had swapped roles. From the optimistic 'activist mum campaigning for release of her son' to the shadows of being under suspicion. Here she was saying, 'I can see this unravelling. My dinner invitations drying up, even the offers of roles dwindling ever so slowly without knowing exactly why. Not much needs to be said, does it? One day you are okay, strong and acceptable and then, just like that, everyone turns their back. If I didn't have my faith, I would go mad. If I didn't believe that I was following my destiny, I would . . .' She stopped abruptly.

'I think you are being unduly pessimistic,' I said, trying to convince myself.

'But I never am,' she laughed. 'All my life I have been hugely optimistic. I have gone ahead with loads of energy, loads of goodwill. Until now. I am stumped. I stay up at night wondering about Oz's future. Will he get through this? I don't know what is going on in his head right now. Will he give up on uni? Will this brand him for life and be on his records? Will he lose his faith or his mind?'

'He is young, he will get over it,' I said with as much conviction as I could muster.

'He had a narrow escape,' her voice dropped to a whisper. 'But what about the others out there? The ones who are really guilty. What do I know about them? As long as the threat is there, there will always be suspects being pulled in.'

'What would Shamil have done?'

She smiled and sat back. 'I wonder.' She took a sip of her drink. 'He would have seen through these militants – that they "fulfil neither a contract nor a covenant. That they call to the truth but they are not its people". He would have gone after the hate preachers who say to the young men of this day and age, "go out and make jihad".'

Interesting that, from her point of view, the leader of one of the longest and most significant jihads in modern history would, if he were alive today, be a supporter of the War on Terror. Unlike Shamil and his highlanders, radical Islamist organisations were inspired by Hegel and Marx, their inner workings ticked along the lines of Trotskyist parties in their suppression of dissent and critical opinion. No wonder that the founders of Political Islam, those revolutionary elite who turned their backs on tradition and worked towards a perfect society, never took Shamil as a role model. Al-Qaeda was a modern phenomenon, with no patience for Shamil's traditional spirituality and utter contempt for the choices he made at the end of his career.

'Oh yes,' said Malak. 'Shamil would have gone after these bigoted preachers. But I don't have his credibility. No Muslim would listen to me. I got some hate mail when Oz's case was mentioned in the newspaper and someone made the connection. "You slut," he or she wrote. "Serves you right for taking off your clothes just to entertain the British public." I don't know what that's about. I've never done a nude scene in my life!'

'Eat,' I said, pointing to the sandwich she had only nibbled at. Eating was a solution of sorts.

She smiled and sounded like her normal self again. 'The only good thing out of all this is that I've lost my appetite.'

Malak invited me to go to a zikr with her. She said that she always attended this particular one when she was in London. It was performed by the same Sufi tariqat that Imam Shamil had belonged to. I agreed to join her for anthropological reasons. The confrontation with religious belief and practice faced every modern historical researcher. We, staunchly secular and sure of ourselves, plunged into politics and economics, ideology and warfare, power and pressures, then hit against the faith of the characters we were studying. The prayer book Anne Boleyn was reading during her last days in the Tower, Genghis Khan bowing in thanks to the sacred Burkhan Khaldun mountain and now, for me, Shamil's Sufism. I had read how the captives in Dargo heard the chants coming from Shamil's apartments when such gatherings took place. To Madame Drancy (who put her fingers in her ears and cried out that she'd had enough) the zikr had sounded like a repetitive song in chorus, a chant of 'la ilaha illa Allah' accompanied by a movement that increased in rapidity until it reached a climax then stopped to restart again with a different phrase, 'astaghfir Allah' or peace and blessings on the Prophet Muhammad.

Malak's modern zikr was held in a North London dance studio. Floor-to-ceiling mirrors, cushions on the sprung hardwood floor, a barre all the way round. We arrived early, before people started taking off their shoes at the door and walking in. She seemed to know nearly all of them and grew more animated with every greeting. The men were wearing turbans and loose trousers, the women in skirts with hijabs or, like Malak, in loose trousers and flowing tops. I was not the only one without anything on my head. 'The man in the navy jumper over there,' Malak whispered, 'is an aristocrat, closely related to the queen.' She pointed out a well-known photographer, an architect and an aromatherapist. Dumpy Asian housewives, extravagantly handsome Nigerian men, hippies and New Agers. I wondered what Shamil would make of this lot. His legacy reaching Britain in this way, tame but undisciplined, capacious and gently accessible.

A haphazard circle of sorts was formed. The sheikh leading the zikr (the German man Malak had identified as an architect) sat cross-legged at the head of the circle. His green turban rose high above his head and matched the waistcoat he was wearing. He held a long rosary in his hand. Stretched around him the men formed an inner circle, followed by another semi-circle. The women sat behind them. I kept shifting away, sliding my cushion back until I drifted further and further from Malak. The lights were dimmed and I could no longer see her. In front of me was a Pakistani woman, her rose dupatta soft in the dim light. The sheikh started with a ten-minute talk, the words of Grandsheikh, he said, and I wondered if he was referring to Shamil's mentor, Sheikh Jamal el-din or a more modern Grandsheikh. It was always a temptation to reach out to the past. To try to grasp what little of it remained.

'Our ego is a wild horse. It is never satisfied. It wants more and more. Tame your ego and ride it. Don't let it ride you.' I tried to concentrate on the lesson but I could not get over the discomfort of sitting on the ground. He went on, his accent appealing, a soothing coolness in his delivery. 'Our souls have unlimited capacity for knowledge and will ever be thirsting for more. As long as the soul is imprisoned by the senses of the physical body, our mind will hold it down. The mind is the guardian over the soul and keeps it passive, inactive. The situation will remain so until we transcend the boundaries of the mind and open ourselves up for the soul's activity.' My knees ached; pins and needles started to tingle in my feet. I shuffled to the back of the room so that at least my back was resting on the wall. When they started the actual zikr, I was far out of the circle.

A few of the men swayed from side to side. Most had their eyes closed. The rhythm of the chant was brisk; it rose, quickened and came to a faltering stop. Then the sheikh led with another phrase. I did not join in but I closed my eyes. My mind wandered to how unfit I was, inflexible. I should care more about my weight, my health in general. I had always been overweight and sedentary. My mother was a child gymnast and when she was older she enjoyed sports and cared about fitness. I ate to spite her, to distinguish myself, and then it became a habit. *Peace and blessings on the Prophet Muhammad*. I could walk out now if I wanted to. Out to the bitter cold. My breathing was slowing down. Perhaps I could try yoga. It could be my New Year's resolution.

I felt heavy on the ground. Like I weighed a ton and I was taking up too much space. This enlargement was subtle and painless. It did not embarrass me. And I could see now that there was too much distance between myself and the outskirts of myself, between my core and the edges. Too much distance to travel on my own. Not much fuel either, no elan. Where did I learn this word from? It was not Russian, but in Russian the same concept existed. With due respect, I would disagree with what I had just heard, though this forum hardly encouraged discussion. Hey Sheikh-Architect, over here, let me tell you that without my mind I do not exist. It is the only part of me I am proud of. It is me.

A curry was served at the end of the zikr, followed by tea. Malak moved closer to me. Paper cups, mint leaves in the boiling water. Moroccan tea, someone said.

I couldn't help with picking up the empty plates, scrunching up the plastic sheet that had served as a tablecloth. I stood apart, waiting and watching. Malak looked as if a load had been lifted from her shoulders. The darkness under her eyes was gone. I was the one sluggish, drugged.

She was smiling when she led me out of the room. My legs were sore and stiff, I almost stumbled down the stairs. She held my arm and spoke to me gently. 'We'll take a taxi. I'll drop you off. Your hotel is on my way.' She was staying with friends in Hampstead.

I dozed in the taxi. The streets were wet with rain, the taxi sped through the night. Malak was humming a refrain from the zikr, something that had a tune, words I couldn't understand. She was petite but she was spiritually strong.

The feeling of heaviness and enlargement followed me to the hotel. I fell into the darkest layers of sleep. It must be because I had inhaled too deeply from the opium of the people. When I woke up in the morning for a split second I did not know where I was. My mobile was ringing. It was Grusha from Sudan, but instead of news about my visa which she had promised to expedite, she spoke softly. 'I am at the hospital with your father. Here, he wants to speak to you.'

I sat up in bed. 'Papa,' I said, 'I will be with you in a few days' time.' I had not spoken to him for nine years. 'How are you feeling now?' I stood up and pulled open the curtains. A remnant of yesterday's heaviness was still in my arms.

'Natasha,' he grunted and then a couple of sentences in Arabic.

'In Russian,' I said. 'I've forgotten my Arabic.'

He needed time to make the adjustment. I could hear Grusha in the background helping him. He spoke slowly. 'You have no business staying on in Britain without your mother. Leave that foreign man and come home.'

I was amused at Tony being the 'foreign man' and my father forgetting that I had grown up.

'Papa, I don't live with Tony. I have my own flat. I have a full-time job and two cars. I'm thirty-five years old.'

'I made a mistake,' he said, as if I hadn't been listening. 'I should not have let you go. I should have kept you here with me. And now I want to set it right. I want my daughter back with me where she belongs. Come over here and I will look after you.' He was upset. Ill, in pain and getting himself more upset. 'People make mistakes. I made a mistake. You don't know how I felt. Your mother blackened my name, she turned me into a laughing stock. That's why I let you go. It was wrong and that's why we need to set this right.'

I felt sorry for him. I said, 'I will come to Khartoum and spend time with you. I am hoping to come in the next few days. But I will have to return. My work is here.'

'Resign. There are jobs here.'

'I can't do that. I'm settled here.'

This made him more agitated. His voice was louder. 'I'm telling you it's a mistake. The biggest mistake. You see because you were her daughter. I couldn't stand even looking at you. That was when I made the wrong decision. Take her, I said. She can go to hell, I said. That is the mistake that needs to be put right. Don't tell me you have to go back. I am your father and I am ordering you...'

Anger surged through me. I did not trust myself to speak. Instead, I threw the telephone across the room. It skidded onto the carpet and the back broke off. All that hard work, all that sucking up, jumping through hoops then proving myself again, all that I had achieved and he called it a mistake.

I picked up my mum's laptop and opened it onto my Staff Profile page at the university. The best photo of myself and next to it who I was. Dr Natasha Wilson, lecturer in history. Next to the photo was my office phone number and my email address. Click to see my profile, click to see my research interests and the research grants I had been awarded. Click to see the modules I taught and a list of my publications.

My body was buzzing. Patches of red floated before my eyes. To calm myself, I should work on the revisions to my paper now. Never mind breakfast, never mind that I could hear Housekeeping up and down the corridor and they would be wanting to clean my room next. I opened the document and began to write.

When in January 1854 Britain and France allied themselves with the Ottomans in the Crimea, Shamil's prospects were strengthened. He had been actively rousing the Muslim minorities in Georgia and Circassia to join the jihad. An Allied advance into the Caucasus would have driven the Russians out of Georgia and the eastern Caucasus. Instead the Allies concentrated on the Black Sea and when Russia lost Sevastopol it turned to the Caucasus and concentrated all its military might on the Muslim insurgents. For only a brief period a large-scale and arguably successful Muslim-led uprising against imperial Russia was a credible possibility.

3. Khasavyurt, the frontier of Shamil's territory, February 1855

In the library of the District Commission, Jamaleldin sat flipping through an encyclopaedia. A painting of a crab held his attention. This particular crab was found in cold waters and due to its size and taste was suitable for eating. It was not an attractive animal, asymmetrical and spiky with too much resemblance to a scorpion. Crabs walked sideways and backwards. This irritated Jamaleldin. No living thing should walk backwards. It was unnatural and gloomy.

Ever since the meeting with Younis and Mikhail, he had felt himself weakening. It was not because his father's men had repelled him – they should have after the distance he had covered, what he had learnt and become. Instead the highlanders promised to drag him down to their level. Threatened him with love and the gravity his father exerted. Without his Russian army uniform, without the tsar's language on his tongue, was he any different from them? They would pull him in and then take him for granted. He would slip and become uncouth like them, leaping over boulders, sitting on the ground to eat, wrapping his head in a turban. He would become wild like them and they were wild not because he remembered them as such but because Russia and Europe said they were. The mountain spirit was in him, it had always been in him but it had been latent all these years, held down by newness and duty. All it needed was a stir and it would thicken. Like a crab, he was edging backwards to them.

David Chavchavadze walked into the room holding a letter. He was ruffled, not agitated. Jamaleldin could read his face now and judge his mood from the way he walked, the twitch of his moustache and the vein on his forehead. Whether it was visible or whether it throbbed was a good barometer. Now David was moderately engaged, which meant that the news was neither good nor bad. David stood tall and began reading out loud, somewhat gratuitously Jamaleldin thought, extracts from the latest letter to arrive from Princess Anna via one of the Georgian servants who had volunteered for the journey to Dargo-Veddin. ' "It is impossible to reason with these people. I have failed to convince them that you cannot offer a greater sum . . . Today, David, I no longer believe that we are destined to meet again in this life. I try, I do try to submit to this trial with Christian humility and to hold on to the hope of that better future promised to the suffering. I will undergo with gratitude whatever may be in store for me here and I will constantly pray that Alexander's fate is better than mine. May God strengthen you in your grief and reward you." '

David's voice started to tremble. 'She does not know that you are here,' he said to Jamaleldin and folded up the letter. 'If she did, she would not be despairing. But they should have heard by now that you are on your way.' He began walking back and forth hemmed in by the shelves of books. 'Delays, delays! First they ask for the sum in gold and I get that ready. Then Shamil changes his mind.'

Jamaleldin winced at the mention of his father's name. He always did, as if it was something intimate that should not be exposed, at least not in that tone, not with that impatience. Yet the name was there, it had to be said. Shamil was the core of the matter. It made Jamaleldin dizzy.

'And why does Shamil want silver instead of gold?' David continued. 'Because the amount would look more impressive were it in silver and presumably he must satisfy the mercenary hordes who seek to gain out of all this. They must be ignorant not to realise that there is no difference, gold or silver, it is the same sum. The trouble I went to find silver! A little bit from here, a little bit from there. It was not easy. I still have five thousand in gold. They had better accept it and not change their minds again.'

Jamaleldin wished he did not have to listen to this. He wished for a companion his age. Twenty-four hours a day he was in the company of David Chavchavadze. They even shared the same room. Was the prince afraid that he would abscond or put a pistol to his head? David certainly hid it well. He certainly conveyed a feeling of trust and gratitude. But why read Anna's letter out to him? So that Jamaleldin would feel sorry for her plight instead of feeling sorry for himself.

'When will this finally come to an end? Our men had to wait a whole month in Dargo because Shamil was away. Then they want to exchange other prisoners as well. That opens more doors of negotiations. Then they tell me: come to Dargo yourself for a visit. A visit! So that you could see your wife and son. And then what? I said. Come back empty-handed? I would not do that. Either they come back with me or not at all.'

Mistrust on all sides. Jamaleldin could see through them both. The Russians believed the Chechens were wily and suspicious. The Chechens believed the Russians were aggressive and treacherous. They were both right, they were both wrong. One led to the other.

'My first offer to him was forty thousand roubles.' David was still pacing up and down. His scalp shone through his receding hairline. 'Would I conceal or keep back one *shaour* when my family's liberty is at stake?' He suddenly stopped and faced Jamaleldin, posing this disingenuous question.

For the sake of peace Jamaleldin replied, 'You would not.' He strained to remember what a *shaour* was. It was a Georgian coin valued at only five kopeks.

'He has still not turned my offer down.' David resumed his pacing. 'Nor has he accepted it.'

A knock on the door and Jamaleldin was saved by a visit from a group of young officers who asked him to join them for a ride. He readily agreed. On a horse he felt more like himself. He could race and exert himself to the point where his muscles trembled and his heart beat louder than his thoughts. He could pretend that everything was normal. Not quite. The mountains were there, up ahead waiting for him. Their forests and snows, their steepness that this horse could not manage, though other horses could.

Why was he thinking of them all the time? Of *him* all the time? In the evenings when he knocked back schnapps and lost money playing cards, Shamil's disapproval ruined his pleasure. He was a marked man. And yet there was the ache to thaw and he wanted more than anything to see how Ghazi looked now. With a brother one would be less lonely, one would stretch out and spar without needing to win. The prospects played out in his mind, secrets soft as dreams. He dreamt of his mother and woke up with the fresh realisation that she was dead. He would not be going back to her, he would not be going back to Akhulgo. The course of the war had altered and his father, who split a man vertically in two halves with one blow of his sword, who could out-run and out-jump friend and foe, must have aged, even if only a little.

On the following morning two highlanders came. They were the official negotiators sent by Shamil. One of them, Hassan, circled Jamaleldin asking him one question after the other. What did he remember from his childhood? What was the name of his mother, his uncle who was long-ago martyred, his father's cook? What was the colour of his father's horse? Jamaleldin's answers were vague, the Avar language let him down. He needed an interpreter. He started to feel bored. There was no point to this interrogation. Hadn't Younis vouched for him already?

Hassan exuded ambition. His thick eyebrows almost met. His copious beard was perfectly black. He was not as old as he wanted to look. 'My commission is to ascertain whether you are really the son of our great imam. I need positive physical evidence. Please bare your right arm.'

Jamaleldin rolled up his sleeve. Hassan grabbed his arm. His hand was rough and warm. 'Yes, I can see the scar.' A smile entered his voice. His grip loosened. He looked Jamaleldin straight in the eye. 'When you were very young, you fell from a mill and wounded your arm. It was the kind of deep cut that would leave a scar.'

Jamaleldin rolled down his sleeve. He did not remember falling from a mill and hurting his arm. The scar had once or twice roused his curiosity but it was neither ugly nor big enough to embarrass him. Now he could make up a story about himself climbing inside a mill in Akhulgo and falling on the straw. Little Ghazi frightened by the sight of blood, running off to tell their mother and Jamaleldin looking at the frazzled stained flesh and willing himself to be brave.

Hassan turned to David. 'You have delighted us with the return of Shamil Imam's son. On my honour, I can now assure you of the return of your family very soon.'

Jamaleldin could see the relief in David's face, the restrained excitement. The highlanders promised they would convey the news to Shamil in Dargo and return in three days' time. I am that close, Jamaleldin thought. Days, not weeks or months.

Hassan and his companion returned as promised but not with a message from Shamil concluding the exchange. Instead the letter read, 'I thank you for keeping your word with regards to my son's return from Russia but do not think that this will end the negotiations between us. Besides my son, I require a million roubles and a hundred and fifty of my men whom you now hold prisoners. Do not bargain with me. I will not take less.'

Jamaleldin watched David's face transform; he saw his hand for the briefest of moments grip his revolver and then let go. 'Is the imam withdrawing his word after he has given it? Can he even count up to a million? I challenge him on that.'

Hassan frowned. 'There is no need for insults.'

'Well, I cannot add another kopek. It is forty thousand roubles or nothing.'

Hassan shrugged. 'Write this down for Shamil Imam and we will take it to him.'

'I will not write another letter,' David shouted. 'Tell him he is lucky I offered forty. I should have said twenty but I didn't think the emperor would permit Jamaleldin's return.'

The wording struck Jamaleldin. It was true, the emperor had permitted his return. Reflect on the decision, sacrifice yourself to save the princess – all an illusion. The truth was that he had been a hostage all these years held by elastic constraints. A rubber band that allowed him to join a regiment, dance in a ball, ask for the hand of Daria Semyonovich. Humiliation pumped through his blood. He could no longer hear David, who continued to shout. The room, the biggest one in the District Commission, began to seem strange, full of eerie sounds and people who were unaware of each other. The aides-de-camp, interpreters, orderlies on the side – all appeared to him as crooked as puppets. He felt someone nudging him; it was Hassan turning towards him with a smile that was itself like a word in a foreign language. 'Don't worry, brother, that's just our way of negotiating. We'll get you out of here soon. Don't worry.'

It was too much. The tears rose to his eyes. 'Worry? You think I'm worried. You don't understand, do you, that I'm not even happy I'm returning. I'm no longer one of you. I've forgotten how to be. If I could, I would turn round and go back to what I know.'

Suddenly David was in front of them, eyes blazing at Hassan, the vein on his forehead stretched blue-grey, spit forming on the corners of his mouth. He pitched in, 'And I will take Jamaleldin back to Petersburg, see if I don't. If by Saturday you don't bring me an acceptance of my offer, I swear by my Creator both of us will leave Khasavyurt. Listen to me. Listen to me well: I will not be played with. Shamil can do what he likes with my family. Yes, he can. Do you understand me? If he makes my wife his slave then she is no longer my wife. She is not. I will renounce her.'

4. Dargo-Veddin, February 1855

When news of Jamaleldin's arrival in Khasavyurt first reached Dargo, it was greeted with celebration. Gunshots were heard throughout the aoul and there was much chanting and thanksgiving. Chuanat rushed into Anna's room to congratulate her and Madame Drancy sank to her knees in gratitude. But it was Zeidat's reaction that turned out to be the most accurate. She stood at the doorway with arms folded and said, 'I don't understand why you're so happy. Does Shamil Imam only have one son? The boy's return is not enough. You will not be released for less than a million.'

It was in itself a torture, this unknown future, this hope that now dangled close. Anna might believe that Shamil truly wanted his son back but Zeidat and the naibs were winning the argument. How much could they get out of David Chavchavadze was the question they were asking themselves. They would push him to the limit. He was doing everything he could – mortgaging, selling and borrowing, but it might not be enough.

And what would become of her if she stayed? More and more often she was thinking along these lines. Anna Elinichna, Queen of Georgia – Shamil had won her with these words, courted her with a dream. These days she was imagining what would have been preposterous months ago. It was a seductive, repulsive path. She would join Shamil's resistance. She would fight with the Chechens for a free Georgia. The prospect was thrilling. It filled her with a dislike of herself but still she could not stop weaving the fantasy. It often threw up surprises. She would contact those relations of hers who had been exiled by the tsar, who had never submitted whole-heartedly to the annexation of their country. David, cautious and pro-Russia, had always urged her to steer clear of them; now she would seek them with an offer of her own. And here in this household there would have to be changes too; the delicious toppling of Zeidat, and Madame Drancy would definitely have to go. Madame Drancy did not believe that Muslims worshipped the same God she did. She would consider Alexander a Christian soul lost to Islam. She would become reproachful and ultimately insubordinate. Her position as governess or even companion would become untenable. It would be necessary to move her to another aoul or seek some way for her to individually secure her own ransom. Unlikely, but there was no other option.

The mountains were filled with the displaced. Here among Shamil's men were captives and deserters. Their wellbeing was a function of how much they integrated or made themselves useful. In Georgia and in Russia, there were also Chechens who had gone over to the Russians. Their survival, too, depended on how easily they fitted in and how valuable they could be. Each with their personal heartache, each with their individual story. The only common thing being that their loyalty would always be suspect, their loved ones far away, their aura tinged with the shame of defection.

One of Shamil's men was a Georgian who had in his childhood been made prisoner. Abid was esteemed by Shamil because of his intelligence and natural fighting skills. His story fascinated Anna. One of the older women in the household had fallen in love with Abid. Shamil approved the marriage in order to strengthen Abid's attachment. If his wife and children were now part of Dargo-Veddin, Abid was less likely to escape. On one occasion when a battle had turned unfavourable, Shamil and Abid were separated from the rest of the troops. Pursued, they galloped until they came very near to the Russian border. 'I have always felt that one day you will leave me,' Shamil said to him. 'If you wish to return to the Russians here is the opportunity. Don't be afraid. No one will follow you.' Abid was adamant that his loyalty was to the imam. Yet he was fated to leave. Years later he fell in love with a Georgian prisoner and when she was, only last month, ransomed by her people, he followed her. Now his children would grow up with a father who had deserted them, a mother who was lamenting her fate. Anna wondered how successful Abid would be back in Georgia. She doubted that he would rise to a position as high as that of being Shamil's arms-bearer.

Alexander came into the room to find her dozing. She was neither healthy nor ill; neither calm nor energetic. 'Mama,' he tugged at her sleeve. She sat up and stroked his hair. He was taller now, less cuddly, less precious.

'Zeidat took me to her room,' he said. 'She gave me sweets and told me that Papa doesn't love me any more. She said it would be better for me if I stayed here. Is it true what she said?'

'No.' She held him by the shoulders. 'No, it is not true. Papa loves you and he is doing all he can to bring us home. And soon we will go home. I promise you.'

He looked relieved. She hugged him to herself and close to her neck he whispered, 'I don't remember which is our house in Tiflis and which is Tsinondali. They are two houses but I think they are one house.'

She went over the differences between them. She jogged his memory. They spent a successful hour regaining their past, shutting out the present. Until a cry was heard from outside and Alexander rushed out to join the domestic drama caused by the mischievous Muhammad-Sheffi breaking the lock of his grandmother's room.

Talking to Alexander had restored her to herself. She felt stronger, her head cleared as if she was waking up from the most vivid of dreams. The promise she made to her son must not be in vain. All that she had told him was the truth. David loved them both and they had a home and a life to go back to. She must not give in to confusion and this sidling astray. Some connections were too deep to be realised, too subtle to be convincing. She was not the Queen of Georgia. She would never be. She was David Chavchavadze's wife, mother of Alexander, and she did not belong here. Her life was on hold. She must speak out and fight; she must say it again and again to break up this deadlock. 'My family do not have a million roubles.'

She went to Chuanat's room and asked for her help. 'I must speak to Sheikh Jamal el-Din. He is the only one who has the strongest influence over Imam Shamil.'

Shamil was surprised to see his teacher coming into his room. He stood up and moved forward to kiss his hand. They had not been alone together since that night they had argued about Princess Anna. Every day he prayed behind him in the mosque and on Thursday nights they sat next to each other in the zikr circle, but they had not exchanged more than greetings and the day-to-day administrative discussions and correspondence that Jamal el-Din was involved in. Seeing him now venerable and grey with his intelligent expression and compassionate eyes, Shamil felt a pang of nostalgia, a longing for their former closeness. He should have been the one to make the first move. Even if he was not ready to apologise, he should have traversed the distance and at least expressed in action, if not in words, some penitence. He bent down now and kissed his teacher's feet. To say out loud that he was honoured by this visit would be to sound formal and formality in itself was undesirable when it was intimacy that was due.

When he was seated cross-legged on the floor and after the customary refreshments, Jamal el-Din asked, 'Are you going to reply to Colonel Williams' letter?'

Colonel Williams, based in Anatolia, was the British commissioner to the Ottoman forces. He had sent a strongly worded reprimand against fighting women and children and demanded the immediate release of the captives. Shamil said, 'I will explain my position and ask him why they did not support me last spring when I intended to march into Tiflis. We could have seized Georgia together. I fear that the Sublime Porte has forgotten us. All we are getting from the Ottomans are medallions and flags!'

'They make the men happy.'

'Yes, but we need more.'

'Unlike Lord Palmerston, the British ambassador to Turkey has never been our steadfast friend. Do not underestimate his power over the sultan. Now he has seized on this business of the kidnapping to label you a barbarian not worthy of association.'

Shamil pondered on this analysis. He would do anything to rebuke the Ottoman sultan face to face. Georgia could have been taken and still it might. If only the Allies would advance onto the Caucasus instead of putting all their effort into the Black Sea. He looked up when his teacher called his name.

'Shamil, I have spoken to your captive. She has assured me that a million roubles will not be raised by her husband.'

So this was why he was here. Shamil became more alert. 'Will not or cannot?'

'Even if Prince David has a million roubles, the tsar will not permit him to give you such a sum. Are they now in the business of financing us so that we can fight them even more?'

'He is offering forty thousand.'

'A huge sum.'

Shamil paused. He did not want to sound contradictory. 'It would be best to receive more.'

Jamal el-Din sighed. 'And if you cannot receive more and there is no exchange – what will you end up with – the princess as your fourth wife? Is this what you want?'

The princess as his fourth wife. Is this what he wanted? Shamil paused again but this time for a different reason. He might have disagreed with his teacher but he had never lied to him. He would not lie to him now. 'I want my son.'

Jamal el-Din smiled. 'Yes, you do. My namesake. Son of Fatima, may Allah grant her mercy. Son of the Imam of Chechnya and Dagestan. Brother of Ghazi Muhammad, brother of Muhammad-Sheffi. The boy belongs here with us.'

Shamil's voice had a catch. 'They tell me he does not speak a word of our language.'

'This is natural. Years he has been away. You must not hold it against him. And he can learn. Be easy on him and when he comes back, insh'Allah, you must let him live as he likes.'

'I will. To have him again safe from the infidels and their crooked ways is all I want.'

'Well, you should be content with the position you forced your enemies into.'

Shamil bent his head. He knew the enemy better than Jamal el-Din did. This was an enemy that could never deliver contentment, a relentless enemy, a force that quickened and grew and devoured like fire. 'What about my naibs? They must not think that I favour my son more than the cause.'

'Your naibs are greedy. They need to be taught a lesson. Money is like grass. It withers.'

'True.'

Jamal el-Din went on, 'We do not serve money, we serve Allah.'

'I know this. But expectations have been raised. I am in an awkward position.'

'One in which you put yourself. Be decisive. Gather the people, tell them that money withers but our deeds last for ever. Strengthen their souls with a gathering of zikr. Remind them that we serve Allah and not our desires.'

Shamil sighed. 'Would you talk to your daughter? Zeidat does not understand compromise.'

Jamal el-Din smiled. 'When a man cannot control his wife it must be the end of Time coming upon us.'

She was going home. It was true. Ameena and Chuanat crowding around her, Madame Drancy in tears, the elderly Bahou hobbling into their room with toothless, wet smiles to babble apologies, to thank them again and again and kiss Anna's hand. It was a miracle, she insisted on explaining as Chuanat translated, Allah had prolonged her life so that she would see her first grandson come home again. Fatima's boy whom she had rocked to sleep and for whom she had chewed the first solid food to pop into his tiny mouth. My daughter Fatima died waiting for him, she explained to Anna and shuffled back to her room, touching the walls for balance, her eyesight dim with tears.

Chuanat insisted on a goodbye party. A gathering in her room of tea and sweets. 'You will forget me, Anna, but I will think of you every day,' she said without reproach. 'You will go back to your busy life and we will be here as we are.'

Anna's head ached from the tension. The fear of even more dashed hopes. Everything to say and nothing to say. Sheikh Jamal el-Din, when he had come to visit her said, 'Child, why are you doing this to yourself? We told you that no harm would come to you. So why all the despair?' He had been taken aback by how poorly she looked, how thin. Now she would go back to David in this state only nine months away but looking nine years older.

And was it real? Would this optimism last? The sight of a splendid white horse in the courtyard was real enough. The children crowded around it. Alexander was given a ride. The stallion with a black star on its forehead was for Jamaleldin's journey home. Everyone in the aoul wanted to touch it.

Men sent to Khasavyurt to count the silver roubles returned satisfied. Shamil decided the day for the exchange. Thursday 11th March.

'You have been so kind to me, Chuanat.'

'You brought us the outside world.'

'I can't believe it,' said Ameena. 'You two are turning this into a gloomy affair.' She was young enough to believe in happiness. 'Look, Anna. Look at the wagon being prepared for you.' It was pulled by horses instead of oxen and the drivers were dressed like Russian coachmen. Carpets were placed at the bottom; a stock of bread and fruit for the journey.

The mandatory black veil covering her face. Alexander sitting on one side, Madame Drancy on the other. She was truly leaving. From the inner to the outer court, they passed through the gate and out of the aoul. They were accompanied by hundreds of men led by Ghazi Muhammad and youths led by Muhammad-Sheffi. No more wooden houses now, no stone towers. She felt the wagon lurch forward, Madame Drancy squealed and they began to descend the mountain. She gripped Alexander's hand. It was one of the first fine days of spring. She lifted up her veil to see flocks of swallows and new green on the mountainside.

Ditches to go over, steep cliffs where they had to temporarily abandon the wagon and go on horseback. A drawbridge and times when they paused for rests. Halfway down the mountain they were joined by Shamil and more of his men. They were in their best clothes, glittering arms and their finest horses. He rode next to her and said, 'According to our custom a father must not go out to meet his son. It should be the other way round. I am here to accompany my guest and prevent any disorder among my men.'

She hid that tether of anxiety that had kept her awake last night. The fear that something would go wrong. Yet he was the one who said, 'I could not sleep last night thinking about my son. I kept praying that everything would go smoothly without treachery.'

Madam Drancy was dozing next to her, Alexander on the horse of one of the men. Whatever she wanted to say she could say now. Whatever she wanted to ask. Instead she said, 'There was another negotiating meeting held last night. What was it about?'

'A request for us not to fire our guns in celebration.'

'Was that all?'

'Yes.'

'Thank you for the costume you gave Alexander. He will remember it all his life.' She had seen him lift her son up to kiss him goodbye, she had seen him bless him.

'And Anna, Queen of Georgia. Will she remember all this too?'

She would not be addressed like this again. It blurred the question that he asked. She said, 'There was indeed once long ago a Queen of Georgia.'

'I know,' he said. 'Queen Tamar. You are like her in many ways.'

She would not be in the company of one who knew the secrets she even hid from herself. Knew the thoughts before they formed into words or wants.

He said, 'I want to tell you that I tried to take care of you as if you were my own ... my own family. It was not my intention that you suffer. You suffered because of my ignorance in how to treat such a noble lady as yourself and my lack of means.'

She must not spoil things by crying. Even her voice must be clear like that of a princess, if not a queen. 'You kept your word, Imam Shamil. I trusted you and you did not let me down.'

The wagon shuddered over a rock and next to her Madame Drancy woke up with a jolt and looked out. 'It's the Russian army,' she cried. There they were, visible across the river, lines and lines of them, a whole regiment. Anna saw a sight that was familiar and should be reassuring. David's army; strong and disciplined, as if they would never tire of war. When she turned her head back towards Shamil, he was gone.

5. Khasavyurt, March 1855

The news of the tsar's death did not surprise Jamaleldin. It only intensified the feeling of an ending. With the rest of the troops, he raised his hand and swore an oath to the new tsar, Alexander II. Jamaleldin was returning to his father without confidence in the success of the highlanders. Mighty Russia would ultimately win the war in the Caucasus. It was one of the few things he was certain about.

David gave him his sabre as a parting gift. 'Do not cut any of our people with it,' he said.

'Neither yours nor ours.' Close now to the mountains he could not ignore the cold-blooded policy with which aouls were razed down to every last chicken and cooking utensil. No wonder the tsar had denied him active service in the Caucasus.

'I hope you will be a bridge between the two sides,' said David.

Jamaleldin's heart sank. A bridge was solid, dependable. Whereas he was like a wafer that could break any minute.

'Talk to your father about peace,' David continued. 'Convince him.'

Just the thought of meeting his father after all these years dismayed him. But, yes, he would talk to him of peace because he would not be able to talk to him about war. Peace was a more dignified version of defeat. He turned away. 'Have the carts been loaded?' It had taken two of his father's men a whole twenty-four hours to count the money. When he asked them if they were afraid that they were being short-changed, their reply surprised him. They were afraid that there was deliberately more money than had been agreed upon, paving the way for accusations of treachery.

David said, 'All is according to plan. The carts have been loaded. Only thirty men from each side will be present at the actual exchange. The rest will stay in their positions.'

The day itself was bright and strange in that it coincided with the funeral of the tsar. In Petersburg they were burying his putrefied, perfumed body, the streets filled with crowds. If it wasn't for all this, Jamaleldin would have been at the lying-in. Instead he was riding out towards the mountains. On the banks of the river Michik, the troops took positions. David was determined that nothing should raise the suspicions of the highlanders but the infantry was ordered to be ready to cross the river and fire if need be. Bayonets in place and the officers raised their field glasses. Through his, Jamaleldin saw the high black banners and what looked like thousands of Chechens. There under that tree the exchange would take place. He saw a horseman gallop towards the tree and when he reached it he waved a pennon. This was the signal. Jamaleldin, David and thirty others proceeded forward with the carts. The dip in the land obstructed the corresponding thirty highlanders who had crossed the river. Jamaleldin could not see his destination. He felt as if he was riding towards nothing. Just more sky, grass, rocks. Slowly, not a word, not a whisper, just the sound of the swallows, horses and the wheels of the carts.

It was time to ride uphill and suddenly there they were. It was their unexpected beauty that caught at his throat. Surreal and timeless. Graceful men on small horses, their guns resting on their right thighs. Their swords decked in silver and gold, insubstantial in comparison to the mountains behind them. The highlanders had sprouted from this soil, this place and nowhere else; men sleek with home, lustrous with what they believed in. And here was their leader moving straight towards him. A young man all in white as if the peaks had anointed his fur hat, tunic and horse with snow. He was smiling at Jamaleldin, he was swinging down from his horse. It was him. It was Ghazi and Jamaleldin found himself hugging him tight, the men cheering, and his brother's face in his hands. It's you, it's you, little brother. I knew it was you.

With reluctance, Jamaleldin turned to see the wagon with the captives. Women covered in black veils, impossible to tell who was who. A child's voice called out. 'It's Papa, it's Papa!'

Ghazi pulled away from Jamaleldin; he went back and lifted Alexander off the wagon and brought him to his father. David held the boy tight, sank his head in his hair. Then he started to walk towards the wagon but Ghazi blocked his path. Ghazi struck a pose and was now giving a speech through the interpreter. Jamaleldin was arrested by the sight and sound of his brother, his slight nervousness, the marks on his skin but still the full cheeks that he remembered as a child pinching until they became red. Ghazi said, 'Prince David, we are not people of treachery and haram behaviour. We are warriors, true believers. My father Shamil Imam gave me orders to inform you that he took care of your family as if they were his own. He is now returning them to you pure as the lilies, sheltered from all eyes, like the gazelles of the desert.'

Jamaleldin understood why David clenched his fist even as he gave a stiff bow. The vein on his forehead was more pronounced than ever. He was furious; the expression in his eyes was straightforward hatred and the desire for revenge. Jamaleldin turned to join Ghazi but the little brother, now turned commander, gestured for him to remain. Not yet.

The wagon with the princess and Madame Drancy rolled closer and the two women took off their veils. He recognised Anna straight away. She held herself rigid, the veil still clutched between her fingers. Their eyes locked. It was as if she knew that his reluctance was due to regret; a part of him had always yearned to return. Her eyes turned towards David and softened, her chin trembled as if she were years older, scoured and undone. It was now possible for Jamaleldin and his party to proceed forward. The three carts with the money, the Chechen prisoners who were part of the exchange, Ghazi and his men, Jamaleldin still flanked by two Russian officers and another aide-de-camp, all crossed the Michik river. Above them were the bulk of his father's troops but no sign of his father.

Ghazi touched his arm. 'He will not see you in these clothes. You must change.'

Jamaleldin was not sure if he understood. Ghazi tugged at his jacket. Another highlander held out a bundle of native clothes.

'Shamil Imam's orders,' Ghazi grinned. 'Time to strip.'

'Here?'

'Yes.'

'I can't.'

Ghazi burst out laughing. 'We'll cover you.'

They formed a circle around him, giving him their backs. He tugged off his boots, he unbuttoned, he pulled down. The cold air on his skin, the snow-capped mountains above and a Russian military uniform fell into a heap on the grass. Here he was between one dress and the other, neither Russian nor Chechen, just naked and human. It was a restful place to be with sun on his back and grass between his toes. He shivered and pulled on the familiar-unfamiliar clothes. Someone had gone through considerable effort to guess his size, to provide the best cloth, the most elegant cut. The long dark cherkesska made him feel regal and feminine, humble and yet daring, supported but unrestricted; the white lambskin papakh reminded him of the one he wore long ago when he left Akhulgo. His feet without the heaviness of boots felt vulnerable, the leather insoles put him in touch again with grass and rocks.

'Are you going to keep us till sunset?' joked Ghazi.

'Don't look.'

'Bashful as a maiden, are you?'

When the circle opened and he emerged, a large number of highlanders broke from their ranks and surged towards him. They shoved and pushed to kiss his hand, the hem of his cherkesska, to get a better look at him. *Because I am his son they think I am special, they think I am more than what I am.* The mob pressed more closely; there was confusion and aggressive jostling. He worried about the Russians around him – they were completely outnumbered, face to face with men who would be happy, at any other time, to slit their throats. The highlanders gazed at the Russians with curiosity; one of them touched the eye-glass of the oldest officer, one of them examined his pistols. With gestures and the little bit of Avar that he could remember Jamaleldin ordered them to step back. It surprised him that they obeyed almost instantly.

Ghazi barged through what had become a mob, swiping away at the men as if he was pushing aside the low branches of trees blocking his path. Another highlander followed with a whip. Some of the men were haggard and painfully thin, their faces scarred with old and new wounds. Some were little more than youths who should be at their lessons instead of in campaigns. But here they were, full of trust. His father's flock. His people, for what else was this soreness and shame building inside him other than the recognition that they looked like him and that he was of them. They were lashing him with the weight of their expectations. He trembled because any minute now he would have to bear his father's eyes on him.

Shamil had retreated under a tree further up from the river. After making sure that the wagon with the princess had crossed safely, he wanted to be alone. He sat and faced the direction of Makkah. He bent and pressed his forehead to the ground. This was a time to feel small and weak in front of the magnanimity of the Almighty. His son was coming home. All the years of waiting and hoping, of feeling helpless and betrayed. All the frustrations of failed attempts and prisoners not valuable enough for an exchange. Soon he would hold him in his arms, soon he would look and look at him again, marvel at the child-to-manhood changes. This was a day to give thanks and because he could not give enough thanks, because no words would be eloquent enough, no amount of praise would be adequate, he wept. Subhan Allah wa bi hamdu. Subhan Allah wa bi hamdu. Years ago in Akhulgo when he gave Jamaleldin up to the Russians he had lifted up his palms and called out for all to witness, 'Lord, You raised up Your prophet Moses, upon him be peace, when he was in the hands of Pharaoh. Here is my son. If I formally hand him over to the infidels, then he is under Your trust and charge. You are the best of guardians.'

The boy was coming back from the hands of the enemy. Jamaleldin had been watched over all along, he had been protected all along. Shamil begged forgiveness for every flicker of doubt, for every moment of impatience, for every flirtation with despair. He cried until his beard became wet.

When he heard the men's cheers, he rose and joined the naibs who had gathered in a wide circle. Shamil sat and waited for his son. At last, there he was, haloed, vulnerable, one of the most beautiful sights Shamil had ever seen. He must not rise and rush towards him. The son should come to the father. Jamaleldin drew near. Shamil saw his mother Fatima in him, saw his resemblance to his brothers. Jamaleldin's face had matured but not changed. He stepped onto the carpet. He knelt and kissed his father's hand. Jamaleldin must greet the others first, all the naibs and elders, Sheikh Jamal el-Din too, he must show his appreciation for the honour they were bestowing upon him by leaving their homes and coming here to welcome him.

At last Shamil took his son in his arms. To have his fill of holding him, to have his fill of looking at him. This was more than an earthly delight, this was a whiff of Paradise. Alhamdulilah, alhamdulilah. I thank Allah Almighty for protecting my son.

VIII
A Thistle Twisted to One Side

1. Khartoum, December 2010

Grusha and Yasha were waiting for me at the airport. I saw them as soon as I rolled my suitcase outside the arrivals hall. Among the crowd they were the only white middle-aged woman and light-skinned son. Besides, they were watching me, searching my face, waiting for the click of recognition, ready to smile. Earlier, when the plane had started its descent, I had been able to make out in the fading light the Nile looping through the desert. By the time we got off the plane, though, it was pitch-dark and I was struck by the inadequacy of the lighting. Even inside the terminal, I was reminded of the flattering candlelight found in romantic restaurants. The exterior of the airport was also dimly lit. Grusha and Yasha did not look at all like I remembered them, so much so that I hesitated in greeting them. The Aunty Grusha in my head dressed like Thatcher. The one in front of me now looked like Hilary Clinton. I thought trousers were outlawed in Sudan? And Yasha, if this was Yasha and he must be, was trapped within layers and mounds of fat. They covered him like a suit of armour. My first boyfriend, nimble and lanky, had become obese.

He took my suitcase and Grusha took my arm. We made our way to their car, a four-wheel-drive that was surprisingly parked only a few steps away, right outside the arrivals gate. I watched Yasha squeeze into the front seat. Beads of sweat on his forehead, his belly pushed against the steering wheel. I looked away. Grusha had aged of course, a slackness in her chin and the way she heaved herself into the car next to Yasha. From the back seat I asked, 'How is Papa?'

They both had their backs turned; I could not see the expression on their faces. Yasha started the engine. 'Not good,' Grusha said at last. I did not want to know more. Not yet. It would come and already the effect was sinking in. I looked out of the window. More traffic than I remembered, a whole row of fast-food chains. Novel to be in a city that didn't have a Starbucks.

Grusha's house was how I remembered it to be. It was neat because Aunty Grusha always kept a mercilessly clean house. We sat in the living room. She said that my father had died the previous night. Mid-morning today he was buried.

I didn't recognise this feeling of disappointment. The sheepishness of arriving too late. 'I needn't have come then.'

Yasha looked down at his hands. His bulk spread over the sofa, immense girth, each thigh as wide as a human being. He would not be able to travel in Economy. I remembered him in swimming trunks, the ripped muscles of his stomach, his thin neck. Now even his face was flattened, his features as if pushed through a slab of dough. It was sadly fascinating. That defeat could manifest itself in such a way brought tears to my eyes.

Grusha put her arm around me. 'At first we didn't know what to do – to catch you before you set out or to tell you in the middle of your travels. Then we decided it would be better if you heard the news from us in person rather than on the telephone.'

Yasha started to speak about my father's last hours but I couldn't focus on what he was saying. I stared at his mouth, the route to his fatness; I heard his voice and it was not the voice of a young man but someone who was confident, experienced, almost jaded. Perhaps I would only rarely see him during my visit. He was a busy man and probably did not spend a lot of time with his mother even though they lived in the same house.

'Your father was proud of you,' Grusha said. 'When you got your PhD, we never heard the end of it.'

It was hard to believe this but she would not lie. We sat in silence. I cried quietly, almost soundlessly. I had wanted to see him again. It was true. I had wanted to argue with him and listen to him rant. He had made me angry on the telephone but when the anger died I was left with the thrill of his honesty. 'I just could not stand the sight of you.' That was exactly what I remembered during the divorce, his hurt that made him repulsive and also frightening, his eyes that looked straight through me as if I didn't exist, all the days and weeks when he didn't speak to me, when he couldn't speak to me, not even hello or good morning or do this or do that. My mother had betrayed him and I was her daughter and he had not been able to rise above that.

I started to feel hot. I peeled off my cardigan, pulled away the scarf looped around my neck. My newly bought dowdy skirt reached my ankles. It irritated me. If Grusha was wearing trousers, then why couldn't I too, and why had that journalist, last year, been fined for wearing them? Or was Grusha exempt because she was Russian? This was one of the irksome things about being an outsider – one never knew the extent to which the rules could be bent. I wanted to initiate this conversation but it was not the right time.

Yasha said, 'Tomorrow I could take you to the cemetery . . . if you like.' My expression made him falter. To see that freshly dug grave, the still-moist earth piled over it. The idea did not appeal to me at all.

'Tomorrow we will go to your father's house so that you can pay your condolences,' Grusha said firmly. 'You must meet your brother. He is twelve, I think. Or eleven.'

I had a half-brother who I never thought about, didn't know what he looked like. 'What is his name?'

'Mekki.'

'Mekki. I can't remember the last time I spoke to a child.'

Neither Grusha nor Yasha responded and I suddenly felt self-conscious. Maybe these were the sort of comments that reminded Yasha of his late daughter. Afterwards, I glanced around for a photo of her, on top of the piano, on the walls, but there were none. I was conscious of the house around me and how familiar it was. Little had been done to make it look modern but as Grusha explained, there was an added separate flat for Yasha upstairs. 'It has its own entrance,' she said. He must have moved in there after he lost his wife and daughter.

When I woke up the following morning, the house was empty. Grusha and Yasha had already gone to work. I set about connecting myself to the internet. Yasha's upstairs flat, I had been told, had the stronger connection, but it did not feel right to try to gain access to it while he was out. After a few attempts, I found that the speed was not bad and after I checked my emails, I started to write to Malak asking how things were, telling her my news, but I lost the connection before I clicked Send. I waited, hoping it would come back but it didn't. After a while I gave up and went in search of breakfast.

In the kitchen a maid was washing the dishes. I chatted to her for a while though my mind was on Malak and Oz. The maid was Ethiopian and had been working here for five years. 'Shall I make you breakfast?' she asked and looked surprised when I said that I would get it myself.

I sat on the veranda with my mug of tea. After the bitterest Scottish winter, the heat and the light felt defiantly foreign, excessive. The small garden was full of flowers and in it stood a large guava tree. I could hear beyond its walls, the sounds of people walking past, the rumble of traffic. All this had existed while I was away. Khartoum as a city, its people, those who had never known me and those who had forgotten me. My mother and I had simply dropped off the radar. After the scandal we had been talked about less and less until, with time, our absence came to be considered the most natural of outcomes. Childhood psychologists say that the first five years are the most formative. I had spent them all here. My mother and father young and in love, easy-going, hopeful. Our day-to-day life an extension of their Cold War romance, as promising as the prospects of an African engineer with a PhD from a Russian university. My father taking me to the river, getting on a boat, afterwards buying peanuts and candy floss; my mother visiting Grusha, the two of them complaining, in Russian, about the weather. My father, during a power cut, peeing in the garden instead of making his way indoors in the dark. My mother lifting her hair to rub an ice cube on the back of her neck. I would always carry this. All the other layers on top could not obliterate this core.

There was a heaviness in my chest when I thought of them. They hadn't been good parents and I hadn't been a good daughter to them. Still, regret was neither attractive nor dignified. My father had sounded pathetic on the phone, wild even. 'I shouldn't have let another man support my own flesh and blood,' he had also said. 'I made a mistake.' And what happened when mistakes couldn't be rectified? Where did one go? To what? To whom? From outside came the sound of a car screeching to a halt, horns and a few shouts. My skin felt more sensitive than usual, my eyes prone to tears; all was vivid and louder. I decided to go out for a walk.

The pavements were narrow and broken and sometimes there was no pavement at all. Toyota pickups zoomed past me. Motorcycles, vans and more four-wheel-drives. Tea ladies sitting in a row. A man stared at me, the whites of his eyes almost yellow. He was squatting in front of a mechanic's yard doing nothing. Rubbish piled on the side of a street; broken chairs stacked on top of each other. Too much struck me as incongruous. A donkey stood in the middle of a dusty street corner with no purpose or owner in sight – I stopped and, like a tourist, took a picture of it with my phone. But I was not wandering aimlessly; I wanted to find Tony's old house. I wanted to see the metal railing with the cut-out letters of the alphabet. If it was still there, if the garden wall hadn't been changed, then I wanted to look at it again. It would be a long walk by my reckoning, but I had nothing else to do and would rather not get on the wrong transport.

The city was larger than I remembered it to be. It stretched out, amorphous and repetitive with the supreme heat of the sun hanging down like a low ceiling. I started to sweat and lost focus. My thighs rubbed against each other; gritty sand entered my sandals and chaffed against my skin. But I did not want to give up and return. I needed to see the alphabet railing, that façade that entered my childhood and changed me. Crossing one street after the other,

I was unfit and my memory was playing tricks on me. I should be there by now.

Suddenly I found myself in front of the Russian Embassy. Its flat exterior, large, solid and unwelcoming. It was exactly as it had been when I was young except for the change in the name board. It was as if time hadn't passed and I was back holding my mother's hand; she had come to renew our passports. The Russian official looked down at me, not with the open curiosity I usually triggered in Georgia but with a knowing look, a thin sneer, veiled disgust. Then my mother's sudden impatience, the pressure of her hand on my arm yanking me outside. She carried me all the way to the car even though I was big enough to walk; she kissed me and hugged me and I wasn't sure what it was that made her feel so sorry for me, but I was happy to be the centre of her attention.

I stopped to ask directions. My rudimentary Arabic made the girl snigger; I tried English and she shrugged. She had no idea what I was talking about. I was the only woman in the street with my head uncovered. An army truck lumbered past full of uniformed soldiers. I turned the corner and there was a pickup truck with a gun aiming at the traffic. It was as if another civil war was about to erupt. My T-shirt was soaked with sweat, my head pounded from the sun, my eyes watered. I acknowledged that I was lost and the most dignified thing to do was to retrace my steps, have a shower and wait for my hosts. I was sure that my feet were covered in blisters.

Late afternoon, before sunset, Grusha and I walked into my father's house. When I had lived here, there was nothing around it but dust and a few scattered villas. Now the whole area was built up, the gardens mature, the newish streets already eaten away by potholes. In my memory the work on the house was still incomplete, it was without adequate flooring, without paint on the walls. Now it was completely unrecognisable. From the outside it looked brand new, ostentatious even. Floor-to-ceiling windows tinted blue, a modern façade and a tiled, spacious porch.

In the shade, a young boy was lounging in a large garden chair, an electronic tablet in his hand. To my surprise, he stood up when he saw us and held out his hand. True, he did all this with reluctance and apathy but still it was an impressive show of politeness. I liked him immediately. 'This is Mekki,' Grusha said and the pleasure I felt was thick and visceral. I looked at his forehead that was like mine, his eyes that were not, his skin that was darker. But I knew, instinctively, before he even spoke that his mind was like my mind and that we were both, mentally, introspectively, like our father.

'I am your sister, Natasha,' I said, in English because if this was one of the happiest sentences I ever said in my life, I wanted to say it in a language I was comfortable in.

His eyes widened and he was no longer bored, no longer wanting to get back to his game. He said, 'My sister Natasha.' His accent was heavy and his smile was one to treasure. This was love at first sight and I wanted to hug him.

He put his tablet on the chair and asked, 'Do you live in Russia?'

'No, in Scotland.'

'Scotland,' he repeated.

It didn't seem to matter what he said or what I said. Just this connection was enough. 'You must come and visit me,' I said. 'You would have a great time. I promise you.'

He listened to me describe the sights he would see, the snow, the castles, ski slopes and football matches. Suddenly I was desperately selling the idea of a visit. He listened, his eyes shining and dimming, a few nods, a few smiles. I kept on speaking until Grusha said, 'Let us go inside to pay respects to Safia and then you two can talk later.'

Indoors the furniture was grotesque, huge and gilded. The house seemed to be full of women. Apparently the men's period of condolence had come to an end and now my stepmother was only receiving women visitors. She was younger than I thought she would be. Mid-forties perhaps, striking-looking, even though she was wearing a plain white tobe. Her complexion was rough but here were the slanting attractive eyes Mekki had inherited. 'I've never really got on with her,' Grusha had said on the way. 'But she is a very capable woman.'

I greeted my stepmother, still hazy from meeting Mekki, already wanting to be with him again. When Grusha introduced me, Safia launched into a monologue, soft at first but then her voice rose. I could not understand what she was saying. The Arabic words bounced off me. I strained to distinguish them from one another, to pin them down to a meaning. I understood the phrase, 'her mother' and concluded that, perhaps, she was not talking to me directly but performing for her friends. They were taken aback, I could tell. She was sounding more and more hostile. A few elderly ladies started to intervene. She ignored them. One of them led me and Grusha out to another, adjoining room. 'Safia is upset,' she explained. 'She doesn't know what she is saying.'

Grusha and I sat in that other, smaller room. There was a large television set and a pair of men's glasses. My father's. There were shelves of books, some in Russian. Who would read them now? There was a walking stick leaning against the door; it was made from warm, high-quality wood. Grusha looked distressed and I assumed it was because she understood everything Safia had said. I wanted to ask her, but my father's room overwhelmed me. Newspapers folded up, a box of cigars, a bottle of cologne. A large print of Vladimir Tretchikoff's *Zulu Girl* was hanging on the wall. I remembered gazing at this print when I was young. I was a fan of Madonna then and the Zulu Girl did not fit into my idea of beauty. Perhaps if I had stayed I would have matured more fully. Perhaps my father could have taught me a thing or two. The room had a bed in one corner with no cover, just a pillow and a sheet. He must have stretched there and watched television.

I stood up to look at the bookshelf more closely. Here was the very same paperback of *Love Story* I remembered my mother reading, with Ryan O'Neal and Ali McGraw on the cover. Here was a box with my Bambi puzzle. We had left these things behind knowing we were going to find better replacements. How had he felt, all alone, seeing what reminded him of us? I picked up a copy of *Hadji*

Murat – he had read it. I would have liked to talk to him about it, especially to discuss Tolstoy's depiction of Shamil. I flipped the pages and found that my father had underlined certain lines and words. Perhaps he read it at a time when he was trying to improve his Russian. I turned to see Safia standing at the door. Another torrent of words but this time the gestures were clear enough: 'Get out of my house.'

In the car Grusha repeated, in Russian, the gist of Safia's outburst. This and what she explained about my father's material circumstances at the time of his death clarified the picture.

My father struck lucky in the last years of his life. He worked with a Chinese petroleum company during the oil boom (likely to come to an end if the South, where most of the oil was, decided to secede in next month's referendum) and he made quick, good money. With it, he revamped the house that I remembered as being half-built with dirt-cheap materials. It used to be in the middle of nowhere, and was now, as I had witnessed, in a popular desirable suburb. Given that my father had passed away, this perfectly decent estate would be divided, as Yasha later explained, according to Sharia law, in descending order of proportions between Mekki, myself and Safia.

I looked back at the scene that took place in the afternoon, furnishing it with what I now knew. Safia the bereaved widow is sitting in her nice house surrounded by relations and friends. In walks her husband's daughter, having just bonded outdoors with her half-brother. After twenty years of absence, after discarding her father's name, after moving further and further away from any semblance of Sudanese identity, this Natasha Wilson has a greater share of the roof that is over Safia's head. It is this that infuriates her. It is this that causes her outburst. 'Now you are coming back?' she says to me in Arabic. 'After it's too late. Where were you when he was ill? Where were you all these years? You disowned your father. Just like that. You don't want his name any more. What does it say in your passport? It doesn't say Natasha Hussein any more. But why should we expect any better of you? Your mother was a slut and you're no better. Don't think we don't hear the rumours about you. Don't think we are simple-minded and gullible. You certainly aren't getting a welcome, not from me.'

If I had understood Safia when she said all this to me, I would have felt more hurt. Instead her Arabic words swept over me only as harsh and as irritating as sand. Hearing them translated by Grusha, they remained somewhat at a distance. My only concern was how all this would affect seeing my brother, Mekki, again. My brother. The words had a clarity to them, an awesomeness that stood out in contrast to everything else.

2. Georgia, March 1855

For her very first dinner in freedom, David made sure that the garrison's kitchen cooked Anna's favourite food. It was, though, the napkins and candles that held her attention, the sensation of sitting on a chair at a dining table; all the mundane things she used to take for granted, were now to be singled out and either appreciated or silently ridiculed. Earlier they had gone to the fortress church to give thanks. It was a relief to do so, her whole body ached; the service was a medley of sounds and sights that were soothing and undemanding. Only when it was time to receive the small triangular holy bread did she start to feel moved by her surroundings. Next to her was David, a stranger who cared about her, who hovered close watching her every movement, her every response. She shied away from his masculinity, from his intent to claim her, and clung instead to Alexander. He was real enough, familiar enough. They would always share this bond. Everyone was saying he was young enough to forget all that had happened but she did not want him to forget Dargo. If he forgot the strangeness of it, who else could she talk to?

Madame Drancy wept and was extravagant in extolling her thanks to the whole of the Russian army. The governess spoke volumes to the officers who asked questions, who wanted intelligence. She elaborated on the position of Dargo, on details of the aoul, on Shamil's house. Anna, next to her, corroborated the information, jogged her memory, mentioned the map she had drawn. There was no alternative. Inside her shadows could shift over layers of secrets, the mind's eye could glance sideways and glimpse other possibilities, as different and as similar as a foreign language, but it was now clear on whose side she belonged, whose loyalty she was committed to. Let Madame Drancy speak; no power could stop her. Describe the specific peaks they had seen from the roof, how many sentries manned each portal, describe the twists and turns they encountered on the way down. Let these good soldiers jot down their notes and do their work. Years later when Dargo was bombed and flattened to the ground, Anna would remember these conversations, the information passed from her and Madame Drancy to the enemies of Shamil.

'What happened to Alexander's hair?' David asked. They were alone now for the first time, watching their son fall asleep. Tomorrow they would start their travels, make their way home to Tiflis. This bedroom was temporary; it was the same one David had shared with Jamaleldin.

With the lightest touch David stroked Alexander's spiky hair. It rose up from his scalp, rougher than it had ever been. Alexander stirred but did not open his eyes.

'They shaved it,' Anna said slowly. The spread of food at dinner had disgusted her. She could only eat very little and now had indigestion. After eight months of abstinence, the smell of wine had gone straight to her head and after two sips she had given up. 'It's their custom this time of year – to make the children bald. Apparently it's the only guaranteed way to protect them from lice and other infestation.'

'Oh you must have suffered!' He drew her to him. Their bodies fitted awkwardly. With the best of intentions, they embraced.

'You suffered too,' she said. He looked older than she remembered him to be, less confident. They had not spoken about Lydia yet. If they did, they would both weep. But she was there between them like a faint colour or a scent.

Even though the room was sparsely furnished, to Anna it seemed cluttered. Her sense of dimension, of bearings, had all been altered. David was larger than she remembered him to be, his uniform bulky – boots, spurs, gloves without elegance. She could not remember if he had always been that pushy and nervous; if his voice had always been this loud.

'You know,' he said. 'I had almost forgotten about Madame Drancy until I saw her today. I thought to myself "Who on earth is this sitting next to Anna?"'

She smiled. 'This is cruel of you. The poor woman was dragged into all this. And she was stoical. Incredibly polite, too, in the most tense of circumstances.'

'She will have to go back to France now.' He paused as if he wanted to say more. To mention their new straitened circumstances, perhaps. He was in debt and they could hardly afford a governess if they wanted to regain Tsinondali.

'I am sure that she would be eager to go home to her family.'

'Not until after we go to Petersburg, though.'

'Why?'

'To thank the emperor in person.'

'Really, David?'

He put his hands on her shoulder. 'It's necessary.'

'I'm so tired.'

His hand cupped her elbow. 'There is no rush. We can wait for the summer. When you have regained your strength. Look at you! Wasted away.' Anger crept into his voice.

She closed her eyes. They were unpalatable to her now – anger and revenge. They were too simple.

'You were so calm during the exchange,' he whispered. 'One would think you were not happy to see me.'

She started to warm to him. 'I was. Of course I was.'

Alexander sighed in his sleep and rolled over. She covered him and moved towards her husband feeling tight and needy, aloof and yet grateful, tainted and not sure what she was guilty of.

'David,' she said.

He looked up at her surprised, hesitant.

'I am a princess in my own right.'

It took time for him to absorb what she was saying, to understand it in his own way. Then he knelt in front of her and kissed her hand.

3. The Caucasus, March 1855–April 1856

The first days had a magical, honeyed quality. Turning to find Ghazi next to him, getting accustomed once more to his voice. Such reassurance in the touch of his brother. And there was more – his younger brother Muhammad-Sheffi, a stranger who turned out to be mischievous, lovable, elusive. His sisters, artlessly beautiful, coming up to him, their eyes shining with trust and welcome. His grandmother, blubbering, caressing him, and he did remember her, her voice, her laugh, and her tilt of the head so like his late mother's. With her, he could sense Fatima close, in this flesh and blood that was surrounding him, claiming him. And there was more. His father saying, 'Let me hold you. I cannot have enough of you.' Shots fired to celebrate his arrival and that of the returned prisoners. Cousins, friends. 'I remember you when you were young,' they laughed. 'You look exactly like Ghazi but paler,' they said and slapped him on the back. The sound of his name tossed about. His little crippled half-sister climbing on his lap. All this uninhibited love falling on him, voluminous and weighty.

He began to unfurl. Slowly. It was peculiar after all these years of hovering in the background to be thrust forward like this, to matter. To be the top man's son, the celebrated warrior's brother, to be gazed at and listened to. He began to speak and move. He began to talk about what he knew and what they didn't.

Railway Trains.

Telegraphic Communications.

Paved Roads.

Sanitation.

Ships as Big as Villages.

Telescopes.

'And how,' they asked, 'can this help us defeat them? Speak to us about what is useful. Teach us what would benefit us.'

This stalled him. Their logic was not his logic. He was saying peace and they were saying the resistance will win. He was saying Russia and they were saying jihad. When Jamaleldin spoke of the modern wonders within reach, Ghazi was in thrall, but their father did not approve. 'We don't need any of these things here. Come, I want to refresh your mind with our ways.'

Shamil took him to the mosque. It was as if time had not moved. To pray again with his father, the Arabic recitations, the movements. But he had become stiff and his heart had crusted. In all his years in Russia, no pressure was put on him to convert to Christianity. He had kept his faith but not practised it. Kept his faith in the sense that Orthodox Russian Christianity neither tempted nor threatened him. Islam in his mind stood the bolder of the two, more refined and complex, encompassing and vital. Its dynamism was rooted in him, his soul's connection to Shamil. Sins were like dirt; they could be washed off. More serious was the core submission, the foundations of belief. But spiritually, he had atrophied. There was no doubt about it. Without the nourishment of practice, Jamaleldin's faith had become insubstantial. After the prayers, his father turned and looked searchingly into his face for the first time. Shamil saw the weaknesses his son was inflicted with. He did not say a single word but the disappointment in his eyes struck Jamaleldin. He walked out of the mosque reeling.

Then the ikon. Jamaleldin walked into the room he was sharing with Ghazi to find Zeidat rummaging through his belongings. The intrusion made him halt at the door, unsure of how to react. Zeidat had been the family member least pleased to see him back; he had yet to figure out a way of dealing with her. Pretending to be shocked but unable to hide her glee, she picked up, from among his belongings, an ikon. What is this doing in your possession? He replied that it was a gift from a friend. An ikon, a gift from the enemy, a Christian friend. She sniffed and stomped out of the

259

room, evidence in hand. An hour later, all his belongings were confiscated. His books, his atlas, his globe – all that he had carefully packed, knowing he would not find it in Dargo, was lost to him. He seethed but it was prudent not to make a fuss. Now that his loyalty was in doubt, he must dodge further suspicion and fit in. *Keep the company of wolves and you must learn how to howl.* This was what the Russian proverb said.

The food in Dargo was ghastly, as was the ventilation and the sanitation. Riding out with Ghazi, who was indefatigable. Dragging himself out of bed for the dawn prayers. Five times a day accompanying his father to the mosque. Jamaleldin fell ill within a few weeks. Then summer rolled in, bringing with it Ramadan. Long days of thirst and hunger, short nights with even longer prayers. In all his years in Russia he had never fasted, never known which Islamic month was which. He was out of practice; fainting from dehydration, vomiting in the evenings immediately after breaking his fast. Zeidat remarked, tartly, that he was just like Princess Anna, completely unsuited to their way of life. The others had noticed the resemblance too and did not contradict her.

Shamil, recognising the challenge at hand, prescribed a rigorous regime of integration. Lessons to relearn the Avar language. Lessons in the Qur'an and Islamic practice. A tour of all of Shamil's territories, accompanied by Ghazi. Jamaleldin fumbled his way through all this with neither enthusiasm nor aptitude. He preferred to spend time with Chuanat, the most fluent Russian speaker in the household. She would tell him about Anna, who was often in her thoughts. And he would speak to her freely of Russia without her interrupting him or judging. He also found comfort in his grandmother's room, lying down with his head on her lap as she sang to him childhood songs, patches of which he remembered. But Bahou could neither speak a word of Russian nor understand his tentative Avar. Their communication was limited and, in time, frustrating.

It was his father whom he yearned to talk to. For this purpose, Jamaleldin was learning his lost language. Learning it enough to be able to urge him towards one thing – peace. But it was not easy to find Shamil on his own. He was constantly flanked by his naibs, his secretary, his translators. They all watched Jamaleldin and shamelessly eavesdropped on every word he said.

'Father, the Russians want peace. They are willing to talk. They are willing to come to an agreement.'

'My men are a suspicious lot.' Shamil's voice was gruff. 'They will think the Russians released you especially for this.'

'But they didn't. You know they didn't.'

'I do not have a favourable opinion of their integrity.'

Jamaleldin pushed on, 'They wish to establish regular commercial relations between our domain and Khasavyurt.' He was proud of himself for remembering to say 'our' rather than 'your' domain.

'This should not fool you. It is pacification by peaceful means.'

'But Father, a new tsar rules now. Change is bound to happen.'

'The sultan is my caliph. I have every hope that he and his allies will triumph over our enemy. This is not the time to negotiate. I would rather mount a large-scale attack but the backing I need from the Ottomans and the British has yet to come.'

Jamaleldin's voice rose. 'What if there is no triumph over Russia? What if there is defeat?' No one could get away with such questions except the imam's son.

Shamil closed his eyes as if the questions bored him. 'Then it is Allah's will and I would submit to it.'

Shamil appointed Jamaleldin as superintendent of administration and judicial proceeding. This freed him from any military duties. However the daily exposure to criminals and the harsh punishments meted out to them dismayed Jamaleldin. Shamil also suggested marriage as a cure for restlessness. Jamaleldin asked for more time in order to settle and build a house. He was eager to move away from Dargo. As much as he enjoyed the company of his sisters and his grandmother, as much as his conversations with Chuanat were fulfilling, it was a relief to escape the scrutiny of Zeidat. She was forever finding fault with him, broadcasting his blunders and, in general, eroding his confidence in himself. More seriously, she threatened to bring an end to his correspondence with any of his old friends and acquaintances. It became customary for his letters to be scrutinised before they were sent; he was advised to keep them short.

He set out designing a new house for himself. This gave him fresh impetus. He enjoyed drawing up the plans, a skill he had acquired in the army. But as soon as the first walls were built, an angry crowd gathered. The structure looked alien, the design, they complained, was in the shape of a cross. It was not in the shape of a cross, Jamaleldin insisted. But it proved impossible to reason with an increasingly hostile crowd. Once the accusation of the cross was spoken, it immediately took root. To appease the mob, Shamil immediately ordered the structure to be dismantled. Jamaleldin watched them tear the whole thing down in a frenzy of self-righteousness and superstition. Public humiliation trampled his spirit.

And there was no reprieve. His father had banned music throughout his territories; anyone caught fermenting grapes or drinking wine was flogged. This was to harden the men for fighting. Entertainment, Shamil believed, would make them soft. Jamaleldin felt this particular deprivation keenly. It was strange not to listen to Chopin, not to visit the theatre or dance in a ball; not even to play billiards or dominos or cards. The day had too many hours; its tone was sombre. 'You need a wife,' everyone said – women being the only pleasure available and encouraged. Ghazi was already married and Jamaleldin was older. The daughter of one of his father's closest naibs was nominated. Jamaleldin shuddered at the possibility that she would turn out to be like Zeidat, mocking his accent, pining for a real man, a warrior, who went out to kill Russians.

'Oh yes, we'll see you married off soon,' he heard them say. Their talk bewildered him; it was an effort to figure out whether they were serious or cynical, whether they were speaking about the near or distant future. He found that he often preferred his own company and started to turn towards nature for relaxation.

He spent considerable time looking at the mountains. On his own he could carry out the sort of conversations he could not have with anyone else. On the merits of Mozart over Schulhoff. On the French translation of 'wide-sleeved linen blouse'. On which of his father's horses could, theoretically, win the Krasnoye Selo steeplechase.

Through the summer and winter, he kept talking to his father about peace. Most of the latter, he spent ill with a fever. 'Your first winter in the mountains,' his grandmother said. 'You will get used to it.' It was only in April that he started to feel slightly better and able to spend more time outdoors. The fresh spring air reminded him of when he had first arrived the year before. Ironically, those first days had been the happiest. Now he was even more tentative, physically weak.

Today he felt a great need to see Shamil and late at night he waited for him outside the mosque. How did his father manage to survive on so little sleep? Long after Isha prayers, when the men dispersed Shamil would stay up with Sheikh Jamal el-Din for more zikr, more Qur'an recitation.

A full moon was burning on the horizon. Jamaleldin followed, with his eyes, the silver and grey shadows on the snow-capped peaks. They stirred in him a feeling of awe. Better still, the night took him out of himself, opened him up to tranquillity. A hand on his shoulder and there was his father next to him reciting, '*Surely in the creation of the Heavens and the Earth, and the alteration of night and day, and the ship that runs in the sea with profit to mankind; and the water Allah sends down from heaven, thereby reviving the earth after it is dead, and His scattering abroad in it animals of all kind; and the ordinance of the winds, and the clouds compelled between heaven and earth – surely these are signs for a people who comprehend.*'

Jamaleldin listened to Shamil explaining the verse and as he spoke, the images came closer and together they weaved their way through the words and out again. So that it was as if Jamaleldin sensed the power of creation; he saw the cargo perched on ships that miraculously stayed afloat. There was no sharper contrast than that between night and day, those long summer evenings and dark winter days. Where would they all be – humans and animals – without the rain? And if you stood still you would feel the change in the wind and know that clouds didn't have free will. They were running their appointed courses, they were subservient and duty-bound; slaves trailed by the winds.

Father and son walked around the aoul. Everyone asleep and for them alone were the stars and the forests audibly breathing. Jamaleldin would have been happy for time to stand still, so that he could be sprayed with this sense of blessing. His father approved of his introspection, of his stillness and desire to spend time outdoors. Jamaleldin would never ride out to war with him. His fate lay elsewhere and he was relieved that his father understood.

If only his father would understand the need for peace. 'Isn't the situation different now?' Jamaleldin asked. 'Now that the treaty has been signed in Paris?'

Shamil nodded. 'Sultan Abdelmajid has made peace with the Russians.'

'Would he not want you to do the same?'

'If he suggests it to me, I shall have no right to reject it.'

This was the best answer he had ever had. Jamaleldin felt a sense of hope. Shamil stopped walking and turned as if he had heard something. A dervish was walking towards them. Jamaleldin had seen him before in the mosque, swaying in ecstasy to the rhythms of the zikr. There were traces of handsomeness on his face but any wellbeing had been eroded by the all-consuming passion that broke off his tie to ordinary life. He neither went to war nor worked nor socialised in a normal way. People gave him plates of food and, once in a while, tossed him an unneeded garment. His clothes were torn, his hair dishevelled. Lurching towards Shamil, the dervish was inadequately protected against the cold, muttering to himself, absorbed in his other-worldly drunkenness. He did not seem to be aware that it was the middle of the night and he did not greet Shamil and Jamaleldin. But he must have known Shamil for he vibrated towards him, circled him a few times in a shambolic loop before veering suddenly into the dark.

'He's mad, isn't he?' Jamaleldin asked.

Shamil did not answer with a yes or a no. He said, 'His inward eye was opened and what he saw was too much for him to carry. It is best to be inwardly intoxicated and outwardly sober.'

'Are you, Father, inwardly intoxicated?'

Shamil smiled but he did not answer this question either. They said their goodnights and parted.

4. Georgia, October 1856

David helped her into the carriage. She was heavier than she had been in previous pregnancies even though there were still months to go before the birth. 'I should stop accepting dinner invitations,' she said when he settled next to her.

'We have two more next week,' he said. Since leaving the army, he had been spending more time at home, concentrating on the family finances with the aim of claiming back Tsinondali.

Anna felt the baby moving, a complete rotation of strong bones and muscles that felt heavy and reassuring. He, she would think of him as a he, a brother to Alexander. Last night's dream still covered her. Shamil putting his hand on her stomach to bless the baby, telling her that his name was Ilia.

'What do you think of Ilia as a name for the baby?' she asked David. The wheels of the carriage rattled over a bump on the road. She held her stomach until the discomfort passed.

'Ilia. Fine. What if it's a girl?'

'I don't know.' She didn't believe that it would be a girl.

'How about Tamar?'

'Yes. I love the name Tamar.'

When they first returned home to Tiflis, the sight of Lydia's toys and clothes had startled them. Anna walked into the nursery early the following morning to find David holding Lydia's christening gown and sobbing. A part of her had almost forgotten that he was Lydia's father, that he felt her loss too. But it was only once that he gave in to sadness. Most of the time, anger dominated him. He wanted revenge.

When they arrived at their destination, Anna moaned as she

stepped out of the carriage. They walked towards the entrance with the wide door and the footman in shining boots. She surrendered to what had now become familiar. The desire for people to see her, to welcome her back, to crow over her. The summer immediately after her release was spent in Petersburg and Moscow. Paying respects and gratitude to the tsar, a ball in their honour, one thanksgiving service after another. More than a year later, and still the topic of the kidnapping was of interest. Every time it died down, something or other would revive it.

Recently, the editor of *Kavkas*, the leading newspaper in Tiflis, published a book-length account of the incident. He had conscientiously interviewed her for a good number of days and written down everything she said, even providing an illustration of Shamil's household. He also did well in correcting many errors published in Germany and elsewhere. She had been mistakenly quoted as saying, 'The highlanders are not human beings, they are wild beasts.' Neither she nor Madame Drancy, before she returned to Paris, had ever expressed such a sentiment. A Prussian author claimed that 'Shamil's people held daggers over the princess's head to force her to write letters to the tsar.' This had never taken place either.

The gentleman seated next to her at dinner, a retired general, spoke highly of Madame Drancy's book. 'For the first time ever, the world is getting a glimpse of the elusive highlanders and the mysterious Shamil.'

Anna sipped her soup. 'Madame Drancy was always exact.'

'The description of the harem is fascinating.'

'She was always taking notes. I am happy that she succeeded in her goal and managed to publish her book.'

'What is astonishing is that you give Shamil a far higher character than anyone ever had done. Even his supporters in Britain.'

'It is all true. No embellishments.'

'But what did he give you in return?' Belligerence took over from curiosity, keener than the fascination of the exotic. 'What did Shamil do to you? Eh? Eight months of captivity. Your property destroyed, you little girl lost for ever.'

She broke down then and there. One minute she was enjoying her soup, the next minute David was helping her out of the room. People's curiosity made them wearisome and thoughtless. She should, really, not accept any more dinner invitations.

In his study, David sat hunched over the accounts. She had come in to ask him if he would like to join her for a walk. It was a clear day and the air smelt of snow. If they went out now they might enjoy a few hours of sunshine. But just looking at his face, she guessed he was not in a good mood.

'Do you know what happened to the forty thousand roubles I raised?'

This was a rhetorical question. He would tell her now and start to tremble with rage. She sat on his lap in the hope that her pregnant weight would restrain him. He did not seem to notice. 'This is how the money was divided. A fifth went to Shamil's treasury. And the rest was distributed among the men who actually took part in the raid! The ones who looted Tsinondali. The ones who broke through and captured my family and burnt—'

She put her fingers on his lips. There was no need for him to get agitated. She worried about him when he did. 'They also have burnt villages and felled trees and crops destroyed. They will use the money to rebuild their villages.'

'Why don't they talk peace, then? It is not as if they have not been given ample opportunities. Instead they are as stubborn as mules, as hard-headed as the rocks they live on.'

Anna heard him but she also heard Zeidat. '... you Russians roll our men's heads like melons on the ground ... you shit inside our houses to humiliate us ...' She did not want to hear Zeidat's voice, to remember her taunts or the looted diamond ring flashing on her finger. Anna felt the blood thicken in her veins, her stomach contract around the baby. She took a deep breath in. 'David, leave them alone.'

He thumped the table. 'Leave them alone! If you imagine that Shamil will be left alone, then you are dreaming ...'

268

She heaved herself off his lap. It had been a mistake to speak to him. She could have been outdoors by now in her coat and muff.

David's voice rose, following her as she left the room. 'We might have suffered in the Crimea but the Caucasus is still of vital importance. Shamil will be captured. His own men are beginning to tire of this war. Believe me, he can't last long.'

Outdoors, she walked slowly, careful not to slip on any unexpected ice patches. The garden lay before her, bare and attractive. Near the greenhouse, she could look up and see the mountains. They were there now, Chuanat and her baby; Bahou and Ameena. She missed them, she could not help it; there was an appetite inside her for them. She wanted them to know that she was going to be confined soon and that Alexander still chanted 'la ilaha illa Allah'.

The snow on the peaks was the colour of cream. *When will blood cease to flow in the mountains . . .* After all these years, would Shamil finally be defeated? She had dreamt again of him last night. She often did. Most of the dreams had neither a setting nor a plot. They were just dreams of his presence. And in his presence was a force, a fullness that was sufficient, an end in itself. Sometimes in the dreams, she did actually see his face. But more often than not there was only his silhouette.

5. The Caucasus, March 1857–July 1858

A rumour was going around that the Russians had given Jamaleldin a slow-acting poison. They had given it to him before his release and only now were its effects showing. He was losing weight rapidly and was always coughing. Too weak to go out riding, he spent most of his time lying down.

Jamaleldin knew better. He knew the first time he coughed and a glob of blood fell on the snow, melting it a little, seeping into a lighter red. It had been the first clear day of spring and he had gone out riding with Ghazi. They carried their falcons on their wrists. He felt the weakness overcome him, a dizziness as if he had not eaten, even though he had. He stopped over the plains and let Ghazi ride on without him. *I do not want to hunt*, he realised. Frost all around him but he felt hot. He veered his horse towards the north and stared down the slopes, out towards Georgia. His other life was there, all the things he knew and missed. But he felt too tired to yearn, the bird heavy on his arm. He slipped down from the saddle and was seized by a violent fit of coughing. The falcon grew restless, it fluttered its wings. His chest was tight; all this mountain air around him and it was a struggle to inhale even a little of it. Perspiration broke throughout his body. He saw the blood on the snow.

'Father, this is not a poison working through me. It is a disease called tuberculosis. I have come across it in the Russian army. There is no cure for it. Because it is contagious. I need to leave Dargo. I have to be alone. It takes a year or so to run its course...' He did not add, '... it usually ends in a painful death.' He would break down if he did and a man of the Caucasus must not be seen to cry.

Shamil arranged for him to move to Soul-Kadi, an aoul hidden behind the massive peaks that made up the Gates of Andi. He gave him a young Georgian prisoner-of-war to nurse him and five armed guards. Shamil was always fearful that Jamaleldin would be recaptured by the Russians; he would not take any chances.

In Soul-Kadi, Jamaleldin found the solitude not only bearable but welcome. The villagers made no demands on him. They left roses at his door, baskets of food. The house he was in was small and bare but it had a roof and when he had the energy, he climbed up and dozed in the fresh air. At night he slept on a cot rather than on the floor – a Russian habit, and when he was weak, that cot was carried up to the roof. On his back he would watch the clouds moving, trailed by the winds.

His father put aside his pride and sent down to the military fort in Khasavyurt for medicine. The medicine came but did not help. It surprised Jamaleldin that his father still had hope. Love clouded his vision. Or else he was simply a powerful man who did not easily give up.

In the middle of winter, Ghazi came to visit. He hung up his gun and slipped down to sit cross-legged on the floor. He sat far away from the cot because Jamaleldin insisted. Ghazi's good health lit up the room with a rude glow. His strength was like a force of nature contained indoors. Jamaleldin kept roses in the room to overpower the smell of illness. Ghazi brought in other smells, of sweat, horses and clothes damp from rain.

'Why are you alone?' he blustered. 'Where's that Georgian prisoner Father gave you?'

'I exchanged him.'

'For how many men?'

'None.'

'What?'

'I got things instead.'

'What?' Ghazi leant forward. The light from the fire flickered on his face.

'Things I need.'

'Medicine, you mean?'

'Sort of. What's your news?'

'It's not going well,' Ghazi said, picking up a yellow rose and raising it to his nose. He meant the war, the battles, the resistance. 'As long as Russia was losing in the Crimea, the men had hope. Now it's all gone, especially after the cholera outbreak. Hidalti said—'

'Who's he?'

'Chief of artillery. There is so little ammunition now. He said, we need to make every bullet work. So we're getting the men to drive an iron nail through each bullet.'

'Is this practical?'

'Not really. All of lower Chechnya is in their hands now. We need to get it back. And there are bad feelings among the tribes, too much rivalry and bickering. Some of them betrayed us and submitted. Then the Russians betrayed them too. They moved the tribes that surrendered to Manych.'

'Where's that?'

'Far north. And it's a dump. Father himself couldn't have come up with a more severe punishment. The other day a Chechen delegation came to him asking to negotiate for peace. He said to them, 'Do you want to go to Manych as well?''

Jamaleldin smiled, 'I'm sure they had no case after that.'

'Of course. Who in their right mind is going to give up their land without a fight?'

It disappointed Jamaleldin to admit it but it was true. 'The Russians don't want peace any more. There was a time when they did. But Father refused all talk of peace. Who has the courage now to talk to him about surrender? I tell you, my illness is a blessing.'

Ghazi smiled. 'You have become a true Sufi. Thanking Allah for your misfortune. All these lessons Father arranged for you must have paid off.'

To laugh would aggravate a fresh bout of coughing. Jamaleldin bit his smiling lips. It was a pleasure just to look at Ghazi, to watch his face. It did not really matter what news he brought with him. 'I have a gift for you,' Jamaleldin said.

'Me?'

'Yes. Look on the shelf over there. Bring it down.'

Ghazi stood up. 'What on earth is this?'

'A music box. You turn it and listen.'

Ghazi sat down and started to turn the handle. He looked like an overgrown child.

'Gently, man,' Jamaleldin said.

The music box was painted in gaudy colours. On it was a picture of the Lake of Lucerne with swans afloat on the shining water. The first notes of 'The Gondolier's Song' filled the room. Ghazi's mouth fell open. When he could speak he said, 'This is beautiful, brother.'

Jamaleldin watched the muscles on his brother's hand as he turned the handle. In exchange for the Georgian prisoner, he had also got books, paintings and an atlas. It would be better if his father never heard about this. He would not understand.

Ghazi listened intently as 'The Gondolier's Song' gave way to 'The Skater's Waltz'. He tilted his head in appreciation. This was the Ghazi Muhammad feared by every Russian serving in the Caucasus. And here he sat enraptured by a toy, simple. His enemies would jeer if they saw him now, they whose pleasures were sophisticated, whose tastes were more refined. Jamaleldin felt a rush of love for him.

Ghazi said, 'We have to hide this.' From Shamil and Shamil's spies. Even the Russian newspapers were confiscated, let alone this devil box.

Ghazi stayed with him a couple of days. He could not be spared for long. Jamaleldin spoke about Russia, about girls skating on ice, about the steeplechase and the railways. Good, kind people, neither devils nor monsters. Ghazi took it all in, fascinated and wanting to learn. No matter what, Jamaleldin would always be his older brother. The one who knew more.

By spring Jamaleldin was emaciated. Shamil sent a messenger to Khasavyurt begging for the army doctor. It was agreed that three naibs would be held hostage in the doctor's absence. Two other highlanders half-dragged, half-carried the unfortunate doctor up the steepest and most terrifying of terrains. By the time he reached Jamaleldin, five days later, he was trembling from fatigue and nauseous from vertigo. Jamaleldin was too ill to apologise. Instead he was happy to see the doctor. At last someone he could speak Russian to, ask for news of friends, go over memories.

There was nothing the doctor could do for him. A few preparations to ease the pain. But the talking was enough; this drawing towards him of his other, Russian life. Days and years that mattered, that could not be erased. His accomplishments, his friendships, the good times, even the disappointments – how the emperor refused to give him permission to marry Daria Semyonovich or to engage in active service in the Crimea. He shared all this with the doctor, indulging in the memories. Listening to the doctor as he narrated the latest military gossip, who lost money to whom and who was called to fight a duel. Bright brief life as he had known it.

After the doctor left, the summer weather enabled Jamaleldin to lie again on the roof. He watched the wind orchestrate the clouds. He saw the sun melt the last avalanches of snow. He turned to look at the local yellow roses he had come to need, delicate petals, proud thorns. When he dozed, it was as if their tenderness and scent fused into him.

Then even to be carried up to the roof became too exhausting. When Shamil visited him, he did not, like Ghazi, stay in the corner of the room. Instead he held Jamaleldin in his arms and prayed for him. The prayers dulled the terror that often flared up as vicious as the disease itself. The prayers lulled Jamaleldin to spaces where the pain subsided and sleep was within reach. His father's hand lay on his chest; it felt heavy and reassuring, a memory of childhood, of other blessings. Shamil propped him up and made him spit, rubbed his back, gave him honey to drink. Jamaleldin saw the sadness in his eyes, the crush. Only three years since his return. Only three years together. Jamaleldin wanted to live, wanted to feel healthy again but death was pulling him away against his will, against his father's will.

Jamaleldin fell into a deep sleep and woke up in the middle of the night to see his father standing up in prayer. He recognised the recitation learnt long ago in Akhulgo. *For truly with every hardship comes ease. Truly with every hardship comes ease.* He thought he had forgotten these meanings but he hadn't. They were buried under the new things he had learnt – French and the poems of Lermontov, how to draw a map, how to buy a railway ticket – but the foundation had remained: there is no god but Allah, Muhammad is His beloved. There are no limits to His Mercy, there is no will except His will. There were colours in the room now and his father growing taller so that his head touched the roof. Sheikh Jamal el-Din was also in the room, sitting on the floor and on his chest was an eye, an open unblinking eye that was looking straight at Jamaleldin. I must be dreaming, the fever gone to my head. Such a great constriction that it was hard to breathe. He heard the chants of the Orthodox funeral services. Were they burying a Russian? They must be. A dear, good friend who had walked by his side and helped him up when he stumbled. Who made him laugh and taught him something useful, something he couldn't now recall because he was dizzy from the room's breaking brightness. How strange that the eye on Sheikh Jamal el-Din's chest was the only light in the room! His father was large, very large, but his voice was soft and Jamaleldin felt the room swell up with angels.

IX
High Torn Banners

1. Khartoum, January–February 2011

I stayed in Khartoum much longer than planned. Throughout the New Year and the run-up to the referendum, which resulted in South Sudan gaining its independence. Safia had hired a lawyer and taken me to court to prove that I was no longer a Muslim and as such deserved to be cut off from my father's inheritance. My first instinct on hearing this was to brush it off and assume that I would be well out of the country before proceedings started. It did not strike me as important enough to postpone my return. When I casually mentioned it to Yasha, though, his reaction made me reconsider.

'Why are you laughing?' he said. 'This is serious.'

We were in his flat. I was spending more and more time there so that I could access the internet. Evening after evening we sat opposite one another; I with my laptop and he spread out on a recliner, with his. Sometimes we worked and sometimes we watched films or I wrote emails to Malak. His flat had modern furniture compared to his mother's downstairs. It was more comfortable too. He had no qualms about using the air-conditioner even when opening the window and putting on the ceiling fan would have been tolerable, if a little balmy. Soon I discovered that after eating the healthy dinner Grusha cooked, he would order takeaways and keep eating late into the night. He drank Pepsi instead of water. No wonder.

'I am laughing,' I said. 'Because Safia's charge sounds deliciously medieval.'

'You have to fight this, Natasha.' He was wearing a white shirt. It flattered him as did the gritty, end-of-the-day look.

I shook my head.

279

He picked up his phone. 'Do you want rice pudding or crème caramel?'

This was the start of the post-dinner bingeing that I had recently been pulled into. He would order more food – kebab, pizza or shawerma – but I stuck primly to dessert. Grusha's cooking was delicious and healthy. The kind of soups I missed: fresh vegetables and tender chicken or lamb. The ingredients were less packaged here, not beaten into submission by supermarket requirements. Often the vegetables were misshapen, twinned and oddly stuck together but their scent was pronounced, their taste more distinct. There was no reason to keep on eating after such a dinner. But this had become Yasha's habit.

'Crème caramel,' I said.

'Anything else?'

'No.' I had to resist the abandonment he was proposing. He put through the order. A large pizza that he would eat all by himself, two kebab sandwiches, pastry for dessert. Sometimes the shops would not deliver and we would have to go there ourselves and pick the food up. I liked these late-night drives, kept secret from Grusha, who would definitely disapprove. Yasha had taken me into his confidence, shared with me his nocturnal guzzling. I never had the heart to lecture him on watching his weight, let alone reducing it. I did worry that he was jeopardising his health but I did not want to embarrass him.

We would drive through poorly lit streets and past the airport. Once we saw a car explode, just like that, orange flames rising up. An excited group gathered. For a long time afterwards, the loud pop of the tyres numbed my ears.

'Safia can't go around making such accusations. It's immoral.' One of the buttons of his shirt had come undone. 'And it's obvious that her motive is greed.'

'I don't want anything.' It was too much drama to be pulled into. But my father's copy of *Hadji Murad* – I would like to have that. Surely it meant nothing to Safia; I doubted she could read Russian.

'My brother deserves it all.' I had been regularly meeting Mekki. Every time felt special, almost too good to be true.

'I am opposed to this apostasy law but if it won't be amended, then the message needs to go out loud and clear that it is virtually impossible to enforce. Safia's position is weak. You will win and afterwards we can turn around and sue her for slander.'

I noted the 'we' in his sentence. It was because he was a lawyer. He wanted to help me in his professional capacity.

Instinctively I switched from Russian to English. 'So let me get this straight. I am to go to court and prove that I am a Muslim? I haven't got a leg to stand on. Nothing. I am not even sure if I am. What is this, the inquisition?'

He had been shaking his head as I was talking. Now he said, also in English, 'That's exactly it. You shouldn't have to prove that you're a Muslim – you are one by birth, by default. You have a right, a human right, to be a bad Muslim, a lapsed Muslim, a secular Muslim, whatever. *She* though, doesn't have any right to excommunicate you, especially when she has something to gain out of it. Believe me, we can get this thrown out of court in a matter of minutes.' He smiled as if this was a case he wanted to sink his teeth into.

'Yasha, this is going to mess up my plans.'

He waved his hand in dismissal and changed back into Russian. 'One week. Trust me. Just delay your return by a week.' He paused and looked at me as if he was noticing something about me for the first time. 'You're the only one, apart from my mother, who still calls me Yasha.'

'It's because, Yassir,' I emphasised his real name, 'I've been away for twenty years. I'm stuck in a time warp.'

'We'll get you out of it.'

I was beginning to like his use of 'we'. I guessed that he had carried it over from Arabic but still there was a grandness about it and a welcome.

The case ended up taking a lot longer than a week. To start with I had to prove that I was my father's daughter. I had to prove that

Natasha Wilson was Natasha Hussein. This required that I obtain my adoption papers from the UK, get them authenticated by the Foreign Office and the Sudanese Embassy in London. To my relief and surprise, Tony, all the way from Aberdeen, was helpful throughout this process. He 'rose to the occasion' as Grusha said and facilitated most of this paperwork.

Week in, week out I waited in Khartoum. Borrowing Grusha's or Yasha's car I would pick up Mekki from school or near his house. He snuck out to meet me behind his mother's back. Lucky for me, he was at the age when he was allowed greater freedom and felt the need to exercise it. Having his own mobile phone also made the logistics much easier. 'Where would you like to go today?' I would ask when he climbed in next to me, his expression deliberately casual, though once or twice he did look over his shoulder to see if anyone was looking.

He would say, 'Take me to Ozone,' or Solitaire, or Tangerine, or Time Out. These were neither amusement arcades nor cinemas nor playgrounds. Instead they were stylish coffee shops and restaurants where we would sit in pleasant, often outdoor surroundings and afterwards I would pay a hefty bill. An eye-opener for me that nowadays a twelve-year-old's treat was a latte. 'Are you allowed coffee?' I once asked but he said, 'I'm a man,' and so I shut up. Most of the time my brother and I spent together was in silence. He studiously dug into his treats and sat back in his chair quite pleased with himself. I, too, once I got over my British need for small talk, relaxed and enjoyed being where I was, looking at him, listening to snatches of the conversations around me. His similarity to me continued to be a novelty; his resemblance to my father would startle me every now and again.

I showed him a photo of my classic Skoda. 'It's a convertible,' I explained. I pointed out the details I particularly liked, the dashboard, the gear stick mounted on the steering column, 'Felicia' written in lower-case cursive. I wanted him to learn.

He asked me about McDonald's and Pizza Hut, Baskin Robbins and Dunkin Donuts. He had heard about them from his friends who travelled to Dubai or Cairo or KL. Sudan was under US sanctions and Mekki had never travelled abroad. 'When you come and visit me, I'll take you to all of these places,' I promised and thought that my colleagues at the university would be amused at how American fast food could be a reason to visit Scotland.

Sometimes I irked him by being predictably adult. 'Stop kicking the table.' 'No you can't have another ice-cream.' 'Have you done your homework?' Sometimes he unnerved me with his blunt questions. 'How come you're not married?' 'When are you leaving?' or 'Why does my mother hate you?' These questions were tempered by his own frankness and gratuitous, though rare, confessions. A story of Safia's quarrel with the gardener, how he once got caught cheating in the Arabic exam, how he lent money to his best friend, never got it back and they were now no longer friends. I liked it best when he spoke about our father. It brought about a slight fizz of envy for what seemed to have been their regular uncomplicated life.

Once, though, he spoke of him in reference to myself and the past. 'He was angry for not keeping you in Khartoum.' The structure of the sentence sounded as if he was repeating something his mother had said.

'I was the one who wanted to leave. He shouldn't have blamed himself.' I would have said this to him in hospital if I had got here in time. Perhaps it would have made him feel better. He should not have felt guilty on my behalf. 'I was sure I wanted to be with my mother. It would have been almost impossible for him to make me stay.'

'Why?' Mekki slurped the last of a chocolate milkshake.

'Why what?' I was thawed because almost everyone around me looked like me. I blended and the feeling was like warm, used bedsheets, lulling, almost boring.

'Why didn't you want to stay?'

'I was afraid.'

'Afraid of what?'

I breathed in. 'Of never seeing my mother again.' I was not sure if this was completely true, if this was the whole story. I remember her bribing me with the promise of a better school in Britain, brighter toys, bookshops. Sharpened pencils, a calculator, a microscope all to myself. I listened to her and believed her because of the alphabet letters on the wall of Tony's house.

A movement caught Mekki's eye and he turned around. Someone had tossed a heavy bag on a chair and it overturned. I was getting upset by his questions; a pressure was building in my chest. For the first time ever, I felt relieved that it was time to pay the bill and take him home. Then in the car, just as I was about to park, he said, 'Teach me Russian. Starting from next time.' What I had said earlier must have made an impression on him – the fact that my father and I always spoke together in Russian.

Yasha stayed away from the cafés and restaurants. His modus operandi was the takeaway, conforming to the Arab cliché that the obese were embarrassed to eat in public. I did not challenge him over this. Besides, my outings with Mekki sufficed. During the day when Grusha and Yasha were at work and I did not have access to a car, I worked on my papers. A number of times, I went by public transport to all the tourist locations – the museum, the camel market, the Mahdi's tomb. These trips left me hot and strangely disappointed. Instead of enjoying what I judged to be well-kept secrets, jewels that the world had overlooked, I felt it unfair that the country remained behind an iron curtain, excluded from the interest of the global traveller.

'Our government has a bad reputation,' Yasha said. 'All the world's goodwill has now gone to the new South Sudan.' He was working hard to protect the interests of the Southern Sudanese who had been living in the North all their lives. Overnight, they had been stripped of their Sudanese nationality and sent packing to the South. Those who could not afford the journey were stranded in limbo.

I liked listening to him rant about his work. This usually started as soon as he arrived home. I would be helping Grusha in the kitchen and he would walk in and stand near the fridge, his bulk filling up most of the space. It was a good thing that the maid left early, otherwise the four of us crowding the kitchen would have been impossible. Yasha would lean on the fridge, which made Grusha jittery as a kitchen chair had recently come crashing down under his weight and the fridge was more precious. He would start narrating his stories of the day – a new client he was defending, a case that got thrown out of court, a petition he was preparing. After dinner Grusha would go out to the veranda to have a cigarette while the two of us lingered at the table. Yasha would be saying something like, 'It's the principle that is at stake here,' while I could see her chunky bare feet propped up on the patio's low table, the glow of the cigarette in the dark. She reminded me of my mother.

He was positive about my appearance in court the next week, assuring me I had nothing to worry about. He sat with one hand over the chair next to him. The other one, which he had been eating with, hovered over the table unwashed. 'Have you ever thought of moving back? Giving it a chance here?'

'No I haven't,' I said. The stage was set for a romance. Every romantic attachment I had ever had ended, like my parents' marriage, with rancour and bitterness. Only Yasha remained a friend.

After almost a month of trying, I finally heard from Malak. It turned out that she was not much of a writer; her emails, few and far between, were a couple of dashed lines or links (where I was merely copied among various recipients) to such things as headshot photographers she was recommending or obituaries of actors who had recently passed away. This time was a response to me telling her about Safia's accusation.

Yes you are a Muslim – fight for it.
Don't worry about Oz.

A day later I heard from him. He had changed his user name. Instead of SwordOfShamil, it was now Osama.Raja.

Hi Natasha,

I'm sorry I behaved poorly that day you came over. I wasn't up to talking much and to tell you the truth, it was because what happened psyched me out. The cell felt as small as a cupboard and for the first two days there was always someone watching me and writing down what I did. Not that I could do much. I was afraid all the time. Even to stand up and pray, let alone ask which direction was the south-east. I couldn't sleep and then after a few days of this, I started dreaming even though I wasn't asleep. My mind played tricks on me. It was weird and disorienting. Then they started asking me questions and as I kept answering I felt that I was lying, even though I wasn't. I kept thinking I must give them the right answer not the wrong answers when the simple truth was that I hadn't done anything wrong. Now Malak keeps saying that 'anything' means anything suspicious, whatever got me into this trouble in the first place. She's mad at me.

I didn't go back to uni when the term started. I'm looking at moving – even changing my degree. Once I get started on filling application forms, I'll put your name down as one of my referees if that's okay with you?

Thanks for coming over that day. It made me remember that I liked your classes and your papers about Shamil. I've been reading them again. I started to think of myself as a student not a criminal.

Apparently I made the news. See ...

I clicked on the link and found myself in a far-right website under the heading *The Stain of Al-Qaeda has Reached Scotland.* Even though he was not charged.

I must have sighed too loudly because Yasha looked up from the kofta sandwich he was eating. I told him about Oz, switching to English. He followed and replied in English.

'That student of yours needs to man up. If he were in any part of the Arab world he would have been beaten, too. He would have come out of this with a broken rib or a broken nose. Or worse. Or not come out at all. He should count himself lucky.'

'Well, he was born in Britain and so his expectations are based on that.'

Yasha snorted. He put down his sandwich and ambled to the

fridge. At home he wore jellabiyas which made him look as regal as a giant. I suddenly felt discouraged from telling him about the police searching my office or Gaynor's complaint against me. Such battles belonged wholeheartedly there.

Yasha and Grusha had an active social life. I was familiar with some of their friends, other cross-cultural families in which the mothers were Eastern European and the fathers Sudanese. I caught up with the news of those in my age group, how many children they had, who was in Dubai and who was in Moscow or Cape Town or Washington or not so far away in Port Sudan. I was shown wedding photos on mobile phones, heard descriptions of holidays spent and family reunions made. So this was the tribe I belonged to, here were my species. They knew my mother and my father, they had known me as a child and this gave them a confidence in their approach. It was hard not to relax with them, enjoying their company, practising that dance from Russian to English to the Arabic words I was now remembering or relearning or a little bit of both.

In three different languages I was told that Yasha and I were truly suited to each other. And weren't you childhood sweethearts too? So what's stopping you? His weight? Help him lose it, take him back to Scotland with you and put him through surgery. What other excuse? Your job? But don't you want to be a mother? Surely you do and you can't keep putting it off for ever.

How easily their words wormed their way through me! I was vulnerable, away from home and instead of resenting their interference in my private life, a sadness would wash over me, a sense that their words were too little, too late. I played a game of 'what if?' – what if my parents' marriage had survived, what if Tony had never shown up? The sensory details around me evoked incomplete memories, half-formed scenes more serene and rosy than I would usually admit. Grusha showed me old photographs of a picnic on the bank of the river. I could not remember any such picnic. And yet here was the proof. My mother in wide seventies-style trousers, orange swirls fuzzy and almost psychedelic; my father's hair like

Jimi Hendrix's. He was carrying me on his shoulder and my mother was looking up at me, smiling, reaching up one arm to hold my elbow as if helping me balance, a cigarette in her other hand. I could not remember being such a happy child.

Quite a portion of Khartoum's social life revolved around weddings from which I was exempt due to my recent bereavement. I would stay behind while Grusha, dressed in her best and still resembling Hilary Clinton, got in her car and headed off. Sometimes Yasha accompanied her or went out with his own circle of friends. Grusha told me how for almost a year after his wife's and daughter's deaths, he kept to himself and shunned company. He stayed at home and ate his way through the pain. She seemed relieved that he was now adjusting.

It had taken me time to find Tony's old house. Whenever I had the car, I would be on the lookout for the metal railing with the alphabet letters. One afternoon, I turned a corner and there it was, on a busy road that bore little resemblance to the one I remembered. But it was definitely the same house. Here, in front of it, my mother had parked and left me in the car to go inside and deliver a cake. Our lives were never the same again.

It was not enough for me to see it from the outside. I got out of the car and rang the bell. I waited and looked at the railing; it had not stood the test of time, it was rusty and the wall beneath it yellow-brown with dust and age. Cracked too, here and there. The letters themselves looked dated, cursive and pretentious. They had captivated me as a child and roused my ambitions. I peered through the gate; there were no parked cars and the house looked deserted, the garden overgrown and unkempt. I had started to turn away, when I heard sluggish footsteps. A tall man in a dirty jellabiya opened the door. He must be the resident watchman. I had not prepared what to say so I asked for Tony.

He shook his head and confirmed that no one was living in the house.

To gain access I lied that I wanted to look inside with a view to buying the house. He let me in. The path used to be strewn with attractive pebbles but most of them had worn away. I walked to the back and found the swimming pool. It was predictably smaller than I remembered and empty, with broken and missing tiles at the bottom and all along the sides. I remembered swimming here with a Tweety Bird inflatable ring while my mother was indoors. In room after room, there was only decay and filth, human excrement and the scurrying, scratching sound of rats. The light fittings and ceiling fans had been either removed or stolen. The bathrooms were stripped down to almost rubble. Upstairs in the master bedroom, the branches of a tree had pushed their way through the rectangular hole where the air-conditioner used to be. There was a horrible smell that turned out to be a recently dead pigeon. I lingered, absorbing it all, feeling it seep into me; it stirred in me an ache I could not at first understand. Only later did I recognise it as homesickness. A yearning for an identifiable place where I could belong.

Later, when I described the court session to Malak, I told her about the small beleaguered judge with crinkly white in his hair. He peered down his glasses at the papers in front of him. He cleared his throat now and again. I would have felt more confident in some kind of jacket, my shoulders straight, a tissue in my pocket. I would have preferred to stand in my sensible black shoes instead of these moist sandals.

'Why did you change your name? Hussein is a good name, the name of the grandson of Muhammad, peace be upon him.'

'Did you become a Christian when you were adopted?'

'Are you or have you ever been married to a non-Muslim?'

'Why do you know so little about the faith you were born into?'

Yasha had coached me on what to say. I went along as practised. The sound of the ceiling fan grew louder, the judge looking up at me over his glasses, down at the papers he was shuffling with his hand. The room and the whole building had a colonial feel to it. There were not many people about. I made a point of not searching for Safia. Was she here or not? I was afraid of her, now, because she was sure of herself, of what she was and what she was entitled to. But Yasha was backing me up and Malak was on my side.

'You are an adult,' the judge said after he ruled in my favour. 'Your father made a mistake in not keeping you by his side, in not bringing you up as a Muslim – but he is gone now to meet his Lord and we must not speak ill of the dead. In fact it would seem that your father repented and admitted his mistake. We can only ask Allah, the Most Merciful, to forgive him. But as I said, you are a mature adult. It is your responsibility now to learn about your religion and to practise it as best as you can. Do you have something to say?'

I said that I was not a good Muslim but I was not a bad person either. I said I had a brother that I wanted to keep in touch with. I said that I wanted to give up my share of the inheritance to him. Apart from my father's Russian books and Russian keepsakes, I wanted nothing. I said that I did not come here today to fight over money or for the share of a house. I came so that I would not be an outcast, so that I would, even in a small way, faintly, marginally, tentatively, belong.

2. Georgia, Summer–Autumn 1859

It became a habit, whenever possible, to walk in the garden and stop at the greenhouse where she could look up at the mountains. Occasionally she would see plumes of smoke, imagine or actually hear a faraway sound of gunfire, but what was actually happening eluded her. There were only things David said and her imagination. A new policy towards the Caucasus, a new Russian leader, Field-Marshal Bariatinsky, who was brilliant and effective. For the first time in all these years, almost overnight, Shamil was losing one battle after another. Aoul after aoul fell to the Russians; the tribal chiefs who had fought by his side were now turning against him.

Anna held Ilia's hand and walked at his pace. His other hand brushed the flowers and bushes along the path. Sometimes he wanted to stop and examine a pebble or a beetle crawling in the mud. The slowness of this walk suited her. It was her first time attempting a full round of the garden after her confinement last month. She still sensed the new lightness of giving birth to Tamar, shifting the weight from her stomach to the outside world, the pressure lifting from her pelvis and lower back. But she was still weak from losing too much blood; once in a while she felt her womb contracting. While the deliveries were quicker, these after-birth pains seemed to get more painful with each successive birth. She had missed Ilia this past few weeks, unable to focus on much other than the newborn and her own health, but he had made his misery and jealousy felt. Crying at times until he sweated and shook; regressing into baby habits he had given up many months ago. 'Ilia is a good boy,' she sang to him. 'Ilia is Mama's friend.' She understood how overlooked he was feeling, how he had been demoted from that important spot of being the youngest in the family. And how special Tamar's birth had been, a little girl again, resembling Lydia so much that it was as if time had looped back. David doted on her, and poor Ilia struggled to gain the attention he had until recently enjoyed.

He leaned forward now to tear up a flower. He shoved it in his mouth. She knelt down to remove petals and dust from his tongue. 'Does it taste nice?' He shook his head, spitting out the rest. 'Ilia, Prince of Georgia.' She looked into his eyes. They were like David's.

He repeated the words after her. This stress on the name and the title as if it were being granted for the first time, this affirmation, was something that Shamil had taught her when he used to say Anna, Princess of Georgia, Alexander, Prince of Georgia. Squatting now on the garden path, she would like to stand up again with some elegance, or at least dignity, without using her hands to push herself up. Her mind wandered to worry again about Alexander's lessons and how his new tutor was a disappointment. She had said to David that she would give him another month, another chance, before starting to search for a replacement. A faint clutch deep in her stomach. She could not help it, she had to pitch herself on all fours before heaving herself up to stand again. The children claimed, it seemed, every part of her body – from mind to womb.

She took Ilia's hand again and they headed back to the house. She repeated, 'Alexander, Prince of Georgia; Ilia, Prince of Georgia; Tamar, Princess of Georgia.' And to herself, she whispered what Shamil had said to her that one time, 'Anna, Queen of Georgia.' How far-fetched all this was. A free Georgia, indeed. Unless it happened one day in the distant future, long after she was gone. But she wanted the children to carry the idea, to know who they were, to not lose themselves completely just because the reality around them insisted otherwise.

News came that Dargo had fallen. The room in which Anna, Alexander and Madame Drancy had been held was now rubble. Shamil and his family had fled to Gunaib, high up in the mountains. There he was making 'one last stand' as David, excitedly, put it. David might have left the army but he still had access to the news. And he was not alone. Georgia held its breath and suddenly everyone was competing to gather information about Gunaib. A desolate rocky plateau, near Shamil's birthplace. Gathered around Shamil were his family and closest allies, his firmest supporters. Day after day the Russians sent envoys to demand his surrender, to negotiate conditions that would be acceptable to both.

'But he's stubborn,' David said over dinner. 'Down to four hundred followers now and he'd rather die fighting than give up. Did you know that on the way to Gunaib, his gunpowder and wagons were robbed by his own people? They hurled insults at him as he passed. I tell you, he's finished.'

The food was straw and cloth in Anna's mouth. These days she avoided company so as not to get drawn into arguments or cause her milk to curdle from aggravation. But she could not possibly get away from David. She must listen to such talk.

'Rewards have been posted for him in case he flees. We want him alive but can one reason with a fanatic who prefers martyrdom?'

In desperation she steered him to their latest disagreement – a governess for Alexander instead of a tutor. The predictable banter was preferable to the news.

But David was relentless. 'Another of his naibs came to his senses and betrayed him, giving us direct access to Gunaib. Every regional commander is there now with his own detachment of men. Shamil is outnumbered ten to one. It's a matter of days now.'

The siege of Gunaib lasted for two weeks. Two weeks of rumours and counter-rumours. It was said that Shamil offered to surrender if he and his family would be released and allowed safe passage to go on Haj. It was said that he challenged the Russian commander to personally come and take his sword away from him. It was said that the final ultimatum was given – unconditional surrender or the death of the whole village, women and children included. And this was not a rumour. This was true.

Anna, standing in the garden near the greenhouse, looking up at the mountains, could do nothing. Through tears – which were in themselves hypocritical, indulgent, ridiculous – she imagined the scene that captured the imagination of the nation. Shamil on his white horse, followed by the remnant of his bedraggled army, their torn banners held up high for one last time. It shamed her that he was lied to. Promised that none of the tribal chiefs who had turned against him would be allowed to be present and yet there they were, gloating. Promised that he would not be disarmed but at the last minute, just before the surrender, they took away his sword.

It was said that his face was impassive. It was said that he was noble in defeat as he had been in success.

Then the newspapers took over. She would sit with Ilia perched on her knees, his arms swatting the pages, and she would read about Shamil's 'triumphal progress' as he left Dagestan, as he descended the mountains and headed towards Stavropol. The young and the curious ran after his carriage, military wives welcomed him with garlands, crowds lined the streets to see him drive past and parks were lit up in his honour, choirs performed... 'A ball at Mozdok railway station!' her voice rose loud and sudden to the extent that Ilia slipped down to the floor in surprise.

David laughed in satisfaction. 'Orders from the tsar himself. Shamil is to be respected and celebrated as a worthy, honourable adversary.'

There was a lot to take in as she nursed Tamar, cajoled Ilia, hired a new nurse, remonstrated with Alexander to obey his hapless tutor. She took to accusing David of exaggerating only to find it a day later in print.

The tsar receiving Shamil during a military parade. The two swap comments on military matters and embrace. Really?

Shamil, impressed by the wonders of St Petersburg, the towering achievements of Russian industry, a visit to the planetarium and the Zoological Gardens, a visit to see the Crown Jewels, a visit to a sugar factory.

Massive crowds camped in front of his hotel (the thought of him in a hotel of all places was in itself bizarre), but here it was in print, crowds waiting just to catch a glimpse of the Lion of Dagestan.

Shamil and his entourage driving up for a gala performance. His son, Ghazi, in tears after the performance of *Les Naiades*, deeply moved by the ballet's sentimental story of unrequited love.

Shamil saying that if he could be born again he would devote his life in service to the empire.

Anna was finding it all more incredible by the minute. 'Are we to believe that now in captivity he loves everything Russian? That he regrets all these years of war?'

David, puffing on his pipe, assured her that she was being unreasonable. 'In his own words Shamil was expecting to be tortured or executed. Now he is getting a taste of Christian mercy and he is grateful.'

'Grateful to be treated like an exotic pet for people to gaze at? And don't tell me that there aren't ulterior motives behind this. They want something from him, David. These people don't give something for nothing.'

This time he agreed with her. 'Yes. They want the whole Caucasus to submit behind him. They want no more challenges.'

She heard Tamar crying and left him to go to the nursery. Her steps quickened as the cries mounted in volume and intensity. It was a joy that she could make her stop crying just by calling out her name, just by picking her up, feeling her dampness, looking into her eyes. Such true need, such anguish. A glistening tear wetting the smallest of lashes. One little tear. Tamar, named after Queen Tamar the Great, the first woman to rule Georgia in her own right. 'Tamar, Princess of Georgia,' she said. 'I'm here. Don't cry.'

Six months later, she found herself in Moscow. 'When the tsar invites you to dinner, how can you refuse?' David said. 'What excuse can you give?' The ball was held in Shamil's honour. A reconciliation between him and the Chavchavadzes, a forging of bonds must be witnessed. Petersburg society would appreciate such a scene. Anna dressed as she would dress to attend a funeral except that she wore all her jewels. Diamonds on black. It aged her but she did not want to look attractive. She did not want to look happy. Why pretend? David's enthusiasm was due to a monetary gift promised by the tsar, a much-needed boost to regain Tsinondali. It had not been easy for him to convince her to travel. They had argued, and because he had won the argument he did not criticise her choice of clothes. If this was a whim, he would humour it.

Shamil looked out of place amidst the wine and dancing. As much as she had been out of place in the aoul at Dargo. He looked fatigued, as if everyone's eyes on him were casting a net to hold him in place. If only they would not gape, these jaded couriers. If only these Asiatic mountain princes, who had switched allegiances to Russia long ago, would not gloat so openly. She could hear them whispering. 'Are there no children for him to play with today?' they sniggered. He survived these functions by withdrawing himself from the adults to spend time with those who were instinctive and pure.

When she walked towards him she sensed his ache for the mountains. The minder by his side, a Russian official, assumed that he must initiate an introduction, jog a memory. But Shamil did not need reminding of who she was. 'Anna, Queen of Georgia,' he said. His voice had not changed, nor his tone.

It was not the correct form of address and the Russian official with all good intention said, 'Princess Anna,' in such a way as to suggest that Shamil should repeat it. A silence as everyone waited for the repetition. The longest moment of silence when she stood like a queen and breathed like a queen, a moment in which Georgia was its own kingdom, not annexed to Russia. This continued until awkwardness interrupted. The air bristled, skirts rustled and someone was clearing his throat. Next to Anna, an aged general changed the subject and drew Shamil away. The guests mingled, saying that Shamil had become hard of hearing and forgetful. And she went home knowing better.

3. Kaluga, Russia, 1859–69

From the upstairs window Shamil could see a church and beyond it the railway station. The houses were in even rows, built on a flat road, tame under a blanket of snow. There were no peaks, no jagged rocks; beyond the hills the forests were pine instead of birch. He had known all along that Russia was vast and different but to find himself living in it was still a surprise.

In this provincial town, south of Moscow, he had been given a three-storey house. For the first few months he was alone without his family, pacing the empty rooms, sensing his minder hovering just outside the door, policing him but not wanting to intrude. Shamil had formed a favourable impression of his *pristav*, Runovsky. The officer was well-mannered and sensitive, genuinely interested in his charge. He wrote down the things that Shamil said and answered his questions about Russian life. It could have been worse, Shamil knew, but he was still wary, understanding that he was now fulfilling a role in his adversary's agenda, a role that was still unclear. All this largess was for the sake of illustration. And once they were done with him, they would change in some way that he could not yet predict.

He told Runovsky how much he admired the Russians for their treatment of him in captivity; they were neither angry nor intent on harming him. The crowds that swarmed to see him off at the railway platform in Petersburg had made him put his hand on his heart and nod to them to express his thanks. He responded to their sincerity, sensed their simple, difficult lives. They hailed him as a hero against oppression because they knew only too well what oppression was. He told Runovsky that he had expected abuse and humiliation. His own men in the Caucasus would hurl dirt on the Russian prisoners and kill them given half the chance. Shamil had prided himself in treating Princess Anna like a guest, but he realised now that from her point of view, he must have been only doing what was right.

It was interesting to discover that Runovsky had served in the Caucasus for several years. Together they went over details of fortresses under siege and battles lost and won. To hear the perspective of his former enemies was illuminating. To recount history in parallel was intellectually fulfilling. And it was not only Runovsky; officers and soldiers who had served in the Caucasus wanted to meet him. Most of them were respectful; even those who had been prisoners of war would bend and kiss his hand as they used to do in their time of captivity. A few, though, made him angry when they told lies. When one lieutenant boasted that he had been given the St George's cross for storming the aoul of Kitouri and capturing the naib Magamoi, Shamil rose to his feet and shouted that Magamoi was already dead by the time Kitouri surrendered. A martyr's name must not be sullied and Shamil trembled as he strode out of the room. That such falsehood could be repeated and believed made him feel old.

Runovsky, in charge of the household, issued Shamil an allowance. It was too much money and every time he went for a walk, he would give it away to the beggars he passed. As the weeks went by, the beggars of Kaluga came to wait for him. He never turned them away empty-handed. Runovsky took him to task for this. They would only spend it on vodka, he said. 'But if I give them too little I would be mocking them,' Shamil replied. 'It says in my Book to help the poor. Does it not say that also in yours?'

Great portions of Shamil's day were spent reliving the fall of Dargo and then Gunaib. He would not talk to Runovsky about this, he could not. In private, in solitude, he wanted to identify the errors made and by whom; he wanted to pinpoint the moment when the tide turned against him. Not for the sake of learning from his mistakes and improving his future performance (he was not in denial) but for the sake of knowledge. Those last weeks before the surrender were worse than the surrender itself. There he was from mosque to mosque preaching, no, begging, bullying, cajoling, for more men to join the jihad, for those who were already enlisted not to drop out. It was no use. Had he not taught that martyrdom was better than surrender? And yet Allah had not graced him with it, had not crowned his achievements in the best of ways. When the Russians gained the peaks above them and that was a sign that they were done for, that the end was near, that even Gunaib, that impenetrable fortress, had been betrayed and was now ready to crumble, he had gone around with fire in his heart pleading with his men to kill him. 'Kill me,' he said. 'I give you permission to kill me before they come for me. Spare me the shame.' They turned away though he held their arms, held their faces between his hands and saw in their eyes helplessness and love. 'If you won't kill me then leave me,' he said. 'Save yourselves. I give you permission to leave Gunaib and I will stay here alone. I will fight when they come; I will fight them until my sword is shattered into small pieces and I will die alone.' But they would not go. These men who had lasted this long and would last for ever. They were the upright, the robust whom the Russians couldn't buy with their 'red and white' coins. By this time, many of his naibs had already changed sides, naibs who had been his friends, naibs he had esteemed and trusted. 'We must be pragmatic,' they said to him but he never listened. 'We must think ahead.' All he knew was that fire is better than shame and he had won before, he had rebuffed them before, decade after decade, year after year, so why was it all slipping away now?

In the last short night, which he spent in prayer at the mosque, surrounded by the moans of the wounded and the smell of the dead, Ghazi came in and hovered. When Shamil turned his head to the right and the left to finish, Ghazi fell to his knees before him. Ghazi wanted to say spare the children of Gunaib, spare the woman you love, Chuanat; spare your lovely daughters, your newborn grandson. Spare the crooked legs of your favourite daughter. The longer Ghazi knelt before him, the more selfish martyrdom became; the longer

Ghazi knelt the clearer it dawned that this was defeat and that defeat was Allah's will. Instead of martyrdom, it was time for Shamil to accept this failure. Disappointment stabbed him like an arrow.

He agreed but he had conditions of his own. First, he and his men would still be carrying their arms when they surrendered to the Russian general. Second, he would be allowed to go on pilgrimage to Makkah accompanied by his family and anyone who wished to join him.

Neither condition was honoured. As he rode out, they came between him and his followers and disarmed him, claiming that the general was afraid of armed men. His sword, which he wanted to keep fighting with until it was shattered to pieces, was taken from him and handed over to Field-Marshal Bariatinsky. And instead of setting out for the pilgrimage, here he was in Kaluga being asked by this pleasant Russian minder about what he thought of the local women's low necklines.

Apparently every officer arriving in Kaluga had strict orders to pay him an official visit. They liked to hear him praise the tsar and Russia, they beamed when he expressed gratitude for the house he was living in. Sometimes they asked to see the fabled seventeen wounds on his body. Sometimes they just stared. He waited to find out what more they wanted from him. Days spent with memories, nights spent in prayer. Often he thought of his son Jamaleldin and longed to talk to him. If Jamaleldin were here now, he would translate for him, explain to him and help him. The son would lead the father. This was yet another thought that made him feel old.

Zeidat covered her ears with her hands. 'Oh this sound is intolerable. Must the Russians have all this clamour to remind them to pray?'

The church bells of Kaluga were tolling. The sound filled the large family room on the first floor, furnished all round with cushions in the Ottoman style. Shamil looked across at Chuanat, who was sewing. He was relieved that she was here, that they were together at last. It had lifted his spirits to have the family gathered around him. They were all here except Ameena, whom he had divorced before leaving Dargo and made sure that she was safely back home with her family in Bavaria. The elderly Bahou, too, had not been able to attempt the journey. Now with him in Kaluga were his two sons, Ghazi with his wife and baby and young Muhammad-Sheffi; his two older daughters and their new husbands, the younger children and their nannies. The house was full of their voices and footsteps. A piece of the Caucasus to wrap around him.

Chuanat looked up at Zeidat, who was now not only covering her ears but swaying from side to side in exaggerated agony. 'You are so rude. When Anna was with us in Dargo, she was often complimentary of the azan and never complained about it.'

He smiled at Chuanat. In the months before she came to Kaluga he was anxious that he would lose her. She could have asked the Russians to return her to her family in Armenia but she didn't. Instead, she chose to join him in exile. Her presence made all the difference. Here she was evoking the memory of Anna. It was right to do so. He said, 'Anna is a princess and she conducted herself like one. You must distinguish, Chuanat, between royalty and a tribeswoman.'

Zeidat snorted. 'I am proud of my heritage, Shamil Imam.' The daughter of Sheikh Jamal el-Din had every reason to be.

'Your heritage should have given you more sensitive ears. Listen to what these bells are saying.'

She made a face. 'There aren't any words, just a ding ding.'

He paused to listen to the bells but not with his ears. 'They are saying "Haqq! Haqq!"'

Zeidat raised her eyebrows. 'Is that what they are saying to you?'

'Yes, they too can remind us of Allah. If you listen carefully you will hear them say His name. Truth! Truth!'

There were quarrels in the house because everyone was cooped up together. The young ones were bored and when they were bored they quarrelled. The air was not as pure as in the mountains. Ghazi's wife fell ill with fever. Permission was granted for Shamil to build a mosque in the garden. Good, resourceful Runovsky facilitated the whole process. As time dragged on the mosque become a haven for Shamil, a place to escape to. He spent longer hours there, reciting the Qur'an in a place where it had not been heard before, kneeling down on a piece of earth that had never been pressed by the forehead of a believer. There was a sense of peace in this. To be told don't fight any more, you have done enough, stand aside, stand aside and worship. That was how he interpreted his defeat in Gunaib. It was a command from the Almighty to stand aside and worship because the years were running out.

Gifts came to him from the tsar and from other dignitaries. He could not accept the gold tea tray and when he found that, instead of returning it, young Muhammad-Sheffi had hidden it in his room, Shamil ground each cup under his feet. He made Chuanat cry when he tore her new green dress. 'When women in Dagestan can afford silk, then you can wear it,' he shouted. A subtle danger was creeping into his household.

Often he thought of his son Jamaleldin. This was the world he had been thrown into when he was eight years old. No wonder it had seeped into him, weakening his resolve, gnawing at him from within. So strongly did he feel Jamaleldin's presence that he was not surprised when on one fine summer afternoon, a peasant woman knocked on the door and said that she had known Jamaleldin. In the reception room fitted for visitors, furnished in the Russian style, she sat across from Shamil, her kerchief knotted around a wide face, and told him that she had been Jamaleldin's nanny, long ago, when he first came from Akhulgo. He listened to her, as the shadows in the room lengthened, describe a shy little boy who could not speak a word of Russian, a child cut off, bereft and still restrained because his mother and father had taught him to be brave, had told him that an Avar mustn't break down into tears. She visited again, bringing an officer who had been Jamaleldin's childhood friend, bringing others who had known him well. These people nurtured his son when he could not and, years later, were still loyal to Jamaleldin's memory. They could not be Shamil's enemies. He owed them friendship and gratitude.

But what did the Russians want from him? To command every fighter in the Caucasus, whether they were Circassians or Chechens or Dagestanis, to lay down his arms? He would. To swear allegiance to Emperor Alexander II? He did. To support the new policy of enforced mass deportations of the highlanders, robbing them of their ancestral lands? He would not.

The best of guests came to stay. Sheikh Jamal el-Din brought with him blustery rainy weather and memories of the Caucasus. The young felt grounded once again. Zeidat was on her best behaviour. While Shamil, in the presence of his teacher, had the chance to feel mature but not old, still protected and not quite an orphan yet.

Jamal el-Din filled him in on the news from home. They were alone in the mosque after evening prayers. Over time, the Tatars of Kaluga had been joining the prayers and the circles of zikr which Shamil led. Now that Sheikh Jamal el-Din had taken over, the feelings in the gathering were refreshed as he added weight and substance to what was already there.

'When the coffin arrived in Ghimra,' he was referring to the recent death of Ghazi's wife, 'people said, "This isn't how we imagined Shamil's family would come back to us."'

'Ghazi took his wife's death badly,' Shamil said. Unlike Muhammad-Sheffi, who embraced Russia and wanted to join its army, Ghazi was bitter and unwilling to change. Often he would lie in bed balancing an unsheathed sabre on his finger, only rousing himself up to pray. Neither old enough to be content with reflecting back on an illustrious career, nor young enough to be flexible, Ghazi's position was unenviable. Shamil worried about him.

Sheikh Jamal el-Din said, 'A new wife would compensate his loss.'

Shamil pondered on the logistics of arranging a marriage while they were in exile. Russian approval would be needed to bring over a bride from Dagestan.

'I heard you were suffering,' Jamal el-Din was saying. 'That's why I came.'

'I am well, as you can see. What you heard must have been

exaggerated reports.' Shamil's voice was low. Not because anyone was around to hear him, but because of a new inner flatness.

Jamal el-Din's eyes looked bright. 'It is good to reassure myself.'

'We are honoured by your visit.' It was more than that. A sweetness in the general gloom, a reason for optimism.

Lightning made him see his teacher suddenly aglow. He was older than Shamil but it was as if he had levelled off at a certain age while Shamil's hair and beard had turned white. With the rumble of thunder Jamal el-Din murmured, '*The thunder extols and praises Him, as do the angels for awe of Him...*'

Shamil listened out for the quickening fall of the rain. It lifted his spirits further, dissolving the distance between earth and sky.

'You have my permission to go on pilgrimage,' Sheikh Jamal el-Din said.

Shamil was taken aback. He thought that he had always had his teacher's permission, that it had been his for decades. It was the tsar he was waiting on. Last year the tsar had turned down his request, saying that the situation in the Caucasus was still unsettled.

'I will join you and we will go together,' Sheikh Jamal el-Din said.

Shamil bowed his head in appreciation. He must write to the tsar again. 'Unless the Caucasus is completely pacified, the Russians won't let me go.'

'They fight amongst each other. The blood feuds which you repressed have now flared up again,' Jamal el-Din said. 'The Chechens have gone back to how they were before they were governed by Sharia.'

'Let their new masters crack down on them now.' He did not feel any grudge or nostalgia for the past.

Jamal el-Din nodded in agreement. 'And those who don't want to be ruled by the infidels are packing up and moving to the Ottoman Empire.'

Shamil sighed. He would go there himself, if he had the chance.

Their conversation meandered. The rescue of Shamil's books from Gunaib, memories of past and better times.

'I ask myself what went wrong,' said Shamil. 'Almost overnight I lost control. One day I commanded thousands, the next day I was on the run and even then my wagons were robbed on the way. Something happened, something changed.'

Sheikh Jamal el-Din closed his eyes. 'You changed.'

'How?' He was fully alert now, his senses sharpened as if waiting in the dark for an enemy to pounce.

'You began to think you were invincible.'

'No man is invincible.'

'True. But you no longer believed that you needed my spiritual support. You began to believe that your naibs were strong and that your tactics were excellent. You began to believe in your own abilities and you said to yourself, what does that old man know about warfare, what does that dervish understand besides mysticism?'

'I have always revered you.'

'And I prayed for you. All through the decades of your success. Then you became arrogant. I am your teacher, you swore allegiance to me. It is my right to chastise you. So I raised up my palms to Allah Almighty and read Al-Fatiha.'

'As if I was already dead.' Shamil did not feel pain, only interest.

'A week later you were captured by the Russians.' There was no anger in Sheikh Jamal el-Din's eyes, no vindictiveness, no malice.

Shamil leaned forward and kissed his hand. He had asked the question and received the answer. Let the Russians think what they wanted to think. Let them understand in their own logic, in their own language how he resisted them for decades and why, almost overnight, he fell. But he had his own answer now, to hold to himself. Without spiritual support, nature took its course. Without blessings, without miracles, one and one made two and an object thrown up in the air fell down; a man could not see in the dark, fire burned and bodies needed food. Without blessing, without miracles, the physical laws of the world govern supreme and those strong in numbers and ammunition sooner or later must defeat the weak.

A crop he had tilled and watched, with pleasure, its vegetation grow green, now lay yellow and dry before him, flaking. There was now only one direction for him to go in, carrying his sincerity and long years of devoted service. One last journey to make.

X
The Castle Then a Tour

1. Scotland, February–May 2011

The news that Oz had dropped out was passed around the department with relief as if we were well rid of him. One of our best students. After yet another dismissive shrug, I hid myself in the Ladies' and cried with anger, ashamed that, even now, I could not stand up for him. I could not say that when he was in my class and I marked essays, I would leave his to the end, just so that I could look forward to it, just so that I could tolerate better the awfulness and apathy of some of the others'. His would be always rewarding, worth the effort I had put into my lectures and worth the facilities in place.

I'm making the right decision, he recently wrote. *I can't go back there now. I don't want to. Malak isn't too happy with me moving to Cardiff but at least it's not South Africa.*

The Non-Academic Complaints Panel, with Gaynor Stead accusing me of breaking her finger, was held immediately after the Easter break. During the run-up to it, I was consumed by stress and lack of sleep. In the end Gaynor could not prove that I broke her finger but the Complaints Panel acknowledged that perching on her desk might have been construed as a violation of personal space. I was admonished to be more careful in the future but without the university declaring that a terrible wrong had been done to the student. Not a triumphant outcome, my confidence was shattered, but I was relieved that it was all over and that I still had a job I could call my own. I developed a stutter and a tremor in my cheek that persisted for a long time afterwards. I supposed my colleagues would have supported me more if the anti-terrorist squad hadn't searched my office after Oz's arrest. Even though this was never mentioned during the hearing, understandably the two things compounded with my being away for such a long time and caused a coolness between myself and my workmates. Natasha Wilson denoted a person who was smeared by suspicion, tainted by crime. I might as well have stayed Natasha Hussein! Even though my laptop and mobile phone were returned to me, even though no formal charges were ever levelled at me, still, it now took conscious effort to walk with my head held high. My voice became softer, my opinions muted, my actions tentative. I thought before I spoke, became wary of my students and, often, bowed my head down.

I kept in touch with Mekki and with Grusha and Yasha more regularly. When I told them that I missed them, I meant it, aware now of that parallel life I could have led if my parents' marriage hadn't ended. I valued the sense of belonging they gave me, the certainty that I was not an isolated member of a species but simply one who had wandered far from the flock and still managed to survive, for better or for worse, in a different habitat. Chatting with them, we would skip from Russian to English to Arabic and I relaxed without the need to prove, explain or distinguish myself. Nor squeeze to fit in, nor watch out of the corner of my eye the threats that my very existence could provoke in the wrong place in the wrong time among the wrong crowd.

A last-minute Call for Papers for an international conference on Suicide, Conflict and Peace Research galvanised me into preparing a submission. I wanted to compare Shamil's defeat and surrender, how he made peace with his enemies, with modern-day Islamic terrorism that promoted suicide bombings instead of accepting in Shamil's words, 'that martyrdom is Allah's prerogative to bestow'. How did this historical change in the very definition of jihad come about?

The Easter break passed in a daze, the days getting longer but the cold still teasing; generous hours of light but the temperature refusing to rise. It was, though, a relatively warm Sunday in May when the telephone rang and it was Malak talking to me as if we had only just seen each other the week before. I could tell from her voice that she was outdoors, somewhere windy.

'I'm not far from you,' she said. 'At Dunnottar Castle. Are you free to come over? I know it's short notice. But you came to my mind, just now, and I thought why not call and see. Just in case.'

And I was driving again, this time with a few drops of rain on my front window. Clouds that started to clear as I neared my destination. I sensed a welcome purity in my motivation, an energy that made the drive effortless, the distance bridgeable. She had always given me a sense of communion with Shamil, oriented me towards the unexpected, and guided me to what could never be written down in history.

I bought a ticket and was told that they would be closing in an hour's time. I hurried down the long path, the castle ahead of me protruding into the water, the sound of the seagulls all around. A number of people walked in the opposite direction, having finished their visit. I was the only one heading to the ruins. It made me feel as if I was running late, that my situation was touch and go, I would either make it in time or not.

The path was narrow and the dark rocky land dipped down straight. The cold wind messed up my hair but I felt warm from the exercise. The grass around me was high and dry, yellow and pale green. When I reached the headland I could see, below, the beach covered in pebbles. Then it was time to climb up until the sea surrounded me on three sides, until looking down at the craggy shoreline with the undulating froth made me feel slightly nauseous. Here – I reached my hand out – were the stone walls on the cliff, thicker and higher now that I was close. Large holes from which guns once stuck out. I passed through the entrance, up slippery ancient stairs, my mind automatically retrieving that Mary, Queen of Scots visited here and that on a similar day in 1652, this was the one remaining place in Scotland in which a small garrison loyal to Charles II resisted Cromwell's army. But I was here to see Malak and she was somewhere inside, waiting for me.

I did not find her as easily as I thought I would. I walked on the cobbled floor, passed through the semi-ruined keep and the drawing room, which was in better shape. Out in the quadrangle the sun shone on the moss-covered walls that rose up in incomplete storeys, upstairs rooms without ceilings. The grass was even here, a lawn, a sense of enclosure, hardly any wind and a stillness as if the seagulls were politely staying away. In front of the chapel Malak sat dressed in what could only be described as a kaftan, wearing a turban on her head. The other visitors must have thought she was in medieval costume; if she popped up in the background of one of their photos, they could claim they had spotted a ghost.

She was sitting on the grass on what I recognised to be one of the small Persian carpets from her house. She was reading a large hard-backed book which, when I came close, I recognised as the Qur'an. I stood watching her for a while, amused by her clothes and sense of the theatrical. What part did she think she was playing? Not that I suspected her of insincerity, but there had always been an attractive self-consciousness about her as if she were trying to please an invisible figure, an unseen audience who mattered only to her.

I joined her on the carpet, listened to her reciting. Not a single word was comprehensible to me. This must be how animals feel when they hear humans talk, this must be how infants experience language long before they are ready to learn it. When she finished the page she was on, she marked it with a brown ribbon and put it in the canvas bag she had at her side. 'I am halfway through,' she said. 'The Qur'an is divided into thirty sections and, over a fortnight, I have read fifteen. Every day I go somewhere different to pray and read a section. I've travelled up and down the country.'

I smiled. 'You're on tour then for a full month.'

She laughed. 'It's probably the most fulfilling one I've ever done.'

'How do you decide where to go?'

'Well, that is the fun part. I've been to spiritual places like Stone-henge, places where I have always sensed a powerful presence. This is one of them, can you feel it?'

I did not know how to answer her. If I said 'No' it would seem ungracious. If I said 'Yes' I might be lying. So I said, 'Centuries ago, people in this very spot worshipped as you were worshipping just now. They believed like you believe.' And centuries ago, as Covenanter history teaches, they also waged wars, resisted and rebelled around issues of faith.

She said, 'Yesterday I prayed further north. In the middle of a suburb which was so artificial and depressing that I almost couldn't bear to be there. But I stuck it out, telling myself that I would be the first one there ever to say the word "Allah".'

'Who heard you?'

'No one. I don't want anyone to hear me. The trees, the wind, the angels. That's enough for me. Sometimes, I can't bear to talk to people, Natasha. Not after what happened to Oz. I can't be the same again. Sorry for not answering your messages. You are the easiest one to talk to because you understand. But I went through days when I did not want to talk to anyone at all.'

'Why, Malak? It's over and done with.'

'I can't let go of the disappointment, it's held inside me like a grudge. I carry it from place to place. It's not that I love him less. Love doesn't change, it doesn't go away. But he was suspected of not behaving with the decency and broad-mindedness I brought him up with.'

'And he was released without charge. So why are you judging him?'

'Because I expected better of him, that's all. He allowed the dark side to distract him even if it didn't win him over completely.'

I smiled at her dramatic choice of words. The dark side. I smelt the sea and heard the seagulls. 'Did you get Shamil's sword back?'

'Oz got his laptop back. And we both got our phones back. But not the sword.'

'How come?'

She shook her head. 'I have no idea. But in a strange way I don't mind waiting. He surrendered it, didn't he? He didn't fight with it and shatter it to pieces. He knew better. He understood that surrender meant humility. He accepted defeat graciously and saw it as Allah's will. There aren't many like him now. Wisdom is in short supply.'

'You never told me,' I said. 'How did your family get back the sword after Shamil handed it over to Field-Marshal Bariatinsky?'

'In 1918 a soldier was captured by the Red Army and it was in his possession. Instead of being placed in a museum it was sold as a trophy and my great-grandfather bought it. But you must tell me about your time in Sudan. It was important, I can tell.'

Yes, it changed me. I might still not have reached home or settled where I belonged, but I was confident that there was a home, there, ahead of me. My homesickness wasn't cured but it was, I was sure, propelling me in the right direction.

When I finished speaking, Malak said, 'You must come with me.' She sounded vague, as if she had not thought it through.

'Where?'

'To Orkney. We could have zikr on the beach; I could read another part of the Qur'an.'

Zikr on the beach. I remembered the zikr gathering she took me to in London. It was powerful, heady. It haunted me, afterwards, for days and nights. I hesitated a little before committing myself.

'It would be good for you,' she nodded, as if the prospect was becoming more real to her.

Sufism delves into the hidden truth behind the disguise. Malak, the teacher disguised as an actor. Natasha the student, acting the part of a teacher. I had come to her today needing to connect, wanting to spend time in her company. Perhaps it was time to acknowledge that what I was after was spiritual. She was ready to be a guide and I would fight my weaknesses in order to follow.

Postscript
Ghazi

1. Makkah/Medina, 1871

After ten years of exile, my father was finally permitted to go on Haj. He was accompanied by Sheikh Jamal el-Din and other members of the family. I, on the other hand, was detained by the Russian authorities. My father spent six months in Istanbul before performing his Haj in Noble Makkah. He then settled in Radiant Medina. There, he sent letter after letter to the viceroy of the Caucasus as well as the tsar explaining that he had been taken ill, that he believed he did not have long to live and that his last request was for his son to join him. It was as if my father's fate was to long for absent sons. First Jamaleldin, then me. He wrote to me too, words that would break the most hardened of hearts. I used to reply with messages of hope, saying that I was leaving in a few days' time, that I would be joining him soon. Eventually after patience wore thin, I lost my temper with the Russian authorities and threatened to escape. It had an effect. They had plans that, in the future, I would become their representative in the Caucasus and so, grudgingly, they agreed to let me go.

From Constantinople I could not travel directly to Radiant Medina. The route was blocked by bandits. So I changed my plans and headed to Noble Makkah, with the intention of proceeding to Medina as soon as I completed my Umra. I was circling the sacred Ka'aba when I noticed from the corner of my eye a dervish, dressed in a green turban and rags, looping in a disjointed way, and as was typical of men like him, preoccupied with the prayers he was muttering, intoxicated by where we were, oblivious to all else. He jerked to a standstill in front of the Black Stone and gave out a cry of pain. 'O Believers,' he shouted. 'Pray for the soul of Imam Shamil.'

I pushed my way through the throng and reached his side. He was rocking backwards and forwards. I grabbed him by the shoulders and forced him to look at me. 'When did this happen?'

He swayed his head from side to side, 'Now ... this dawn ... last night.'

'My father is in Medina, twelve days' march from here – how can you know?'

Instead of answering, the dervish started to cry. He shuffled away from me, back into his inner world. And all I could think of through the din of grief was that I was too late, too late to see him and he wanted to see me, he was ill and he made them twist his bed so that it was facing the door, so that he would see me as soon as I came in. Now I was too late and it was the Russians' fault, as it had always been their fault for every misfortune that beset us. 'Forgive them,' he told me before he left Russia. 'I order you to forgive them.' And I argued with him, saying, 'I cannot control my heart.' He said 'I know more than you. Forgiveness is for your own benefit, not theirs.'

I set out for Medina on that very same day. I walked barefoot on sand as hot as coals but not as hot as what I carried in my breast. We belong to Allah and to Him we return. I could not believe that I would not rush into my father's arms, that I would not tell him my news, that I would not wait for the approval to shine in his eyes.

When my father left Russia and arrived in Istanbul, it gratified him to turn down the hospitality of the Russian ambassador and say, 'I am a guest of the Ottoman sultan.' Sultan Abdelaziz received him ceremonially and offered him a choice of palaces, all too ostentatious for my father's taste. Crowds lined the streets to cheer him and men kissed the ground that he walked on. On finding out that the sultan was preparing an army against Ismail Pasha of Egypt who had just opened the Suez Canal and was showing signs of rebellion, my father offered himself as a mediator. He travelled to Egypt where Ismail Pasha honoured him by coming off his throne and seating Imam Shamil on it. My father reasoned with him saying, 'If war breaks out between you and the Ottoman sultan, it would delight the infidels.' Ismail Pasha took heed of his counsel and, on his suggestion, sent his *son to wed the sultan's daughter. A war between Egypt and Turkey was avoided and everyone rejoiced.*

On the steamer back to Istanbul, a storm broke out and the waves raged up high and fearful. My father wrote a prayer on a piece of paper and asked that it be thrown overboard into the water, without touching the ship. It was and the sea calmed down.

When my father first arrived in Noble Makkah, the crowds that gathered were such that the police had to intervene and protect him so that he could perform his prayers. An elderly ailing scholar who was a descendant of the Prophet Muhammad, peace be upon him, insisted that his children carry him to meet my father. He said that the Prophet Muhammad, peace be upon him, had told him in a dream to expect a distinguished guest.

I missed his funeral prayer. Vast numbers walked in the procession. Those who couldn't touch him, lay down on the ground in the hope that his body would be carried above them. It was said of him that he passed through life like gold through fire until Allah Almighty elected his soul.

When I was able to, I arranged, in his memory, a charity meal for all Chechen pilgrims. I said to them, 'My father once governed you. When you return to your homeland ask its people to say a funeral prayer for him and request that they forgive him and pardon his severity.'

Later I heard that on the night of his death, the sky above the Caucasus turned a bright red.

My father did not die a martyr but his life ended with the greatest of honours. He was buried in the Garden of Baqi near the grave of Al-Abbas, the uncle of the Prophet, peace be upon him. Shamil Imam, who followed the path of truth, the fighter in the way of Allah, the learned, the leader. May Allah Almighty purify his soul and multiply his good deeds. Al-Fatiha.

Acknowledgements

I am very grateful to the following for their feedback, advice and, at times, inspiration:

Arzu Tahsin, Elisabeth Schmitz

Stephanie Cabot

Dr Christine Laennec, Professor Michael Syrotinski

Vimbai Shire

Khadijah Knight, Bruce Young, Zvezdana Rashkovich, Natalia Fadlalla

Nadir Mahjoub

For researching the life of Imam Shamil, these books were the most helpful:

The Sabres of Paradise by Lesley Blanch (John Murray, 1960).

Let Our Fame Be Great by Oliver Bullough (Basic Books, 2010).

Captivity of Two Russian Princesses in the Caucasus, tr. from the Russ. [of E. A. Verderevskii] by H. S. Edwards (General Books LLC, 2012).

Highlanders by Yo'av Karny (Farrar Straus Giroux, 2000).

'The Shining of Daghestani Swords in Certain Campaigns of Shamil' by Muhammad Tahir al-Qarakhi in *Russian-Muslim Confrontation in the Caucasus: Alternative Visions of the Conflict Between Imam Shamil and the Russians, 1830–1859* translated and edited by Sanders, Tucker and Hamburg (Routledge, 2004).

Read on

On *The Kindness of Enemies*

In the 19th century, the tall, jagged ranges of the Caucasus Mountains separated India from Imperial Russia. The Muslim tribes of the mountains resisted Russian invasion and in doing so gained the support of Queen Victoria. Their leader, Imam Shamil, was praised in the British press for his bravery and resilience. By maintaining the independence of the Caucasus, Shamil was protecting British interests in India from the threat of Russian encroachment.

Thousands of feet above the Caspian and Black Seas, the Caucasus rose into misty, snowy summits. Rivers looped around the rocks. Imam Shamil's villages were like rock fortresses, the houses embedded into the mountains as if they were a part of it. This world of stone resisted the Russians. Their soldiers struggled to climb, dodging the sharpshooters who threw burning logs and rocks down at them. They slipped trying to use the stony ledges as footholds. Shamil's horses were trained for the steep, twisted ascent but the Russian horses collapsed with the effort.

A world apart from the Tsar's court, the mountain tribes lived a life connected to the seasons and rhythms of their surroundings. When threatened, they hid in stone caves

323

and birch forests. The moss-covered boulders and syca-more trees were as intimately known to them as the barren rocks and stretches of sandstones. They were fighting to keep hold of their homeland and their traditional way of life.

In *The Kindness of Enemies*, Princess Anna and her family are kidnapped from their estate in Georgia and dragged up the mountains to live as captives in Shamil's harem. They are to be exchanged for Shamil's son, Jamaleldin, who had been held hostage by the Tsar since he was eight years old.

On her long, arduous journey up the mountains, Princess Anna is given horses trained to swim across streams and climb vertical, zigzagged paths. When the horses are tired or the paths too dangerous, she must wade in deep mud or crawl on hands and knees over ravines. Although it is the beginning of a hot summer, there are avalanches of snow that will not melt until mid-July.

She passes villages embedded in the rocks, the houses peculiar in their design, they appear higgledy-piggledy. Entering one of them, she finds a hill inside a courtyard and rooms, like caverns, without windows. It takes three weeks of steady climbing before Shamil's rock fortress looms up into view. Before the final climb, the Princess is surprised to find herself in an area surrounded by ferns and waterfalls. The rugged, harsh Caucasus Mountains are also home to azaleas and nosegays.

The kidnapping of the Princess tarnished Shamil's reputation in Britain and, in 1859, after more than thirty years of resistance, the Caucasus fell to the Russians. Armed and riding his white horse, Imam Shamil surrendered to the Russian commander. In his descent from the mountains, he was followed by the remnants of his bedraggled army, their torn banners held up high.

Leila Aboulela

2015

A version of this article first appeared in the Metro *as* *'A Mountain of Resistance' on 10 August 2015*

Q&A with Leila Aboulela

Q: You were born to a Sudanese father and an Egyptian mother, raised in Sudan but then moved to Aberdeen in your twenties. What were your first impressions of Scotland? How did you find the process of adapting and integrating into a new community? Were you homesick?

A: I arrived in Scotland with a four-year-old son and a two-week-old baby. My husband, Nadir, was working off-shore on the North Sea oil rigs and it was our first time living alone, as we had been living with my parents since we got married. So, it was an exciting start but it wasn't easy. I had romantic ideas about Scotland. It does have a romantic landscape, so does Sudan but that is one of the very few things they have in common! I was extremely homesick and unable to integrate into the mums and toddlers groups and school-gate friendships. For a while I taught statistics, which is what I had studied, but I wasn't fulfilled. I felt that I was at a crossroads and started to look for other ways of fitting in.

Q: When did you start writing and how has your journey influenced your writing?

A: The place that gave me happiness and comfort when I first moved to Aberdeen was the Central Library. Growing up in Sudan with a scarcity of books, I deeply appreciated the luxury of being able to read in abundance and to read for free. Then for the first time ever, I tried my hand at writing a short story. I remember that when I surprised Nadir with it, he was impressed and said, 'I can't believe you wrote this!' I started to attend creative writing workshops at the University of Aberdeen and then at the library. Those were led by the writer-in-residence, Todd McEwen, who encouraged me and showed my stories to his editor. All the other writers I met at the workshops were welcoming and genuinely interested in my writing. For the first time since arriving in Britain, I started to make friends and to feel that I belonged.

Q: Where did your inspiration for *The Kindness of Enemies* come from and how did the novel evolve in your mind? Did you conceive the two narrative strands – one contemporary and one historical – from the very beginning?

A: A few years ago, I wrote a BBC radio play, *The Lion of Chechnya*, inspired by the life of Imam Shamil. There were some aspects of the story that I wanted to develop into a full-length novel, namely that of his son, Jamaleldin.

Jamaleldin was taken away from his father at the age of eight and brought up by the Tsar as his godson. Hurt and humiliated, Shamil did everything he could to bring his son back. But how did Jamaleldin, after experiencing modernity and sophistication, feel about re-joining the mountain tribes? Russian and Western historians cast him as a tragic figure but my instincts were that Jamaleldin's position was more complex; he too belonged to Chechnya and he too, eventually, returned to Islam.

Although I had never been to the Caucasus, researching Shamil's life threw up many wonderful descriptions of the mountains, details which I wanted to work with and shape as a backdrop for a novel. I read those of Tolstoy's works which were set in the Caucasus and watched Russian YouTube films and serials. It didn't matter that I couldn't understand what the actors were saying; the landscape was what I was after.

When I started writing *The Kindness of Enemies*, I introduced a present-day character to act as a bridge connecting us to the past. Natasha Hussein is a half-Russian, half-Sudanese lecturer of History, living in Scotland. In 2011, I was intrigued by articles in the British newspapers which reported that, under new anti-terror legislations, university staff would be expected to inform on Muslim students vulnerable to radicalisation. What if Natasha, eager to distance herself from being Muslim, sets out to inform on those of her students who were 'at risk'?

Q: Your novel explores ideas of religion, language, culture and identity that seem particularly relevant in Britain today. What does it mean to be a Muslim in a secular society? Do you think that questions of allegiance and belonging are more urgent now than ever?

A: To be a practising person of any faith nowadays is to swim against the tide. But it also means having access to ancient wisdom and guidance that modern society devalues but is unable to replace.

The rise of terrorism and the ability of groups such as Al-Qaeda and ISIS to inflict destruction and mass murder puts Muslims living in the West under scrutiny and suspicion. But there is a more positive narrative taking place in parallel to this tension. Slowly, Muslims are joining the mainstream. Whether it's Asda selling halal meat or a greater awareness of Ramadan – the trend is heading towards a time when, instead of a negative stereotype, the word 'Muslim' could carry infinite possibilities and relate to people from disparate backgrounds who may practise in different ways or even not at all.

Q: Who are your favourite writers and who influences your writing?

A: When I was growing up in Sudan my favourite writers were Dostoevsky, Charlotte Brontë, and Daphne du Maurier. I also read a lot of Somerset Maugham. Later when I moved to Britain, Tayeb Salih's *The Wedding of Zein* became the novel about Sudan that best expressed what I was homesick for. But I would say that my writing is mostly influenced by women writers such as Anita Desai, Jean Rhys, Buchi Emecheta and Ahdaf Soueif – all of whom I read after I started writing.

Q: What are you working on at the moment?

A: I am finishing up a collection of short stories about women in various stages of their lives. Schoolgirls falling out, first love, a teenager avenging her father's murder, a single woman joining a revolution, another in her thirties meeting a prospective suitor, a bride getting used to her new life. Then morning sickness, parenthood and divorce. In the story I am working on at the moment, a successful middle-aged woman meets her favourite author fifteen years after the writer had snubbed her at a literary event.

I'm also planning a new novel about three Muslim women on a road trip around Britain. As they bicker and banter, the tensions between them grow, and through modern methods of communication and social media their lives stretch out to loyalties in different continents.

For Discussion

- '. . . we have to grope our way through so much filth and rubbish in order to reach home! And we have no one to show us the way. Homesickness is our only guide.'

    Why do you think Leila Aboulela has chosen these lines from Hermann Hesse's *Steppenwolf* as an epigraph to her novel?

- Natasha believes that she has an 'unfortunate name' in Hussein and nags her mother and stepfather to change it when she arrives in London in 1990 (p.4). How important are names in the novel? Do they determine identity?

- What do you now understand by the term 'jihad'? How does this compare with your thoughts prior to reading *The Kindness of Enemies*?

- How are the contemporary and historical narratives woven together in *The Kindness of Enemies* to reveal deeper insights into identity and belonging? Consider especially how Anna's story, that of a stranger in a strange land, mirrors Natasha's.

- What does it mean to be a Muslim and a woman in the world today? Does anything surprise you in Leila Aboulela's presentation of Malak, a single mother and actress who is devoted to keeping fit? Compare and contrast Malak with Shamil's women.

- Explore the relationship between Natasha and Oz. What do you think they derive from each other?

- 'Shamil and his people were the goodies; the Russians were the baddies.' (p.14) Do you agree with Oz?

- 'The Stain of Al-Qaeda has Reached Scotland' (p.286)
  How do the media, reportage and hearsay distort truth throughout the novel?

- 'The mountains were filled with the displaced. Here among Shamil's men were captives and deserters. Their wellbeing was a function of how much they integrated or made themselves useful . . . their loyalty would always be suspect, their loved ones far away.' (p.229)
  Consider immigration today. How far does this statement hold true for those moving from one country to another?

- Natasha yearns for an 'identifiable place' where she can 'belong' (p.289). How does she begin to reconcile the complexities of her upbringing by the end of the novel? Does Jamaleldin attain any peace by the end? What does it mean to belong?

If you enjoyed *The Kindness of Enemies*, you might also like . . .

Hadji Murad by Leo Tolstoy

Purple Hibiscus by Chimamanda Ngozi Adichie

Good Hope Road by Sarita Mandanna

The Moor's Account by Laila Lalami

The Narrow Road to the Deep North by Richard Flanagan

The Year of the Runaways by Sunjeev Sahota

The Kite Runner by Khaled Hosseini

The Lowland by Jhumpa Lahiri

The Map of Love by Ahdaf Soueif

If you enjoyed The Kindness of Enemies, you might also like . . .

Have you read *Lyrics Alley*?

Longlisted for the 2011 Orange Prize for Fiction

It is the dawn of the 1950s and from the bustling streets of Khartoum to cosmopolitan Cairo, the sun is setting on the British Empire. Mahmoud, the head of a powerful Sudanese dynasty, has grand ambitions. But there are tensions between his wives: one is bound to traditions which confine her to an open-air kitchen, whilst the other is a modern Egyptian woman intent on dividing the household. Then Nur, Mahmoud's brilliant son and heir to his business empire, suffers a near-fatal accident, leaving the family to face an uncertain future.

Moving between Sudan and Egypt, this is a heart-wrenching portrait of a family in turmoil, a love lost and history in the making.

'Beautiful' *Marie Claire*

'A story for all the senses, one to be savoured and enjoyed'
Financial Times

'Evoking the alleyways of Sudan, Egypt and Britain, this novel ... traces the hidden pathways of the mind and heart'
Sunday Telegraph

LYRICS ALLEY

LEILA ABOULELA